I0662417

Hearts
Journey Home

Book one of the Journeys of the Heart trilogy

Ashley Elisabeth Crook

Trestle 2 Treasure
Sinclairville, New York
www.trestle2treasure.com

Hearts Journey Home
Book one of the Journeys of the Heart trilogy
Copyright © 2008
Ashley Elisabeth Crook

All scripture quotations taken from, or adapted from, the King James Version.

Library of Congress Control Number: 2008909898

Published by Trestle 2 Treasure
Sinclairville, New York
www.trestle2treasure.com

Printed in the United States of America

Cover design by Ashley Elisabeth Crook with assistance from Ethan Ledden
Cover copyright © 2008 by Ashley Elisabeth Crook

ISBN–13: 978-0-9822133-0-8

ISBN–10: 0-9822133-0-1

For my wonderful
Savior, Jesus Christ

And my dad and mom, who introduced me to
Him and nurtured my love for Him

"One must first endure some rain in order to see the rainbow."

"My little children, let us not love in word, neither in tongue; but in deed and in truth." 1 John 3:18

Note from the Author:

Though we may not see it, our lives influence those around us more than we believe, for good or for bad. Some we may find out about. Others may remain undiscovered until we reach eternity where, perhaps, God will reveal them to us. We are to be held accountable for our every word and action. I wish mine to be a pleasure to remember. How about you? As you read this story, remember that you are impacting people's hearts and lives even if you don't speak directly to them. Who knows, a smile in passing may fill someone's day with joy or change someone's decision that his or her life is too miserable to go on. Show others you care. Even if you feel like you are a failure, if you have smiled even once or given one kind word, you have ministered to someone's heart. Keep up the good work! Take heart and purpose to do more. Each little step to minister to others leads you toward a more joyful life. Persevere! It will be worth it!

Today, I was driving along in the countryside and happened to glance over as I passed a white farmhouse where there were two people speaking to each other in the driveway. One was turned towards the road, laughing. It sent a warm thrill of joy through my heavy heart, making me smile. That person may never discover that they brightened my day, but they did it. By being cheerful, and showing it, they passed that joy on to me, and perhaps many others. God's word says, "A merry heart does good like a medicine." How true that is. Even if you don't believe in God, you have to agree that it is a true statement. Let us be always ready with a smile, and to look on the good side— the harder of which it is to find, the more joy it brings when you finally do.

Now go and make a difference in people's lives. A good difference!

A special thank you to all those who encouraged me to write

Historical Note:

There were some orphanages still in use when this story takes place in the early 1950s. Though by that time, few of them would have been like the orphanage in this story is depicted. Most of them were respectable establishments and foster care was becoming more widely used than orphanages.

❧ ✹ ❧

Hearts Journey Home

❧ ✹ ❧

Chapter 1

Sorryl hunched closer to his brother and pulled his arms into his shirtsleeves in an effort to keep warm. The five-year-old glanced up at his brother. Trey was still trying to force himself to eat the moldy crust they had discovered in a garbage heap. Hunger pangs gripped his stomach and Sorryl reluctantly pulled one arm from his shirt and took another nibble of his bread. He swallowed without chewing so he wouldn't have to taste it.

Trey glanced at his little brother in understanding and wrapped an arm over his shoulders as they tried to lend each other warmth and strength. In order to ignore the taste of the bread he was attempting to eat, Trey allowed his mind to wander, something he usually avoided these last weeks. The six-year-old tried to keep his thoughts on the present lately. The past was too painful, and the future too frightening and lonely to dwell on.

Suddenly, Sorryl leaped to his feet, "Trey, watch out!"

Trey's head snapped up, but he was too late. An older boy roughly grabbed him and pulled him to his feet, sneering, "Whad'ya know, Albert. I think this is just the type of boy we were looking for." His raspy voice broke off in a harsh laugh as the boy smirked at Sorryl. "And you, I'm sure you want us to let this boy go, 'ey?"

Sorryl clenched his fists at his side and threw his chin up, "Yes. You put him down now!"

"What is he? A friend? Why should you care what we do with him?"

Sorryl's eyes flashed, "Let him go!"

Albert spoke now, "We-e-e-ll." He drawled. "Maybe we'd let him go. But you'd have to do us a favor first."

Sorryl just bore his eyes into the boy.

"So, you think you're tough, do you? Brady, look at the little spitfire. He's trying to shoot daggers through me!" Albert mocked.

Brady laughed and shook Trey, "It seems your little companion thinks he can get you free."

"Leave him alone!" Trey growled through clenched teeth.

The boys just laughed, "You youngsters sure do like to think you're tough. But you're really just sissies. You'd never get away from us."

Sorryl could stand no more. Recklessly, he lunged at the boy called Brady. He caught the tormentor off-guard, but Sorryl's small body was not enough to have much effect on the bigger boy.

"Sorryl, don't!" Trey pled, but he was too late.

Albert seized Sorryl and dangled him above the ground. His voice took on a coaxing tone, "Now, we know you want your little friend released, but you'll have to do what we tell you or we won't let him go."

Sorryl just let out an infuriated yell and kicked the boy in the shins.

Albert dropped him and his voice grew threatening, "Now. You will go and get that money box on the corner there. When you give it to us, we'll let this other boy go."

Sorryl's eyes flew wide. He leaped to his feet. They were asking him to steal? His mind raced as he groped for another option, but none presented itself. He mutely glared at the boys, trying not to show how terrified he was. Albert shoved him in the direction of the vendor with the money box and demanded, "Go! You know there's no other way."

Sorryl hesitated and glanced at Trey.

With an evil grin, Brady twisted Trey's arm. Trey clamped his lips shut in an attempt to keep from crying out, but a strangled yelp escaped anyway.

Sorryl's chest burned with anger and fear, yet felt limp in helplessness at the same time. Reluctantly, he moved off to do his detestable duty... or whatever it was.

He entered the crowded street and crept toward the money box. He could feel his heart hammering within his chest. Pausing a few feet from his target, he glanced around to be sure no one was looking before he took the last few steps and reached up. He grabbed hold of the box. Now to get away with it. Suddenly, Sorryl jumped as rough hands locked about his small arms. He twisted around to see who it was and a gasp of despair escaped him. Inwardly, he panicked. *No! It can't be! I'm done for now!* Sorryl strove to break free of his shock and cried, "No, sir! Please! I won't take it!"

"You're right, you won't!" growled the New York City police officer, shaking the boy he had seized. Suddenly, there was a shout and clatter of feet in the ally nearby, but when the officer turned to see what it was, the only thing that met his gaze was an astonished boy lying in the filthy street.

When Trey saw his brother in the policeman's grasp, he leaped to his feet again, his heart pulsing. Flames of anger tore at his chest. He glanced behind him to see where Albert and Brady had gone, but the cowards had already fled around the corner. He turned back to this new trouble, gulping down the anger. *It won't do you any good to stay upset, Trey. You'd better just calm down and figure out what to do,* he silently reprimanded himself. *Jesus, please help me!* For a moment, he hesitated. What should he do now? He made his decision with a burst of courage and determination, "Sir! Sir! Please!" The officer grabbed Sorryl's ear and he cried out. Indignation burned in Trey's chest. He shifted his gaze from the pink spot spreading across his brother's ear to the officer's irritated back. *How dare that officer.* Resolutely, he squared his shoulders and pounced onto the policeman.

"Hey! Y-you scoundrel!" the officer yelled, catching his balance just in time. He glared angrily at the two street urchins.

Suddenly, shame flooded Trey. He knew he was supposed to respect the officer, but he had been so desperate to rescue his brother. A vision of his mother rose before his eyes and he drew in a sharp breath. *I'm sorry, Mama,* he sobbed inwardly. Her image's eyes met his, full of sadness and love. Trey's heart clenched within him. No matter the desperate situation, he should have had more respect toward the officer. He silently cried, *Mama! Why can't you be here to help me know what to do?* No answer. He had known there wouldn't be, not from his mother. Not ever again. He clenched his eyes shut. Oh! Why had the world suddenly become so cold and unfriendly these last weeks? Why?

Trey's next words carried this lonely ache and a plea for help into their respectful, though desperate tones, "Please leave him be! It wasn't his fault! Those boys made him. Oh, please!" His voice broke and he tried to choke back a sob. Why did those boys have to find them and harass them? Didn't they know it was already hard enough to live?

The police officer only sputtered angrily and shook the boy off his back, catching hold of him as well. "I saw no other boys! Where are your mother and father?"

At this question, pain filled the brothers' eyes. They looked down with a choking sound, but gave no other response. How could they speak? If they opened their mouths, the boys feared all the built up pain and sorrow that chiseled relentlessly away at their hearts would burst out. The officer definitely would not take kindly to that. So the dark-haired brothers clamped their quivering lips and blue eyes shut and mutely awaited their fate.

At their silence, the officer pressed on in half-accusing, half-sarcastic tones, "Afraid to tell me, huh?" He paused to growl under his breath, "Little troublemakers," then impatiently rattled Trey, who seemed to be the more vocal one, "Better tell, it'll be better for you that way."

Trey laboriously worked his lips, but no words would come. Finally, he stuttered brokenly, "Th-they're g-gone." He gulped down a sob that caught in his throat.

"Oh, likely excuse," the policeman pressed on. He was tired of all these street kids making trouble. "Have they left on vacation without you?" he scoffed.

"N-no s-sir."

"Well, then, where are they?"

Trey gulped, swallowing around the lump in his throat. He *must* make his voice work and answer the officer. He finally managed to whisper, "I-in... H-Heaven, s-s-sir."

The officer muffled an incredulous guffaw, "Oh, so you're an original. Usually they say, 'a long ways away, sir,' looking ever so innocent."

Sorryl watched his brother, unable to speak. He wished he could help him, but... no words would present themselves.

Trey swallowed hard. "I-I m-m-mean, s-sir..." he halted painfully.

Believing the stubborn boy might actually be acknowledging the truth now, the officer gave him a prompting pinch on the cheek.

Trey flinched, resisting the urge to place his hand over the stinging cheek. The officer shouldn't know how it had hurt. Instead, he drew a shaky breath and continued with difficulty, "I mean that they're..." He gulped, "D-dead." Trey's face contorted in inward pain for a moment before it relaxed into an unreadable expression as he shoved his hurt deep down. He thrust out his chin in determination against the wave of grief that endeavored to rise to the surface once more.

At last, the officer understood, "Well then, you are orphans, and belong in the orphanage." He paused a moment. He hadn't seen many street kids this well mannered, even considering his perception of the older one's obstinate attitude. He couldn't help but think they must have had a good mother long enough to adopt some of her gentleness and learn some good manners. Yet, they would probably soon be tough and hardened like the rest of the unfortunates running around. He could see it happening already. He'd best get them while he could. With this last thought, the officer began dragging them in the direction of the Children's Home.

Fear gripped Trey and Sorryl's hearts anew as they were pulled along.

Sorryl silently berated himself for even attempting to steal, even if it was to save his brother. Now he had gotten Trey in trouble with the officer too. But it was too late for regrets now.

He *had* done it, and because Trey had tried to defend him, now his older brother was forced to pay the consequences with him.

Their hearts throbbing like the frantic fluttering of trapped birds, Trey and Sorryl strained against the police officer in an attempt to escape. They had heard dreadful stories of the orphanage and it struck terror within their souls. But it was no use to struggle. The officer was too strong for them.

Trey felt as though his heart was dying within him. Glancing at Sorryl, he knew his little brother felt the same way. It seemed as though their world, which they had thought had already been completely destroyed when their parents had disappeared, had found some way to further crumble around them in this one, short, yet torturously long, afternoon.

Growing irritated at the boys' struggles, the officer tightened his grip, striving not to let them wiggle free. Suddenly, he felt a restraining, though gentle, hand laid on his arm.

He turned with a scowl toward whoever dared interfere and was met by the imploring blue eyes of a young lady. Her chestnut hair curled about her face in soft waves. Though she barely came up to his shoulder and her carriage was somewhat shy, he instinctively knew there was power behind her words, perhaps more than his six foot frame held. It seemed her purpose was so set that anything in the way would melt before it. Her gaze that held so much... peace?... struck him and he averted his eyes.

"Please, sir," she began, summoning all the courage her heart could find. "They're so young," was all she managed at last with a glance at the trembling boys who were standing taught and dry-eyed.

Despite the vagueness of her plea, the officer understood, "Well, all the better for them to be in the orphanage. They can't stay on the streets." His answer came rather roughly because he was still irritated with the boys, though this stranger's manner made it impossible for him to remain angry with her for interceding for these waifs.

"Well, what if they have relatives who could take them," she insisted. She cast up a silent plea, *Oh, Lord. Please help me! If only I could penetrate the hard shell I sense You telling me bitterness has created in this officer and reach that caring heart that is hidden beneath!*

6

"Listen, lady, the orphanage will find out about details. My job is just to keep 'em out of trouble. They're lucky I'm not lugging them off to jail."

The soft-spoken lady was not to be discouraged so easily. She suppressed a shiver at the thought of the small boys being put in jail and pressed on, "May I speak to the children a moment, sir?"

"I don't know why you'd want to." After an undecided pause, he grudgingly gave in, "Guess it can't hurt. But don't blame me if you find something missing. I caught the little one swiping a money box."

"I know. I saw," the young lady murmured. She blinked back tears as she stooped down in the dirty street. She didn't want the boys to have to look up to see her. "What are your names?" she asked tenderly. They looked at her with matching blue eyes; eyes full of honesty... and pain.

"I'm Trey. He's Sorryl spelled with a 'y', ma'am," the older boy answered, heroically stifling the flow of tears that *would* prick his eyes. This lady reminded him of his mother. Besides being gentle and caring, she even looked a lot like her. And her eyes, her eyes seemed so kind.

"What beautiful names!" she exclaimed with a feeling smile, barely keeping her composure as tears assailed her once more. She dreaded bringing up the subject she knew she must. It seemed they hadn't been orphans for long and the last thing they needed was to have a wound torn open again. Finally, she continued reluctantly, "Do you still have a house, where you lived with your mama and papa?"

Trey's searching eyes met hers. "No. We were in a..." his voice trailed off as he sought for the proper word. He finally ventured, "...in a sharing house. And the owner threw us boys out when they found out Mama and Papa were dead and weren't paying anymore." His answer was uttered nonchalantly in a detached tone, but the shaky sigh that followed gave him away, piercing the lady's heart to the quick. With her motherly instinct she could see the barricade he had thrown up. *Someone so young should never find need for such a thing,* she thought sadly. She glanced at the smaller boy. Trey had said his name was Sorryl... spelled with a 'y'. Apparently, that was very important to them. She nearly smiled, but its shadow quickly disappeared as she observed the small boy. He was trembling a bit, but his lips were clamped tightly shut, for he, too, was trying to ward off the pain in his obviously tortured heart. She sighed.

The officer shuffled his feet impatiently, still holding the boys' arms tightly. This lady reminded him of his mother, who couldn't bear to see a child suffer. He had once been that way, too. But now... Well, now he didn't quite know what the matter was, but he somehow felt... dead inside.

The lady glanced up at him in a mute request for his patience, and then turned back to the boys, "Did your family have some friends?"

"We just came here, we didn't know anyone yet, and Grandma and Gran'pa died in the sickness." Trey answered, unable to keep the pain from venturing into his voice and eyes once more. He bit his lower lip to stop its quivering. His heart felt as though it would burst any moment.

Sorryl startled them by finally speaking as the pain and confusion in his heart throbbed into words, "And Mama and Papa are gone, 'cause a man with beer ate them in his car." A solitary tear stole past the little boy's self-constructed barrier and sparkled down his cheek, leaving a clean trail upon the noble face.

Suddenly, the lady had to glance away from him. She could no longer bear the pain in his young eyes that looked far too old.

"He means they were in a car accident, really," Trey explained, holding his chin higher and blinking rapidly as he felt his barricade weakening.

The officer cleared his throat and shifted uneasily. He was beginning to see a painful image of himself in Trey, and even in the quieter Sorryl. With a pang, he suddenly realized that it was not rebellion which caused the older boy to thrust out his chin, but rather determination not to reveal the pain that was tormenting his young heart. *Something I understand all too well,* he thought almost bitterly. He could still feel the pain weighing in his chest like a hard rock. It hadn't become that way all at once. No. His heart had gradually callused over his thirty-three years of life as he harbored the pain in a hidden corner of it that he strove to pretend was nonexistent.

Still waiting for the lady to finish her conversation, he glanced down at the boys and suddenly noticed the redness of their arms where he was gripping them. Without knowing why, he quickly loosened his hold, still keeping enough of a grasp that they would not manage to slip away, and averted his eyes, ashamed for the first time in a long while of his learned insensitivity.

"All right. Let's be off now," he ordered, softening his tone a bit, but still speaking rather shortly as he swallowed the rising lump in his throat. He glanced at the lady, who stood as he began pulling the boys in the direction of the orphanage, "If you want to talk with the rascals, go to the children's home." And, with that, he pulled the pain-filled boys down the street, a little more gently this time. Sorryl glanced back at her, stumbled, was righted by the officer, and then disappeared around the corner.

A warm tear slid down Annaleah's cheek. Her heart swelled as she stared at the place she had last been able to catch a glimpse of the officer and boys through the crowded streets. "Poor dears," she whispered, meaning the police officer as well as Trey and Sorryl. Finally pulling her eyes from the corner around which they had disappeared, she suddenly remembered the shopping she was supposed to be doing and turned toward the store. All thoughts of her mission had fled when she had encountered the police officer and boys. She wished she could have done something more for them.

Finally, she finished her shopping and distractedly made her way home. She knew she had forgotten at least one item, but no matter how much she tried, she could not force her mind to focus on the task at hand. As she walked through the crowded city streets she allowed her thoughts to linger on the boys. The buildings that loomed above her and the mud on the sidewalks went unheeded as she swept along with the afternoon throng. Someone jostled against her shoulder, causing her to almost lose her balance. Glancing up as she steadied herself, she caught sight of another man carrying some large boxes and stepped aside just in time to avoid another collision. She sighed and inwardly scolded herself, *You'd better pay attention to where you're going or you'll get run over, Annaleah.* She grimaced. She disliked the bustle and cramped feeling of the city just as much as her husband did.

Despite her self-scolding, her mind took flight once more, playing back the scene that had taken place only an hour before. She groaned inwardly as she wondered if somehow she could have stopped the officer from carrying the boys off to the orphanage. But then, she couldn't have just left them in the street, prey to other relentless persecutors. She could have taken them home if they would have come with her... but then, what would Spencer have said to that. She smiled. What would he say if he knew she had confronted the police officer? She could see the smile that always played about his lips when her fiery spirit emerged from her usually quiet demeanor. She remembered the first time he had observed it. He had just looked at her for a moment, trying to hide his surprise, and then smiled that smile which was now so familiar. Now two years later and after seven months of marriage, she still loved that smile.

Suddenly, Annaleah glanced up. With a laugh, she realized she had passed her house. Shaking her head at herself, she retraced her steps, then let herself into the house and put away her purchases. Her mind flitted back to Trey and Sorryl as she took up a dust rag and attacked the furniture. There must be something they could do for those children. There had to be! Her mind searched for solutions. One by one, they presented themselves. And one by one she discarded them. The boys' sweet, yet troubled, faces persistently rose before her, their names etched forever in her memory. "Trey – loyal and brave. Sorryl – gentle and sweet. Trey and Sorryl – noble, and in need of help..." *But what help can I give?* Her heart wrung within her at her helplessness. Suddenly, her dusting hand stilled as she stood up straighter. *Yes! Yes! That's just the thing! Perhaps we could! I'll talk to Spencer as soon as he comes home. Well, after I let him rest. He needs it after working in that factory. Thank You, Lord! An answer! Well... if Spencer agrees. It really is a wild plan. I wouldn't blame him if he ran out of the house as soon as I told him what it was.*

Spencer Trestle paused on his doorstep to release a sigh and shook off the heaviness he felt from working at the factory.

When he opened the door and entered the house, Annaleah rushed to greet him.

He hugged her close, enjoying the lavender aroma of her hair. Then he held her at arms length and looked deep into her eyes as he always did, "To see how she had fared that day," he always told her. He smiled to himself. Despite her attempts to hide it, he could tell Annaleah was trying to push something aside that was pressing on her heart. "So, what is it, Annaleah?" he asked almost playfully, yet with a touch of earnestness.

"What?" she answered, trying to affect an innocent attitude as she gave him a peck on the cheek, blinking back tears in spite of herself.

Spencer just looked at her with searching, green eyes.

She laughed, "I can never hide anything from you, can I? I was planning to let you have a rest first, but now I see you won't take one until you know what is troubling me. Come take your coat off and get cleaned up, then I'll tell you."

An amused smile twitched the corners of Spencer's mouth, "What? You don't like me when I'm dirty?"

Annaleah laughed again, smacking his shoulder with a twinkle in her blue eyes as he took his light jacket off. "No, it's just I want you to be comfortable first, instead of barraging you with more to think about as soon as you come home." He smiled and pulled her into another hug before heading to the bathroom.

11

He quickly washed his hands and splashed water onto his face, which was blackened from the greasy machines he worked with. He wondered what could have so preoccupied Annaleah. Well, he would soon find out. He finished drying his hands and returned to the hallway where Annaleah had hung his coat. He smiled when he saw that she was still there, thoughtfully staring at the ceiling as if in conversation with the Lord. He gently took her arm and led her to the living room where he seated himself on the couch and pulled her down next to him. "Now. What seems to be the trouble?" he asked.

Annaleah sighed and attempted a smile, "I was out shopping today... "

A grin played about Spencer's lips, but he knew Annaleah had something serious on her mind, so he resisted the urge to exclaim in pretend shock, "Wow! How amazing! When did you learn to do that!" Annaleah loved it when he teased her, but now was not the time, so she was allowed to continue without interruption.

"...And I saw this dear little boy, his name turned out to be Sorryl – spelled with a 'y' – attempting to steal a money box."

Spencer nearly chuckled at Annaleah's description of a 'dear little boy' who was stealing a money box. But she didn't notice his reaction.

"Then I realized his brother, Trey, was being roughly held by some rich-looking boys, but they threw him down and ran away when the police officer showed up..."

When she had finished her account of what she had witnessed, she exclaimed with feeling, "Oh! It pierced my heart!" She paused a moment before continuing, "I felt so awful for letting the officer drag them off to the children's home. It just seemed I could have done something more."

Spencer smiled, "A couple years ago I would have been astonished to see the quiet Annaleah confronting a police officer. I know better than that now. You never could stand to remain still if someone was being wrongly treated. You did more than many others would have done."

"But that doesn't make it enough. It isn't the minimum I should reach for, but the maximum."

Spencer put his arm around her, "Well then, what is the maximum?" He suddenly wondered if he would regret asking. Annaleah sometimes had wild ideas, though usually good ones.

"Well. I puzzled and puzzled. And all of a sudden the verse came to my mind where God says to take care of the orphans and widows..."

Spencer blinked. So what exactly was she proposing? That they somehow help the orphanage the boys had been taken to? When Annaleah remained thoughtfully silent, he prodded, "And?"

Annaleah looked up and locked her gaze with his. She could feel her heart racing within her. Now she would find out what he would think of her proposal. *It's all up to You after I tell him the suggestion, God. Even I thought it was crazy at first.* With a deep breath, she plunged forward, "My idea was that we could adopt them." The words dropped like soft, yet shockingly cold, snowflakes and the room was filled with silence when they drifted away.

Spencer sank into his seat and blinked. His mind silently repeated her words in astonishment, *Adopt them?*

Annaleah's voice was quiet when she spoke again, almost to herself, "When the idea came, I felt like God was telling me, 'These are the children I have given you to take care of for me, Annaleah.' As I thought about it, I realized we had the space and—"

Spencer's mind reeled and he didn't realize he interrupted her until he was already speaking, "But the space is for *our* children. Remember? We wanted a big family."

Annaleah met his troubled gaze and quietly said, "Well, couldn't these boys be part of it?"

Spencer fought to rise above the shock surrounding him. He sighed. "It's a pretty major decision. Besides, there's millions more just like them."

"Not *just*," Annaleah clarified in a quiet voice, toying with the rug at her feet. *Did I hear you wrong, Lord? I didn't mean to shock him so badly.*

"Well, in the same plight, or nearly the same," Spencer defended. His chest clenched within him as he clutched the ideal dreams he had held since he married Annaleah. He felt as though they would crumble if they took in these street kids.

Annaleah sighed. She understood her husband's struggle in accepting the idea of adopting orphans off the street. She knew she probably would feel the same way if she hadn't seen the two children with her own eyes. It just seemed as if God had gently spoken to her heart, telling her, *My daughter, here are some blessings for you. Take them. Cherish them. Train them. Give them a merry heart. They need it. As I have said, 'A merry heart does good like a medicine.'*

Finally, Annaleah paused in her methodical foot-brushing of the rug and sat up straighter, tucking her hand within his, "I'm sorry. I didn't mean to shock you so. Perhaps it wasn't as great an idea as I thought. I was scared when the idea first struck me, but I felt so like it was what was meant to be…"

Spencer squeezed her hand and tilted her chin so her down-cast eyes were once more gazing into his, "How about we at least go to the orphanage and see if they found any relatives or friends. Meanwhile, I'll think about it some more. And pray," he added with a smile.

Annaleah wrapped her arms about him, "Spencer, did I ever tell you you're just the most wonderful husband a girl could ask for?"

Spencer smiled and playfully tweaked her hair, "Many times. I'm afraid soon I shall have too high an opinion of myself if you say it many more times."

Striving to shove his misgivings aside, he rose to stoke the fire. It was so difficult to comprehend the idea of taking in an orphan who had been caught stealing, and one that lived right in their city on top of it. Annaleah and he had thought of adopting foreign orphans, but adopting one from their own city? That thought had never occurred to him before. He sighed. Maybe he would feel differently if he could see the boys who had so easily captured Annaleah's heart. For reasons he could not explain, he felt a deep down hope that it would be so.

Annaleah spoke from the couch, "I suppose we had better wait a week so they have time to find any relatives, though. Hadn't we?"

Spencer shoved a log onto the fire, "Yeah, I suppose that would be a good idea."

Annaleah sighed as she gazed at the leaping flames that matched the tumult within her heart. It was going to be a long wait.

Chapter 2

Finally, the next Saturday arrived and they eagerly started for the children's home. As the couple walked side-by-side, they stepped lightly, enjoying the warm, spring day with the birds filling the air with their music even in the crowded city.

As they approached the orphanage, the couple could just make out the lifeless letters on the building within the gates, "Containment Home for Homeless Children".

Spencer glanced at Annaleah. "The word 'home' somehow seems out of place here," he commented wryly.

Annaleah nodded her agreement as she continued to stare at the foreboding words painted in drab gray, gloomily harmonizing with the dark brick building looming before her. Somehow she didn't seem to be able to speak around the lump in her throat.

With a sigh, Spencer said, "Well, we may as well go in."

Annaleah fought a sudden urge to turn and run the other way, but as images of the two hurting boys rose before her, she resolutely set her face toward the iron gates with a determined nod. If Jesus could endure the cross for her, she could go in there for those boys.

Spencer took a deep breath, slipped his protective arm within hers, and led the way to the formidable gates. For a moment, he stood there awkwardly. Was there some sort of bell to ring, or should they just open the gates?

Annaleah indicated a button embedded in a stone pillar, "How about that?"

Spencer followed her gaze and then gingerly reached out to press the button, quickly withdrawing his hand as if afraid his finger would freeze to it if he left it there too long.

They waited in silence for someone to come and open the gate.

Finally, Spencer turned to Annaleah, "Maybe we better try another time. It seems no one is going to come."

Annaleah nodded, "Perha—"

"How may I help you?" a dull voice interrupted her.

Annaleah jumped and grabbed Spencer's arm. Then she sent the new man a wobbly smile.

Spencer was speechless for a moment. Where had this little man come from? Covering his surprise, he answered, "We would like to see the person in charge here."

Without a word, the man drew a large key from his pocket, turning it in the lock. The great gate creaked ominously as he swung it open just enough for them to squeeze in one at a time, then it clanked shut behind them with frightening finality. Annaleah unconsciously tightened her grip on Spencer's arm.

The man pointed toward the towering building, "The gentleman over there will help you." This said, he quickly disappeared into the little shed-like building from which he had emerged, as if he could not stand to see their faces any longer.

Bewildered, Spencer and Annaleah slowly took in their surroundings. It seemed as if the sunshine had suddenly faded and even the birds had become melancholy. All at once, they found it difficult to breathe or even move. It felt like a heavy cloud had descended to smother them. Finally, Spencer slowly led the way down the walk.

Annaleah shuddered when she took in the tall fencing that lined the walk on either side. "It's almost like a prison," she whispered.

Spencer only nodded.

Pushing the fences from her mind, Annaleah began to search for Trey and Sorryl within the enclosure looming high above them. When she sighted them sitting dejectedly in a corner of the yard, she stopped abruptly and pointed, pulling Spencer to a halt as she did so. Her heart went out to the little boys. They seemed so small, especially compared to the rest of the children, and so helpless. She blinked back tears once more. *Maybe it wasn't such a good idea to come here*, she thought with a shiver. However, she quickly changed her mind. Perhaps they could get those little boys out of here.

As she lifted her eyes to Spencer's face, her gaze fell upon a sign posted on the fence behind which the boys were locked. It read in foreboding, red letters, "Beware, crime children within." She glanced at Spencer with a puzzled expression, hoping he would refute what she thought it must mean.

Spencer turned his gaze to the opposite side of the walk, where another fence stood. He pointed to the sign fastened to that one. "Orphans/Unfortunate Children," it read. As he turned back to the 'Crime' fence, he concluded with an involuntary shiver, "Must be those are the ones they caught breaking the law or something."

Annaleah only nodded and continued gazing at Trey and Sorryl. That was exactly what she had reluctantly decided. "Well, that's them," she said at last, swallowing around the lump that suddenly formed in her throat. "The little ones."

Spencer immediately knew which ones she was speaking of and his eyes were riveted on the helpless boys. Finally, he tore his gaze from them. "We'd better go," he nearly whispered.

Annaleah let him lead her to the steps where they were met by the stony-faced man the gatekeeper had directed them to. It seemed like agonizing hours since they had started toward him.

"Yes?" the man addressed them with a superior air.

Spencer hesitated a moment, "We want to see the one in charge…"

The man smiled, but it seemed more like a grimace, "Follow me."

He led them into the building, which was equally as dismal as it had been outside. Their steps echoed hollowly down the cold, grimy hall, sending shivers up Spencer and Annaleah's spines. The man glanced back at them, seeming to laugh silently at their discomfort.

18

Finally, their crusty guide stopped and, with another of his grimace-smiles, opened a door, ushering them in. Annaleah's mouth nearly fell open. It was so warm and cozy in the room. Elaborate paintings and lighting fixtures graced the comfortable office. It seemed out of place, almost like an entirely separate world from the orphanage.

Their escort cleared his throat and informed them, "This is Mr. Minor." He grimaced at them once again before taking a seat on the far side of the luxuriant room.

Mr. Minor did not even look up, but continued scribbling on a piece of paper behind his huge oak desk.

Glancing around a little uncertainly, Spencer cleared his throat in an attempt to get Mr. Minor's attention, but the man still gave no indication that he even knew they existed. Finally, as it seemed to be his only option, Spencer spoke, placing a reassuring arm about his young wife's shoulders, "We have come to inquire about two boys who were taken in last week for stealing. Their names are Trey and Sorryl. I believe they are brothers."

Mr. Minor glanced up and grudgingly turned toward them. "Last Saturday... let's see," he mumbled, shuffling through some papers. "Ah, yes... Very troublesome boys... What did you say you wanted with them?" he asked methodically, unconsciously twirling his graying mustache with his forefinger all the while.

"I don't believe I said," Spencer responded, nearly letting a chuckle betray him at Mr. Minor's absentminded air. "But we want to know if you have found any family or friends belonging to them yet."

After briefly consulting his sheet, Mr. Minor glanced back at Annaleah and Spencer, "Nope." He continued in an unconcerned tone, reading from the papers and never ceasing to twirl his mustache, "All evidence leads us to believe they have none. Their previous landlord informed us that they just moved here from a city near Houston, Texas. Supposedly left the town where the last of their family had recently been taken by a serious illness."

"Thank you. How long before you complete your search?"

"Now. We're done," came the matter-of-fact reply.

"Thank you, uh… Mr. Minor," Spencer stumbled, surprised at the man's blunt and unconcerned answer.

"Can I help you with anything else?" Already Mr. Minor was turning back to his work. The large, padded chair creaked under his wait.

Spencer's mind raced. *Lord, should I ask to adopt them?* His heart pulsed in uncertainty at the thought. Dared he make such a commitment for complete strangers? Was he willing to give up his dreams of a family – with children of his own – by speaking the fateful words 'Could we adopt them?'. Glancing up at Mr. Minor's bored face, he heard himself reply, "No thank you. Good day, sir."

Annaleah sighed and her shoulders sagged a bit as she looked at him questioningly. She had hoped he would at least ask to see the boys… or something. Weighing heavier and heavier upon her heart was the impression that they should adopt Trey and Sorryl.

Spencer glanced at her and sighed himself. *What?! Why had he said that?* He knew instinctively that it was because he had allowed fear to rule his heart. Fear of the uncaring, blunt Mr. Minor, fear of the unknown and what these children would be like. He could have at least asked to see the boys so he could make a better decision. But Annaleah had already met them, and she seemed to know they would work together as a family. He shoved his self-reproaches down, yet one rebellious one rose to the surface to voice itself before it simmered into submission. *How must Mr. Minor treat the children if this is his attitude towards you?* Spencer suppressed a shudder. He didn't think he wanted to know. With sudden conviction, and in spite of his fear, he opened his lips to voice the question that would change his life forever. But before he could utter a word Mr. Minor waved his hand at them as if they were pesky flies, and the couple was quickly ushered back into the dark hallway, which seemed even gloomier after the cheerful room they had just vacated. He was too late.

Once outside, Annaleah and Spencer's gaze again fell upon the two small boys within the 'Crime' gate. They were now bravely trying to join a game of tag. But the bigger boys rudely pushed the smaller two off to the side, peppering their rough shoves with mocking taunts. The man who was apparently supposed to be keeping order seemed to take no notice of the bullies.

Spencer gently pulled Annaleah toward the gate and she reluctantly tore her eyes from Trey and Sorryl.

When they reached it, Spencer glanced around for the guard, but he was nowhere to be seen. Hoping the gate would open for him, he pulled on the steel bars, but it stood unyielding.

Panic began to rise within their chests at the realization that they were locked in this dreadful place. Their hearts squeezed within them as they thought of how the children kept here must feel like they did now... perhaps tenfold.

Spencer glanced at the run-down shed the gatekeeper had disappeared into and led Annaleah toward it. "The gatekeeper's probably still in there."

Annaleah nodded and breathed passionately, "I sure hope so."

When they reached the small building, Spencer raised his hand uncertainly and knocked. When it finally opened a crack with a suddenness they hadn't expected, they nearly jumped.

Annaleah glanced at Spencer with a shaky half-smile. This place sure activated your nerves. Neither of them were normally so jumpy.

"What do you want?" the gatekeeper asked sharply.

"We were wondering how to get out," Spencer answered with unusual timidity in the face of the keeper's almost accusatory tones.

The man laughed cynically, "You want out already? I can't believe it." With that, he pompously withdrew into his shed, letting the door slam in their faces.

Annaleah and Spencer stared at each other in dread. Was he actually going to leave them locked in there? Spencer glanced around for any way they might be able to escape, but it seemed there was no possible way to get out except through the securely locked gates. On all sides, cold iron bars stretched high. Spencer sighed hopelessly and Annaleah gripped his arm tighter.

Suddenly, the man emerged from a side door, carrying a key. He laughed harshly when he saw their relieved faces, "Thought I was gonna leave you in here, didn't you? Well, maybe we should have a tour of the place and make the folks spend the night. Then maybe someone would adopt one of these poor children, or at least find a way to make it a better place to live." The gate-keeper's voice softened as he finished speaking and he turned the key in the lock.

At the man's words, a pain shot through Spencer's heart. How could he have let fear and selfishness keep him from asking to adopt Trey and Sorryl?

As the gate swung open a crack, Spencer and Annaleah sighed with relief. They hurriedly squeezed their way out into the sunshine and bustling sidewalk.

The gatekeeper paused a moment, sticking his head out into the sunshine. He drew a deep breath of fresh air before shutting the gate with a clang.

Spencer reached up and brushed his forehead. In surprise, he looked at his damp fingers and wiped them on his shirt. He had been sweating! He turned feelingly to Annaleah, still protectively holding her arm. "What a place to live," he muttered.

Annaleah only managed to nod, one tear escaping and trailing down her cheek. She glanced at Spencer to see if he had noticed and hastily swept it away.

That evening, Spencer and Annaleah sat on their green couch, trying to read the Bible. But images of the two small boys and the miserable orphanage relentlessly floated through their troubled minds. Before long, they sat in silence.

Spencer stirred and finally spoke, "Maybe we should go back. I'm beginning to think God meant us to have those boys. How can we just leave them there? We have to help give them merry hearts. You know, the kind that 'does good like medicine'."

For answer, Annaleah just hugged him, a tear of joy sparkling down her cheek. After a short silence she spoke, smiling gently through her tears, "That's exactly what I felt God wanted us to do, help them get merry hearts. They certainly could use some healing!"

"Yes, they could! You really thought the same thing?" It wasn't really a question, just a wondering statement. He should be used to how God often impressed the same thing on their hearts, but he still often felt surprise when it happened. After a moment, he said, "Let's pray about it tonight to be sure." After an uncomfortable pause he continued with a sheepish grin, "We should have done that in the first place, but I guess I was too set on what I wanted."

Annaleah just smiled, she didn't even nod.

"That's just like you not to say 'I told you so'. You're the best wife," Spencer said with a fond smile. He paused another moment, "He's such a gentleman, God is. He doesn't make you do things, He just asks or waits for you to invite Him. And He always wants the very best for us."

This time Annaleah did nod.

Spencer took a deep breath and began, "Okay, Lord, we know, in keeping with Your compassionate nature, You want us to take care of the orphans. We can see that You have brought Trey and Sorryl... spelled with a 'y'," he added with a smile, "to our attention. I'm sorry for being selfish and stubborn at first. Thanks for keeping on working in my heart." Another sheepish grin spread across his pleasant face. "Please help us to know if You really want us to do this, although I think You've already shown us that clearly enough, but please give us the *courage* to do this is maybe more what I mean. And the courage to go back to that... place. And please be with Trey and Sorryl and all of those children in the Containment Home. Please be a Father to them and provide some way for them to have good homes and to know about You and Your love. I ask this in Jesus name."

Annaleah's heartfelt, "Amen," showed her agreement. Then the two lapsed into silence for a moment before climbing the stairs and attempting to catch some sleep amidst the horrible memories of the properly named 'Containment Home'.

Sunday, after church, Spencer sat staring into the fire as Annaleah watched him with an affectionate smile.

Finally, he swept a hand across his eyes and nearly burst, "I feel more and more sure we should adopt those boys, what about you?"

Annaleah nodded and murmured, "So do I," though she knew he was only asking as a way of bringing up the subject and already knew her thoughts on the issue.

Spencer began eagerly thinking aloud, "Okay, so tomorrow morning we go to the orphanage, and, if they're still there, try to adopt them. I'll call work to see if I can get off."

Annaleah's heart filled with joy and, at the same time, apprehension. She had been the second child of two and never had younger siblings, though she loved children. But she really didn't have much experience with them and was not sure how she was going to do this.

A gentle, calming voice seemed to whisper to her tumultuous soul, *Don't worry. Remember? You can do all things through Christ, because He gives you strength... Let me 'do', you 'follow'.* Annaleah took a deep breath and determined to trust her Savior, who had already proven Himself so faithful. For one, he had died to save her, then had risen from the dead, and was still alive today. What power and love! She sighed deeply. He would take care of her, and she would strive to love these boys as the Lord Jesus loved her – she didn't think that part would be hard at all – and to teach them what she had learned about how much He loved the whole world.

Drawing herself from her reverie, she happily put her arms about Spencer, "It sounds like a good plan. We'll do our best for them!"

Monday morning dawned overcast and dreary. Spencer glanced out the window with a sigh and returned to brushing his hair. When it rained outside of the city, it seemed refreshing and even made one want to splash around in it. But it was different in this big, crowded city. Rain just made everything seem even duller. Maybe it was his outlook, because he didn't really like the city anyway. As Spencer tried to lift his spirits and think on more pleasant things, he caught the wonderful aroma of frying eggs wafting up the stairs from the kitchen and sighed again. Shaking his head to clear it of gloomy thoughts, he quickly dressed and dashed down the stairs a few moments later.

As he descended, Annaleah glanced up from the stove where she was frying the eggs he had smelled, her cheeks flushed from the warm burner, "It's almost ready."

Spencer kissed her rosy cheek and then began setting their places at the table. As he worked he spoke quietly, "When I was reading my Bible earlier, I came across the verse that says, 'Whoso stops his ears at the cry of the poor, he also shall cry himself and shall not be heard.'"

A fork slipped out of his hand and clattered to the floor. Spencer paused, glancing at Annaleah with an impish grin before he stooped to recover it. As he went to the drawer to procure a new fork, he continued, "It made me feel more than ever like those boys were crying out for help, and wonder how I could fail to listen…"

His face grew thoughtful, "I wonder what would have happened if we hadn't listened to Him asking us to help them. Probably they would end up like the rest of the orphans." He remembered with remorse how he had nearly turned them away. "I hope we're not too late."

Annaleah smiled at him, "Don't worry about it, Spence. We're going now."

Spencer smiled his thanks at Annaleah's attempt to comfort him, "I think I might deserve to feel this way."

Annaleah just smiled tenderly as she flipped an egg. How she loved Spencer. His heart was so big. And when he realized he was wrong, he always admitted it, though sometimes she thought he was too hard on himself.

After a reflective pause, Spencer added playfully, "And then, you talked me into it." He continued with a good-natured laugh, "The Bible does say, 'a prudent wife is from the Lord.' "

Annaleah's tinkling laugh joined his as she set the eggs on the table and took a seat. *Giving the credit to someone else as always,* she thought fondly. "I think God talked you into it, not me. If you remember, I was scared about it, too," she said with a sweet smile.

"Yup. But he used you to talk to me," he said, kissing the top of her head before he sat down.

As soon as they were through with their meal, Spencer and Annaleah dashed about the house, preparing for the trip to the orphanage. Excitement mingled with nervousness in their hearts. The couple doubted they would be permitted to take the boys home that day, but they wanted to begin the process as soon as possible.

Nevertheless, the moment they stood before their door, ready to depart, their eager hearts began racing as the seriousness of what they were about to do penetrated their beings. The sun had emerged, cheering them a bit, but each took a deep breath to summon courage. Spencer turned to Annaleah and grasped her hands, "Let's pray before we start out." She smiled agreement and bowed her head with him.

"Lord, we know we're doing what You want us to, but somehow we're still afraid. Please be there with us today, direct our speech and circumstances, and bind Satan. Don't allow him to have any influence here. And... please bless us with Your peace. And most of all, may Your will be done. In Jesus name... amen." Spencer squeezed Annaleah's hands and smiled at her, then released her right hand and they started forward.

When they were once more standing before the unfeeling gate, Spencer reached up and, with a burst of courage, pressed the button in the cold, stone wall.

A few minutes later, the gatekeeper appeared. Dully, he questioned, "How may I help you?"

"We came to see Mr. Minor," Spencer answered a little apprehensively. What if they weren't allowed in a second time?

The gatekeeper squinted. "You were here a couple days ago. You still want back in?" he asked incredulously.

Spencer nodded a little uncertainly. If there was any way to adopt those boys without entering this formidable place again, he'd probably do it.

The gatekeeper almost eagerly opened the gate for them – a little wider this time. He watched as they made their way up the fence-lined path.

Annaleah shuddered involuntarily and moved a little closer to Spencer. The children did not appear to be in the fenced yard this time, so she reluctantly followed Spencer to the steps where the same man who had ushered them into the building on Saturday grimaced at them and inquired in superior tones, "Yes?"

"We would like to see Mr. Minor," Spencer said.

"Follow me."

They were once again grudgingly conducted into Mr. Minor's office. This time the man glanced up when they entered and grunted, "Back again?"

"Yes, sir. We wanted to inquire about adopting a couple of boys," Spencer replied in excitement even as a tiny lump of trepidation pulsed within his heart.

At these words, Mr. Minor seemed a bit surprised and suddenly sat upright. His chair groaned in protest as he leaned this way, then that, clearing off his desk. "Any ones in particular?" he questioned in a businesslike tone, neatly folding his hands in front of him on his now clutter-free desk.

"Yes, Trey and Sorryl, brothers who were brought here two Saturdays ago," Spencer answered, trying not to feel intimidated.

"Ah. Those ones. Lucky for you most orphans here don't have such names as those. I know who you're talking about. Most folks have to go and point out the one they want." The 'most folks' he spoke of consisted of a few do-gooders who decided to try and adopt an orphan or two but usually returned them promptly. The street children knew that, if once they entered the dreaded 'Containment Home', they would most likely be there for the rest of their young lives until they reached eighteen, unless they somehow managed to escape.

Mr. Minor easily swung into his businessman mode now, "Good boys, those." In his eagerness, he forgot that, on Saturday, he had told the couple standing before him they were 'troublesome boys'.

Amused, Annaleah glanced at Spencer. Lucky for this man, they had no need to be talked into adopting the children. They had already made their decision. They had discussed the risk of what they were about to do since they knew nothing about these boys, but both were confident in their decision. They were now sure God wanted them to do it and would therefore have His blessing.

"So, how do we go about adopting them?" Spencer finally asked, a little bewildered when Mr. Minor did not say anything more, as well as a bit apprehensive, fearing that the man would not allow them to adopt *any* of the children.

"Oh. Well..." Mr. Minor paused, leaning over to retrieve some of the papers he had cleared from his desk. The chair creaked ominously and Spencer winced, afraid the man and his chair would topple over at any moment.

Mr. Minor sat upright once more with some papers in his hand, "Here, fill this out. We make it easy for you here," he boasted with a grin.

As he handed the paperwork over to them, he squinted a bit. "Say, do you happen to be their relatives?" He had quite forgotten that he had just informed them they had completed a search and found none. "You both look like 'em".

Spencer glanced at Annaleah, "Not that I know of." He chuckled. "But that's nice anyway. That we look alike, I mean." Spencer let out a silent sigh of relief – it seemed Mr. Minor was willing to let them adopt as many children as they pleased. *I wish we could adopt them all*, he thought. His heart ached as he realized that was quite impossible. Catching Annaleah's little sigh, he knew she was thinking the same thing. He squeezed her arm comfortingly and she sent him a wobbly smile before she turned to the paperwork Mr. Minor handed her. She was surprised by how little there was. She carefully looked it over as she and Spencer began filling in the required information. Suddenly, her eyes locked on the words they had nearly passed over. She never noticed Spencer's wondering gaze as she stared intently at the names recorded as Trey and Sorryl's parents. All she could see were the letters that formed the words 'Anna Ruth (Welden) Carter'. The letters swam before her and her mind raced back in time.

She was three years old. It had been a weary year with Mama sick and Papa trying to take care of the fields and the home, and to care for his wife as well. Yet through it all, she and her six-year-old sister, Anna, had held a sort of hope in their young hearts that all would soon be 'right' once more. They clung to each other with fierce loyalty and found a sense of security as their sibling bond deepened.

And then it happened. With no warning at all, her sister had disappeared. Anna had died. With a pang in her heart too deep to release itself in tears, Annaleah had run to her room and thrown herself onto her little bed, clutching her aching heart and clenching her dry eyes tightly shut.

Three years later, she and her father were on their own, for her mother had passed away. She wondered at a sort of regret her father seemed to carry. A regret she couldn't discover the source of.

Annaleah's mind flew to seventeen years later, only one year before she had married Spencer. It was four days before her twenty-third birthday.

"Annaleah."

The weak voice of her once strong father drew her to his bedside. "Yes, Papa?"

"I must..." he broke off in deep emotion. "I must tell you something."

She waited in silence, the urgency in his voice drawing curiosity, but strangely no fear, to her heart.

"Go to my bureau. Second drawer down, you will find a photo at the bottom of my shirts."

Obediently following his instructions, she wondered what could be so important to her father. She could hear him trying to catch his breath after the effort of so much speaking. He hadn't said so much for days. She could feel his eyes on her as she felt underneath his shirts and drew a photograph from their depths. The face that peered at her from its surface froze her as she prepared to turn back to her father's bedside. Her heart leaped within her. It seemed to be her own face, only brown eyes shone from the features instead of her blue ones and the cheeks were fuller than her own. Was it? Could it be... Questions tumbled through her mind as she turned to her father with wide eyes, not daring to hope. Suddenly, she realized he was crying.

"Papa! Papa? What's wrong?"

He shook his head as if to tell her not to worry about him. When he finally spoke, she wondered how he had known what she had been thinking. "Yes, Annaleah. You are right. It is your sister."

She could do nothing but stare at the picture of her beloved Anna.

"Your mother was too sick to take care of both of you. Someone offered to take Anna and raise her as their own and I finally agreed." He spoke now almost as if to himself, "I always wondered if I did the right thing. I begged them to take you as well, because I knew it would break your hearts, young as you were, to be separated and they planned to move to Texas somewhere near Houston where I knew you would never see each other again. They refused." His voice grew almost teasing, "Because you were too unpredictable for them. They said you were sly — I suppose because of your quiet nature that would be lost behind your fire if you found need for it." He laughed softly and placed a large hand over her smaller one, "I've always been glad they refused. I don't know what I would have done without my little joy-giver and gentle pillar of strength and comfort." His gaze traveled to the photo Annaleah was holding and she handed it to him.

"This was sent to me with a note from the people who had taken her — the Weldens I think was their name — on her seventeenth birthday. I couldn't bring myself to show it to you, for that would mean I would have to admit to you my lie." He looked into her eyes, "Can you ever forgive me?"

Tears flooded Annaleah's eyes. "Oh, Papa! Of course I can!" she breathed as she leaned over and encircled him in a gentle embrace. She didn't know what she was going to do when he was gone. They had been everything to each other ever since her mother's death. But she also knew he was in much pain and found comfort knowing he would be much happier in Heaven with the Lord he had waited so long to see—

Suddenly, she jerked her eyes from the words as Mr. Minor impatiently cleared his throat again. She smiled an apology and then leaned over to Spencer as she pointed at the name of Trey and Sorryl's mother, "Do you remember my sister I've been searching for more information about?" Her voice threatened to tremble, "And that her name was Anna Ruth Welden?"

Spencer's eyes grew wide as he realized what she was saying. The name he had taken little notice of on the sheet before him now stood out boldly – 'Anna Ruth (Welden) Carter'... He remembered well the photo of Annaleah's sister they had hanging over the mantle.

Annaleah looked up hastily at Mr. Minor, who was looking on with great curiosity, something she hadn't seen in him since they met.

"Where did you say the parents were from?" Annaleah asked eagerly.

Mr. Minor's answer came provokingly slowly. He paused a moment to twirl his moustache while searching his papers.

But he did not have time to respond before Annaleah discovered the answer on the sheet before her and gave a shout, which came out as a squeal because she was trying to hold it back. Rocketing from her seat, she danced across the room in her enthusiastic style, the papers fluttering in her hands as she spun in the middle of the floor. Suddenly, with a sheepish grin, she danced her way back and made herself sit down. Sadness crept into her heart at the knowledge that if this were her sister, she would never see her again. But the joy in knowing her sister's sons would soon be her own and a part of her sister would live on overshadowed her sorrow.

Spencer watched Annaleah's reaction with a delighted smile, but Mr. Minor ignored it all and answered complacently, as if he did not know she had already found the answer, "A small town near Houston, Texas." Then he looked up as if asking, "What's this all about?"

"I think I just found out that these are my lost sister's sons," Annaleah announced with a smile she could not contain.

Mr. Minor nodded and smiled, satisfied now that he knew what all the excitement was about, then he sat impatiently twirling his moustache until they returned to signing the papers.

As she scanned the paperwork and signed where required, Annaleah's heart pulsed with gratefulness and wonder of how God had brought her lost sister's sons right to their city and now into their home.

After the paperwork was filled out, Mr. Minor said, "There, now you can take them home any time you wish." He leaned forward eagerly and added hintingly, "Now is good." This said, he sat back again with a satisfied smile.

Spencer and Annaleah looked at each other in astonishment. Their house wasn't even ready yet. They had expected it to at least be a couple of days before they could take the children home. They'd have to find and set up a bed for the boys before that evening so the youngsters could have somewhere to sleep.

Spencer's head was spinning. "Perhaps we should wait until I'm out of work since I was only able to get half the day off today. Then I can have tomorrow off and be there the whole first day," Spencer suggested a bit reluctantly, not wanting to leave the children there any longer now that he knew he didn't have to.

"And I'd have time to get the house ready for them and find a bed and clothes somewhere in town," Annaleah agreed just as reluctantly. She shared Spencer's sentiment but knew she would have to be running all over town finding a used bed for them and whatever else they might need.

Spencer nodded and turned back to Mr. Minor, "Can we come get them this evening around six o'clock?"

"Well, if you're sure you don't want them now. They could be gone by the time you return you know."

Spencer shook his head with more decisiveness than he felt, "We'll come back later today."

At these words, they were unceremoniously ushered out of the building.

The couple saw that the children were still not outside, so they headed down the walk, which seemed like a valley hemmed in by ruthless fences instead of majestic mountains.

When they reached the gate, Spencer stood still for a moment before starting toward the shed. He had only taken one step when the shed door swung wide and the gatekeeper stepped out, bearing a key. He seemed a bit more cheerful and pleasant and Spencer and Annaleah wondered at the change.

However, as the gatekeeper drew near, he seemed disappointed and the slight smile faded from his lips. After casting an almost reproachful look the confused couple's way, he sullenly unlocked the gate and let them out without a word.

Spencer and Annaleah eagerly breathed in the sunny, fresh air as they began their walk home, shaking off the heaviness that seemed to cling to them like an unpleasant odor when they entered the 'Containment Home' gates.

"I wish we didn't have to leave them there," Annaleah mourned softly.

"Yeah, I know. Maybe we shouldn't have. But it's done now. We'll go back as soon as we can after I'm through with work," Spencer answered regretfully. If they had brought them home right away, Annaleah would have had to take them all over town with her in search for a bed and some clothes for the boys. He sighed, "This is best, though."

Annaleah nodded and blinked rapidly to ward off the tears she felt rushing to her eyes. Spencer was right. What was decided was decided. She would find what the boys needed and be ready when Spencer returned from work.

Chapter 3

Spencer dashed through the door after work that evening, calling as he flung the door open, "I'm ready!" He was halted abruptly when he collided with something. Blinking rapidly, he attempted to recover his vision to find out what new object Annaleah had placed in the hall. To his astonishment, his gaze met Annaleah's laughing eyes. "Oh! Hello. I guess you're ready, too. Are you all right?"

Annaleah laughed, "Yup. I'm fine." Then in a teasing voice she added, "You'd think you were only five years old or something, the way you came crashing in here nearly knocking me over in your excitement."

Spencer ran his fingers through his hair with a soft laugh, "Yeah, I guess we're both pretty excited and acting rather childish. Sorry about running into you."

"I don't mind one bit," Annaleah's soft, tinkling laugh sounded once more.

Spencer smiled, "Well then, should we go now? You *are* ready, right?" he added eagerly.

"Yup, I'm ready," Annaleah laughed.

"Then what are we waiting for?" Spencer wondered impatiently, pulling Annaleah out the door and to the car.

When they stood before the towering gate, Spencer rang the bell with a little more confidence than he had the last time, but still pulled his hand away rather rapidly.

The gatekeeper appeared and looked at them, first with hope, then irritation. He didn't even ask what they wanted, but just opened the gate barely enough for them to slip through and let them make their way up the fence-lined walk.

The man at the doors recognized them and motioned them to follow him, "Right this way," he almost ordered.

They entered the now familiar office and stood before Mr. Minor as he twirled his mustache.

Mr. Minor finally glanced up and, upon seeing who it was, immediately sat up straight, ordering, "Walsh, go get the two little ones in the crime ward." He looked Spencer and Annaleah's direction, "We should have them in a few minutes for you."

The couple nodded and took a seat as they anxiously waited, wondering at the uncaring way Mr. Minor spoke of the children.

Suddenly, the door swung open and Walsh returned, leading two small boys by the hand. "Here they are, sir," he said, going to his corner once more until his services would be of use again.

Spencer and Annaleah half rose as Trey and Sorryl entered, but dropped to their seats once more as Mr. Minor addressed the boys sternly, "These are your new family. They are very kind to take you. You must be very good for them."

"Yes, sir," the anxious boys answered, trying to stand tall in the middle of the floor where Walsh had unceremoniously left them.

Mr. Minor nodded to them coolly and turned to Spencer and Annaleah, "Well, they're all yours."

Spencer and Annaleah looked at each other. That was it?

"They *are* the right ones, aren't they?" Mr. Minor questioned apprehensively.

At Spencer and Annaleah's nod, Mr. Minor sat back in his chair, relieved.

Annaleah glanced at him once more, then stooped and spoke reassuringly to the boys as she struggled to stem the flow of tears that sprang to her eyes as compassion filled her heart, "We're going to take you home with us and you can live with us, how's that sound?"

Neither boy answered, but just stared searchingly into her face with matching, blue eyes. They remembered her from the street, but only vaguely. Their minds had been too tormented to retain much.

Annaleah invitingly held her hands out to them, coaxing, "Well, come along, we'll take you home." After she said it, she realized they probably had no idea what 'home' would be.

Trey slowly reached out, nervously taking her hand, but Sorryl retreated behind his older brother and refused to budge. He did not give his trust freely. But once he did, the receiver was sure to have his deep loyalty for the rest of their life.

Annaleah sighed, glancing at Spencer. He shrugged and then smiled encouragingly at the two boys, taking Annaleah's free arm to lead them out the door. The new parents glanced back to make sure Sorryl was following, but they needn't have worried, for the brothers were not about to let each other out of one another's sight.

When the foursome exited the building, Trey and Sorryl moved a bit closer to Spencer and Annaleah despite their fear of their new parents. The formidable fences posed a much worse threat in their young eyes.

The brothers warily watched these people who were leading them down the path. What were they doing? Mr. Minor had said they were their new parents. But... how? And what did it mean? Sorryl suppressed a shudder as he glanced at the fences. At least whatever it meant, nothing could get worse than it already was... Or could it?

As they approached the gate, the keeper rushed out of his little shed, clasping Spencer's hand warmly. "You're taking them?" he asked eagerly.

Surprised, Spencer felt his eyes widen in disbelief, but he quickly recovered enough to nod.

The gatekeeper wrung his hand even tighter, "Thank you, thank you, thank you!" he exclaimed happily. "I'm sorry about my attitude before. When you left without any children the second time, I figured you were turning more kids in or something."

Spencer didn't quite know what to do, so he just murmured, "I forgive you. And you're welcome." Then he added with a laugh, "But you should be thanking God, He's the one that convinced me to do this."

The gatekeeper nodded smilingly, "Those two were the ones I was most worried about. Now I just need to pray in parents for all the rest of them."

Spencer smiled, nearly laughing at the man's optimistic attitude, "We'll pray, too."

The gatekeeper beamed at them, then turned to the boys, who were looking on with wide eyes, "You'll love your new home. You're perfect for each other." He shook his head in wonder, "God sure does know how to match them up." He turned to open the gate, swinging it wide this time.

"Goodbye," Spencer and Annaleah waved as the gatekeeper continued to beam at them while he reluctantly closed the gate.

As soon as they were outside the iron gates, Trey and Sorryl sighed deeply, feeling as though they had been set free. But a cautious air still clung to them as their young hearts wondered what would happen now.

When they reached the Trestle vehicle, Annaleah helped Trey into the back, and then turned to assist the wary Sorryl. Finally, after a glance at Spencer who gave her a nod, she hopped into the back with the boys and they began the silent drive 'home'.

When they entered the house, the boys stared in awe. Even though it was not really a big house, it seemed so to them compared to where they had lived their entire lives.

While Annaleah prepared supper, Trey sat on the couch with his arm protectively surrounding his little brother, who had one little finger stuffed in his mouth while he snuggled fearfully against his 'big' brother. From their haven, they looked curiously about the room, not making a sound. The picture above the mantle especially held their attention. It looked familiar, somehow sending a warm glow to their hearts, but they knew not why. After a while, they turned their attention to Annaleah, who was bustling about the kitchen, and warily watched as she finished preparing supper.

But when the tempting food had been placed before them, they brightened without delay. The hunger pangs that gnawed at their insides intensified at the aroma. The brothers gazed at the food fearfully. Would they be allowed to eat some? Or would it be like it had been in the orphanage, where they had been given only small portions and had met with slaps from the older boys for diving in before the bullies had gotten more than their fair share.

Noticing their fearful, yet hopeful faces, Annaleah prayed they weren't too scared to eat.

Spencer looked compassionately on the boys, not quite knowing what to do, then bowed his head and began to pray for the food.

Both boys stared at him for a moment. Then Sorryl glanced at Trey. He remembered doing something like this not too long ago… only with his Mommy and Daddy. With a last glance at his brother, who had folded his hands, closed his eyes, and bowed his head, he followed Trey's example. When Spencer and Annaleah peaked at the boys, the new parents glanced at each other in surprise.

When the prayer was through, the boys paused a moment, then dove in as if they had not seen food for a year. Annaleah smiled, pleased they weren't too afraid to eat after all.

After he had taken a few hurried gulps, Sorryl cast a worried glance at Spencer. He vaguely remembered living in a home and eating at a cozy table like this, but that was forever ago, wasn't it? What if this man was going to clobber him just like the boys in the orphanage had? However, the man gave him a soft smile, calming the fears that had beset his young heart, and he returned to his food with no further reserve.

That evening after supper, Annaleah and Spencer joined their new children in the living room. After a glance at each other and then at the boys seated by the couch, they settled on the throw rug in the middle of the room.

Annaleah glanced at Spencer, silently asking, *Now what?*

He shrugged with a mischievous grin and proposed, "You wanna play hot potato? ...If you remember how. If they see us playing, maybe they'll feel better about us."

Annaleah smiled, feeling a bit silly, "I think I remember how, let's try." She rose and left the room for a moment, returning with a little ball. She seated herself across from Spencer on the floor and handed the ball to him.

He smiled, "Ready? I think we're supposed to say something like, 'Hot potato, hot potato, who's got the hot potato...'" he began tossing the ball and Annaleah picked up the chant as they continued tossing it back and forth.

"...Who's got the hot potato? Whoever's got the hot potato, you are *out!*" She thrust the ball at Spencer. He caught it just as they called 'out'.

Annaleah laughed and glanced at the boys, then they began again.

Trey and Sorryl curiously watched from a safe distance, Sorryl peeking from behind the humble couch and Trey sitting next to him beside the couch.

"I haven't done this for *years!*" Spencer chuckled.

Annaleah giggled, "Me either."

Keeping a close eye on the adult's actions, Trey cautiously crept a foot closer. When Spencer looked over and winked at him as he tossed the ball back to Annaleah, Trey suddenly scuttled for the back of the couch to join Sorryl. That man had such big, penetrating eyes. But, somehow, they seemed full of something wonderful... just like the lady's were. Something that made him feel all warm and special, that abated the fears battering relentlessly within his chest.

Annaleah laughed softly at Trey's antics, although her heart still ached for both of the boys. These children were fun already.

At the pleasant sound, Trey curiously poked his head out again. In Annaleah's tinkling laugh, he detected that sound of whatever it was he could see in their eyes. What was it? He caught Spencer looking his way and dodged behind the couch again. But it wasn't long before his chestnut head reappeared, peeking around the side of the couch, curious to discover what that something was.

Spencer saw him and made a funny face, pleasantly surprised when Trey smiled tentatively back.

In a couple minutes, Trey had scooted nearer again, just out of reach of Spencer and Annaleah. All of a sudden, he scampered back to Sorryl's side, whispering in his ear and beckoning him to come over with him. Sorryl furiously shook his head. His searching blue eyes were wide with fear. He had seen and heard that something, too. It reminded him of his Mommy and Daddy. Nevertheless, these were strangers, and strangers were something to avoid at all costs.

Trey slowly made his way back to Spencer and Annaleah alone, looking back every once in a while to beckon Sorryl forward. But Sorryl refused to come closer.

Finally, Trey reached Spencer and Annaleah and plopped himself down between them. Maybe it was love that he saw. He tentatively returned Annaleah's smile, then spoke for the first time that evening.

"I'll play with you," he said as if he was doing them a great favor, which, in truth, he was.

Annaleah and Spencer tried not to laugh for fear they would scare him, but they soon lost the battle and a chuckle escaped them.

Yes, that's what it was, love. Like his Mommy and Daddy had had.

Trey looked back and forth between them for a moment, and when Spencer smiled at him, he returned it with a shy half-smile. Spencer tossed him the ball and he caught it with a grin, then passed it to Annaleah. He left the chanting of the words to the adults, but eagerly passed the ball when his turn came. Though he was enjoying the game immensely, he never forgot his little brother behind the couch, and often glanced his way to be sure he was okay.

Sorryl peeked timidly from his hiding spot. Catching Annaleah looking at him with that same thing shining in her beautiful eyes, he quickly ducked his head, diving behind the couch out of sight.

Trey trusted them. They had not done anything to him yet. In fact, they were having fun with him. And there was that sound in their laughs again. Was it joy? Yes, they had joy. But there was something else...

It was not long before Sorryl cautiously peeked around again, this time with a playful smile barely touching his lips. Maybe they would play with him, too.

When Annaleah looked at him again, he dove back behind the couch in an almost playful way. He appeared a moment later with an even wider smile. Maybe he could trust them... just a little.

After a few minutes of peeking around then diving behind the couch in a shy but playful way, he finally ventured to the middle of the floor, where he sat watching the little group with great interest.

Trey glanced up and spotted his brother, "Hey! Come and play!"

But Sorryl just gazed at them with searching eyes and stuck a nervous finger in his mouth. He didn't know if he was ready to trust them *that* much yet.

Annaleah finally broke off from the group on the throw rug and scooted slowly toward Sorryl. He watched her intently, like a deer ready to spring at a moment's notice. What was she going to do?

Annaleah halted and smiled at him, perceiving that he would dart away if she came any closer. Oh! How she longed to catch the tender boy up in her arms!

He tentatively returned her smile, revealing a single dimple in his left cheek.

Slowly sliding a little closer, Annaleah invitingly held her arms out. The movement suddenly reminded him of his mother. That's what the something was! It was love! Oh, how his heart yearned for love! He nearly ran into her embrace, but quickly caught himself and stiffened. He glanced at Trey, who was watching them closely.

Returning Sorryl's look with an inviting smile, Trey nodded to encourage him on.

After hesitating a moment longer, Sorryl scooted so he was sitting next to Annaleah. He longed to cuddle in her lap, but he could not bring himself to trust her enough to put himself in that vulnerable position. He remembered wrapping his little arms around a lady he had seen in the street after his parents had mysteriously disappeared. Everyone told him a drunk man ate them with his car, but he somehow thought they must be lying. He had thought the lady was his mother, but she had looked down at him, shrieked as she swatted him on his tender cheek, and begun calling out for help, for someone to save her from 'this malicious thief'. Bewildered, Sorryl had heartbrokenly stumbled away, holding his stinging cheek and longing for someone to hold his aching heart.

Annaleah smiled at him again, her heart warm with joy. She slowly offered her hand. He hesitated a moment, then laid his little palm within hers. She smiled that smile so full of what he had discovered was love and gently led him to the others. He sat down next to Trey and smiled at Spencer.

After playing with the boys for a while longer, the new parents spoke to them earnestly. They wanted Trey and Sorryl to understand what had happened that day.

"Do you know why we took you to our house today?" Spencer questioned softly.

Trey looked at him with questions in his deep eyes and shook his head.

Sorryl's chestnut head gave an almost imperceptible shake.

Smiling gently, Spencer continued, "We brought you home because we have adopted you. Which means now you're our sons. And we're your Mommy and Daddy and will love you forever, no matter what. It's like what God will do for us. We can become sons of God and then He is our Father… and you won't find a better one anywhere. Then we have two Daddies."

Sorryl stared. So that was it. A new Mommy and Daddy. Would these ones suddenly disappear some day too? He steeled his heart against the ache that rose in his chest. Well. These seemed like nice people, but he wasn't so sure he wanted a new Mommy and Daddy. He'd have to wait and see if he could trust these strangers before he accepted them that way. He understood what the man had said about God. His other Mommy and Daddy had taught them that too, and he and Trey knew God had adopted them when they decided to trust Jesus to clean their sins from their hearts. Sometimes during those last hard weeks he had thought he would die if it weren't for knowing his Father in Heaven was there. He knew Trey felt the same way.

Trey studied the man and lady before him. These were to be his new Mommy and Daddy? Did this mean he belonged to someone again? Though he didn't fully trust these people yet, his heart somehow felt more peaceful knowing he and his brother weren't on their own any longer. It felt so nice to belong.

When it was time for bed, Trey permitted a delighted Spencer to carry him upstairs, but Sorryl would only allow Annaleah to hold his hand and help him up. His loyal, but wary, heart wanted to be sure he would not be betrayed before he trusted someone that much again. He could not forget the shrieking lady in the street, although this lady's voice was much nicer than that lady's had been.

Annaleah had found a used bed for the boys and decided to put it in her and Spencer's room at least for that night. They tucked their new children in and then prayed with them. Annaleah knew Spencer was longing with her to give each of the small boys a tender kiss on the forehead, but neither dared. Not so soon.

"Goodnight," Annaleah whispered instead.

Spencer echoed her, "Goodnight."

The boys were silent for a moment before Trey ventured timidly, "G'night." Oh! How wonderful it was to be 'home' again! Without rough boys shouting at you after lights out, and then blaming the noise on you when the overseer came storming angrily in. Where frightening noises weren't echoing up and down the cold corridors and the beds weren't hard and lumpy, if you were lucky enough to get a bed.

At his sweet tones, Spencer and Annaleah smiled at each other and headed for their own bed. They somehow knew they were in for a spectacular adventure full of wonderful rewards.

A piercing scream broke the silence of the night. Annaleah sat up abruptly, wondering what had awakened her.

"No! He-e-elp! Mama! Mama! Oh, Mama!" the desperate cry ended in a wail.

Annaleah flung the covers back and leapt out of bed. She hurried to the boys' bedside.

The screams began again, "Oh! No! Please Ma-am! I just wanted my Mama! Mama!" Sorryl tossed on the bed as if struggling to break free. His tones, full of heartbroken despair, brought hot tears to Annaleah's eyes.

She paused a moment, afraid she would frighten him more if she woke him since he didn't really know her. But how could she just leave him there, heartbrokenly crying out and struggling in terror to break free from a relentless, though imaginary, foe. In a moment, she gently swooped him into her arms with silent tears glittering in her own eyes.

Instantly, Sorryl's eyes flew open. He began fighting to break free from her. Annaleah nearly dropped him, but Spencer leapt to her side and caught the frantic boy just in time. In a moment, he placed Sorryl back in Annaleah's arms, because Sorryl seemed even more scared of him. Annaleah's lips trembled. She didn't know what to do for the suffering boy.

His cries pierced the night once more, "No! Please! I thought you were Mommy! Help! Mommy!" His breath came in ragged gasps as he fought to free himself and rise above the fog that was making his movements sluggish.

Lord! What do I do for him? Spencer cried silently. "Sorryl, it's alright," he whispered when Sorryl paused to take a breath.

Sorryl's cries ceased for a moment and he glanced Spencer's way. But new terror gripped his small frame and he began crying and struggling once again.

"Sh-sh-sh. It's all right," Annaleah attempted to calm him when she could finally find her voice.

At the sweet tones, Sorryl paused in his struggling. He looked up into her face with terror in his eyes. Where had that voice come from? The fog encircling his mind began to lift as he focused on the face of this lady who was holding him. Some of the terror seeped from his heart.

Annaleah hesitated a moment, then finally whispered reassuringly, "Mommy's got you."

Sorryl suddenly stopped whimpering and gazed at her more closely. He searched her face as he evaluated her remark for truth. Finally, he took another shaky breath and wrapped his arms tightly about her neck, relaxing in her embrace.

Annaleah gave a sigh of relief. She smiled as she cuddled him and began talking to him in soothing tones.

Spencer sighed too. The poor little guy. He caressed the shaking boy's chestnut hair.

Sorryl looked up at him. After a moment, he sighed. A deep, restful sigh. He somehow vaguely remembered something pleasant and comforting about the man now that he was not in hysterics.

Annaleah glanced at Spencer and smiled. "I think he's going to be okay," she whispered.

Spencer nodded.

After that night, Sorryl clung to Annaleah, and soon to Spencer as well. Having decided they could be trusted, the small boy gradually adopted them as his new mother and father. It didn't take Trey long to become just as fond of them.

When the boys had settled in a little more, Annaleah enthusiastically pointed out the portrait the boys had noticed above the mantle.

Trey and Sorryl turned to gaze at it once more.

"See? That's your Mommy up there, when she was younger. Do you know she's my sister?"

Sorryl stuck a finger in his mouth, contemplating. His new Mommy was his Mommy's sister? Like he was Trey's brother? He glanced between the picture and his new mother and decided to believe her.

Trey gazed and gazed at the portrait. So that was why it had stirred something within him! That lovely lady in the picture was his Mommy! And his new Mommy was her sister.

A few days later, as Spencer watched Sorryl's clinging arms clasp first Trey and then Annaleah about the neck, he smiled happily. *Lord, thanks for leading me to adopt these boys,* he silently breathed.

Trey dashed over to Spencer then, holding his arms up.

Spencer smiled and swung him gently into his arms, then turned to beam at Annaleah over Trey and Sorryl's heads.

Annaleah returned his smile. They knew they would never regret their decision to follow God's call to take in these boys who had become so dear to their hearts in such a short time. They also knew there were many struggles and adventures ahead of them.

Chapter 4

One Month Later...

Annaleah was at home enjoying her busy day with the two boys. Much had happened in the last month and she couldn't believe how close the four of them had grown. She had always hoped Trey and Sorryl would become just like real sons, but now that it had actually happened, she could hardly believe the change.

She ventured to the kitchen, gathering materials to prepare lunch. Suddenly, she dropped the spoon she had taken up and clutched her stomach, barely keeping herself from vomiting. Something in that region had been bothering her a little lately, but she hadn't thought it was serious, though it had gradually grown more bothersome. Bracing herself, she glanced at the boys who were constructing houses out of blocks for their 'people', which were actually flowers from the yard outside.

"I'll wait until Spencer gets home," she resolved with a deep breath as she clutched her stomach once more and tried to calm her fluttering heart. In spite of her resolve, a moment later she hurriedly reached for the telephone. Her hands shook as she desperately dialed the operator and barley managed to ask for Spencer's work place.

"Hello, Factory one-twenty-five, Maria speaking, how may I help you?" the motherly receptionist answered.

Annaleah took a deep breath and managed, "May I speak with Spencer Trestle please?"

"One moment," Maria replied.

After what seemed like hours Spencer picked up the phone, "Is that you Annaleah?"

"Yes," she barely croaked out.

Sensing the pain in her voice, Spencer grew anxious and his fingers involuntarily tightened about the receiver, "Oh, honey! What's the matter?"

"I... can you come home?" Annaleah managed weakly.

"Hold on, I'll find out," Spencer hurriedly glanced to Maria to see if she could contact his boss and obtain permission for him to leave.

But, before he could speak, she told him, "Go ahead Spencer, I already called and he said it was fine."

Spencer urgently spoke into the receiver, "I'll be there as soon as I can, Annaleah." Then the receptionist gave him an encouraging pat on the shoulder and he hurriedly dashed to the car.

It seemed like a torturing eternity before he finally pulled up in front of their home. When he dashed through the door, he found Annaleah collapsed in an easy chair. "What's the matter?" He asked softly, striving with all his might to keep anxiety out of his quavering voice. Her pale face and the way she was clutching her stomach terrified him.

"I... my stomach hurts terrible," she whispered weakly, unable to say anything more.

Spencer realized he needed to get her to the hospital without delay, so he helped the boys, who were worriedly hovering over their mommy, put their shoes on. Then he gently helped Annaleah out the door. A rock of fear settled in his stomach. *God! Please help us! I don't know what's wrong with Annaleah, but please show us what to do! Please!*

Just as they labored their way off the porch and onto the sidewalk, a police officer walked past their home. He stopped suddenly, recognizing the lady being helped toward a vehicle in obvious pain. Giving another start as he glimpsed the boys hovering at her side, he hurriedly began walking again. But he had gone no more than a few paces when he halted abruptly. After a severe inward struggle, he resolutely turned back. As he retraced his steps, the officer shook his head in wonder. He couldn't believe that she actually had those boys with her. When he reached them, he cleared his throat nervously, then hesitatingly but gently took Annaleah's other arm and assisted Spencer in helping her the rest of the way to the car.

The boys looked up at him fearfully, remembering their experience with this man not too long ago. Was he going to lug their new Mommy off to that horrible place too? Trey nearly attacked him to defend his Mommy, but the officer smiled gently down at them just in time, trying to reassure them as his heart smote him for afflicting these two boys so. Trey hesitated. This wasn't how he remembered the man.

As the policeman gently took her arm, Annaleah glanced up and managed to send a sweet smile his way in spite of her pain. She noticed that his face seemed softer, and her heart filled with joy for him even amid her physical pain.

Spencer looked between them, realizing they recognized each other, but made no inquiries at the moment. He was too busy worrying about Annaleah, so he just respectfully nodded his thanks.

When Annaleah was safely in the back of the car, the officer paused awkwardly a moment, perceiving that the family was headed to the hospital, and then asked tentatively, "Would you like me to come with you?"

Spencer glanced at him and, after a brief pause, nodded his agreement.

"I'll drive if you want to sit with her," the policeman offered.

Spencer couldn't find his voice, but took the back seat next to Annaleah and the boys and tossed him the key for answer. He still did not know this man's name, but, in his anxiety over Annaleah, he forgot to worry that this could be a robber, or anything else, disguised as a policeman.

When they reached the hospital, Annaleah was whisked away and the rest were left to wait anxiously in the waiting room.

"I should get back to work now," the officer observed regretfully. Suddenly, he held out his hand and offered warmly, "I'm Joe Reaper, the officer that found the two boys— if your wife told you about it."

49

Spencer nodded and shook Joe's hand heartily, "She did. Mine's Spencer Trestle, her name's Annaleah. We'd be happy to have you visit sometime," he added, sensing that Joe needed some camaraderie. He had taken a liking to the man immediately, though he wasn't sure exactly why. Perhaps it was the silent plea in the man's eyes for someone to understand and allay the pain hidden there.

Joe nodded his thanks, paused a moment, then finally said awkwardly, "I'll be prayin' for you."

Spencer nodded his thanks and Joe left, feeling with a strange sense of joy that perhaps he had found a new friend, though he did not realize that he had also begun a wonderful yet challenging journey of opening his heart again.

The boys watched this exchange between their Daddy and the policeman with great interest, wondering at the difference in the officer.

When Joe had disappeared out the door, Trey and Sorryl crept to their father and perched on his lap, each toying with a lock of their daddy's deep chestnut hair while they all three anxiously awaited some news. It seemed as if they had been sitting there for an eternity. Wouldn't the doctor ever come out and tell them what was wrong?

A moment later, the door opened softly and the doctor beckoned Spencer in. He rose, carrying the little boys with him.

When the door had closed behind them, the doctor spoke quietly, "Annaleah has an infection in her uterus. It seems to have completely taken it over although, miraculously, it has not spread anywhere else." The doctor paused a moment before continuing compassionately, "We feel we should perform a hysterectomy before the infection spreads."

At Spencer's blank look, the doctor realized what he had said must not have sunk in. He spoke again, "In other words, there is a bad infection in her womb and we feel the womb should be removed as soon as possible. He paused again before continuing gently, "This would mean she could not have children, but it would save her life."

Spencer worked his jaw, but no words came. He wanted to scream out at God, *This isn't right! We're supposed to have lots of chil-*

dren! But he swallowed hard and ground his teeth together instead, managing to ask softly, "Does she know?"

The doctor shook his head, "I figured you would want to be with her when she found out."

"Thank you," Spencer whispered brokenly.

Trey looked at his daddy worriedly, "Mommy?"

Spencer looked at the boys' anxious faces and kissed the tops of their heads as he tried to steady his voice, "She'll be okay; we just have to fix her." The words wavered at the end despite his determination. In those words, it sounded so simple, and yet... it was far from being simple.

The doctor smiled compassionately and turned to lead them down the hall to Annaleah's room.

As they walked, Sorryl reached up and wiped a tear off his daddy's cheek, "You're cryin'," he observed in comforting tones.

Spencer smiled sadly and nodded his head in acknowledgement. When they reached Annaleah's room, he took a deep breath and followed the doctor in.

Knowing Spencer wouldn't be able to deliver the news, the doctor paused a moment when they had entered, then began explaining to her.

Spencer tenderly watched Annaleah's expression as she heard the sad news. She fixed her eyes, now brimming with tears, on Spencer's face, drawing comfort from him.

Spencer went to her side, taking her hand comfortingly in his as the doctor continued.

The two boys, not really understanding what was happening, but knowing something was amiss, hung worriedly around his legs.

When the doctor was through, Annaleah whispered heartbrokenly, "Why?"

After a pause, the doctor quietly said, "I'll be in the next room when you need me." Then he added, "Would you like me to take your boys with me?"

At those words, the boys clung more fiercely to their daddy's legs and Sorryl let out a whimper.

Spencer tenderly looked down at his sons and shook his head as he swung them into his strong arms, "Thank you, but I think they'll be fine."

The doctor nodded his head in understanding and softly closed the door behind him as he left.

Silence reigned.

"But the Lord knows what He is doing," Annaleah said determinedly, breaking the silence.

"Yes," Spencer agreed quietly, for that was all he could say. He swallowed, trying to get rid of the lump in his throat.

"And I'm glad it's just my womb, and not all of me," Annaleah added, attempting a smile.

Pulling himself out of the pit of self-pity he was digging for himself, Spencer tenderly brushed back a dark curl that had fallen across Annaleah's forehead. "I have a wonderful wife," he said, smiling affectionately into her eyes.

She smiled softly back at him as a tear traced its way down her pale cheek.

Spencer gently wiped it away before he asked reluctantly, "I guess we better do it, huh?"

Annaleah hesitated a moment, then nodded. Oh! It was so hard to trust God, but she realized that she needed to embrace the grace He was offering now, as He always did for anyone that would accept it.

Throughout the next few, draining weeks while Annaleah recovered from the surgery, Spencer and Annaleah battled with deep pain and sadness. How could it be they would never have children of their own? That Annaleah would never know what it felt like to have a little person growing within her.

"But, you know, the Lord has been so good," Spencer spoke from a deep silence one evening. "He knew you wouldn't be able to have children, and Trey and Sorryl would need parents, and gave us to each other to fill the needs in each of our hearts and lives. I still don't know why these bad things happen other than that this is now a sinful world and must have sorrow because of it." He sighed. "I must say, I can't wait for Heaven."

Annaleah listened to her husband as peace began to spread through her heart. "You're right. He's always so faithful!" Annaleah said, a soft light beginning to glow in her eyes. "And yet so often all we see are the bad things."

After a thoughtful silence, Spencer spoke quietly, "I think we really ought to stop dwelling on the things that bring pain and try to find the joys. I know it'll be a hard journey that requires some stiff resolve, but..." his voice trailed off.

Annaleah leaned her cheek on her husband's strong shoulder and whispered, "Yes. I think you're right. No. I *know* you're right."

He put his arm about her shoulders and nearly whispered, "Then let's start right now with a verse to remind us when we begin to forget, 'Let us come before His presence with thanksgiving, and make a joyful noise unto Him with psalms.' I love the song that says, 'Count your blessings, name them one by one. Count your many blessings, see what God has done.' Perhaps we could do that each night before we go to sleep."

"Yes, let's. Let's count our blessings. One is that I am still alive."

"And we have two wonderful boys."

"And a house and..."

One evening, a couple weeks after Annaleah's surgery, Spencer answered the door to find Joe standing on their doorstep. The officer was twisting his hat in his hands, not sure he would be welcomed.

Joe shifted his feet anxiously, "Hi. Uh... do you remember me? I'm Joe Reaper, the police officer that—"

"Of course I remember you!" Spencer interrupted, immediately giving Joe a warm welcome, thus banishing the man's fears as he ushered him in.

Everyone except Annaleah, who was curled up on the couch with a warm blanket, was in the middle of a rousing game of snake tag in which participants must slither around like snakes. The boys were disappointed that their mommy couldn't join them, but they were growing used to her weak state after the surgery and understood that they needed to be gentle with her.

The boys were still racing around when Joe entered, but as soon as they caught sight of him, they ran and hid behind the couch.

Joe grimaced, wishing he had not been so harsh and unfeeling toward them. After a moment of awkward silence, he drew an enticing red yo-yo from his pocket and began performing fancy tricks with it.

Soon, Trey laughed as Joe swung it once again about his head.

As he continued to flip it through the air, Sorryl finally giggled.

The boys glanced at their parents and, seeing that Mommy and Daddy weren't afraid of him, they ventured over to Joe.

"How do you do that?" Trey asked in awe, looking up at him.

Joe laughed, "Like this." He demonstrated once more, drawing another giggle from the boys.

Sorryl looked at Trey and their gazes met. Joe must have changed somehow. *And I think I rather like him now,* Sorryl thought. Watching Joe's smiling face as he swung the yo-yo in seemingly impossible patterns, they nearly forgot the incident on the street. They trusted their Mommy and Daddy, and since it appeared their Mommy and Daddy trusted Joe, why couldn't they?

"Hey! Will you play snake tag with us?" Trey suddenly asked.

"Yeah! It's fun!" Sorryl added.

When they kept begging, Joe finally relented, "Okay, okay, I'll give it a try."

The boys whooped. The more players there were the more fun the game.

Joe laughed as he lowered himself to the floor. "I can't say I'll do a good job though," he warned, beginning to slither about the floor with the boys. Indeed, the regal police officer was a bit rusty and embarrassed at first, but he finally decided to cast aside his self-consciousness and just have fun. It surprised him how much he enjoyed himself after that.

When they were all too worn out to continue their game, Spencer helped the boys to bed. Then the adults seated themselves before the fire.

Breaking the thoughtful silence that reigned at first, Joe exclaimed with a shake of his head, "They look just like you! I can't believe they aren't really yours!"

Annaleah smiled rapturously and looked over at Spencer, who then related to Joe the story of how God had worked amazingly when they had adopted the boys and discovered that Trey and Sorryl were actually Annaleah's long-lost sister's sons. "In fact, that's their birth mother's picture above the mantle," Spencer added.

As the story unfolded, Joe listened with great interest, and sorrow that he had made it so difficult for those sweet boys now special to his softening heart. He could only shake his head in awe of what God had done in spite of him.

From then on, as soon as Joe walked through the door, the energetic little boys bombarded him. Joe was overwhelmed at first as he realized how the family treasured his friendship, but it felt so wonderful to be surrounded by their love. And he soon grew used to their vivacious and original games and open show of affection, though he was a bit unpracticed and stiff with these things himself. Being with this young family was doing his sore heart good and, he realized nearly subconsciously, made opening it much easier.

The boys were delighted when their mother finally grew stronger and could once again join them in their games.

"Now Mommy can play too, 'cause she's not sick," Sorryl exclaimed happily, unable to refrain from clapping at least once.

"I hope I don't get sick and then I can't play," Trey added with deep feeling.

Spencer looked at Annaleah and laughed, "I hope not too."

Chapter 5

Two years later...

"Oh! I forgot! We need some bread or the boys won't have anything to eat for breakfast tomorrow. I couldn't bake since all the baking stuff is packed," Annaleah said. She straightened from bending over the box she had been packing. "I'd better run and do that before it's too late."

Spencer glanced at the clock. He couldn't believe it! Time was flying these past few days. It was already eight-thirty in the evening. They'd better hurry; there wasn't much time left to pack for their move to West Texas in two days. He and Annaleah hoped to give the boys a better environment in which to grow up in Texas, and they both missed the open land where they had been raised. They couldn't wait. Spencer stood and stretched too. "Okay, I'll finish up this room while you go do that. I'd go, but it would probably take me half an hour just to find the bread. I need to learn where everything is again," he finished with a little laugh.

"That's all right, it's mostly heavy stuff left to move anyway. I couldn't get it all by my self," Annaleah answered with a twinkle in her eyes.

"Okay, we'll see you, then. I can get the boys to bed if you're not back on time. Unless I forget because I'm packing," he added with a grin.

Annaleah laughed good-naturedly at his qualifier and hugged Spencer, then the boys.

"You be good now, okay? I should be back soon," she told the boys as she gave them each a tender kiss on the top of the head. "I love you!" she called as she opened the door.

The others returned her affectionate words and 'I love you's!' echoed through the house, which was rapidly growing emptier as they packed their scant possessions into boxes.

After Annaleah departed, Spencer turned back to packing, keeping an eye on the boys as he did so.

It seemed as if he had just returned to his boxes, though at least a half hour had passed, when he heard someone burst through the front door. Puzzled, he cautiously walked to the front room. *Who on earth could that be? I hope it isn't some sort of burglar.*

When he rounded the corner, Joe nearly ran him over. He was more distraught than Spencer had ever seen him before, "Spence, you're okay!"

Spencer stopped and stared at his friend. *Why wouldn't I be okay?* He wondered to himself.

Before he could question him, Joe hurried on, "Are the boys here with you?"

At Spencer's bewildered nod, Joe rushed on, "Whew! At least *they're* safe!" He stopped. Steadying his voice, he resumed his collected policeman demeanor, "You'd better come with me, Annaleah's in trouble."

Shocked, Spencer stood still for a moment before calling the boys to come with him. He fought to keep his mind from imagining all sorts of crazy things that could have happened, but it was no use.

Joe helped them into his patrol car and sped through the streets as he explained, "I was on motor patrol when I saw these police cars and ambulance by the Narrows. There were even coast guards from the Hudson there. It was then I realized there was a car in the strait."

Spencer's eyes flew wide and he clutched at his seat. He brought his concentration back to Joe's words with difficulty.

"I stopped to see if they needed help, but they had already gotten to the car and no one was inside." He turned to Spencer with compassion and fear in his eyes, "From what I saw of the car, it looked like yours."

Spencer nearly choked. His already spinning mind seemed loathe to respond, "Did they find Annaleah yet? Are you sure it was our car?" he managed to ask. In all its imaginings his mind had never dreamed of something like this.

It was a moment before Joe could speak, "Yes. I'm sure it was yours now. They found some shoes and a purse in the car." He glanced at Spencer. The man was staring at the road with a clenched jaw as if his life depended on it. Joe continued huskily, "They were Annaleah's shoes, and her name was in her purse, too. They hadn't found her yet when I left."

Trey and Sorryl sat in the back seat with wide eyes. They knew Mommy was in trouble, but... where? And how?

Sorryl whimpered.

Spencer glanced back at them. He crawled into the back seat with his boys and put his arms comfortingly around their trembling shoulders.

As the car sped its way through the darkened streets, now illuminated by beams from the street lights, first agony, then anger rose in Spencer's chest. Why? Why did everything have to happen to them? Why couldn't it have been someone else? Or even him. Why did Annaleah, the joyful, fun-loving, sweet Annaleah, have to be the sufferer? If only he had gone for the bread instead of her, then she could still be safe at home being her old energetic self, taking care of the boys. And he was sure she would have done a much better job raising them than he was going to do if she died. Spencer groaned and dropped his head into his hands. He choked back tears as he pushed that thought aside. Surely she wasn't dead. She must have swum ashore and was probably with the police right now. Finally, he raised his head and took a deep breath, trying to calm his aching heart. Then he placed his arms once more about the boys and whispered brokenly, "We'll pray."

When they arrived, police lights were flashing and there were several spotlights bouncing along the shore and the middle of the water. When Joe led Spencer and the boys toward the police and reporters that were gathered around the car, an officer started to command them to stay away from the scene of the accident until he recognized Joe and inquired who was with him.

"The husband, eh?" the policeman questioned, peering closely at Spencer with an almost pitying expression. "To the best of your knowledge, was your wife the only occupant of the vehicle?"

Fear knotted Spencer's stomach. He nodded and glanced about for a sign of Annaleah. There was her car, pulled onto the bank. It was dripping water and looked alone and forlorn. Tears sprang to his eyes. Quickly, he blinked them back. Trying to rise above the mist clouding his brain, Spencer slowly forced himself to listen to the policeman, who was addressing him somberly.

"... In fifteen minutes we'll call it off until tomorrow."

Spencer stared blankly. What was the man saying? He should've been listening. His heart silently pled, *Oh, God! Please! Please help Annaleah! Let her be safe!* He forced his voice to work, "So did you find Annaleah?"

Blankly, the officer gazed at him, "Didn't you hear anything I said?"

Looking down, Spencer slowly shook his head. He glanced at the boys. They looked terrified.

Trey looked up at him imploringly, "Daddy, Mommy's drownded!"

Panic flooded his being. With a severe scolding to his bleeding heart to stay focused, Spencer turned questioning eyes to the officer who explained again, more thoroughly this time.

"We were called in about a vehicle in the harbor, but when we arrived the car was submerged. It must have been there for at least twenty minutes. When we got to it, we discovered that it was empty and the driver's window was rolled down." Holding up a pair of shoes and a purse, he continued, "These were in the car. The only thing we can figure is that the occupant tried to crawl from the window and was swept by the water current into the ocean. It's running fast and high because of that big storm yesterday."

Horrified, Spencer choked at the sight of Annaleah's shoes and the news the officer had just given him. Desperately, he pled, "But maybe she crawled out of the river –"

The officer was already shaking his head, "We had a team scour both banks. We'll comb the river tomorrow. It's too dark to continue tonight. The coast guard will be watching the shores for a sign of her all along the Narrows and the Lower Bay and even the shores where she might be swept ashore from the ocean."

Spencer blanched white. He reached for Trey and Sorryl's hands. Their faces were drawn and frightened.

Suddenly, the police chief came up and laid a hand on Spencer's shoulder. Seeing Spencer's dazed expression, he spoke with a glance to the terrified boys at Spencer's side, "We're doing all we can to find her. Right now maybe the best thing for you to do is go home and get some rest. We'll all be leaving in ten minutes or so anyway. Tomorrow morning, we'll comb the river as soon as it's light enough. There's no way she could be alive unless she was already ashore anyway, and we have people watching the city for her." He looked beseechingly to Joe who spoke up quickly, wondering if maybe he should have waited and just told Spencer after the police left and not brought him here until the morning. But he knew deep down that Spencer wouldn't have stood for staying home all night and not even going to look at the accident scene. He spoke, hoping Spencer would now listen to reason since he had looked on the scene and could be satisfied that nothing more could be done until daylight, "And besides, we've got to get the boys in bed."

Spencer looked down at Trey and Sorryl. They weren't going to be able to sleep. But Joe was right, he had to get them home and talk with them. Much as he'd rather stay and search for Annaleah, he couldn't leave the boys. And with the high waters and darkness, it wouldn't be safe to keep them here. With a despairing glance toward the rushing water, he realized that it would be fruitless to continue to search in the darkness anyway. The police and coast guard had already been looking for more than half an hour. Finally, Spencer sighed and nodded in resignation. "Yeah, you're right."

The police chief placed a comforting hand on Spencer's shoulder once again, "We'll call you if we find anything."

Spencer nodded and numbly followed Joe to his car.

Back at home, Spencer took Trey and Sorryl on his knees and talked with them, answering questions with a confidence and peace he didn't feel. When they finally fell to sleep in his arms, he held them all night, somehow gaining comfort from their little arms clasped about his. Poor things, they'd already been through so much. Now another Mommy was missing. Stubbornly, he forbade his mind to finish the last thought, "or dead".

Spencer must have finally fallen to sleep, because he awoke to the morning sun streaming in the living room window. He sat with the sleeping Trey and Sorryl for a few moments, talking to God and trying to trust Him, until the boys awoke with questions about where Mommy was and whether they were going to go find her now.

Spencer was grateful for their eagerness to be off. He couldn't stand to wait a moment longer either.

Just before he dashed out the door with Trey and Sorryl, he remembered he was supposed to be at work. He turned back and picked up the phone, dialing his work number. With difficulty, he explained what had happened. After a few moments of talking with his boss, he hung up the receiver with relief and leaned against the counter. Thankfully his boss had been understanding. He didn't need to go to work today. Or the rest of the week.

"All right, let's go boys," Spencer said. He took their hands and left the house, locking the door behind him. He was prepared to walk, or run, the entire way, but Joe pulled up beside them when they had walked only a few blocks and told them to get into his patrol car.

When they arrived, the search team was just getting organized. Spencer and his boys quickly joined them.

His brain spinning, Spencer's desperate gaze swept the shore. Relief flooded his heart when he didn't see a lifeless body resting on the shore. But a nagging fear clutched at his chest as he held the boys' hands and began searching the banks more thoroughly.

His heart wanted to say it wasn't necessary; that she wouldn't be in the water; that she was safe at home.

Unconsciously, he was searching for an alive Annaleah, just wounded on the shore. All up and down the water he could see others searching while boats and divers combed the deeper waters. Instinctively, he knew they were looking only for a body, not a living person.

As the day wore on, his search became a routine and he found his heart seemed numb. He almost forgot it was Annaleah he was searching for. Yet, deep down, an anguish he could not describe filled his being. Looking down at his children, he realized pain filled their weary souls too. Reaching down and taking their hands, he led them to a grassy area and sat down with them. He took them on his lap. None of them spoke. Their eyes just followed the forms of the people dotting the riverside as the search went on while their hearts sunk to the river bottom. After some time, they rose and began searching again. Still, none of them spoke as their sad eyes swept the terrain and water.

When the day was over, nothing had been found. There were people on watch in the city in case by some chance she had swum ashore and tried to make her way home, but no one had seen her. Spencer didn't even realize he had tucked the boys in and prayed with them. Or that he lay in his bed to toss and turn, dreaming of finding Annaleah under the water, miraculously alive.

For three weeks the search went on, but nothing more was found. Spencer joined the search with his boys after work. He didn't want to work, he wanted to be with his boys. But they had to eat and live somewhere. And without work, they would soon be homeless… and close to beggars. So each day he picked the boys up after school and they headed for the Narrows. His boss had adjusted his hours so he could be with his boys when they weren't in school. Joe watched them on Saturday and if Spencer didn't get out of work soon enough during the week Joe picked them up and took them on patrol with him. Trey and Sorryl enjoyed going on patrol with Joe, but Spencer knew it wasn't that safe. What if Joe had to arrest someone when they were with him? *Oh, Annaleah!* his heart cried, *Why can't you come back? Why can't you be here? God! What have you done? Oh Lord, I'm sorry. Maybe someday I'll understand…* He choked on a sob.

Spencer's heart wanted to be glad that his searching eyes found nothing by the ruthless Narrows, but it found no relief, for he knew it was more possible for her to have been swept into the ocean and never again seen than for her to have swum ashore and be in the city somewhere… alive. The officials said she was dead and must be in the ocean somewhere. There was no way she could be alive and not have been found. His heart refused to believe them.

When they held the memorial service, Spencer shed no tears. It didn't seem real. And the drawn out search had somehow slowly hardened his heart so that it could not understand. He hoped his boys were not so messed up as he, but as he looked into their young eyes, he knew they were. He hugged them closer, purposing to talk to them that evening.

When the service was over, Joe went to them and wrapped his arms about them, choking back his own tears.

For over a month, Spencer, Trey, and Sorryl haunted the city and the river, still hoping to find something, but to no avail. Finally, Spencer realized he must agree with the officials. His Annaleah was dead. Gone.

It was only then that the tears came. In the early morning stillness, or as still as it got in that busy metropolis, Spencer shed the first tears he had in a long while. They were refreshing and healing and somehow he felt freer after his tears were shed.

Spencer wasn't sure the boys really understood that their mother was never coming back. He sighed and hoped they did. He didn't know how to explain it to them. His mind hurt too much and seemed to be spinning in circles now that he had accepted that she was gone. It seemed so strange without Annaleah.

More than once, Spencer found himself silently crying out in agony, *Why, God?* He knew God had reasons for everything. He tried to tell himself it must be that Annaleah had completed her mission and God had lovingly called her home – out of this miserable, painful world. He tried to remember that, sometimes, God took His children home before they were old just as farmers sometimes picked their vegetables early because they knew they wouldn't get any better, and neither would their environment. He reminded himself over and over that it was God's mercy that had caused Him to bring Annaleah home, but an ache still settled within his heart. It would take a long time to heal. With a sigh, he swung his legs over the side of the bed and decided to tell his boys they would search the city and river no longer.

Through the following days, Spencer tried to help the boys understand, tried to work through the pain he knew dwelt within all their hearts, but he did not manage to talk much about Annaleah's death. Often, he still couldn't bring himself to believe she was really gone. If only he could have seen her. Then maybe he could come to terms with it. But with the feeling that she was just out there somewhere… it was horrible. Sure, they had conducted a memorial service for her, but something still seemed incomplete. Perhaps that was half the reason he had continued to search for her. If he could have found her, he would know he'd done all he could. Now there was no closure or realness to it. It was just that Annaleah had been, and now wasn't.

Finally, Spencer decided to move to Texas anyway, as they had planned. He had to think about the future of the boys. They would put a little stone in memory of her in the cemetery the town they were moving to had. He knew others might think it was silly, but he didn't want to forget her. Not his dear Annaleah.

School ended for the boys shortly after they stopped searching for Annaleah. Their good grades had dropped dramatically after their mother's accident. Spencer knew it was hard for them to cope with their grief and their rough schoolmates as well, so he was glad that school was over for them, even though it meant he had to quit work. Joe couldn't watch them all the time, and there was no one else they knew there that he could trust. Besides, they had to make plans to move. They set the moving date for a month later, July twenty-fifth.

Joe was there for Spencer and the boys every step of the way and even helped them find a car before they headed to Texas since theirs had been too far damaged by the water. When the time came, he bade them a teary farewell. He was going to miss these dear people and the sunshine they seemed to bring to his life.

The Trestles had already chosen the house. Annaleah had explained in her animated way how it would be wonderful, even though Los Ciegos, the town in which the new house was situated, didn't seem to be a very active or happy place. Spencer had finally agreed, and Annaleah had begun enthusiastically exclaiming over how they could fix up the house and make it 'home' as she lightly danced from room to room. The boys had joined her in prancing about the house, and even Spencer caught her enthusiasm and followed her around the house, adding his own ideas.

A couple months after the accident, after Spencer had ceased searching the riverside, Sorryl asked worriedly, "When's Mommy coming back?" His lip quivered.

Trey looked eagerly to their daddy as he waited for the answer.

Tears rushed to Spencer's eyes and he took the boys on his lap. He sighed. So they still didn't understand. Or else they were in denial of the truth as he found himself doing quite often. He swallowed hard, "Do you remember about your other Mommy and Daddy?"

Sorryl nodded.

Trey replied with a quivering lip, "They're in Heaven. Mommy said that's where they would go when they died, 'cause they knew Jesus, too."

Spencer blinked rapidly to stem the flow of tears that rushed to his eyes. His voice wavered as he spoke, "Well, your Mommy has gone to Heaven with them. She's not coming back. We'll go to be with her someday though." He almost angrily swept away a tear that had escaped his barricade.

Trey and Sorryl stared at him with wide eyes for a moment, and then tears began softly sliding down their cheeks.

Spencer finally gave in, letting his tears mingle with theirs as he hugged the boys close. Somehow, it felt good to cry.

Chapter 6

One month later...

"Hey, Trey! Come see what I found!" seven-year-old Sorryl called.

At first the boys hadn't known what to do with the space and fresh air at their new home just outside the small town of Los Ciegos located in West Texas near El Paso, but it had not taken the adventurous boys long to discover the intriguing nooks and crannies of the nearby small mountain. Feeling as if they had been set free, they eagerly explored the area surrounding their new home.

Eight-year-old Trey scampered curiously over to where Sorryl was peeking into a foreboding cave.

"I wonder if there's a bear in there," Sorryl whispered breathlessly.

"I don't think so," Trey said with a valiant show of bravery, or perhaps foolishness. "Let's find out. But we have to be careful." He picked up a stick and cautiously poked it into the cave. "Nothing's growling at it. Maybe it's okay," he said, taking a tentative step into the dark hole. Sorryl stole in behind his brother.

They hadn't ventured far when Sorryl whispered with a touch of fear in his tones, "We need a flashlight or something." Somehow, with the suspense and darkness, it seemed proper to whisper. "M-maybe we should go home and get one." The eerie echo that sounded when Sorryl spoke spooked the city boys even more.

"Good idea," Trey said.

When they arrived at their small, frame home, they ran around the back where they could hear their daddy working on the shed. Spencer glanced up and smiled as they scampered into the small barn to find a flashlight. They knew Daddy wouldn't mind. He was used to their adventures by now, and he also remembered how much he had enjoyed them as a boy. In fact, he still loved tramping around in the fresh air and even joined his boys when time permitted. Trey and Sorryl loved to be with their daddy and often helped him fix things. But today there was nothing they could do to help, so they happily embarked on a new adventure.

After a long search for the misplaced flashlight, Trey's voice shouted from under the work bench, "I've got one!" His last word was suddenly cut short as he let out a painful groan.

Sorryl, standing on top of the work bench as he used it for a stool in order to search the upper shelves in the shed, felt the boards beneath his feet jiggle. He dropped onto his belly and hung his head over the edge of the workbench to peer at his brother, "What'd ya do, Trey?"

Trey didn't speak for a moment, but Sorryl could see that he was holding his head. Finally, Trey giggled a bit and answered, "I just bumped my head. I got too excited and jumped up because I forgot I was under here."

Sorryl giggled with his brother, and then just watched him for a moment, savoring the feeling of hanging partway upside down.

"I'm a bit hungry," Trey suddenly announced, rubbing his tummy with an exaggerated air, forgetting about his head.

"Me too. How about we go get something to eat," Sorryl suggested as he righted himself and hopped off the work bench.

Trey crawled out from under the work bench and followed his brother to their house.

When they arrived, Trey began searching the refrigerator shelves. "Maybe we should just take some bread, we can eat that on the way back and then we won't waste time," he suggested, suddenly sticking his head back out of the refrigerator.

"Okay. Good idea," Sorryl agreed, grabbing a piece after Trey retrieved the loaf. He took a bite and then dashed for the door.

As the boys climbed the rocky incline toward the cave, Trey offered, "I'll go first with the flashlight." He figured it was better for him to go first in case something *was* in there, that way Sorryl would have more time to run.

"Sure," Sorryl said, relieved he didn't have to venture in first. The he added, "I'll get a stick and follow you in." He wanted to be prepared to help Trey should the need arise, so, true to his words, he picked out a long, sturdy stick and began dramatically practicing his swings.

The brothers cautiously re-entered the cave, Trey in the lead. He carefully shone the light all around, trying not to be afraid. *Maybe this wasn't such a grand idea after all,* he thought. Finally, his fear abated some as he realized nothing dangerous was in the cave. He turned back to Sorryl, who was gaining confidence as well, "Wow! It's neat! And there's no bear. It's wonderful! Not that big, but it's got plenty of room."

"Hey, this is bigger than our other one, how about we use *it* for our fort now!" Sorryl exclaimed.

"Yeah! And, besides, you can see our house from this one! And there's even a hidden entrance! Great idea, Sorryl!"

The boys began transporting their fort furnishings to their new cave. All fear had fled. Once, Sorryl thought he saw something slinking away from their new fort and the fear returned to prickle his skin, but he decided he must be wrong and promptly forgot about his concern as they carried their scant furnishings to their new cave.

"Here, you'll have to help me," Trey grunted as he struggled to lift one of the old tree stumps they were using for seats.

"Okay, then we can come back for the other one and the candles. Ooof!" Sorryl finished as he took an end of the stump.

They soon returned for the other stump, grunting as they carried their heavy load to the new cave.

"Whew! There, that's all done," Trey sighed as they wiped sweat from their faces. The boys couldn't help but feel important as they thought of the great task they had accomplished. A feeling of pride that they were somehow more like their beloved daddy, who was always working so hard, made them stand tall with importance. They didn't stop to puzzle over how their daddy balanced getting all his work done with spending time with them. It was enough for them that he did it.

Suddenly, both boys jumped and then glanced at each other with a giggle.

"It's only Daddy ringing the bell for supper," Sorryl said.

Trey looked at the sun in surprise, "I didn't know it was that late!"

With the air of one practiced at telling time by the sun, Sorryl glanced toward it too, "Well, I guess it *is* time for dinner, or past it. Hey! Look! You can see Daddy from here! I wonder if he can see us!" He began waving his small arms with vigor.

They were both small for their age, unlike Spencer, who was just over six feet tall, though he had started out small, too. The boys knew they didn't really belong to Spencer, but they still admired their handsome father and hoped they would be like him when they grew up.

"He doesn't see us. Oh well. I'm starved," Sorryl said, finally giving up and scurrying down the mountainside with Trey close behind.

When they arrived at the house, Trey dashed up to Spencer and threw himself into his daddy's open arms. "What's to eat?"

"Pizza," Spencer answered with a sparkle in his green eyes.

The boys looked at each other in excitement, and then cried in unison, "Hoorah!" Beginning a happy jig, they pulled their daddy around in circles with them.

When they finally let go of his hands, Spencer said, "I didn't have time to make something today, so I thought we could drive to town and pick up a pizza together."

This was met with more enthusiastic shouts and Sorryl leapt onto Spencer's broad back, proclaiming in his animated, yet quiet, way, "Let's go, Daddy!"

So the happy trio pranced to the waiting vehicle. Only to topple back out and into the house to get cleaned up. Spencer had discovered a wide smear of dirt on Sorryl's cheek and a smaller one to match on Trey's nose, not to mention the dirt all over their clothes. Before long, they paraded to the car once more.

"Daddy," Trey spoke up over the rumble of the engine when they were seated in the car, three across the front with Sorryl in the middle. "We found a cave! And there was no bear, and we can see the house from it…"

"Well, I'm glad there was no bear. Do I get to see it sometime?" Spencer asked with a playful twinkle in his eyes and an affectionate smile playing about his lips.

"Of course!" both boys exclaimed together.

"And, Daddy, guess what?" asked Sorryl.

"What?"

"When you rang the dinner bell, you looked even smaller than we are!"

Spencer's tanned face crinkled up as he tried not to laugh at his sons' antics. "Is that so?" He looked down at his sons. Sorryl had managed to end up squeezed next to him, and Trey, smashed up against Sorryl, made the Sorryl sandwich complete.

"Well, here we are!" Spencer said, pulling up next to the pizza shop.

Both boys catapulted themselves out the door like twin torpedoes, giggling.

Spencer smiled at their excitement as he led the way into the pizza shop.

It was good to hear their young, carefree laughter again. For a couple months after their mother's death, they had been unusually sober. The pain went so deep, and yet there was a joy that ran even deeper and it held them above despair. It, along with Jesus' love, carried them on.

The pizza shop door banged shut behind him.

"We would like one large pizza with cheese and pepperoni please, Jerry," Spencer announced with a majestic air.

"One moment, Spenc… uh, I mean, sir!" the spry little owner acknowledged, mirroring Spencer's mood.

The boys giggled and Jerry winked at Spencer. This was the third time they had come for pizza, and they were beginning to become acquainted with each other. Jerry, now so jolly, had not been so when they had first met him. But with this irrepressible trio around it was difficult to remain in low spirits for long. Jerry had begun looking forward to their visits, finding they raised his sorrowful spirits.

"Here you are, dear sirs!" exclaimed Jerry as he brought a wonderful-smelling pizza from the oven with a proud flourish, "Fresh from the oven."

"What do you say, gentlemen? Shall we dine here tonight?" queried Spencer.

The boys were about to shout their replies when they remembered the roles they were supposed to be playing. So, with many suppressed bounces, they replied in unison, "I don't see why not."

Spencer and Jerry nearly laughed at the careless fashion, as is typical of proud, high-class folks, the boys had assumed. The smudge on Sorryl's cheek Spencer had chanced to overlook made it even more comical.

Jerry suppressed another smile as he said with a respectful bow, "Right this way, gentlemen."

The boys swallowed giggles and followed Jerry to a gray and blue booth, walking as straight and tall as possible.

As soon as they were seated, Spencer said, "It doesn't seem like you're very busy this evening, would you join us, Jerry?"

At this remark, all the acting was ended.

"Oh, please, please? Will you?" the boys begged as hope filled their large hearts.

Sorryl was bouncing up and down, "Please do! Please, please won't you? Ple—"

He landed on the floor with a thump. Looking up in surprise, Sorryl just stared back and forth between Jerry and Daddy. *How did that happen?*

Jerry lifted him to his seat with a good-natured laugh.

When he found himself once more properly seated on the bench, Sorryl sat with wide eyes a moment, striving to recover a piece of his lost dignity. Then he eagerly asked, "Please?" He turned hopeful eyes to Jerry's.

71

Jerry gazed fondly at the small boys and their father. His heart filled with joy to see how much they already cared about him. Since when did people in Los Ciegos ask a server to join them with their meal! He had never met anyone in this small town as cheerful, caring, thoughtful, and animated as these. It almost seemed as if they were out of place, like a colorful parrot would be in foggy England. But he was glad they had come, and hoped they would stay.

Los Ciegos was considered a religious town and was esteemed as holding one of the most righteous groups of people around, but he couldn't help but feel these newcomers were closer to Heaven than any of the townspeople were. He knew Spencer and the boys believed in God, he had seen them pray before they ate their pizza. But it wasn't the kind of stiff prayer he was used to. No. It seemed like they were actually talking with a God they believed loved them rather than one who expected them to follow a whole mess of rules and go about like little machines, who they thought was waiting for them to make a mistake so He could pronounce judgment upon them. It puzzled him.

He also found it hard to believe they had lost their wife and mother not so long ago. There were moments when he could see the pain in their eyes, when they began missing her, but that didn't last long, especially if Jerry could help it. He had not heard their story, but it was known to the town that this strange trio was without a woman, and this put them in a bad light to many in the town. The strange newcomers were supposed by most to be reckless, dirty, rugged, without manners, and headed straight for Hell. They didn't often find opportunity to come into town since Spencer was so busy fixing their home, so they had not been able to right this opinion and were a great mystery to the town, as well as a favorite topic among the tongue-waggers residing there.

Suddenly, he realized three pairs of eyes were still eagerly looking to him for his answer. The unaccustomed joy within his heart bubbled into his words, "I'd love to join y'all!"

"Hooray!" the boys shouted as he took a seat.

"Hey, Jerry," Spencer said after they prayed.

Jerry looked up from his pizza.

"I've been wondering how this town ended up with 'Town of Los Ciegos' for a name.

Jerry laughed. "When I first came here I wondered the same thing. I found out it means 'Town of the Blind'. It was actually named that because, when the town was first established, there were four blind people living here, and that's not counting the founder of the town, Mr. T. J. Caldwell," he said the name with a flourish, "who was blind himself. It was actually to honor the blind, and to show that they weren't helpless if they learned to 'see' through other people and through different means than just their eyes."

Trey grinned, "That's cool! Too bad there aren't any blind people here now. They'd sure be proud to live here!"

Spencer smiled, "I'm sure they would be if they had learned to see in different ways."

"Yeah, 'cause if you're blind, and don't think about whether there's something else out there to do while you're blind, you wouldn't realize there was more to life than blackness… right?" Sorryl asked.

Spencer smiled, "I suppose not. It'd be easy enough for me to just sit around and mope in my own little world if I were blind."

As they neared the end of their supper, a young lady arrayed in a dull, gray dress entered the shop. She would have been beautiful if it weren't for the stiff and haughty, yet sad, manner with which she carried herself. The same attitude seemed to preside over the entire town, seeming to proclaim in solemn resignation, "If one is to get to Heaven, one must not have fun but must spend their time helping the poor and in solemn gravity. Therefore, there should be no spontaneity, and definitely no flash or enthusiasm."

This accounted for the proud, stiff manner. But there was still that trace of sadness and purposelessness which seemed to say, "There isn't much to life. Life is something to bear, not enjoy." Yet this lady had an element about her which the others they had seen seemed to lack, as if she were extra stiff and felt awkward and out of place.

Embarrassed to be caught sitting at one of his patron's tables, Jerry leapt up as if he'd suddenly realized he was sitting on a hot burner. He hurriedly composed his features back to a blank despondency and slipped behind the counter, hoping to affect an inconspicuous attitude.

The young lady gave the unusual trio in the corner a curious glance and then stiffened, if that were possible, as if reproving herself. She sauntered up to the counter. "I would like a small cheese pizza, please."

Trey, always friendly and ready to get acquainted with new people, bounced from his seat and flashed over to the lady. "Hello, I'm Trey. What's your name?" He stuck out his hand in a friendly gesture.

He puzzled at the lady's startled look. She stared at his hand for a moment, and then moved her gaze to his face. A smile slipped into her eyes and began to spread to her lips, but it quickly faded as she seemed to scold herself again. Slowly she reached out her hand to shake his, evidently only to be polite.

He flashed a smile. It spoke of joy, yet held a hint of sadness as well. The lady felt as though she had caught a glimpse of his very heart and quickly diverted her gaze, unaccustomed to this sort of openness.

"My name is Starlight," she responded dully, her voice sounding strained as if it were hard work to keep it that way. She took her hand away, shook it once, and turned back to the counter.

Jerry was still standing there, watching her with an eager expression on his face. She gave him a stern look as if to say, "Well, aren't you going to cook my pizza?"

He turned abruptly to place her pizza in the oven, then she handed him his money and crossed her arms, stiffly waiting for her pizza. She carefully avoided looking at the Trestles.

Trey had slowly made his way back to his seat, somewhat subdued and feeling quite dejected.

Spencer, wanting to make him feel better, plucked the cheese off the last piece of pizza and, flipping the piece over, stuck it on the bottom. Then he proceeded to offer Trey a bite.

Trey squirmed and a peculiar sort of noise escaped him as he pressed his lips together in an attempt to hold in a giggle. A drip of sauce landed on his plate with a silent plop, causing Sorryl to giggle too.

Starlight allowed herself a glance in their direction, but she soon forgot it was only to be a glance as she curiously watched the interesting threesome.

Sorryl laughed silently and pointed at the pizza. His eyes danced. "Da-a-addy," he laughed softly.

Trey giggled too.

"I want a bite. Does it taste different that way?" Sorryl asked.

A twitch tugged at the corner of Starlight's mouth and she absently reached down to adjust her gray skirt. Until that moment, she had stood frozen in awe with a wistful look as she observed this unusual spectacle.

Spencer laughed and offered the pizza to Sorryl, "Try it and see, though I doubt it does."

Sorryl eagerly took a bite and chewed thoughtfully for a moment, then swallowed and, with a confident nod, proclaimed, "Yup, it tastes different. It tastes backwards... or something," here his confidence fled, to be replaced by confusion.

Trey's curiosity was roused now. "Here, let me taste it," he requested, leaning over the table for a bite.

When his father handed him the pizza, he bit into it and thoughtfully chewed. Then, swallowing, he ventured, "It *does* taste different. It's like... I don't know, the sauce and cheese are separated and, well... maybe it tastes more like breadsticks... or something." He faltered and his tanned face scrunched up in perplexity.

"Well, now you've got me curious!" Spencer said half-playfully. "I'll have to take a taste now." Without further delay, he proceeded to copy the two boys. When he finally swallowed, his eyes were wide in amazement. "Wow! It does taste a bit different, especially if you're looking for it. Like a different combination of flavors... or something," his voice trailed off. The flavor somehow seemed indescribable.

This was the undoing of Starlight and her eyebrows ventured very high upon her forehead in her effort to suppress a laugh.

Jerry chuckled and quipped, "Perhaps I'll begin making a different kind of pizza. Such as... um... split pizza. Yes, that's it, split pizza!"

Starlight made one last attempt to compose herself before she gave up and said in a teasing tone that somehow seemed to fit her and yet be out of place at the same time, "That'll be popular around here." Meaning it wouldn't be since no one liked change in that town. Then she nodded for a goodbye, as if afraid to speak any more lest she trespass upon something she was not supposed to do, took her pizza from Jerry, and sallied out of the shop.

When she was safely in the street, she gave a disconcerted shake of her head, muttering sternly to herself, "Now Starlight!" and proceeded toward home. The truth was, Trey's expressive, yet lonely, smile had brought tears to her eyes. She couldn't understand it, but it had touched her heart.

Once she had carefully shut her door, Starlight sat down to have her meal. After a quick, stiff prayer, she opened the pizza box and took a bite. As she raised her pizza to take a second bite, she paused with it in midair. Did she dare? She studied her pizza as she debated. Finally, she set down her pizza and gingerly pulled off the cheese, slowly flipped the pizza over, and put the cheese on the opposite side. "What a mess," she mumbled as she shook her head in amusement. "Oh well." She complacently took a small bite and began to chew thoughtfully. Suddenly, she exclaimed aloud, "Why! It really *does* taste different!"

At that moment, the front door opened. Starlight glanced up and saw that it was her mother. Quickly, she set down her pizza and carefully wiped her hands on a napkin. "Oh, hello Mother," She greeted in familiar monotones, rising from her seat. "I was just eating. I thought you were going to be at Mary's."

"Well, she came down with something." Emma Bolton walked into the room and indicated the pizza, "Is there enough for both of us?"

"Of course." Starlight took another plate from the cupboard for her mother and sat down at her place again. She reached for her pizza and suddenly realized her predicament. There was her silly piece of 'split' pizza unabashedly sitting on her plate. *Well, I suppose the best thing to do is try to eat it without Mother noticing,* she thought. *Whatever will she think if she sees it?* Endeavoring to act as if nothing was out of the ordinary, she picked up her pizza and took a bite. She could just imagine her mother's face if she happened to notice the pizza. It would probably have a look on it as if she had just seen a cat with fins. Starlight smothered a laugh in spite of herself and tried to focus on what her mother was saying.

"…I came directly home again, since I didn't want to acquire Mary's ailment."

"Sure," Starlight responded, grateful she had heard enough to make a suitably intelligent reply.

After this, they lapsed into their normal, dull silence during meals.

Starlight took another bite. Would she ever finish that big piece of pizza? It would do no good to try and put the cheese back on top, that would attract more attention, and the sauce would still be all over the bottom.

The next thirty seconds felt like twenty minutes to Starlight as she concentrated on finishing her pizza and hoped her mother wouldn't notice.

Suddenly, the silence was shattered, "My dear! What *ever* is the matter with your pizza?"

Starlight gulped and nearly dropped the offensive piece in alarm. She answered in the most casual manner she could muster, "It was, ah, an experiment." She couldn't help noticing her mother's expression. Yes, she certainly did look as though she had seen a cat with fins.

"An… experiment?" Emma asked with a choking sound as if she had never heard the word before.

"Yes," Starlight answered conscientiously, her heart sinking. *Am I ever in for it now! And I thought I was through astonishing people and had finally collected myself! Oh dear!* How she hated to disappoint or displease people.

Emma just stared at her daughter in surprise. "Dear," she paused, bewildered. "I thought you had finally learned to be normal. I should have changed that preposterous name your father gave you, maybe that would have helped. He insisted the name matched your lively, blue eyes. After a pause, she said sternly, "I… Oh dear," she broke off with a relinquishing sigh. "You managed for two years, anyhow. Why, you're twenty-one years old, you should have learned by now. You're just like your father. All the rest of the children learn it from birth. Even your older sister knew how to be normal! You are doomed to… to… to not make it to Heaven I am afraid." She finished by sorrowfully shaking her brown head, now dusted with grey.

Starlight sighed and ventured in a subdued tone, "I'm sorry, Mother. I saw someone at the pizza shop do it and I just couldn't resist." She pleaded with her soft eyes for her mother to understand.

But Emma Bolton brushed her silent plea aside. "Resist temptation," she said reproachfully.

"Mother, how can splitting pizza possibly be wrong? It doesn't seem like God wants us to sit around pretending to help the poor and keep ourselves out of trouble while we follow all sorts of confining regulations that seem to have no meaning." Starlight stopped abruptly, embarrassed. She looked down as her mother's gaze bore into her, "I'm sorry."

"You should be," Emma retorted.

Starlight just gazed at her hands, now folded in her lap. Suddenly, she noticed a smear of sauce on her thumb and nearly laughed. She didn't know why, other than that she had felt the happiest she had in two years when she had displaced the cheese on her pizza.

After a pause, Emma continued testily, "And just who was it that dared to switch their pizza around! Just look at what a mess it makes!"

"I know, but—" Starlight started sheepishly.

"Just who was it, then?" Emma interrupted once more.

Starlight realized she had gotten herself, or, rather, the new family – the Trestles was it? – into trouble when she mentioned that someone else had done it. She tried to avoid having to tell who it was, "Well, it wasn't their fault you know…" Starlight halted abruptly at her mother's reproving look. Letting out a troubled sigh, Starlight reproved her unusually hasty tongue. "Okay," she relented, "It was that new family."

Emma sniffed indignantly. "Oh, those new people, the peculiar ones. I would hardly call them a *family*. I don't understand why Jacob had to sell his home to them. They will corrupt our town before we even know what's happened. I've seen them pray, but have you seen all the preposterous things they do? Jacob could have chosen someone who fit in," she finished testily.

"Well, he had to sell fast, he couldn't really be picky," Starlight said. Really, she didn't think what the Trestles did was all that preposterous, but she wisely kept this thought to herself.

"I suppose," Emma let out a deep, troubled sigh. "They'll probably leave soon anyway, once they find they don't fit in," she finished in a satisfied tone, taking another bite from her pizza.

Starlight somehow doubted this, but refrained from saying so. Her mother was already riled enough and her conscience smote her for causing such distress to her mother. She shoved down frustrated tears and resolved to do better.

"Well, I think it's absurd to eat your pizza all mixed up like that, what good does it do anyway?" Emma began again, still somewhat annoyed.

"It does taste different," Starlight answered, taking a bite to renew the flavor so she could describe it better. "Like, maybe... breadsticks," she finally fell back on Trey's explanation. "But... not exactly," she added in a faltering voice.

Emma gazed at her in puzzlement for a moment and then declared in ornery tones, "I don't see how it could taste different. It's the same stuff! Here, let me taste it and I'll put your imagination to rights."

Starlight obediently held out the altered piece of pizza and Emma calmly took a bite.

"Oh my!" she exclaimed, her serenity shattered. Then, attempting to compose herself, she conceded, "Well, I suppose it does have a bit of a different flavor. But you didn't really need to find out about it. I trust you will be normal, now that you have found out, and stop jeopardizing your salvation?" she asked, sounding a bit worried. She was afraid Starlight would grow increasingly 'weird' and perhaps do something that really would keep her from Heaven if she didn't get back to normal soon.

Starlight hesitated before saying quietly, "I'll try, Mother." She felt somehow that what she had done was not affecting her salvation, that there was some other way to Heaven than following, or trying to follow, senseless rules, but she didn't know what it could be.

"Try!" Emma was all in a huff again. "That's what you did for nineteen years. I hope it doesn't take nineteen more to get back to where you were before those preposterous people showed up. You better avoid that new... family," she finally allowed, "if this is the effect they have on you."

After Starlight had taken her leave, the occupants of the pizza shop laughed merrily over the 'split' pizza.

Spencer stood up, still smiling as he held his hand out warmly to Jerry, "Well, I suppose we better be going."

"All right," Jerry said. "Goodnight then."

"Goodnight, Mr. Jerry!" Sorryl said, giving the spry man a hug around the legs.

"Here, we can do better than that!" Jerry laughed, swooping both boys into his arms and hugging them tight. A warm feeling spread through his heart.

"Goodnight, Jerry, I hope we see you again soon," Spencer said as Jerry released the boys and they headed for the door, completely unaware of what they had just begun.

Chapter 7

"Daddy," Sorryl whispered.

Spencer turned back to his son and went to his bedside. He had already turned off the light, but the full moon shown gently through Trey and Sorryl's window, casting a soft, blue glow on the boys' features and illuminating the room. "Yes?"

"Um," Sorryl continued in a hushed tone. "I was wonderin' if you could sing to me."

"Why's that?" Spencer asked, caressing Sorryl's deep chestnut curls. Curls that were so like Annaleah's.

Sorryl's lips quivered, "'Cause I miss Mommy tonight. And she always sung to us." A small tear trickled down his cheek, sparkling in the moonlight as it settled on his quivering chin.

Why didn't I think of doing that before? Spencer reproved himself. He heard a weary sigh from Trey's side of the bed. "You, too?" he asked tenderly.

"Well… Uh-huh," Trey finally assented.

"Why don't both of you come in my room. The bed's plenty big. Well, as long as we scrunch," he added, getting a smile out of Sorryl. "Then I can sing to you."

The boys clambered out of bed and followed their daddy down the hall to his room where they climbed onto his bed and snuggled under the warm covers. Annaleah had sewn the comforter herself, and put lots of butterflies all over it, because she loved butterflies. Trey reached out and stroked the biggest one. It had blue wings with black and yellow spots.

"Now for the song, then I've gotta get ready for bed, okay?" Spencer said, smiling gently.

This was the first time the two boys had really said much about missing their mother. He had seen it in their eyes a few times, but the look had quickly passed. It seemed it was finally sinking in to all three that Annaleah was truly gone and that they would never see her again on this earth.

I don't really know how to comfort those dear boys or what to say, other than to take them on my lap and cuddle them whenever I see that look begin in their eyes, he mourned. *What do I do, Lord? Please help me! I feel so helpless sometimes. I try not to show my grief too much around them. I need to be strong for them, don't I?*

My son, if they see your grief, it will help them realize it's okay for them to hurt, and they will let go of it easier and find healing... and so will you.

Spencer clenched his hands and blinked back tears in spite of himself. *I suppose you're right.*

Not knowing how to comfort them wasn't his only problem. He sometimes worried about Trey and Sorryl on their adventures in the hills and had instructed them to stay within hearing distance. He had told them if they could hear him pounding with the hammer they were okay. But were they really? He wished he could spend more time with them. He wished they had a mother. He wished Annaleah was still here.

Why did you let her die, Lord? Why? He felt as though a crushing weight was pressing upon him. Only it came from the inside, sending fiery pain throughout his veins. A tear escaped, but he let it fall, remembering the Lord's admonishment. *Oh, Lord! I need your strength and healing!* There was complete stillness for a moment, and then a cool flood washed over him, quenching the flames that had torn at his veins. There was still a pulsing pain in his heart, but he no longer felt overwhelmed. *Please help Trey and Sorryl to find healing and strength from You too, Lord.*

Realizing the boys were gazing at him, he made an effort to shake himself out of his reflective mood and asked, "So what song shall we have tonight?"

Sorryl said, "He is able. That was Mommy's favorite."

Trey nodded in agreement and brushed a tear away.

"Okay, I'll try, though I don't sing as well as Mommy," Spencer said. His voice caught, but he began singing in his rich baritone anyway. When he finished, tears stood in all their eyes. The words whispered a balmy salve across their hearts: *He is able, He is able, I know He is able to carry me through.* Yes, Jesus *could* carry them through all their problems.

"Mommy used to sing all the time, even when she weeded the garden out back by the house," Sorryl said. His eyes grew distant as the sensation of a billowy breeze and the aroma of soil filled his senses. It felt almost as though he could reach out and touch his mother. He could see her. He could even smell that wonderful smell that could only be Mommy. But he realized with a pang that it was only a memory, and could never again be anything more.

Trey's voice cut into his dreamy thoughts, "And she laughed when I put a ladybug in her hair and said 'every girl should have such a lovely hair adornment'."

"And she loved to dance with us all!" Sorryl added. A spark of enthusiasm lit his eyes.

"Yeah," Trey said. "And she made Daddy twirl her!" He spun himself in a circle to illustrate his words.

"Yes, and you tried to twirl her once and you both would have fallen if I hadn't caught you," Spencer said, a smile tugging at his lips.

"Hey! Can you twirl me?" asked Sorryl.

"Sure!" Spencer swooped both boys up and swung them in circles. Finally, he fell onto the bed with them, gasping for breath, and rolled onto his stomach. Trey and Sorryl weren't tired though, and they tussled with each other, rolling over Spencer's back. They ignored the heavy rise and fall of their playground as Spencer strove to catch his breath.

"Okay, boys," Spencer finally laughed. He stood slowly, dumping the boys off his back. "Time to actually *sleep* now." He paused dramatically before adding with a twinkle in his eyes, "We've got a big day tomorrow."

For a moment, nothing was said. Trey and Sorryl sat on the edge of the bed, studying their toes as they tried to remember what would put such significance into those words. Suddenly, Sorryl leapt up and ran to Spencer. He threw his arms around him with a grin. Trey sat a moment longer, then understanding dawned and his eyes suddenly grew merry.

"All day, Daddy?" he asked, jumping off the bed.

"Yup, I can spend all day with you. We should have saved pizza for tomorrow, 'ey?"

"No, no, no!" both boys exclaimed in unison.

"We can just have it again!" Trey suggested.

"And so can Mr. Jerry!" Sorryl added with a bounce.

Spencer's laugh rang out at his sons' enthusiasm. It warmed his heart. "I'm surprised you forgot."

"Well, we did so much today we forgot tomorrow was to-morrow… I guess," Sorryl faltered.

Spencer chuckled as he scooped up his sons and set them in bed. "Now, it's time for me to get ready for bed and you two to sleep."

But he was continually bombarded with questions all through bed-preparations. Truth was, *he* had forgotten about tomorrow, too, or he would have saved pizza for then.

"Will we go in the pond?" Trey queried after a moment of trying to keep quiet.

"If you like," Spencer answered from the bathroom.

"Can we show you our cave?" Sorryl asked, bouncing out from under the covers, then right back in again as he suddenly remembered he was supposed to be in bed.

No wonder Annaleah never liked it when I got the boys going just before bedtime, Spencer mumbled to himself with a chuckle. "That'd be wonderful!" he said aloud. After a slight pause he demanded, "Hey! Trey, where are you going?" He tried to sound stern, but nearly failed.

Trey paused abruptly in the doorway of the room. He turned back to the bed with a sheepish grin, "I forgot, Daddy. I was just gonna get a rock I found in the cave."

"It'll wait 'till tomorrow," Spencer reprimanded gently.

Reluctantly, Trey climbed back into bed. After about forty seconds of silence, in which Spencer could almost hear the squirming which was being contained, Trey suddenly burst, "And we can go on the other side of the hill, and further than where we can hear you?"

Spencer gulped down a laugh at the way the words erupted from Trey. With dismay, he realized his effort to swallow his laugh had caused him to clench the toothpaste tube in his fist. He looked at his toothbrush. Toothpaste plopped from the bristles into the sink. There was even a blob on the mirror. Spencer shook his head at himself even as silent laughter from over-tiredness seized him.

The bathroom was at the wrong angle, so the boys could not see him from the bed. They heard only complete silence, broken once by something that somewhat resembled a snort.

"Daddy?" Trey tried again. He managed to stay in bed even though it felt like a magnet stronger than any he had ever seen before was pulling him toward the bathroom.

Spencer took a deep breath and replied as calmly as he could, "If we get time." Those boys sure could be funny sometimes, but why had Trey's eruption seemed so humorous to him? Probably because it reminded him of Annaleah, and that reminder brought with it a rush of sweetness filled with pain. This overwhelming emotion demanded some sort of outward expression, and he'd rather laugh than cry.

Frugally, he tried to force the toothpaste back into the tube, only managing to smear the paste all over it. Finally he shrugged and wiped his sticky fingers on his shirt. With a final look at his toothbrush, then at his shirt, he shrugged again and raised his brush to his mouth. The minty paste stung at first. He'd never tried brushing with so much before.

"And we can go to town and meet people. Right, Daddy?" Sorryl asked. He was always eager to make new friends, even though he was usually shy at first. But as long as his brother was there to do the talking until they got acquainted, it worked out just fine.

No answer.

He tried again, a little louder. "Right, Daddy?"

But there was still no answer, other than some weird noises emitting from the bathroom.

"Daddy?" both boys ventured once more. A touch of worry etched their query.

A weird sound, as if someone were trying to talk with cottonballs in his mouth, issued from the bathroom. The boys glanced at one another, then simultaneously dashed out of bed and to the bathroom doorway. They halted and stared wide-eyed at their father who was standing over the sink, foam bubbling out of his mouth and dripping into the sink. Occasionally, he paused to spit some of the white foam out before brushing some more.

Spencer suddenly caught sight of the boys and muffled out what they guessed was telling them they were supposed to be in bed, but sounded something like, "'Ey, mft fpoof t b en bfd?" The sounds had a desperate tone to them because he was striving not to spray the room with foam.

The boys, relieved that their daddy was okay, giggled as they obediently made their way back to the bed. Spencer overheard Sorryl tell Trey, "Mommy would have laughed and cleaned Daddy up like she used to do with us."

At least this successfully ended the boy's endless questions about their coming day with Daddy, but a good while was lost in muffled laughter.

When Spencer finally came to bed, smelling very much like a mint patch on a spring morning, they all had one more laugh, then lapsed into a merry silence so unlike the somber one of just a half hour before. The trio finally fell into slumber as images of three people dashing along the mountain slopes and splashing in their pond flitted across the fathomless air of their dreams. A warm feeling stole across their hearts even as they slept.

Chapter 8

Sorryl stretched and yawned. His eyes inched open to gaze at his hazy surroundings.

"Where am I?" he wondered, rubbing his eyes.

Finally, his confused gaze fell on Daddy, then Trey, who were sleeping on either side of him. Understanding dawned; he was sleeping in Daddy's bed! The night before came back to him and he remembered that they were to spend a whole, entire day with Daddy today! He gave an excited bounce before he remembered the sleeping forms on either side of him. He glanced at them. Good, he hadn't wakened them. *Now to get out of bed without bumping them around too much.*

Sorryl crept toward the end of the bed so he could hop off there. Once, his knee came too close to Trey and the bed sloped away from him, joggling him. Sorryl froze in place as he anxiously watched his brother. Trey stretched and shifted, then lay still again. Sorryl proceeded. He felt like he was trying to follow a very wobbly and unpredictable valley. Finally, he reached the end of the bed. He smiled in triumph and hopped off, but his foot got stuck in the covers and he landed in a heap on the floor. For a moment, he lay there, then he slowly picked himself up and peered over the end of the bed.

With a smothered shout, he leapt backwards, then he giggled and crept back to the bed. "You scared me, Daddy! It was supposed to be your feet, not your head!"

Spencer chuckled and gave his son's back an affectionate scratch, "You didn't know I could turn around so quietly, did you?"

Sorryl giggled, "No, I guess not."

Spencer picked up his Bible, leafing through the worn pages. He loved Sorryl's giggle, though it was so like Annaleah's that he often found himself needing to force a smile and blink back tears when he heard it. He felt so incapable of watching out for these boys when all he wanted to do was run to the mountains and cry. He wondered if they wanted to do the same thing. Once in a while, he could see that their laughter was to cover up what would have been a sob. It pained his heart, but he didn't know what to do. *Lord, I feel so… inadequate.*

My strength is made perfect in your weakness, dear one. The words were almost a feeling rather than someone speaking.

Spencer sighed and almost smiled, *Yeah, I do know that… it's just so easy to forget there's a strength other than mine.*

He felt almost like a Heavenly chuckle rumbled across his heart.

Sorryl had climbed up beside him, forgetting the labor he had gone through to get off the bed. There wasn't a point in being off the bed now, when he could be with his daddy who was awake.

Spencer smiled at him before he turned his attention to the words before him. Sorryl climbed onto his back, watching as Spencer read. For some reason he felt protected there.

Before long, Trey stuck a tousled head next to Spencer's.

"Want me to read to you?" Spencer asked.

"Yeah! Please!" both boys agreed.

Spencer flipped through his Bible. This was a daily occurrence, except usually he read by himself before he came to the living room where Trey and Sorryl clambered onto his lap to hear him read the Bible. "How about Esther's story?" he asked, even as he gulped down tears. He couldn't help but think Annaleah was the one responsible for their love for reading the Bible. She had read it so enthusiastically, as if she realized the characters within were real people and that the stories had actually taken place. As her musical voice breathed life into the words, you could almost feel the dust swirling about your sandals, hear the

clamor of the marketplace, detect the stench of fish by the sea...
Spencer sighed.

"Oh, yeah! Esther's a fun one!" Trey exclaimed.

Sorryl agreed, so Spencer began reading. The boys were transported to another place and time, where the people of Israel were in danger of being wiped out; where a queen decided she was willing to pay the ultimate sacrifice, if she must, to save her people... her people whom her own husband had decreed should be killed. It wasn't his idea. No. A wicked traitor had plotted it all and convinced the king to sign the decree. And now, now she must do her part to save her people... nay, to save the *Lord's* people.

When the story was through, the three stayed huddled together on the bed for a moment.

"We should be like Esther was," Trey said.

Spencer smiled, "How so?"

Trey thought a moment, "Well, we should be brave because we know God will help us. And we should do what we can to tell people about Jesus so they don't die... I mean the death of going to hell and never being with God again."

Spencer nodded, "Yes. Yes, we certainly should."

"Esther was kinda like Jesus," Sorryl said.

Spencer looked at his son and raised an eyebrow.

Sorryl answered his father's silent query, "Esther was willing to die so that the rest of the people wouldn't have to. Jesus *did* die to save us, to keep *us* from dying. Only He's alive again," he added with a sparkle in his eyes. "'Cause God is stronger than death and made Jesus alive again."

"You're right, Sorryl." Spencer smiled.

They sat in silence for a few more moments, then Spencer said, "Well, let's pray together and then get dressed. We've got a lot to do today!" He winked at his sons. They squirmed in delight and, after talking with God, they scampered to their rooms.

When they came downstairs, Spencer had breakfast ready and they ate quickly.

"Hey, can we have a picnic lunch?" Trey asked as he cleared his breakfast plate. He wiped a smear of ketchup from his cheek.

"Of course! Splendid idea!" Spencer exclaimed, entering into the boys' excitement as he resolutely threw off the somber mood that was threatening to overcome him.

"You can start to gather what you want." He caught the mischievous twinkle in Trey's eyes just in time and added, "... *food* stuff." He smiled as he imagined what treats the boy must have been planning to stow away. He was twenty-five, but he could still understand a boy's thought pattern. *Almost too well*, he thought with a grin.

Trey tipped his head at an 'oh well' angle and proceeded to gather the food items they would want.

"And we can get pizza for supper, right?" Sorryl asked with dancing eyes.

"We'll see," Spencer managed to answer as he tried to shove the napkins to the other side of the small table without dropping the picnic basket and plates he was balancing in his other hand. *How did Annaleah do this?* He tried to remember all the things they had packed on their 'picnics' to the city park back home.

"Can we get some ice cream for the picnic?" Trey asked, popping his head out of the refrigerator for a moment.

"It'll probably melt." Now Spencer was trying to hold the jam and peanut butter in one hand and lift the basket lid while holding the butter knives with the other.

"Then could we have brownies?" Sorryl asked.

"Brownies then! Brownies!" they both suggested now. Trey tried to hand Spencer the bread, but he was busy struggling to pack a picnic blanket around the jars in the bottom of the basket and only subconsciously heard the boys.

So Trey decided to try balancing the bread on Spencer's back instead, since it was conveniently bent over at the moment. The excited boys continued their request for brownies and it quickly grew into a song as Spencer stuffed the last rebellious corner of the blanket into the bottom of the basket.

"Brownies. Brownies. Brownies. Brownies..." They were marching around the table now. Trey quickly righted the loaf of bread every time he went by, for it was attempting to slide off Spencer's back.

Success! Spencer stood up, relieved and hot. Trey made a sudden dash for the loaf of bread. Sorryl was in his path, so he landed on the floor for the second time that day. Trey missed the bread, dove in a last valiant attempt at catching it, and landed on top of it instead.

Spencer looked down, surprise written all over his features. As far as he could tell, the boys had been suddenly thrown to the floor and a chair had ended up by the stove instead of next to the table by some unseen force. Worry etched his brow for a moment until he realized both boys were giggling and must not be hurt too badly.

Trey carefully stood up and rather sheepishly handed Spencer the squashed loaf of bread. "It was on your back, and when you stood up…" the culprit gave up, dissolving in laughter.

That was all the explanation Spencer needed in order to understand. He laughed along with them as he helped Sorryl to his feet. The boys clung to each other and kept giggling.

Spencer took a deep breath; this was a lot harder without Annaleah. He wiped the perspiration from his brow and asked, "What else do we need?"

The boys quickly recovered themselves in order to think, remembering so many things they 'needed' that they could have fed a den of bears.

"Wait a minute, wait a minute!" Spencer chuckled, holding up his hands for them to stop. "We don't *have* all that stuff! Besides, we'd never be able to carry it if we did."

"Alright," the boys assented, eliminating most of the items they had hurriedly listed off.

"Well, I hope we've got everything," Spencer proclaimed, letting his breath out in exasperation. "Your mother always made it look so easy."

The boys just looked at him. It hadn't been hard, it'd been fun!

"Well, let's be on our way," Spencer finally said, recovering his jolly spirits now that the packing rush was over. They trooped out the door with an important air.

"Oh! Brownies!" Sorryl exclaimed, suddenly remembering the most important part of their meal.

"Ah, yes," Spencer said, vaguely recalling having heard a request for brownies.

Trey giggled, "Now that you aren't all tied up with the picnic blanket," he paused uncertainly for a moment. "I mean, of course, *busy* with the picnic blanket. And your head isn't buried inside the basket anymore... well, not *actually* buried," he stumbled. "Well, anyway, you can hear us ask about brownies," he finished.

Spencer chuckled while Trey and Sorryl anxiously awaited his answer.

"Of course we need brownies. I saw some yummy-looking ones in the bakery last time we went there for bread, so we should be able to get some in town. Shall we walk or drive?"

Walk! Walk!" both boys exclaimed.

"Okay, let's leave the basket here. We can come back for it when we have the brownies," Spencer said.

They eagerly started off toward Los Ciegos, doing everything but walk.

"We can get our brownies, go to the mountains and explore a while, of course leaving our picnic lunch in your cave, and then eat lunch by the cave. And after that we can go to Mommy's grave, then home and swim in our pond, and when we're through with that, we can head off to town and get some supper and then look around a bit," Spencer said.

"Pizza? Can we have pizza for supper?" the boys instantly pounced upon him.

"Perhaps," Spencer replied, still not committing himself. Details being settled, they began chattering, often pausing in the road to have a playful scuffle or chase.

The townspeople could not help but notice the trio as it made its merry way down the road. This was the first time the Trestles had really been in town during its busy hours, and thus the first time for many of the citizens to truly lay eyes on them. And a jolly group they were, for they were going on a picnic!

A joyful yelp from a ways up the road that led into town pierced the normal hustle and bustle noises of the small town. One head after another turned to where the sound had originated. Even the children of the town rarely made such a 'racket'. What met their gaze was a grown man chasing a little boy around in circles in the middle of the road, while a smaller boy clung to the man's back, managing with great difficulty not to become dislodged. They were obviously just having fun. The man, who was really Spencer, suddenly spun around and the boy ran into his grasp before he could stop himself. Spencer swung him above his head, then set him down and proceeded on the way to town. The sound of joyous laughter floated on the breeze, reaching the disbelieving peoples' ears. One by one, the townspeople returned to their work, embarrassed that they had stared so long.

Starlight stood in the middle of the road with her mother, delightedly watching the fun. But she was rudely awakened when her mother nudged her in reproof. Instantly, Starlight erased her smile and set off to purchase some fresh fruit from a vender while Emma stepped into the general store, the owner of which had come to the door at the playful sounds floating into town from the road.

The Trestles continued down the dusty road, pausing now and then to exclaim over a flower or colorful pebble. The townspeople attempted to ignore them with stalwart determination, but the little group was such a novelty that they could scarcely refrain from turning to watch the trio.

Presently, Emma re-emerged from the general store, shaking her head as she glanced the travelers' way. "Total misfits," she muttered disconsolately to herself. They reminded her of her late husband, George, and of how Starlight used to be.

Her mind flew back to the time when she had fallen in love with George when he had accompanied his sick father, who had been sent to the desolate town to recover in fresh mountain air.

But instead of helping, the town had caused him to grow worse, so they had left for another, happier town within three months. But not before the two young people had exchanged addresses. They had kept in contact, and when his father died, George had come to marry Emma. She refused to go to his home and leave her town and her family, so he had moved to her town.

When their second daughter, Starlight, had been born three years after their marriage, the little girl had possessed the same love and joy in life as her father had. When Starlight was only six years old, and still as jolly and carefree as ever, though her father had become more like the townspeople, George had died from an unknown disease. Starlight had been inconsolable, for her father had been the only one besides one other child in the town who would play with her and be merry. It seemed everyone else was too busy following rules to enjoy life. She had thought it strange that he had become so dull, and only romped with her once in a while when no one else was around.

When he was gone, she had no one and longed for one of the rare playful times she had enjoyed with her daddy. But there was no way to squelch *her* spirits, until she finally mastered the art of stoicism when she was quite a bit older. And even then she was not completely changed. She had only suppressed her imagination and joy; they had not been thrown away.

These strangers painfully reminded Emma of him whom she had loved. He was the only one she had ever accepted that was different and full of life. "My daughter had finally managed to quit being outlandish and now here come these intruders, making her back into what she used to be," she quietly fumed. Her husband had changed, so she figured these new people would either decide they didn't fit, and leave, or they would change as well. But she didn't like the change she saw in her daughter.

Emma stopped a moment and observed the littlest boy. He stooped to pick a flower and then dashed to his father, who added it to their growing bouquet.

Suddenly, she glimpsed Starlight amidst the crowd of shoppers. She was standing there with a delighted smile on her face. With a shock, Emma was reminded of her as a little girl, when she used to bring her mama wild flowers, until she realized Mama didn't want flowers. She remembered Starlight's confused and hurt face when she had sternly told her that flowers didn't have a place in the house and to bring the bouquet right back outside where it belonged. She had found it two days later under her husband's pillow, where he had placed it when he found Starlight tearfully laying it on the porch railing. That was the first indication she had had that he was missing his joyful home and it had touched her calloused heart. She had allowed Starlight to set flowers on the table from then on, until George died, unless they had visitors – she would have been considered less righteous if she had been found with flowers on her table. Flowers were considered frivolous and an unnecessary bother. Because of this, her husband's had been the only grave in that town where flowers had been planted. Starlight had done it, watering them with her tears.

Not liking where her thoughts were leading, Emma pulled herself from her reflective mood. Going to Starlight, she took her arm and drew her away to do more shopping.

She stared at the basket Starlight carried, "Why did you buy blueberries? I told you to get strawberries."

Starlight looked down a bit sheepishly at the blueberries she had bought and blushed, "I-I forgot which one you told me to get," she faltered uneasily.

Her mother sighed, "You haven't forgotten which I wanted you to get for months, dear. We always get strawberries the first of the month."

Starlight only blushed again and followed her mother.

By now the trio was very near the town. Trey looked up from their play. "Wow! I didn't know there were so many people in the town!" he exclaimed.

"I better carry you so you don't get lost!" Spencer laughed as he swooped the boys onto his back and continued on to the bakery. The boys were having too much fun to notice all the stares of the townspeople at first, but Sorryl presently grew aware of them and buried his blushing face in Spencer's broad back. Trey saw them too and rested his chin on his father's shoulder, averting his eyes. Spencer glanced around and began wondering if something was wrong with him and his boys. He reached up to be sure he had really shaved. He let out a sigh of relief. He had.

Sorryl lifted his head a bit and whispered in his father's ear, "I think we're too colorful." He hurriedly buried his face again.

Spencer raised an eyebrow in surprise and looked around at the rest of the people. Sure enough, they all looked wilted and forlorn, as the few others they had met had, but this was a totally different feeling, being surrounded by them. It was like being confronted by a confusing wall of different shades of gray, dotted with pale faces that seemed almost devoid of life. The only color seemed to be the fruit and vegetables the forms in gray were carrying. The living food shone like beacons of hope.

Spencer shrugged his shoulders, then laughed and said in a low voice, "Never mind. If they can be different, so can we. Just smile back at 'em. They think we're weird now, but they'll get used to us."

Trey readily pounced upon this idea and beamed his friendly smile. Sorryl followed suit with his own shy, but sincere, smile.

Suddenly, Jerry poked his head out of his shop door and exclaimed, "Hello, Spencer! Come back for pizza again?" His deep laugh rang out.

Astonished heads turned the pizza maker's way. His smile faded and he slipped back into his shop.

"Hey! There's that lady!" Trey exclaimed, pointing to Starlight. He had taken a liking to her despite her indifferent response to his greeting.

"So it is!" Spencer answered.

Sorryl smiled at her and gave a little bounce. He had liked her too. "Where do we get brownies?" he asked.

"Right... here," Spencer answered as he walked into a shop and the aroma of fresh bread wafted around them.

"Yummy! It smells like when Mama used to bake!" Trey exclaimed lifting his head and sniffing delightedly.

"Oh! It smells sweet! Oh, Daddy! Can we get that instead of brownies?" Sorryl requested, leaping from Spencer's back and pointing to some doughnuts.

"Oh, yes, Daddy! Those look yummy! I forgot about doughnuts! Do you remember Mommy made them once?" Trey asked.

Of course he remembered Mommy had made them once. "All right," Spencer agreed with a little laugh. "Doughnuts it is!"

"Could we have the white ones, Daddy?" Trey asked.

"Sure!" Spencer smiled at his boys.

"Yes!" Sorryl exclaimed. He turned around to dash toward the doughnuts, but he was abruptly halted when he ran into someone. He looked up shyly into the hard, stern, and now astonished face of Martha Geller. All traces of enthusiasm quickly fled from his young frame. "I-I'm sorry ma-am," he managed to stammer.

"And well you should be," the lady fumed. "Children have no business hopping around in such a fashion! Hasn't your father taught you what is right?"

Her stern words pierced Sorryl's heart and he blinked back tears. "Of course he did. Daddy knows all what is right and tells us," he answered meekly.

Spencer came up behind his son and encouragingly placed his hands on Sorryl's small shoulders.

Martha was astonished at this boy's reactions and her heart smote her at once. "Well, I suppose I forgive you," she assented, softening her tones a bit, choosing not to add that she was sure the little boy's father did not know all that was right and that she was certain he knew much that was wrong.

Joy swelled Sorryl's heart when he heard her words of forgiveness and, before Martha could respond, he had wrapped his tan arms about her in a joyful hug, "Thank you ma-am! Here, you can have these. We got them along the road." Sorryl held their bouquet of colorful flowers out to her. Martha automatically accepted them before she realized what she had done. His mission accomplished, Sorryl turned and leapt into his father's protective arms, watching her curiously.

Martha stood stunned for a moment, then, shaking herself out of her stupor, she walked to the counter with her purchases.

The shopkeeper had enjoyed this spectacle much more than he cared to let on. Martha was a very stern and uppity lady and would normally have severely reproved a child for such a display of affection and for being so lively, more so than would any other person in the town. He was greatly surprised when she let the boy alone after her first reproach, assuming it must be because he was a stranger, though she had shown no qualms of reproving even adult strangers before. Of course, the town had never seen such people as these before. They kind of threw your brain into a fuzzle. Other visitors had soon become as subdued as the rest of the town. Not these people, they seemed simply insuppressible.

Starlight, who had been reprimanded by this lady more than once, had just entered the shop with her mother when Martha began her lecture. At first, she trembled for the little boy, who was much like she had been as a small girl. But she soon relaxed, for he did not receive such a piece of Martha's mind as Starlight once had.

Emma just shook her head in amazement, thinking disconsolately, *Well, if* she's *not going to put them to rights, I don't know who will!*

When Trey, Sorryl, and Spencer had each chosen a doughnut, they stepped to the counter to pay for them.

The shopkeeper winked at Sorryl. He didn't know why, he just couldn't help it. He shot a hasty glance toward Martha's departing figure to make sure she hadn't seen. If she had, she surely would have huffed back to give him a piece of her mind.

On the way out of the store, Trey said, "Daddy, they should put the sugar *inside* so it doesn't get all over."

A few people chuckled in spite of themselves before they realized what they were doing and recovered their somber moods.

The townspeople were all considerably shaken by this whirlwind that had come upon them so suddenly. Most managed to recover almost completely, but not quite entirely, and complacently continued their day. But the incorrigible trio left many bewildered people in their wake.

"Now to the mountains!" Sorryl exclaimed, leaping off the ledge of the bakery doorway. Townspeople paused to look at him and found their mouths involuntarily lifting in smiles. Quickly, they forced the corners of their mouths downward into disapproving frowns.

The Trestles walked along the road out of town.

"First let's visit the cave," Trey suggested with sparkling eyes. "'Cause we have to put our food in it." After a slight pause, he asked hopefully, "Say! Couldn't we eat our doughnuts *right now?*" He grinned convincingly.

"I don't think so, little tyke." Spencer answered, affectionately ruffling his son's hair.

Chapter 9

When they had retrieved their picnic basket from the house and added their now somewhat squashed doughnuts to it, they started the climb to the cave the boys had discovered.

"See, Daddy? See the little black hole up there?" Sorryl said, pointing a small finger.

Spencer squinted, straining his eyes to see where Sorryl was pointing. He finally shook his head.

"Right there!" Sorryl instructed again.

Spencer glanced at Trey. He appeared to be having just as much difficulty finding it. "Nope, I don't see it," Spencer said, playfully tousling Sorryl's hair.

"Me neither," Trey said, still struggling in vain to see the opening.

"Are you sure you really see it?" Spencer asked.

"Yup. Right there," Sorryl persisted, indicating the spot again.

Spencer and Trey followed his finger with their gaze, then, suddenly, a huge bird alighted from the side of the mountain and soared off into the sky.

Sorryl giggled.

Spencer smiled fondly and asked, "Was that eagle your hole?"

Sorryl nodded and continued to giggle at himself.

Trey joined in as they continued their way up the mountain and Spencer laughed too, "That's a perfect example of how we sometimes see what we want to, not what's actually there."

Sorryl smiled, "Yeah, and then you get embarrassed for being so sure. Only it's worse if you're thinking wrong of a person, because then it hurts them."

Trey added, "And sometimes it hurts you too."

Spencer nodded with a sigh, "Yeah. Unfortunately that's true. I have two very wise boys."

Trey and Sorryl's faces flushed with pleasure.

After climbing a little further, the boys stopped and pointed, "There it is!"

Spencer was about to follow them, but he suddenly stopped. Had he just seen a man dash away up the mountain? His anxious gaze searched the open face of the mountain, but he couldn't find anything. He finally gave up, laughing at himself and his sudden fear. He had boldly explored the woods and hills as a boy, what was the matter with him? He must have lost his familiarity with the wilderness while he was living in the city.

The boys were talking to him, "Can you find it, Daddy? It's right there in front of us."

Spencer stepped forward to join his boys, but he still couldn't see a cave. He stooped down. "Oh! Now I see it!" he said, realizing the opening was covered with vines. "Well, that is certainly a well-hidden fort!" he exclaimed in genuine appreciation. "Any boy would be proud to claim such a place as his own."

"And, see, if you step out of it and over this way a teensy bit, you can see our house!" Trey said, demonstrating.

"So you can! That's really neat!" Spencer exclaimed. "Now, let's just stick our basket in here," following his own instructions, "And head off to explore our terrain."

The boys whooped and were about to dash off, but Spencer stopped them, "Hold up a second, boys. First, a rule: make sure you *always* know where the other two people are, okay? Stay pretty close together."

Their eyes sparkled, eager to be off, "Okay, Daddy."

This taken care of, the three adventurers set off to explore, whooping and hollering as they ran first up one steep grade and then down another.

Sometimes, one of their shouts would carry on the clear, mountain air down to the little town, where the townspeople wondered what could possibly be going on up there. The three explored the area all around until they knew it quite well, and then they began playing chase over its various invisible trails.

"Now I'm an Indian, a friendly one, but you don't know it," Trey began when they tired of their game of chase.

"And we're trappers taking our furs to the nearest town," Sorryl said, indicating Los Ciegos below them.

"Okay. Sorryl and I will go a little ways up the path. You can tell we're lost, so you track us, looking for an opportunity to assist us. But you have to be very careful that we don't shoot you, because we might mistake you for an angry Indian 'cause we're invading your land," Spencer agreed, joining in the boys' fun.

So the two set off down the trail while Trey shadowed them, looking for an opportune moment to reveal himself without getting himself shot.

This went on for quite some time, with Sorryl struggling to hold back his giggles and not look back. But they were shortly caught up in the game and played their roles magnificently. By now Spencer and Sorryl 'knew' that Indian Trey was following them and naturally assumed their lives were in real danger. The mountain now grew quiet as they crept along silently, the Indian hoping for an opportunity to show himself, the trappers seeking a way to save their lives. Presently, Spencer and Sorryl slunk around a curve and walked smack into a real mountain goat, which immediately took to its heels and fairly flew up the steep grade. Spencer and Sorryl jumped in genuine surprise, and the Indian took this chance to creep around to the front and show himself.

"Welcome," the Indian solemnly greeted with a thick accent and in a much deeper voice than would be expected to emanate from him.

Still pretending, Spencer gave an exaggerated start and drew his 'gun' out, leveling it at the 'Indian stranger'.

Sorryl leapt onto Spencer's broad back, hiding behind his shoulders.

"You are lost?" the Indian asked in a still thickly accented voice.

Spencer looked guarded and continued to hold the gun ready, though he lowered it some. "We're looking for a way down the mountain," Spencer answered evasively with a tremor in his voice.

"To the village?" the Indian questioned, pointing to the town. After a brief hesitation, Spencer assented, "Yes."

The Indian cautiously stepped forward, "I am Sequatut," holding his hand out in the English manner. "We will be friends?"

Spencer slowly put his gun away, then took the Indian's hand and gave it a hearty squeeze.

Our pretended native grimaced, for it had been a little bit too hard of a squeeze.

"Friends," Spencer agreed, smiling an apology.

"Good," Sequatut smiled gravely. "Then I show you the way. Follow me." With a friendly wave of his hand, he boldly turned his back to show he trusted them and they slowly began their descent. When they were to the bottom of the mountain, he pointed straight across the grassy plain to the village and then vanished into the bushes.

"Wait!" Spencer cried after him, running into the bushes with Sorryl astride his back once more. "How will I find you again?"

But the Indian was gone. Spencer searched for some sign of the native while Sorryl gazed around from his perch on Daddy's shoulders. The boy had entirely disappeared! All at once, Spencer felt something seize his ankle, and then he heard a muffled giggle at his feet. Looking down, he saw a slim arm reaching out from behind the bushes. He bent down, peering between the branches.

Now Trey laughed outright. "Indian Sequatut hungry," he announced.

Sorryl and Spencer agreed that they were hungry too, so the three trooped over the mountain and headed to the cave for lunch.

When they reached the cave, Sorryl went in to retrieve their picnic basket. His voice echoed from inside, "Hey! Someone took our candle!"

"Oh, I saw it was gone when we came the first time, it's over there, on the other stump. I figured you moved it," Trey said.

Sorryl came out of the cave with the basket. He tilted his head, "Maybe. Anyway, I'm hungry!"

Spencer laughed and took the basket from Sorryl. *Maybe I really did see someone*, he thought. *Maybe I shouldn't let the boys up here anymore…* He paused in thought for a moment, then shook his head. *I'm just being silly. The boys probably left the candle in the wrong spot. And what I saw earlier was probably just another mountain goat.* He sat down and opened the basket to get their food out.

Sorryl wiped jelly from his mouth and asked, "Now is it time to visit Mommy's grave?" The three called it a grave, though they knew it was only a stone. Somehow it helped to say 'grave'. It made it seem like she was here and not in the bottom of the ocean somewhere.

"Yup. Let's go," Spencer said as he gathered up the lunch articles. When the picnic basket was packed once more, they set off for town.

"Let's leave our picnic basket at the house," Spencer said when they reached their home. "Wait here while I put it inside."

Trey and Sorryl picked some flowers for their mother's grave while they waited. When Spencer returned, they continued down the road to Los Ciegos.

Sorryl found an orange flower on the way and added it to their growing bouquet, "I gave the other flowers to that lady in the store. But that's okay, 'cause it would have been wilted by the time we got it to Mommy."

Spencer smiled and ruffled Sorryl's hair, then he stooped to pick a large white flower, "This one's to show that your mommy is in Heaven, where everything is pure and there's no sin or anything evil."

Sorryl looked up at him with a wobbly smile, "It helps to know that... that she isn't just... gone, that she's where I'll get to see her again." He kicked a pebble with his foot and glanced down, blinking back tears.

When they entered the graveyard, Trey suddenly stopped. "Look!" he pointed at a gravestone, "Nobody had flowers before, but now one does."

Spencer followed Trey's finger, "Hmm. I wonder whose that is?" He curiously walked over to the grave, "George Bolton," he read. "I don't know who that was. But the graveyard looks a little brighter now that there are some more flowers in here. Let's put ours on Mommy's grave."

The boys followed Spencer to their mommy's special spot and Sorryl slowly placed the colorful flowers at the foot of the stone and removed the old ones, now dry and brown. They seated themselves on the grass beside the grave and lapsed into a thoughtful silence.

Finally, Spencer stood, "You ready to get going, boys?"

The young boys looked up at him, tears trembling in their eyes.

Spencer tried to smile and knelt back on the grass, holding his arms out for Trey and Sorryl. They ran into the comforting embrace and he curved his arms around them. After a moment, he kissed the tops of their heads. "She's in a wonderful place. We'll get to see her again," he whispered tenderly, tears gathering in his eyes too. "Do you wanna talk about it?"

Trey shook his head.

"No. It hurts more to talk about it. I just needed to cry a minute," Sorryl said. He sniffled and wiped his nose on his sleeve.

Spencer's voice was gentle, "I know it's hard, but we can't just keep the pain inside. If we do, it'll just grow and get worse, even if it doesn't feel like it at the moment."

Sorryl attempted a smile, "I know, Daddy. But talking doesn't seem the right thing to do. You just have to... feel."

Spencer hugged the boys closer, "Yeah. I know what you mean."

They sat there for a few more minutes, then Trey plucked a piece of grass and began chewing it. He gazed at the gravestone in front of him. "Why do they use stones? They seem so... cold and unfeeling. I'd rather plant a tree or something that's alive."

Spencer smiled and stood up, "I don't know why they use stones. But I'm kind of glad that little tree is growing next to Mommy's stone."

"Me too," Sorryl agreed.

Trey nodded, "Yeah. It makes it nicer that way."

Spencer stretched, "So are we ready for a swim?"

The boys stood and Trey said, "Yeah. It's getting hot! I didn't notice earlier."

Spencer smiled and took their hands.

"Volcano!" Trey shouted as he ran and jumped off their makeshift dock into the cool water.

"Whale!" Sorryl cried, following Trey and spraying water all over.

"Dolphin!" Spencer called. He gracefully dove in and came up next to Trey without making the slightest splash.

Sorryl climbed back onto the platform. "Now I'll try something different." He backed away from the water, his wet feet pattering on the boards of the platform. "Butterfly!" he called in a high-pitched voice, meant to sound like his mother. He ran forward, flung himself into the air, and clumsily fluttered his arms, succeeding in a belly flop.

Spencer couldn't help laughing as Sorryl sputtered to the surface. He swam over to him, supporting the boy in his strong arms, "Are you all right?" he asked when Sorryl stopped coughing.

Sorryl nodded as he rubbed his stinging stomach, "Uh huh."

"Good thing. We wouldn't want your belly turning inside out or anything."

Sorryl giggled.

Here," Spencer said, climbing out of the water, "Is this what you wanted to do?" He paused a moment on the dock and yelled, "Butterfly!" He gracefully swooped into the air, fluttered his arms, then smoothly tucked his head and skimmed across the top of the water. It was Annaleah's special dive she had performed back home in Joe's pond, where they had each adopted their own way of getting in and a name to go with it.

"Yeah!" Sorryl exclaimed, clapping his hands together. "You did it good!"

"Mommy and I used to do it together, remember? Only we called it 'Twin Butterfly' because there were two of us," Spencer reminded.

"Uh huh," Trey answered, lapsing into a pensive silence.

Sorryl was quiet for a moment too, then he said, "Let's play Blind-Man's-Bluff!"

Trey smiled, "Good idea! That game's fun in the pond!"

"Yeah, because it's hard to find two people in such a big space," Sorryl agreed.

"Okay! Trey's it first!" Spencer said.

Trey shut his eyes and began counting. He heard someone splash real loud, and then all went silent. "Ten!" Trey finished. He began swimming around, trying to find Sorryl or his daddy. After a few minutes, he decided that was fruitless and resorted to flailing his arms and making sudden dashes in random directions. Finally, he gave up and shouted, "I've received my sight!" His eyes sprang open and he immediately pounced on Spencer, who had been right next to him, hoping Trey wouldn't decide to make one of his random dashes in that direction.

Spencer laughed, "Jesus must have come and healed you, 'ey?" he said, water streaming down his cheerful face from the dunking he had received when Trey pounced on him.

"Yup," Trey nodded, laughing too. Then, looking around the pond he queried, "But where'd Sorryl go to?"

A giggle sounded from behind Spencer and Sorryl peeked around him.

"Hey! That's not fair!" Trey exclaimed playfully, leaping for Sorryl.

But Spencer swept him out of the way and they retreated across the pond, laughing, with Trey in hot pursuit. Water flew everywhere and joyful yells bounced over the rippling surface, carrying to the little town and arousing critical curiosity once again.

When the sun hung low in the sky, Spencer said, "Supper time boys! Get out and dry off!"

Eagerly, the boys followed their daddy out of the water and grabbed towels, hurriedly drying themselves before dashing to the house to throw on their clothes. Sorryl pulled his shirt on backwards in his haste, but it went unnoticed because everyone else was in just as much of a rush.

Finally, they were all ready and tromped off to town, smoothing their wet hair as they went. But it was a fruitless effort, for they romped about so much on the way that it soon became dislodged again.

When they entered the town, Spencer inquired of the little boys, "Now, good gentlemen, what shall we have for supper?"

"Pizza!" Trey said.

"Pizza it is!" and they waltzed into Jerry's now busy pizza shop and right to the end of the waiting line. It was the dinner hour and many townspeople had stopped there to eat.

"Do we want anything special?" Spencer asked. "Like breadsticks?"

The townspeople stared at them, trying not to smile. Why on earth did this annoying family always have to make them smile? Their hair was wet... how on earth could that be? And it stuck up in odd angles in a couple places. To top it off, they realized Sorryl's shirt was on backwards. But they all had good manners... or so it appeared.

"Oh, *can* we have breadsticks? I'd love to!" Trey said.

Sorryl started to exclaim in excitement. But he suddenly stopped himself. Clearing his throat he said, "That would be grand, kind sir," in an awkward accent. He was supposed to be a beggar whom Spencer had taken in and was buying food for.

Spencer quickly caught on and answered, "As you wish."

With an effort to copy Sorryl's accent, Trey added, "Yes, 'twould be lovely, sir." They were obviously beggars who had once been high-class, for they had the speech of the well learned and the accent of one accustomed to living on the streets.

When it was their turn to order, the 'beggars' stood respectfully back while Spencer ordered their pizza and breadsticks with the flourish of a wealthy man, which he was not. Jerry stifled a laugh and prepared their order while the wet-haired trio found a seat.

"This one's the best!" Sorryl said, "Can we sit here, Daddy?"

"We sure can. It doesn't look like anyone else is sitting here," Spencer answered.

Sorryl sat down and one of his wayward locks of hair bobbed a couple times. Suddenly, he straightened himself and rose to walk sedately up to the counter. In his newly-acquired accent, he said, "We would like sauce with the bread sticks as well, sir."

Jerry smiled, "Why, of course, sir!"

To which Sorryl whispered loudly in a confiding tone, "I'm a beggar, you don't need to talk to me like I'm a gentleman! *And,* I'm only a little boy, and you're grown."

Jerry laughed, "Ah! But it pleases me to!"

When the Trestles had their pizza, they carried their steaming food to their chosen seat in the middle of the room. Suddenly, Spencer noticed the boys' tousled hair. He tried to smooth it down. As he struggled with one of Trey's locks, it unpleasantly occurred to him that his own hair was probably in the same disarray. He suspiciously reached up, smoothing it as best he could, but it had partially dried in the wrong position and stubbornly stuck to it. He finally gave up, thinking it must have come to some semblance of order.

Sorryl giggled and pointed at Spencer's hair, "You still have a cowtick... I mean, cow*lick*."

Spencer reached up and pushed his hair down, but he knew it sprung up again by Trey and Sorryl's giggles. He tried once more, then gave up with a grin. "I guess the cowlick's going to stay there." he said. "Let's thank God for this wonderful day... and the food." They bowed their disheveled heads in greatly contrasting respect to their wonderful Lord.

When Spencer finished, they each took a slice of pizza and began talking about the adventures they had enjoyed that day.

Trey finished the bite he was chewing and swallowed, "I wish we could do this every day."

Spencer smiled a bit wistfully, "Me too, but we can't, because I have to work. But at least we get to work together lots of times, right?"

Trey nodded, "Yeah, workin' with you is fun! Besides, we'd probably get bored of always just having fun all day. We need to work. It always makes me feel more... useful."

Spencer smiled, "That's a good mindset to have."

After a moment of silence, all three looked at each other.

Sorryl grinned.

Trey grinned back.

Spencer winked at them.

At this, they each peeled back their cheese and transferred it to the bottom of the pizza.

Puzzled customers gazed at the eccentric newcomers' 'split' pizza with critical eyes.

Jerry silently smiled to himself. He could see that some of the townsfolk couldn't hide a spark of interest that lit their eyes behind the criticism. His life certainly was more interesting since the Trestles had arrived.

"It's yummy that way," Trey said, finishing his last piece of pizza.

Spencer laughed and handed him a napkin, "Here, I think that 'split' pizza got us more messy than usual."

Sorryl looked at Trey and giggled when he saw the sauce on his brother's face.

"Ah. Ah. Before you laugh you ought to have a look at yourself!" Spencer warned in teasing tones.

This promptly sobered Sorryl and he accepted the napkin his father offered and vigorously wiped his face and hands.

"Well, I guess we better get going," Spencer said when they were sufficiently cleaned up. He rose from his seat.

The boys followed him to the door where they bade Jerry a cheery good evening and sailed into the dusty road with still-damp hair in order to have a better look at the town. Several wondering pairs of eyes followed their retreating figures.

Chapter 10

The first place the explorers visited was the general store, which was full of people doing their last minute shopping for the day. There was a dusty checkerboard in the far corner for shoppers to play on, but it looked like it had probably never been used. The shopkeeper had set it up because, where he came from, the general store was a hangout place for the town and the citizens had often played with it there. The three were not long in finding it, and they promptly sat down for a game.

"Who's playing first?" Spencer asked with a twinkle in his eyes.

"How 'bout you against *both* of us," Sorryl suggested.

Spencer's deep laugh rang throughout the store. He winked at them, "Two of the finest players against one? I hardly think that's fair!"

Trey and Sorryl giggled. They knew Daddy was a much better player than either of them.

"Well then, you boys can take the first move," Spencer said.

After that, silence reigned, broken once in a while by intermittent giggles and quiet exclamations from the boys.

Spencer was winning. It was Sorryl's turn and his face puckered in concentration. He gazed long and hard at the board. Suddenly, a shadow fell across the table and Sorryl felt someone leaning over his shoulder. He looked up into the face of the shopkeeper, Charlie Kwen.

Charlie whispered something in Sorryl's ear. Sorryl glanced at the board and looked back at him. Flashing the storekeeper a delighted smile, he took his turn, jumping clear across the board, capturing four of Spencer's men on the way.

Spencer playfully looked up at Charlie as if to say, "Hey! They've already got two on their side!"

He hopelessly lost the game, for the shopkeeper remained at the boys' side, except when he had to leave to take care of a customer, and coached them as Spencer sometimes had. But Charlie was much better at the game. Hadn't he watched players hack away at each other all evening long for three years in Lottie, the town he had come from?

Puzzled shoppers tried to keep their minds on their business. But it appeared to be a fruitless effort, for the players soon had a crowd gathered around them. Every minute or so, one of the members of the group would give a start and tear themselves away from the game to resume their shopping, pretending not to notice the players anymore.

Presently, a lady possessing an air of self-importance stepped into the shop. Her criticizing eyes fell on the game-players with disdain and she haughtily turned her head from them, giving a disgusted sniff.

The onlookers needed no more encouragement to remember their place. They had soon dispersed and, in place of the cheers and anticipation of the next move that would be taken, there were many a sniff and reproving shake of the head in the player's direction.

Spencer glanced up, wondering why they had suddenly lost all their onlookers. With a puzzled quirk of his eyebrow, he returned his attention to the game.

After a moment, a lady approached them and kindly whispered in his ear, "We consider that to be sinful. We're a high-minded, religious folk. We refuse to stoop to such measures."

Now Spencer understood why everyone had left and nodded his understanding before he replied with a soft smile, "I don't see how developing a good relationship with my boys in a fun game can be a bad thing. In fact, I see it as a good thing. They're learning to think and work together, and having a good, fun time deepening their relationship with each other and their daddy."

The lady stood and puzzled a moment. Finally, she nodded to show she thought he made sense and then, ducking her head under the scrutiny of the other shoppers, she turned and walked to the counter to make her purchases. Charlie followed her and rang up her groceries.

By the time they were through with the game, the Trestles were well acquainted with the shopkeeper. He decided he liked these new people. After six years of this town it had begun to rub off on him, but he had been reminded of the good old days in his previous town when these three had enthusiastically seated themselves at the board and begun playing. And once he joined them, well, he was done for.

"We'd better be off," Spencer said, offering a friendly hand to Charlie.

Charlie took it in a firm grip, "Be sure to visit again."

"Oh, we will," Trey said, peering up at the shopkeeper with shining eyes.

Charlie chuckled. "Good."

Spencer was nearly to the door when he turned, suddenly remembering another of his reasons for coming to town. "Charlie?"

Charlie turned back to him.

"Could you use any help around here?" He paused a moment, "I'm going to be finished working on my house soon and am looking for a job."

Charlie laughed, "I was just planning to start looking for a hand. I've expanded a bit and would like help stocking shelves and sorting products and such. And I was hoping maybe I could get a break now and then," he added with wink. "When would you be able to start?"

Thank you, Lord! Spencer breathed silently. He hadn't expected to find a job so quickly, and he already liked this man who he would apparently be working for soon, "I could probably start in about a week." After thinking a moment, he added apologetically, "Trey and Sorryl would have to come with me until school starts. I can't really leave them at the house by themselves."

Charlie grinned and winked at the boys, "Oh, don't worry. They can help out a bit. And we can have some more good times together. 'Ey, boys?"

"Yeah!" they said.

"It'll be fun to help, too," Trey added.

Charlie chuckled, "Then I'll see you next Monday?"

"Sure thing. Oh. How much would you pay?"

"How much you willing to work for?"

Spencer laughed.

They ended the deal with another warm shake of the hands and the boys gave Charlie an enthusiastic hug, then they were off to explore the rest of the town.

"Where to next?" Spencer asked as they exited the store.

"To the houses," Sorryl said.

Spencer laughed, "Sounds like a good idea! Let's walk along and, if we find anyone on their porches, maybe they'll say hello and we can go and talk with them. Though we already saw lots of them in the store," he added

"Yeah, but most of them didn't really talk to us. They kinda seemed unfriendly after a bit, and they left before our game was over," Trey said.

Spencer smiled, "Well, maybe we'll find they're friendlier when they aren't in the middle of shopping."

They started up the road, the boys skipping along next to Spencer.

The first house they passed, Sorryl saw Martha Geller seated on the porch swing. "Hello, ma'am!" he called, smiling at her.

Martha glanced up from her sewing, startled, "Hello, young man. You shouldn't skip. Hasn't your Daddy taught you that?" she scolded.

"No," Sorryl answered, his brow furrowed in confusion, "Daddy does it too. It's fun. I can teach you." Then, at her look of displeasure he added, "Don't worry, you won't get hurt." By this time they had come up to her porch steps and could see she was working on a quilt.

She only sniffed, "Why aren't you doing something productive? You should be doing something to help the poor." The lady adjusted her glasses and bent her demeaning gaze over the rims on the three gathered at the base of her porch steps.

"Oh, don't worry, ma'am. That's what we're doing. We're gonna make all the down-turned faces be... be... bright-turned faces," Trey spoke up comfortingly.

Martha sniffed again and readjusted her glasses. After a pause she said shortly, "Have a seat," and patted the bench next to her. "Now, here is what I'm talking about. I'm making this quilt for the poor box, it's my twenty-first quilt," she added proudly. "Now, all the other children, while you were busy making all those screeches up at your house doing I-don't-know-what, have been working on some project for the poor box as well. Don't you feel ashamed?"

"Well... we had a lot of fun, and we were jumping in our pond. But," Trey added reflectively, realizing he wasn't really answering Martha's question, "I suppose I don't feel ashamed... because I didn't know you could do that here. And besides, now I'm doing something like that too," he added, brightening. "You see, I'm making a quilt for people's insides, by being cheerful and loving them." Trey patted Martha's hand, trying to comfort her troubled heart. He didn't realize she was attempting to reprove him. He could only sense the confusion and feeling of lack of fulfillment that was within her.

She didn't sniff this time, but shook her head. With a half-smile, she reached over to pat his hand and mumbled almost to herself, "Maybe you people *will* do this town some good." Then she sat up straight and resumed her sewing.

"Yeah! And we can go and cheer everybody in this Town of Glooms and bring them all some cookies!" Sorryl said.

"Humph!" Martha answered.

Spencer reached over and ruffled Sorryl's hair. When had his son come up with that name for the town?

"But I know the person who needs help first," Sorryl spoke again.

"Who?" Martha wondered in spite of herself.

"Why, don't you know? You're the one helping everybody," Sorryl exclaimed in amazement.

Spencer nearly laughed at this remark, but managed a gentle smile instead.

Martha frowned and said, "It must be your brother."

At this, Sorryl laughed. In his innocent heart, he thought she was teasing him, for it had never occurred to him that his brother would need the sort of help he was thinking of, which was helping someone to laugh and to know what it was to really live and know Jesus. "No, no, no!" he giggled.

Spencer smiled to see his son so merry. It was becoming more common for the boys to be able to laugh from their hearts now. It made him glad. "Who is it then?" he asked.

"Well, I don't 'zactly know his name," Sorryl answered reflectively, "But he lives in that big house at the front of town."

"Oh," Martha said knowingly. "That's Daniel Brendt." She paused, "He doesn't need help. He's got lots of money and he's done the most of all of us in the town. Buying materials for quilts and dresses and such, goes to church every Sunday, doesn't miss a day – even when he's sick. Wears his suits just perfect, he presses them every day you know. I'll say, if anyone's getting to Heaven it's him."

"Oh! But that's not how it is!" Trey exclaimed incredulously.

"Well then, sir. Tell me how it is!" Martha retorted.

"Well, you don't get to Heaven that way. See, don't you know that God sent Jesus to earth and He lived perfect for us because God knew we couldn't?"

"Of course I know Jesus came to earth. And I also know He died on the cross and rose again and then went up to Heaven. I read my Bible. But what does that have to do with it?" she huffed sourly. Oh! The idea that this little boy should think she, a very religious person, did not know *that*.

"Right!" Trey said, the worried creases in his forehead disappeared, "so you *do* know!"

"I know what?" Martha said in her grumpy way.

"That you don't get to Heaven by your good things and going to church and stuff. That's way harder than it really is! Really, you just need to see that Jesus lived perfect for you and died to take away your sins. And when you know that, you decide to let Him forgive your sins and wash them all away and ask Him to come and live inside you and help you live right. Then you get to go to Heaven!"

"Humph. I don't know that."

"Well!" Trey exclaimed, confused, "But you just said you knew that Jesus was on earth and died and..."

"Yes, of *course* I know that!" Martha replied, "But I don't know that He is the one that gets you to Heaven. We have to do our job you know."

"Yes. But our job is to not make God sad by refusing His gift. Our job is to accept it and follow Him, then we do good because we love God, not to get to Heaven."

"I *do* follow God. I do all those good things and go to church."

Trey stared at her for a minute, "But if you don't give your life to Him and have Him in you, then you can't get to know God and be friends with Him. Besides, having Jesus living in you is the only way you can be good enough to get to Heaven because God says everyone has sinned. Then, when Jesus is in us, God sees His righteousness instead of ours, which to Him is like rags you used to clean your bathroom or something."

Martha looked at him, appalled. She repeated, almost to herself, "Rags I used to clean my bathroom..."

Martha returned Trey's gaze. She was silent for a moment, then she said, "Well, I guess I've given my life to Him, seeing as I follow everything He says to do, and more."

Spencer watched Trey to see if he would have an answer for her. He was ready to answer if his son couldn't, but he felt it was better if Trey finished.

"But do you do it because you love Him, or because you want to get to Heaven?"

"You sure are persistent. What's the difference?"

"Well, if you do it just to get to Heaven and to look good to other people, then you haven't given your life to Him, 'cause you're still serving yourself, not Him. Like Paul in the Bible said, 'Do I seek to please men? 'Cause if I seek to please people, I'm not the servant of Christ.' Really the whole reason for accepting Jesus is to have a relationship with Him anyway."

Martha sat quietly for so long that Sorryl finally peeked into her face to be sure she was still awake.

Martha peered back at him. Then she gently, though a bit stiffly, put her around him. For a moment, he sat there uncomfortably, but soon the feeling of having a lady hold him, like his mother had, overcame his shyness. He hadn't been cuddled by a lady since his mother died. He gave her a wobbly smile and leaned his head on her arm. "That's where Mommy is," he said quietly.

"Where?" Martha wondered.

"In Heaven," Sorryl replied, almost in a whisper.

Martha sat in silence a moment longer until she felt a warm tear drop onto her work-worn hand. She glanced down at Sorryl and gently ran her hand over his chestnut waves.

Sorryl suddenly looked up, brightening a little, "And then I'll see both my mommies. When I go to Heaven, I mean."

Martha smiled at him. "Both your Mommies?" she asked, puzzled.

"Yes, my Mommy before the Mommy that adopted me and then my Mommy that adopted me. I had another Daddy too," he added, trying to clarify things, but only managing to muddle them further.

Spencer decided an explanation was in order, "Their mother and father died in a car accident when they were five and six years old. Annaleah, that's my wife that just passed away, found them on the street and we took them in."

Martha's heart smote her for preaching to these people about ministering to the poor. Had she ever taken in an orphan? "Oh," was all she could say as a lump rose in her throat. Silently she wondered, *Does God have a family for every orphan, but when He brings one to someone's attention, they dismiss His call to help them?* She was remembering a homeless orphan boy who had come to her door a few months ago. She had sent him away with a crust of bread that she wouldn't want to eat anyway, thinking she had done her duty and earned one step further into Heaven.

Martha stirred, "I'm so sorry about your mommies. I don't see how you can love God if he did that to you."

Sorryl looked at her with pain in his eyes, "Yeah, it's hard to understand. But God's the one that is making me feel better. He gives me hugs, sort of, when I need them. Hugs on the inside where nobody else can. He always is there when I need Him, and I know I can trust Him. That's why it's worth it to give my life to Him, 'cause He gave His for us, and He loves us lots and is always there when you need Him if you let Him be."

Martha just looked at him. She had never seen a child with such grown-up thinking before.

"Besides," Sorryl added, "Dying isn't really dying, it's going home to Jesus. This is just where we have to stay while we wait to go to Heaven, or Hell I guess, if you don't trust Jesus. I'll see my mommies in Heaven again."

Spencer's smile was bittersweet, "That's right, Sorryl. They're waiting for us with Jesus."

Martha was quiet for a moment. This family intrigued her. She could see the pain in their eyes, but behind that pain was something sweeter, something stronger. Was it because they had 'given their lives to Jesus?' She looked up at them. *And I've been gossiping about how unruly they are because they don't have a woman… and because they aren't religious.* Suddenly, she felt a twinge of regret. Maybe she had judged them too quickly. They still appalled her with their weird ideas, but now that she had spoken with them, they didn't seem so heathenish to her. *In fact, they just might be closer to Heaven than I am… or even than Daniel Brendt is,* she thought. *That's ridiculous!* She retorted to herself, *they don't even follow all our rules! They have too much fun. If they really knew God, they'd be more serious.* Even with this thought, she found herself standing to lay a hand on Spencer's broad shoulder, "If you ever need help with anything, I'm usually here." After a pause she added wryly, "Most of the town is usually here. We don't get out much."

Spencer chuckled, "Thank you. We've had a nice visit. But I guess the boys were hoping to meet a lot more people today. I suppose we better get on."

"Good luck," Martha replied in friendly sarcasm.

Spencer chuckled and grinned, "Yeah." Then he added with feeling, "God bless you, Martha."

120

She was silent a moment, then nodded as if accepting the blessing and, after a pause, added, "God bless you, too."

As the three made their way back to the road, Martha stood and reflected for a moment, then whispered to herself, "I think He's already blessed me today, though I hadn't thought of Him as a God who would bless people before."

The Trestles traipsed further down the street. They hadn't gone far when they saw Starlight weeding the vegetable garden outside her house where she lived with her widowed mother, Emma. The trio had quickly learned that flower gardens were considered a vain waste, so vegetable gardens were planted across the front of the townspeople's homes instead.

"Hello!" Sorryl and Trey called together.

Starlight paused and looked up, startled at the children's cheerful voices. It was a new, but pleasant, sound. The three were standing in the road. When she looked their way, the two smaller ones waved. She returned a rusty smile and waved back, but the younger one kept waving. She was thinking of waving again when he suddenly exclaimed, "Hey! Look at my long arm! It's longer than yours!"

Spencer looked at Sorryl's arm and noticed its shadow. It reached all the way to Starlight and was just brushing her shoes. He chuckled and stuck up his arm. "Not anymore," he teased.

Sorryl looked up at him, "Hey!" He grinned, then looked back at his shadow and began waving his arm again, "I can tap your shoes, ummm... Miss," he finally said, not sure how to address her. "Or maybe Mrs. But maybe ma'am would be better. Well, anyway," he finished, "I can pat your shoe!"

By this time Spencer, and even Starlight, were chuckling.

Trey had begun waving both of his arms about and said, as soon as Sorryl finished speaking, "Well, whether you're a Miss or a Mrs., I can give you a hug from way back here!" He swung his arms together so they seemed to go around her waist.

Starlight laughed softly and said, "Oh, but you went right through my middle, because both your arms are clasped in front of me now, not behind me."

"No, my arms didn't go through you, you're just invisible there," Trey said.

This brought a hearty laugh from Spencer.

But Starlight straightened her face and said sternly, "Why did you make my middle invisible? Did you just want to see the food I ate for supper?" and crossed her arms with a frown.

Now it was Trey and Sorryl's turn to break out in giggles.

Trey said, "No, I just wanted to see if you had drunk enough water today."

Starlight managed to keep a straight face and asked, "So, did I?"

Trey peered intently at her for a moment, as if evaluating the quantity of water in her stomach. Finally, he gravely answered, "I'm afraid you haven't. You have your choice of solutions for this serious problem. We can either soak you with that hose," he said, pointing, "Or you can get another drink of water."

Starlight laughed and glanced at the hose, and then at Spencer with a silent question in her eyes. He smiled and nodded his head so she slipped her shoes off and grabbed the hose, shouting, "I'll take the soaking... if you let me soak you!" and dashed for the spigot to turn the water on.

Trey and Sorryl leapt at her, laughing as she fell with their arms clasped about her legs. Then they began fighting over the hose. Seeing his chance, Spencer dashed to the spigot to turn on the water.

Water hit Trey, Sorryl, and Starlight. They leapt backwards and screamed. Brushing water from their eyes, they looked up and saw Spencer dashing away from the spigot. Immediately, they realized what had happened. With a shout, the three who had been fighting against each other only a moment before suddenly became allies. All three pursued their tormenter with the hose. But he was too fast for them.

They dashed on at top speed. Suddenly, they were thrown to the ground when the hose ran out and came up sputtering and giggling as they received another showering.

"Hey! You have to come back, Daddy! We can't get you over there!" Trey yelled, struggling with the hose as he tried to make it go an inch further.

Spencer laughed, but didn't budge. He stayed tantalizingly just out of reach.

Hearing an odd commotion outside their house, Emma finally put down her quilting. "I can't imagine weeding the garden could make somebody shout so," she muttered as she went to the door and poked her head out. She stared in shock as she beheld three soaked people picking themselves up off the ground. "What on earth possessed those people to take over our yard!" she mumbled to herself indignantly. She was about to yell at them to get out when she gave a sudden gasp, "Why! That's Starlight! I wondered where she'd got to." Then she hollered, "For shame, Starlight! What on *earth* are you doing!" But nobody heard her.

Sorryl had found a bucket full of weeds and brought it over to the end of the hose. Trey and Starlight's eyes took on a sudden gleam when they saw it and they quickly dumped out the weeds, replacing them with water. Then the three resumed their pursuit.

Spencer saw their plot and took off around the back of the house.

With a gasp, Starlight shouted, "Wait! Stop! Uh. Mr.!"

But he never slowed down. Just as he rounded the corner of the house, they heard a surprised yelp muffled by a loud splash. All three continued running, Sorryl carried the bucket, water sloshing over the sides. Starlight slowed just before she turned the corner and there they saw Spencer sitting up to his shoulders in a pond. He had obviously tumbled all the way under, for there was a lone lily pad perched on top of his dripping hair.

As soon as she saw he wasn't hurt, Starlight began laughing.

Sorryl took the bucket of water, which was only a quarter full now, and waded into the pond. He unceremoniously dumped it on Spencer's head.

Spencer just sat there and laughed. After a moment, he asked, "How deep is it in the middle?"

"Oh, about five feet just beyond where you are," Starlight answered. "Why?"

In reply, Spencer picked up the already-soaked Sorryl and tossed him into the water. He came up laughing and cried, "Again! Do it again, Daddy!"

"Next do me!" Trey requested eagerly, wading into the pond.

In the house, Emma nervously dashed up the stairs to locate her shoes, "Oh dear! That Starlight! No telling what they're doing now!" she muttered to herself.

The children around the neighborhood were perking up one by one and going to the windows to see what the commotion was. Mothers and fathers looked too, shaking their heads at what they saw.

One mother turned to her children at their request to join the happy group in the pond, "Most certainly not! You children aren't even going out there!"

Starlight saw the mother that lived to their left shoo her children inside and shook her head, mourning to herself, *Oh! How I wished so many times I could see them dashing around! But no, they always walk with their heads hanging. It's so refreshing to actually see joy radiating from Trey and Sorryl's faces.*

Her face suddenly lit up when she saw John racing toward them. *His mother would be the most likely to let him come. I remember she showed me her marbles and let me play with them once,* Starlight thought to herself.

"Hi, Starlight! Mama said I could come!" John told her when he reached her, excited for the first time she could remember.

"Good!" Starlight responded. She didn't know what else to say.

John went over to Spencer, "Can I have a turn?"

"Sure!" Spencer said, holding out his arms for John. He had to support the boy and be careful when he tossed him, for John, like the rest of the children in the town, had never learned to swim.

"Oh, dear me! It just gets louder and louder out there!" Emma worried grumpily. "I can't believe Starlight is doing this," she shook her head miserably. "I mean, I can, but I wish she wasn't." She paused a moment. "Or maybe I'm glad she is," she said at last, now undecided. She was hurrying to exchange her slippers for her shoes. She would never dream of going outside barefoot, or even in slippers. But the more she hurried, the slower it seemed to go. One of her laces snapped and she disgustedly held it up between her finger and thumb, "Now look at what you've done!" she reproved the unyielding shoelace. Then, with a sigh, she gave up as the noise emitting from the backyard grew. She pulled the shoe she had successfully secured on her foot back off and dashed down the stairs for the first time in her life. She slowed herself when she reached the door and made herself walk composedly to the back yard. What she witnessed there completely astonished her. Awe-struck, she stopped and stared for a moment before she could speak, "Starlight! What on *earth* are you doing?"

Starlight stopped short and whirled around. Her gaze immediately fell to her mother's bare feet. It was her turn to stare now, "You have no shoes on, mother!"

This totally dismantled Emma's dignity and she uttered nothing further for a moment. Starlight stood gazing at her as her dark curls dripped water onto her blue shirt.

At last Emma gathered her resolve and said weakly, "You don't either."

"No, I don't, but I go without shoes all the time. Remember when I was younger? I always used to lose them somewhere or other," Starlight said with a laugh.

Emma didn't know what to do, "Well, I expect the weeding to be done tonight," she finally ventured, and turned to huff her way back into the house. She tracked mud across the floor as she went after a towel to wipe her feet with, muttering furiously the whole way. "To think they made me go out there without any shoes!" she fumed.

Suddenly, a picture of the scene in the backyard replayed in her mind. A smile began in her eyes and started spreading to her mouth. Quickly, she turned it to a frown and glanced around as if afraid a nosy townsperson had eavesdropped on her humor. *It seems funny I'd suspect them of eavesdropping,* she thought, *but not of... playing in a pond. Seems to me eavesdropping is worse, but we think we're doing pretty good by being... stoic and helping the poor."* She stood in the middle of the floor for a moment, contemplating. Finally, she dismissed it with a shrug and went to clean up the mud she had tracked into the house.

Trey had heard Starlight's mother say the weeding had to be done that night. He looked up as she made her way back to the house, "I'll help weed!"

"Yeah, me too!" Sorryl volunteered.

"I guess if they're so willing to help, so will I," Spencer said.

"Well! I never saw anyone so eager to weed a garden. But I'll be glad for your help. Thank you!" Starlight replied as they made their way to the front of the house where the garden was.

John followed, not quite sure what to do. Whoever heard of volunteering to weed a garden?

"Now, let's play I'm the daddy," Trey said, "and Starlight is the mommy, and you guys are her kids."

John just stared at him, still unsure what to do. None of the children in the town had ever played this way or been given occasion to use their imaginations. But Starlight had exercised hers plenty and so had Spencer, and, with their help, John joined the game and was playing it famously by the end.

"I'll harvest the hay, 'cause it's the hardest job and the daddy should have the hardest part," Trey continued in a deep voice. There was not really any hay, but he was pretending, as he was with all the tasks he assigned. "And the mommy can do the chickens, 'cause. Umm. Well, because..."

"Because I can reach the eggs," Starlight supplied.

"Yeah, thanks—" he broke off, forgetting her name once more.

"Starlight," she supplied again, wondering at the Trestles nonchalant response to her name. Usually people stared at her in awe and could hardly pronounce it.

"Yeah, thanks, Mommy Starlight," Trey finished, laughing. "Okay, and then John," he continued, pointing to him, "can do the sheep. And Daddy... I mean, Spencer," he quickly corrected himself, "can mend the fence, 'cause he's the strongest." The entire garden was sectioned off and assigned to each person and they vigorously set to work.

As they steadily worked away, making noises to suit whichever task they had been assigned, Emma looked out the door. She was about to scold, "Now you all go home and do your work and let Starlight do hers," when she noticed that they were all energetically working in the garden. She had never seen children working in such a manner before. The children of the town had always treated almost everything they did as a duty and done it with as little energy as possible. She stood and stared in amazement for a moment, then quietly made her way back into the house to puzzle over what she had seen.

The gardeners soon completed their task.

Sorryl sat back on his heels and surveyed their work with satisfaction. Then he said eagerly, "We need to go see the Mr. in the big house at the front of town today. He's the one that really needs the most help you know."

Spencer laughed. "Okay, I guess we better get going. We had a good time," he said with a chuckle as he glanced at his damp clothes and muddy knees, then at the boys' wet hair.

"Yeah! We had fun! Can we come over again?" Trey and Sorryl asked.

"Sure, any time!" Starlight beamed.

"Hooray! Thanks, Starlight. We had fun today," Sorryl said.

She smiled, "Thank *you* for stopping by."

When they arrived at Daniel Brendt's house, dusk was fast turning into night. The porch light was on and, as they approached the stairs, he emerged from his house to retrieve his newspaper.

Sorryl called, "Hello, sir!"

He glanced up, startled. No one ever ventured to speak to *him*. He never wanted to talk anyway. He grunted in reply and turned to go back inside.

Sorryl hurried to inquire, "Is it your bed-time, Mr. Brendt?"

Mr. Brendt paused with his hand on the doorknob, then turned back to them and answered grumpily, "No. Not my bed time. What do you need?" he asked shortly, assuming no one would bother to talk to him unless they needed something.

"Nothing, sir. Well, I mean I *do* need something, but not from you. I need a new pair of clothes 'cause I got mine dirty," Sorryl said, now nearly whispering. He had suddenly grown shy of this imposing man.

"Come up on the porch, how's a body supposed to hear you from way back there?" Mr. Brendt growled.

Spencer and Trey obeyed without delay, but Sorryl would only come as far as the stairs. He stood with his heart beating fast as he peeked through the railings.

"Now, repeat your sentence please," Mr. Brendt continued as if he were a schoolteacher.

Sorryl's lips quivered. He opened them to speak, but no words presented themselves.

Mr. Brendt cleared his throat impatiently.

Trey began to respond for his brother, but Mr. Brendt interrupted him gruffly, "I asked him, not you." So Trey quickly snapped his mouth shut.

Sorryl finally worked up the courage to stutter, "I-I said that I d-didn't n-need anything from y-y-you, but I n-need a-a, I m-mean, s-s-some, a. Oh dear! I mean, I need a new pair of hair, or, no, clothes because mine got all dry. No, they got all wet and muddy," he finished in a rush.

"Come on up here with the rest of us," Mr. Brendt ordered.

Sorryl went.

Mr. Brendt sniffed, "If you don't beat all," he muttered, surveying the group before him.

Trey spoke up excitedly then, "Yeah, we all need new clothes. It's a good thing it's all dark, 'cause you can't see what a mess we are. We had a water war and went swimming in the pond at Starlight's house. And then we helped her weed the garden. That's why we're all muddy. And it was really fun!"

"At *whose* house?" Mr. Brendt replied incredulously.

"At Starlight's house," Trey repeated.

"Was her mother there?"

"Oh, yes. And she came out in her bare feet to see us!" Sorryl said, taking heart now. Somehow, Emma's bare feet had left a deep impression on him because of Starlight's reaction.

Spencer tried to shush his son before he delivered the astonishing news that Emma Bolton had been outside in bare feet, but he was too late.

Mr. Brendt's eyes went wide with astonishment and he grunted, "Indeed. Well, is that all you needed?" When they did not reply right away, he grunted and stepped inside, leaving three bewildered people on his porch.

"Well, let's head home, it's almost time for bed anyway," Spencer said, holding his hands out to the boys.

They took his hands and began the walk back home.

It was now dark and, since they had walked to town, they had to walk back in the dark. They didn't mind, but Spencer kept an eye out for animals.

They were nearly to the porch when Sorryl stopped abruptly, his heart racing. "Daddy," he whispered, "Something's over there! On the porch by the door!"

Spencer followed the direction of Sorryl's finger. He could just barely make out a dark shape slouching in the shadows. "Get behind me boys," he ordered quietly, hoping it wasn't a dangerous animal or a man, like the one he thought he had seen on the mountain earlier that day. He stared a moment longer. The shape gave a whimper.

"Stay back here boys," Spencer instructed quietly. He cast up a prayer for safety as he slowly advanced until he could see that the shape was a German Shepherd dog, lying with his head on their doormat. It weakly wagged its tail once, then lay still. Spencer cautiously reached his hand out and felt the dog's side. "He barely has any meat on him," Spencer muttered to himself. "Poor thing is starved." He was quite sure the dog wouldn't hurt anyone, and didn't think it could, even if it wanted to. "You can come up now boys. It's just a poor dog who hasn't got enough to eat."

Trey and Sorryl slowly made their way up the steps and followed Spencer into the house, "Whatcha doin'?" Sorryl wondered, sticking his hands in his pockets. "Can we help him? He might get cold."

"Yeah, Daddy, we can't just leave him out there."

"I'm getting a blanket to lay him on, so he can be comfortable," Spencer answered.

"And he can have my breakfast, 'cause he's really hungry," Sorryl offered, his heart going out to the dog.

"We'll get him his own breakfast so we can all have some. How's that."

"Good! Only maybe he wants some supper now," Sorryl suggested, following Spencer and Trey back into the living room as they carried a blanket for the dog.

"I think that's a good idea," Spencer answered. "Why don't you boys put some cereal and that left over hamburger in a bowl for him while I carry him in." It was the best thing he could think of to give the poor thing.

"Okay!" The boys scampered importantly back into the house. They were going to help a poor dog just like Mommy and Daddy had helped them when they were stuck in that containment home.

When Spencer tried to pick the dog up, it looked up at him and licked his hand. He tensed, ready to spring back if it tried to bite him, but it lay its head back down again.

When he had gotten it safely inside and laid it down on the blanket by the stove, the boys tried to feed it the cereal, but it wouldn't even lift its head.

"Here, let's see if he'll take the hamburger," Spencer suggested. He held the meat in front of the dog's nose. It sniffed once and attempted to move, but soon gave up with a pathetic whimper.

"Here, let's try this," Spencer suggested, breaking a chunk off and holding it in front of the dog's mouth. It eagerly took it, then whimpered again.

"He wants some water," Sorryl said, running to bring him some in a big kitchen bowl. Annaleah would have promptly sent him back for an old bowl they wouldn't use any more, but Spencer never gave it a second thought. They tenderly held the dog's head up so he could get a drink. It took a little, then began whimpering again and flopped its head back onto the floor.

"Poor boy. Poor doggy. You're hungry, eat somethin'," Sorryl soothed as he ran his hand along its matted fur. He couldn't understand why it refused to eat.

"I'll brush him, maybe he'll like that," Trey suggested, dashing off to get his hairbrush.

"I'll help you," Sorryl offered, running to retrieve his brush as well.

This time Spencer did protest, "Wait a minute, boys! If he's got ticks, we don't want you to get them. Use that old brush in the cupboard."

"Okay." They obeyed, veering off to Spencer's room where the old brush was located.

When they returned, they gently brushed the dog's matted fur. Every once in a while they paused to offer him some food and water.

Spencer finally stretched and yawned, "Okay, it's time for bed now. We have church in the morning you know." This was the first time they were going to church since they had moved.

"But the doggy doesn't want to be out here alone all night," Sorryl said, fondly stroking the dog's head. "Could we at least stay out here to sing and pray?"

"I have a better idea. Let's all have a slumber party out here with him," Spencer said.

"That's a good idea, Daddy!" the boys both exclaimed. They ran to fetch their pillows and blankets.

When they were all situated on the floor and had prayed together, Spencer asked, "What song shall we have tonight?"

"Let's sing 'He Is Able', so the dog will know God is able to make him well," Sorryl suggested.

"Okay," Spencer agreed with a chuckle. "Let's all sing it together."

Soon after the song had ended, the boys fell asleep with anticipant dreams of their first day of church in the new town.

Chapter 11

When Spencer woke the next morning, the boys were curled up with the dog. Their pillows were thrown aside and they were using the dog as a headrest instead. All three were still sleeping soundly. He smiled.

"There goes my hope of not getting ticks by using the old brush." With a yawn, he mumbled sleepily to himself, "Seems we've got ourselves a dog."

Spencer stumbled into the kitchen to prepare some breakfast. "Boy! I guess I must be getting old. That floor wasn't so nice to me as it used to be," he mumbled to himself, massaging his aching back. "I Guess I'll do eggs this morning." He glanced at the clock, "Got two hours before church." Sleepily, he cracked an egg and threw the shell into the bowl. He stared at it a moment, then blinked, trying to collect his thoughts. Suddenly, he laughed at himself, "That'll teach me to cook when I just woke up. Must be the hard floor, usually I'm fine." Good-naturedly, he fished the eggshell out of the dish and was more careful with his next egg. He stepped over to the trash can to throw the next shell out. Just as he was about to head back to the table, he heard a crash.

"Boys!" he started to scold as he spun around. Then he saw the dog. It was eagerly lapping up the eggs that had spilled from the bowl that had just been knocked onto the floor. Spencer shook his head. "You got your breakfast I guess. Now what are we humans gonna eat? 'Ey, trooper?"

"Yeah, Trooper, you have our eggs an' now we gotta eat your cereal," Sorryl said with a yawn as he appeared in the kitchen doorway.

"It's okay," Trey soothed the dog, reassuringly patting his head, "We don't mind, 'cause you need the eggs more than we do. Maybe you haven't eaten in a week."

Spencer laughed, "I'll get some more for us. At least he's walking. I thought he'd never get enough strength to live."

The dog ignored all this except to briefly glance up at each one as they began speaking.

"I think Trooper'll be all right, Daddy. He's waggin' his tail," Sorryl said, stroking the dog's head.

"I hope you're right," Spencer replied. He especially hoped so for the boys' sakes. He could see they already loved him a lot. He had to smile at the way Sorryl had adopted the name Spencer had used for the dog. "Okay, let's hurry. We haven't got long before we have to leave for church."

"Oh! Church! Church! Hooray! I forgot today was church day," Trey exclaimed, dancing around the floor with the newly christened Trooper following him.

"I'll do the next egg, Daddy," Sorryl offered. He lifted another egg from the carton and banged it with all his might on the bowl.

Spencer tried to warn him, but it was too late. Egg was spilt all over and Trooper was eagerly lapping it up.

"Well. At least Trooper'll clean it up for us," Sorryl giggled. "I'll do it gently this time."

"Okay. Be careful. Eggs break easily; you don't have to hit 'em too hard," Spencer said.

"Okay." Sorryl tapped the egg lightly on the edge of the bowl. And tapped, and tapped, and tapped. He glanced up at his father. "I have to go a little harder," he appealed solemnly.

Spencer smiled and nodded. He watched as Sorryl tapped harder, remembering how deftly Annaleah had cracked eggs and even made entire meals. He shook his head. He feared Trey and Sorryl weren't getting as good of meals since their mother wasn't here to prepare them. Spencer tried to cook, but somehow it never came out as good as Annaleah's meals had. Sometimes he grew frustrated and would have given up if it weren't for Trey and Sorryl's sakes. They needed food. Trey and Sorryl helped him sometimes. Usually it actually did help, but other times… A smile played about his lips as he remembered how Trey had once put a whole cup of salt instead of sugar in some muffins. The boy's face sure had looked funny when he tasted it. But they were gradually learning through their blunders.

Finally, the egg cracked open.

"I'll do the next one," Spencer told them. They didn't have all morning.

When they had eaten, Trey and Sorryl dashed about trying to find the right clothes.

"Daddy. I don't have any shirts a' tall," Trey called, after searching his closet.

"I don't think we unpacked our nice clothes yet. We haven't had time. And we haven't gone to church yet. We'll have to look in the boxes." *My how unorganized we are!* Spencer thought. *I've been working so hard on fixing the house up we haven't taken the time to unpack. I'll have to work on that this week.*

Sorryl went to look in the boxes.

Trey went into the bathroom to wash his hands. Something gooey that had been on one of his shoes in the closet had gotten all over them.

"Got some of them, Daddy!" he heard Sorryl yell from the living room. Suddenly, there was a crash and surprised yelp from Sorryl.

Spencer raced to the living room. He looked with dismay at the boxes strewn across the wooden floor. "Oh! Sorryl! What happened?"

"Well…" he looked down sheepishly. "I tried to stack all the boxes on top of each other to see how high they could go. But when I found the shirts, I forgot to watch it. And Trooper didn't catch it."

Spencer had difficulty keeping a straight face at Sorryl's last remark, "Okay, don't do that any more. You could get hurt or break something, 'kay?"

"Yeah. At least it was just the dishes and not our pictures, right Daddy?"

Spencer nodded, "Yeah, good thi—" suddenly, he realized what his son had said. He dashed over to the boxes that had been on top and pulled back the flaps. With a sigh of relief, he sat back on his heels. The dishes seemed to be okay. "Yeah, at least it wasn't our pictures," he said with a tiny chuckle. "And you didn't get hurt," he reached over and ruffled Sorryl's hair.

"Daddy! Daddy! Come quick! The sink won't drain!" Trey's panicked voice echoed from the bathroom.

Spencer rolled his eyes and dashed away, Trooper and Sorryl close on his heels.

When he arrived at the bathroom, Trey looked up at him, "I dropped the soap bar in, and it won't come out, and I couldn't remember to turn off the water. Only now I did." There was water up to the brim of the sink. Spencer didn't dare reach his hand in to pry the soap out of the drain.

"I'll hold up Trooper so he can drink it out. Then it won't spill," Sorryl offered, attempting to put the dog's front feet up on the sink.

"No!—" Spencer moaned in despair as the dog's foot slipped into the water, splashing them all. Helplessly, he ran his fingers through his hair, trying to think what to do. "I'll get it out with a cup," he finally said.

The boys ran off to find a cup. Trooper's nails clicked on the floor as he trotted after them.

Spencer leaned against the wall. *Oh, God! I need help! My world is falling apart and I just need help!* he silently cried. He took a deep breath, "Okay, so, actually this is really funny," he said to himself. "I may as well see the funny side of this. Like the Bible says, *'a merry heart does good like a medicine.'* And boy do I need some medicine for my soul right now." He crossed his arms and looked at the sink again, "Really it is funny! I mean... who else but us could get into so much trouble in one morning... and... a *soap* bar in the sink..." he began to chuckle.

When the boys returned with Trooper, Spencer saw that they had secured the cup over one of his pointed ears. Occasionally, the cup would twitch when the dog shifted his ear.

Spencer laughed. "All right boys. Let's not torture him too bad," But the dog seemed to enjoy it. When they removed the cup, he rubbed his head against it as if to say, "Hey! Put it back!"

Finally, the three were ready for church. They headed off to town in the car looking very well, especially for having no mother to put them in order. Trooper whimpered and followed them a ways down the road. But he tired quickly and couldn't keep up with the car, so he gave it up and went back to lie dejectedly on the porch where they had left a blanket and bowl of water for him.

When the Trestles entered the church, almost everybody had already arrived.

"Hey! Hello!" they heard someone greet quietly from somewhere towards the front of the church.

"It's Starlight!" the boys said. They headed in the direction of the voice.

"Hello, Starlight! We had fun at your house yesterday! Oh, and hello, Mrs. Starlight's Mama," Trey added when he saw her at Starlight's elbow.

Emma cleared her throat, "That would be Mrs. Bolton to you, young man," she corrected sternly.

"I'm sorry, I didn't really know your name," Trey apologized.

"That's all right, seeing as you didn't know, I suppose," Emma Bolton replied.

Trey continued, "After we left your house yesterday, we visited Mr. Brendt. He told us to come on his porch and we did, but he didn't talk to us much. I think he was afraid he would laugh if he talked to us too long. Maybe he thought that would be rude."

"Mr. Brendt invited you onto his porch?" Emma Bolton queried incredulously.

Spencer nodded, "That he did. Though I'd say it was more like a command than an invite," he chuckled.

Emma's eyes grew wide, "No one ever even ventures onto his *lawn*. He doesn't speak with anyone except on business. I can't believe it of the uppity man. He *is* the best of us all, but he needn't act like he knows—" She stopped abruptly as she spotted the subject of her speech entering the church.

The Trestles noticed that nearly everyone went to their seats right away. The church was mostly silent, because, if anyone ventured to speak at all, it was in very hushed tones.

As Martha Geller walked past them on her way to her pew, Sorryl greeted her and held out his hand.

She paused and turned to take his hand affectionately, "Hello, young man. And how are you today?"

"Fine, thank you. I think you're good too," he replied, gazing up into her face with a sweet smile

Martha smiled at this and nodded her assent, then turned to greet Trey and Spencer as well.

As Mr. Brendt walked stoically by them on his way to his accustomed seat, Trey and Sorryl smiled at him and greeted, "Hello, Mr. Brendt!"

The gruff man only glanced down at them and sniffed, then continued on his way. Their hellos caused a wave of whispers to spread across the unusually noisy church, "Saying hello to that old crank?" the parishioners whispered incredulously. "Now they must have learned that he won't stand for anyone saying hello to him."

Just then, the boys caught a glimpse of Jerry as he entered the church. They waved, but refrained from calling a hello. They knew they shouldn't shout across the church. He saw them and made his way towards them, a smile breaking over his wrinkled brow. "Hey, y'all! How are you doing this morning?" he asked as soon as he was near them.

"Oh! We're good. Especially since Mrs. Geller is good," Trey spoke for them all. He took hold of one of Jerry's hands and Sorryl claimed the other.

"You can sit with us!" Sorryl offered with a beaming smile. "I'd love to sit with you!" he finished.

Jerry chuckled. This once again resulted in whispers across the usually silent church.

Sorryl pulled Jerry into a pew with him. The others were about to follow when a lady appeared at the end of the pew. She looked down her nose at Sorryl and said indignantly, "This is my pew, young man. Out you go!" Then she grumbled under her breath, "These spot stealers! I tell you!"

Sorryl glanced up fearfully.

"Who are you rascals anyway!" she scowled down at them.

Before Spencer could answer, Trey spoke up, "Oh, we're the new people. I thought everybody knew us. They're always talking about us and staring at us." His eyes grew sad for a moment; it was hard when everyone always stared at you like you were painted with orange dots or something. And it made it even worse when they wouldn't talk to you and looked at you with mean eyes. His daddy had told them they needed to love the people anyway, like Jesus does. He knew he was right, and he tried to love them like Jesus did, but it wasn't always easy.

The lady just stared at him. She didn't know what to say, for she was one of the gossipers and had spread many a tale about this strange family.

Trey shoved his sad feeling aside and smiled. "Well," he continued politely, "I'm Trey. And that's my daddy. His name is Spencer," he added in a confidential whisper.

Spencer chuckled.

Trey continued, "And that's my brother Sorryl, he's shy. But he loves people, even though he doesn't talk as much as me. And my mommy and my other mommy aren't here, but my mommy's name is Annaleah," he finished. Sorrow touched his tones, but he perked up in a moment when the lady still hadn't responded. "What's your name, ma'am?" he asked.

The tall, stern lady hastily held out her hand to him. "I'm Mrs. Ruth Hock," she answered, pursing her lips.

"Pleased to meet you, Mrs. Ruthock," Trey replied, taking her hand.

Spencer smiled at Trey's mistake, "It's Ruth," he paused exaggeratingly, "Hock."

"That's what I said, Daddy, Ruthock."

Spencer gave up with an apologetic smile in Ruth Hock's direction.

"So, you are still in my seat," she grumped for an answer, looking pointedly back down at Sorryl.

"Do all the seats belong to people?" Sorryl asked worriedly. "Where can visitors sit? Do they have to stand?" he gazed questioningly into her face.

"I'm sure we'll find somewhere to sit, honey," Spencer said, holding out his hand. "Please excuse us," he nodded in Ruth Hock's direction.

"You can sit by me," Jerry finally managed to break in, smiling at the way he had been pulled into someone else's seat without being able to protest. "I think there's enough room where I usually sit."

Ruth watched them go before seating herself with a satisfied twitch of her head.

When the service was through, the boys made their way out the door. They greeted the pastor on their way.

"Good afternoon, Pastor. I liked to hear about Jesus coming back, but I think it'll be more cheerful than that. Well, at least for those who have Jesus. And you made the lights to rattle!" Sorryl finished in awe.

Spencer smiled. Sometimes his shy little Sorryl could be almost too bold. He turned warmly to the pastor, "It was a good sermon, a beautiful reminder of what those who know Christ have to look forward to."

As soon as they had greeted the pastor, the boys eagerly leapt out the door into the sunshine.

The Trestles soon joined the throng walking home. They smiled at everyone who chanced to glance their way, but no one seemed inclined to talk with them.

When they veered off from the rest of the group toward their home outside the town, Spencer allowed his thoughts to wander. He wished he knew how to take better care of the boys. He just didn't know what to do. Maybe they shouldn't have moved, at least they'd know the people around them then. *Well,* he thought to himself, *I guess we didn't really know anyone back in New York other than Joe either, but at least someone smiled once in a while. Here it feels like we've entered a gloomy wilderness.*

Chapter 12

The following Monday, Spencer stared into the mirror. Today he started his new job. He began shaving, his thoughts churning. He had finished repairing the shed and the house and the boys had helped him unpack the last of their things, or at least the important ones, last week. It felt good. They could start putting pictures and drapes up today after he was through with work. He tried not to imagine what trouble the boys, not to mention the dog, would stumble upon as they tried to put the things up. He would try to do it the way Annaleah had been picturing it before she died. He winced as he nicked himself with the razor, then reached for a rag and returned to his thoughts. Annaleah's plans for the house had seemed so beautiful. He hoped he could remember how she had envisioned it. Even then he doubted he could get it to look right, it needed a woman's touch. He shrugged, "Oh well," he mumbled to himself. But that was far from what he was feeling. He couldn't pass it off with a casual 'oh well'.

His thoughts ventured to the job he would be starting that day. *I hope I can give Charlie the help he needs. I'm sure the boys will find some way to be helpful too.* He smiled sadly. Yes, they were always eager to help. To be 'like Daddy' – big, strong, capable… He smiled again. It felt good to have sons that thought those things of him, even if their view was somewhat exaggerated. He sighed. *If only Annaleah were here.* It pained him that the boys were having to grow up without a mother. His heart clenched tight. *Dear, dear Annaleah. Why did she have to die? Why?* He wished with all his being that he could understand. *Why, God? Why her? She was so good and sweet and... Oh!* he moaned silently.

A quiet voice whispered across his being like a fresh breeze, *There is evil in this world. It won't be perfect as long as Satan has rule over it. He will bring as much pain and sorrow and evil upon it as he can, while he still has the chance. But hope, dear son, wait for the time when your Savior, Jesus, shall reign. Then will be peace and light and love.*

Spencer squeezed his hands into fists. He silently cried, *Oh! But it's so hard! Why her? I still don't get it. I know, I shouldn't be asking why. I know You do what is best for us all. I just read this morning, 'All things work together for good to those that love the Lord, to those who are called according to his purpose'. And then, 'For I know the plans I have for you, declares the Lord, plans to prosper you and not to harm you, plans to give you a hope and a future.' I must admit I got mad at You at first when I read that. It sure doesn't feel like we aren't being harmed. But I know You aren't letting any of this happen just to hurt me. I can feel Your love and compassion if I pause and let You through to me. But I still wonder, why this!*

The gentle whisper spoke again, *My dear son, I do not mind if you ask why, I love when my children speak with me and tell me what they are feeling. Don't despair! I can see the whole picture. I am here with you, 'A very present help in trouble'. I'm working here. Won't you wait on me, trust me, be of good courage?*

Spencer leaned on the sink in anguished silence for a moment, struggling to release his burden. Finally he sighed. *Alright, God,* he choked inwardly, *I'll try to trust You. You've proven Yourself before. I'll try. But... please help me! Help me! Help me!* a hot tear slid down his cheek. He pressed his forehead into the wall.

A moment later, a sleepy Sorryl stumbled into the bathroom. Spencer hastily swiped the tear away.

"I'm sleeping walking," Sorryl informed him drowsily.

Spencer tried to smile.

"Oh! You cut yourself, Daddy!" Sorryl said, coming more awake as he rubbed the sleep from his blue eyes.

Spencer only nodded and finished shaving. "Ready for breakfast?" he asked, making an effort to pull himself together for his sons' sakes.

"No. My tummy's still sleeping," Sorryl answered with a yawn as Trey came up behind him.

"Mine wakes up first thing, even before my brain," Trey spoke up, rubbing his tummy, "I'm starved."

Spencer smiled, "Okay, I'll start making breakfast. We've got to hurry this morning. We have to leave for the store in forty-five minutes. Run and get dressed," he said, playfully smacking their bottoms as they turned and dashed for their bedroom.

"You're gonna be done first today," Sorryl laughed as he pulled his pants on. "I've gotta fix my shirt, it's wrong side out."

Trey giggled. "Well I can't find my socks, so maybe not," he answered. He walked around the bed, looking for some socks. Then he crawled under it, then over it. Still, he couldn't find them. He finally gave up. "Can I borrow yours?"

"Sure, if they fit," Sorryl said with a giggle, trying to tug his shirt on. One arm was still inside out and he got stuck. He began to giggle again. "Oh, bother! I'm all stuck in!"

Trey pulled one of Sorryl's socks onto his own foot. It nearly fit, but not quite. He wiggled his toes and shrugged.

"Here, I'll help you," he said. He went over to Sorryl and tugged at the sleeve. They were used to these problems. At least, they were used to them since their mother had died, but this morning seemed to be trying to throw all the problems at them at once.

"It won't go!" Trey grunted. He gave an extra hard tug on the sleeve and stumbled backwards, tripping on a shoe. The boys started giggling and Trey tried once more to free Sorryl. He finally gave up, "Daddy! Sorryl's stuck and he won't come out!"

Spencer flipped his last batch of toast onto a plate with a small smile. "What could those boys have done this time?" He buttered the toast, then went to the boys' room. When he got there, he took a moment to survey the scene before him. Trey was seated on the floor, or, rather, on a shoe. Trooper was prancing around Sorryl, who had his shirt stuck over his head and was struggling to free himself. Spencer couldn't help smiling. "Boys! You silly gooses. Here, I'll help you out of there, Sorryl," he chuckled. "How do you manage to get yourselves into such fixes?"

When Sorryl's shirt was on properly, Spencer hurried back to the kitchen to finish breakfast. He called over his shoulder, "Only half an hour left boys!"

"There! Now we're all ready, except you have a cowlick, Sorryl. Here," Trey said, leading him to the bathroom sink. "Let's get it wet. Stick your head in the sink."

Sorryl obeyed. Water splashed out of the sink, spraying them. Trey took no notice. Sorryl took his head from under the faucet and water dripped down his face.

"Now we'll brush it down," Trey said.

"What are you boys doing?" Spencer called from the kitchen with a worried glance at the clock.

"We're fixing Sorryl's head... I mean his hair!" Trey shouted back.

"I think I should be worried. It sounds like they gave the bathroom a shower," Spencer mumbled to himself as he flipped an egg from the pan.

"Ouch! Don't brush my head off! Here. I can do it," he heard Sorryl shout in pain and mild anger.

Shortly, the boys entered the kitchen, looking as if they had run through the sprinkler with their clothes on. Spencer shook his head despondently. They didn't have time to change. "We have to hurry up and eat. We've got to leave in twenty minutes," he said, hurriedly putting everything on the table. They prayed and then ate as quickly as they could.

"Now to clean up," Trey said, taking his plate to the sink.

Spencer was relieved to see that their clothes were drying pretty quickly.

"Okay, get your shoes on, it's time to go!" Spencer stooped down to pull on his own shoes, then glanced up to see how the boys were getting on. *Good,* he thought, *Sorryl's almost got his shoes*

145

on. His relief lasted only a moment. "Oh!" Spencer moaned, dropping his head into his hands for a moment. He didn't need this, especially not this morning. Why did these things always happen when they were in a hurry? "Sorryl!"

Sorryl hurriedly glanced up at him. A silent question flitted across his face, *What did I do?*

"Your pants!"

Sorryl glanced down and saw that there was a large blob of ketchup on his pants leg. He stared at his pants a moment in surprise, then he glanced back at his father with big eyes. "How'd I do that?" he wondered.

A bit of anger crept into Spencer's voice as he grabbed Sorryl's arm a little too roughly, "Hurry. Run and change. Here, I'll help you." They dashed off for the bedroom, leaving Trey and Trooper in the entry.

In a moment, they came puffing back and Spencer whisked the boys out the door. Once they were outside in the beautiful morning air Spencer closed his eyes for a moment and took a deep breath. Peace flooded his weary soul and he opened his eyes again.

As they started down the road, Trooper began to bark indignantly. He quickly caught up with them, seeming determined not to be left behind again.

"Okay, we'll see how you do in town," Spencer conceded.

Trey nodded excitedly and grasped his Daddy's hand.

Spencer glanced worriedly at Sorryl, who usually held his other hand. But now he was on the other side of Trey, looking sadly off into the fields. He hadn't even perked up when Trooper joined them. Spencer sighed. He shouldn't have gotten angry at the boy, it wasn't his fault he had spilled ketchup or that a million other things had gone wrong that morning. He slipped his hand from Trey's and stepped over to Sorryl.

Sorryl glanced up at him, then set his jaw and looked the other way.

Spencer started silently calling himself names for not keeping control of his temper, but he stopped himself. That wasn't going to help. He could see Sorryl had set his jaw to keep from crying.

The boy was hurt. Gathering his courage, Spencer placed a gentle hand on Sorryl's shoulder. He was so tiny and young!

"Sorryl?" Spencer peered down at him.

Sorryl glanced up, then swallowed hard and looked the other way again.

Trey glanced at them, then he dashed off to pick a flower he had seen at the edge of the road.

Spencer swallowed too. "Sorryl?" he tried again. He slowed his pace, slowing Sorryl with him. "I'm sorry I got angry with you back at the house. You didn't really do anything wrong. And I shouldn't have gotten mad even if you did." He sighed, "I guess the morning was just rough, and I was worried about being late." He paused a moment, searching Sorryl's now upturned face, "Forgive me?"

Sorryl gazed at his daddy for a moment. When he spoke, his voice was quiet, but sincere, "Yeah." He held his arms up to Spencer.

Joy pulsed through Spencer's heart. He reached down and swung his son into his arms. He carried him a little way as he held him close.

"Hey, Sorryl! Look at this stone!" Trey exclaimed, suddenly skipping to their side.

With another fond squeeze, Spencer set Sorryl down and the boys kept pace with him as they examined the stone for a minute.

Once again, Spencer took a deep breath, smelling the wonderful breeze as it brushed his skin.

Glancing up at him with a smile, Sorryl copied him. "It makes you feel better when you do that," he said. "Do you feel better now, Daddy?"

Spencer smiled as tears sprung to his eyes at his son's caring words. He had to work to keep his voice from sounding strangled, "Yeah. Yeah, I do, Sorryl."

Sorryl smiled at him and squeezed his arm, "I'm glad, Daddy. I feel better too."

Spencer ruffled Sorryl's hair, "I'm glad you feel better too. I was asking God to help you 'cause I could tell you were feeling bad."

Sorryl smiled at him, "Thanks, Daddy. I was too mad to talk to God earlier…"

"But you're not now?"

"No."

"Good." Spencer squeezed Sorryl's hand. "Now I'm thanking Him for helping us."

"Me too."

The three walked in silence a moment longer. Finally Spencer said, "Well, today is our first day of work." He had told Sorryl the truth, he did feel better, but the despondent feeling that had gripped him that morning while he was shaving was still trying to cling to him.

Suddenly, he paused and guided the boys to the side of the road. He smiled a bit sheepishly at them. "We forgot something very important this morning since we were in such a rush."

The boys looked at him inquisitively.

"We didn't talk to God or read what He has written for us in the Bible together."

"Oh, yeah. That's probably why I got all mad, huh?" Sorryl asked. "Let's talk to God now. We can ask Him to help us the rest of the day, and thank Him out loud together for helping us when you asked Him to, Daddy."

Spencer smiled at the boy's eagerness. "Yes, let's," he answered as they joined hands to pray.

They arrived at the store just in time to meet Charlie as he opened the shop, "Hey, boys! How are my little gems?"

"Fine! We get to help you today!" Trey declared proudly.

"And we won't get into anything," Sorryl added brightly, back to his cheerful self again.

Charlie laughed and bobbed his head, "Good, good." Suddenly, he noticed Trooper, "Hey! Where'd that beast come from?"

Sorryl's eyes brightened, "Oh, he's our dog. He was sad and hungry and went to sleep on our door-rug, so we fed him and now he's ours."

Charlie laughed. It seemed just like the Trestles to take in a hungry animal. Anyone else in the town would have shot him or thrown him into the woods to die. He addressed Spencer, "Well, come right in and I'll show you what to do." He dug in his pocket, "Here, I'll give you the extra key, though I don't know why I ever lock the place," he chuckled to himself.

The boys excitedly followed the men around as Charlie showed Spencer all he could think of that his new helper would need to know. "I keep the grain in the back, it's all labeled and the customers know what they want. They'll tell you and all you have to do is go back, find what they asked for, and bring it up. And of course," he added, "For the ladies, I always carry it outside to their transportation."

"And we can help carry it sometimes," Trey spoke up excitedly, indicating Sorryl and himself.

"Well, maybe you boys can help keep the shelves dusted, and carry smaller things and hand out baskets for the shoppers. You can walk around and make sure everything stays in its place and the customers find everything they need, how 'bout that?" Charlie asked.

"Oh boy! A job just for us!" Trey enthused importantly, jumping up and down. He turned to take Sorryl's hands and danced him in a circle.

"Now, you have got to be real professional like and gentlemanly, especially to the ladies," Charlie reminded, wagging a finger at them.

At those words, the boys immediately ceased dancing in circles and straightened their shirts, which were a little wrinkly from their morning dousing.

A few moments later, a lady entered the store. Trey went up to her, Sorryl following close behind. Trey asked, "How are you today, ma'am? Can we get you a basket?"

She paused a moment, unaccustomed to such a greeting. Finally, she shook her head, "No, thank you."

A bit later, another lady entered and Trey and Sorryl approached her. They recognized her as the lady whose seat they had 'stolen' in church, but couldn't remember her name at the moment. After a confused pause, Trey ventured, "How are you today, ma'am. Could we get you a basket?"

Ruth Hock paused, then responded stiffly, "I could use a basket, I left mine at home."

Sorryl ran off to fetch her one. He soon returned and handed it to her with a shy smile.

This continued with any customer that entered, and Sorryl even managed to approach a few people and ask them if they needed help.

Later that afternoon Mr. Brendt arrived, gruff and curt as usual. He was the first customer they had already met besides Ruth Hock.

Trey and Sorryl approached him a bit timidly, unsure of how this strange man would respond to them.

"Good afternoon, Mr. Brendt. Do you want a basket?" Trey asked, indicating the one Sorryl was holding.

It seemed for a moment that Mr. Brendt thought to just walk away, but he changed his mind and said gruffly, "No, thank you," and walked up to the counter. He glanced around the store with a puzzled expression, looking for Charlie.

Spencer smiled, "Hello, Mr. Brendt. If you're looking for Charlie, he's out at lunch."

Mr. Brendt nodded, "I see. Well, I need some poultry feed. For layers."

"Sure, I'll be back in a minute."

The boys followed Spencer into the back room. It was the first time they had found a need to go back there. Spencer walked up and down the rows of feed, mumbling, "Where could it be? Where on earth is it?" All the while, the boys shadowed him, pretending to read the packages in the dim light. Spencer had almost given up when Sorryl said, "Daddy, this one has a chicken on it. That's what he wants, isn't it?"

Spencer retraced his steps and looked more closely at the bag his son was examining, "I'll be! So it is!" he chuckled, relieved that he didn't have to go and find Charlie to ask him where it was after all. He ruffled Sorryl's hair and swung the bag onto his shoulder.

"We'll help, Daddy," Trey offered, jumping up as he tried to reach the bag.

Spencer swung it off his shoulder so it would be lower and the boys could 'help'.

"Here you are, Mr. Brendt," Spencer said, appearing with his boys from the dark back room.

"Took you a long time," Mr. Brendt grumbled.

"Yeah," Spencer assented with a sheepish laugh. "That's the first time I've been back there, I couldn't find it for beans. But Sorryl finally saved me," he added, tousling his son's hair. "And they were both good helpers carrying it out with me," he chuckled. "Is this all?"

Mr. Brendt nodded.

Out on the street, the citizens were buzzing about the change in the shop. "I walk in, and here's these two boys. They come up to me and ask, 'How are you? Would you like a basket?' My, how surprised I was. I gather Charlie hired their father and they had to come along since they have no mother."

"And did you see the shelves? Cleanest I've seen 'em in forever!"

"The little boys' shirts were wrinkly," one ventured to grump. "They need a mother."

"Well, their manners are good enough," another countered.

"All the ribbon was rolled up nice and neat. It only took me thirty seconds to find the right one, instead of thirty minutes," a lady added, changing the conversation back to the original mood.

A man's voice spoke up wryly, "That's the first time I've gone in there near lunch time and didn't have to ring the bell."

And so the talk ran through the streets. The plain houses along the street stared at the commotion in the road in seeming astonishment. This was the most enlivened the people in that town had been for a long, long time.

As the day came to a close, Charlie showed Spencer how to close up the shop. "I'll see you folks tomorrow then. And maybe we'll be able to play checkers," he added to the boys in an undertone.

Trey grinned, "That'd be fun!"

Sorryl nodded, then said, "I like helping here. It's really fun! And it makes you feel 'dustrious too."

Spencer and Charlie smiled.

"Did we do good?" Trey anxiously asked Charlie.

"You did excellent. We had more customers today than I remember ever seeing before." He chuckled. "'Course, I think that was on account of curiosity," he added with a wink.

"But you're starting school in two weeks and won't be able to be here all day anymore. You can probably still help on Saturdays, though. That should be fun, too," Spencer added, hoping they wouldn't be too disappointed.

"Yeah! And we'll meet the other kids and everything!" Trey exclaimed happily.

Spencer hoped it would be as good as the boys imagined, but he somehow doubted it. Everyone here was so strange!

Chapter 13

The following days went more smoothly as the boys grew accustomed to leaving for the store every morning. Spencer also made it a priority to get with his boys and talk to God with them each morning and read the Bible to them. He answered their questions as best he could, but he often had to tell them he didn't know the answer. Then they would search it out and talk about it together.

Two weeks later, Monday dawned a clear, crisp day. Trey and Sorryl's first day of school in Los Ciegos.

"I wonder what it will be like," Trey said, excitement etching his tones as he buttoned his blue-checked shirt.

"I hope the teacher is like Miss Susan," Sorryl said, working on his own buttons. She had been Sorryl's teacher in the city and he had become quite fond of her. "We can be together in this school," Sorryl added excitedly.

"Yeah! And not just for recess!"

Spencer's voice carried to their room, "Breakfast's ready!"

Sorryl's fingers fumbled with his last button, "Oh! Hurry! Can you help me with my button? This one's not working."

Trey complied, then they dashed to the table. They sat side-by-side. They had decided to match that day, so they each wore a blue-checked shirt and a pair of jeans rolled up at the cuffs.

As they ate their breakfast, Spencer asked, "Are you excited about school?" He really didn't need to ask. Their faces told it all.

The boys nodded, their mouths too full to answer.

Spencer stifled a sigh. He was worried about the boys. The children were different here; it wasn't going to be easy for his boys.

"What's wrong, Daddy?" Sorryl asked with concern, noticing his father's pensive silence.

Spencer just shook his head and resumed eating. He didn't want to dampen their excitement or make them dread school before they even started.

"I'm gonna miss you," Sorryl spoke up again, sadly this time.

Spencer tried to fend off the lump he felt rising in his throat.

"Would you say hello to Mr. Brendt for me, please?" Sorryl asked. "He needs someone to say hello to him."

"And to the lady with the black hair. You know, who always has a scarf," Trey added.

"Okay, I'll do that," Spencer said with an affectionate smile.

Trey suddenly exclaimed, "Hey! Why don't we write notes for them!"

"Yeah!" Sorryl clapped his hands.

"But not today, you don't have time," Spencer reminded, pointing the direction of the clock.

This silenced the boys at once and they returned to their food.

"I'll come with you today," Spencer told them as they hurried to put on their shoes. "I should make it to the store just in time if I hurry back."

All three skipped out the door and down the road, though Spencer didn't feel at all like skipping. But he didn't want to pass his mood on to the boys, so he let them pull him along.

The schoolhouse was just the other side of the little town. When they walked up to the schoolyard, many children were already there. Trey and Sorryl watched them, slightly puzzled. The children weren't playing in the yard like at their old school, they were slowly filing into the schoolhouse.

Spencer brought Trey and Sorryl inside. The school walls were a dull brown and bare, except for a map hanging on the north wall next to the blackboard. He approached the teacher, who was standing at the front of the room. The man was a medium height with a slight build. His graying hair was balding on the very top and his hawk nose and narrow eyes gave him a stern look.

Sorryl gulped and squeezed his father's hand tighter. This man wasn't at all like Miss Susan.

Spencer cleared his throat and said to the teacher, "These are my boys, Trey and Sorryl." He tried to swallow the relentless lump in his throat. Now that he saw the teacher and schoolchildren, his fears leapt even higher. And a niggling worry that, like Annaleah, they would never come home again lurked in the back of his mind.

"Hello, Trey and Sorrel. I am going to be your teacher. You may call me Mr. Grey."

Trey nervously squeezed his father's other hand.

"We will begin in a moment," Mr. Grey said pointedly, clearing his throat.

"Alright, boys, I've gotta get to the shop. May God be with you," Spencer hugged the boys and gave them each an encouraging pat before he started off for the store.

When he was halfway to the shop, he finally remembered to cast his cares on Christ and began to pray. Gradually, he felt peace seep into his soul, but it was still difficult not to be at least a little anxious.

When he walked into the store, Charlie looked up from behind the counter. "Hey, what's the matter, long-face?" he teased, trying to lighten Spencer's mood.

Spencer waved a dismissive hand in Charlie's direction. "Guess I'm feeling like a mother," he answered, trying to grin. He almost completely failed. "I wish I could teach them myself."

"Awww. They'll be all right. I've got something new here," Charlie added, brightening.

When Spencer didn't answer, he continued, "Somebody wanted me to get these chains. You know I've got the big ones, but every time someone wants smaller ones, they have to wait until I can order them, so I decided to keep them in the store. They all fell off the roll and now it's tangled, so we have to roll it back up. Hopefully before Mr. Brendt gets here." He was trying to distract Spencer, but it wasn't working very well.

Charlie shook his head at him, "Aw, c'mon, Spence. You'll see 'em this afternoon. They'll even be out of school in time to help at the store some." He paused and Spencer nodded, trying to cheer up. They were working on the length of chain now. Charlie spoke up over the clinking, "I know the kids here are different, but they'll be okay. The teacher's kind of stiff, but they'll probably get by just fine. I think." He was sadly blundering in his attempts to make Spencer feel better.

"I know. They were so scared. And it makes me miss..." he gulped, "Annaleah." The chains now lay forgotten in his hands.

Charlie assumed Annaleah was Spencer's deceased wife. He nodded his head in understanding and stole a glance at Spencer. He was fingering the smooth metal of the chains in his hands.

Finally, Spencer spoke, "You know, sometimes I get mad at God. But I don't want to be. I feel so much more— I don't know. I guess... peaceful, when I'm close to Him. You know, you can't really physically get any closer to Him, but you just feel like He's right there beside you."

"No, I guess I don't know. He seems to me like He's up there checkin' up on me and ready with a big stick to, 'whamo!', crack me a good one if I mess up. I guess that's pretty much how all of us in this town feel," Charlie said. His frustration at the rules they had to follow, and at having to watch his back all the time, crept into his voice.

Spencer didn't know what to say. He'd never thought of anyone seeing God like that before. "I. Well..." he was at a loss for words. "I suppose you must feel that way because you don't really know God. I mean, you know about Him, but you don't know Him," he peered at Charlie to be sure he wasn't offended, but the man was listening intently, hungry to hear more. "Sure, God can't abide evil or sin, because He is holy. But He loves us and is full of mercy and compassion, too. That's the reason He sent Jesus, His own beloved son, to die and then rise from the dead. He wanted there to be a way for us to have contact with Him, but there had to be a payment for our sin before we could have that, so Jesus died *for* us, and His death paid for our sin. Now God is holding out that gift, Jesus' payment for our sins and a relationship with Him, for all who will accept it. And you just have to reach out and take it. Then God makes us new creatures and shows us day by day how to be more like Jesus. It's that simple. Jesus even told us that we had to become like a little child in order to enter the kingdom of Heaven. I think that's because, one, we have to be humble and confess that we have sinned and choose to rely on God to change us, and, also, it's too simple and we have to stop thinking it's supposed to be hard. We need to just trust God."

Charlie listened intently. He finally spoke, "You mean getting into Heaven isn't all about being good and not doing wrong and…" he drifted off.

Spencer smiled, "Do you remember the story of the Good Samaritan? The kind man who stopped to help a traveler that was beaten up and left to die? This man was completely helpless, wounded, unconscious. He couldn't help himself except to cry out in anguish, 'Please help me!' That's how *we* are. Satan has lied to us, stolen from us, left us open to more attacks. Jesus comes and pours oil on our wounds. He paid the price of His blood to get us restored, just as the Samaritan paid his own money for the wounded man. It's all what Jesus has done that enables us to go to Heaven and have a relationship with God. Those who have accepted God's gift should do what is right, but that doesn't get them any closer to Heaven, to a relationship with God. They live righteously because they love Him and are grateful for what He has done – He picks us up on the road of life like the Samaritan did for the injured man, keeping us from certain death. And we also do what is right because He has instructed us to follow Jesus' example."

"Goodness!" Charlie mused. "You mean, I just have to take that gift, and God is holding it out to everyone, to me, right now?" wonder filled his countenance.

Spencer nodded.

"Well, I want that gift. But how do I take it? I mean, it's not something I can just grab with my hands."

Spencer chuckled, "No. You need to believe that Jesus was truly God's Son and lived as a man here on earth, died for you, that His death paid for your sins, and that He rose again and lives today, redeeming from sin everyone who asks. Realize that you need *Him* in order to be able to go to Heaven and that you can't do it on your own, because, like the Bible says, 'The wages of sin is death', not life in Heaven. And 'All have sinned and fall short of the glory of God', even the most righteous person has sinned sometime in their life and our own righteousness is like filthy rags next to the holiness of God."

"I believe that. And I guess, from what you said, now I believe that *is* the way to get to Heaven, to be able to talk to God and be... His special own. And it makes me feel even worse for all the bad I've done to know Jesus had to die because of it," Charlie said. He looked down sorrowfully and rubbed the chain he still held.

Spencer was growing excited as he saw this friend so near to finding the joy he himself had. "Wonderful! Then you can tell that to God and ask Him to save you from the certain destruction you are headed to now, and you're His adopted child! A sheep in His fold that He loves and takes care of."

"Right here? Not in church?" Charlie inquired incredulously.

"Of course not, God doesn't care where you are. He can hear you no matter where you happen to be," Spencer assured Charlie.

Charlie took a deep breath. "Well, God, I guess you can hear me right here, huh?" Methodically, he rubbed his hands across the chain. "Well, I want to thank You for the gift of Jesus that You are offerin' me. And I want to let You know I'll take it. Here I am God, a broken, beat up, dreadful man. I realize that I am, even though I've tried to be good all my life, and really I'm sorry. But, oh! I'm so glad that's not the way to You, trying to be good, 'cause I wouldn't make it if it were. So I ask You that You would reach down to this poor old man and save me from the destruction I've been headed for. Thank you so much Jesus, God. I guess I don't really know how to pray, but from what Spencer says, You aren't that particular. I just talk to You, that's all it is." He paused a moment, then let out a joyous whoop. "I guess I know what you mean now, Spencer! About feeling God close to you! Whooeeeee! Oh! Thank you God! Thank you Jesus! Thank you!" he was elated, he was filled with God's love, peace, and joy. He'd never realized how stressful it was to have all the weight of making his way to Heaven on his shoulders. Now it was God's responsibility to get him there. He just had to trust God and follow Him.

Spencer laughed and jumped up from the floor with Charlie.

Charlie wiped a tear of joy from his wrinkled cheek, "I've been waiting all my life to have this! And I didn't even know what it was I needed and didn't have! Now I see how you and your boys can be cheerful, even though you've lost your Annaleah."

Spencer laughed, "Sometimes I get to feeling all overwhelmed and like I can't live another day, but God always comes through. He's always there when I need Him, but sometimes I forget to invite Him to help me."

Charlie looked down at the abandoned chains, "You know, I feel like those used to be all wrapped around me… and now they're suddenly gone!" Then he added as someone entered the store, "I guess we better get back to winding it up, you get the customer, I'll keep working on these."

"How are you this morning?" Spencer asked the lady who had just entered the shop.

"Fine, thank you. Where are those boys?" she asked curtly, as if it was a crime for them not to be there.

Spencer smiled wistfully, "In school, I'm afraid."

All day long, customers constantly wondered, "Where are the boys?"

When Mr. Brendt arrived, he paused at the door a moment, surveying the room. Finally, he stepped into the shop, but he didn't speak a word.

When he approached the counter to get his things rung up, Spencer told him, "The boys had to go to school today, but they wanted me to be sure to tell you hello for them."

The shadow of a smile played about the old man's stiff lips, but he only nodded. After some thought he added, "Tell the chaps hello back."

"I sure will. They were mighty sad not to be here today. They're sure to bounce in after school, though." Then he added as if to himself, "Of course they will. Nobody's at home for them."

But Mr. Brendt's sharp ears heard anyway, though he gave no indication that he had caught Spencer's quiet words uttered with a touch of pain. He lifted his hand in goodbye as he left the shop. It was more than he had done to reach out to someone else in a long time.

Chapter 14

When their father left, the boys shyly made their way to the seats the schoolteacher indicated were theirs. It was a completely different setup from what they had been used to back home in New York. There the students had all had their own desks and each grade was separated into different classrooms. But here, two students shared a desk, and the whole school, which was the size of one of their classrooms back home, shared the same room and the same teacher. The boys were glad to find that, even though they were in different grades, they were to share a seat for now.

Mr. Grey stepped behind his desk and tapped his stick to gain the children's attention, though it was really unneeded since everyone was already watching him, even if it was with a dull, uninterested gaze. He cleared his throat importantly. "Today we have two new pupils," he announced. "Would Trey and Sorrel please stand."

The boys obediently rose to their feet, not daring to look about them.

Mr. Grey scrawled their names on the blackboard as he mumbled, "Trey… and Sorrel…"

Sorryl looked up. Even the way the teacher said his name sounded wrong. He stared at the dusty chalk lettering and timidly raised his hand.

Mr. Grey turned to him, a bit irritated, "Yes?"

The boy replied respectfully, "Excuse me, Mr. Grey. My name is spelled S-o-r-r-*y*-l."

The students snickered and Mr. Grey stared at him a moment. Finally, he turned to change his 'e' to a 'y'. White chalk dust drifted down to settle on the floor. When he was finished, he turned back to the class and continued, "The taller one is Trey, the other is Sorrel."

"Hello, Trey and Sorrel," the students chimed in unison.

Thoroughly embarrassed, Sorryl sat down as soon as the greeting had been uttered.

The teacher gave him a harsh look and said pointedly, "You may now be seated."

Relieved, Trey dropped to his seat. He glanced compassionately at his brother. Sorryl's sensitive face had turned quite red.

"Now, today we will begin with..." The teacher began in monotones.

Trey and Sorryl tried to pay attention, but it was a trial when the lesson was not interesting and the teacher's voice seemed to be lulling them to sleep.

Sorryl was staring intently at the teacher, trying to listen and understand. The room blurred before his eyes and he blinked to bring it back into focus. Suddenly, he felt a sharp prick in his back. He leapt to his feet with a pained yelp.

"Sorrel. You will please remain seated," the teacher ordered harshly. "Another such display and I shall call you up here to wear the dunce cap." He shook his head. He wasn't used to such displays. The children of Los Ciegos rarely yelped or moved suddenly, they were plagued with the same apathy and disinterest as the adults.

Sorryl gingerly seated himself again. Trey gave him a quizzical look, but Sorryl just rubbed his sore back and glanced at the black-haired boy seated behind him. He didn't dare speak. He sat with his muscles tensed, waiting for another prick. Sure enough, there it was again, digging further and further into his back.

The boy behind him had been delighted at the unexpected response Sorryl had given. He had expected a scowl at the most, for that is what any of the other students would have done. Then they would have beaten him up at recess when no adults were around to witness the fight.

Sorryl held his breath. Striving with all his might not to jump up, he braced himself against the pain. He inched forward in his seat, but caught Mr. Grey looking at him in a displeased fashion, so he sat back again. The pain intensified. Finally, he could stand it no longer. He leapt out of his seat and an agonized squeak forced its way between his tightly sealed lips.

Trey leapt up too. Now he realized what had happened. Menacingly, he faced Sorryl's tormenter with a defiant look.

The boy only smiled as if to say, "What are you looking at me for?" though inside he was quaking in terror as this newcomer's gaze bore into him. Maybe he had gone just a little too far. He'd rarely seen siblings stand up for each other and hadn't expected to have two to fight against. No matter, the rest of the students would be on his side.

Mr. Grey turned on Sorryl. He almost growled, "Sorrel, I warned you. I don't know what they allow you to get away with where you come from, but we certainly don't allow this."

Sorryl tried to tell the teacher the reason for his behavior, but his quiet, respectful voice was interrupted.

"No excuses, young man. Come up here immediately. I will say, this is the first time I have actually had to do this and you ought to be very ashamed of yourself."

By this time, Trey was red with anger. He contained himself with difficulty. He knew he shouldn't attack the boy who had hurt his brother, and especially not the teacher, though he dearly wished he could. But that would only make things worse. Instead, he clenched his teeth and repeated over and over to himself what his mother had taught him from the Bible and had further impressed on him by her example, "Love your enemies, love your enemies, love your enemies... A soft answer turns away wrath, a soft answer..."

He remembered just before the teacher turned back to his pupils that Mr. Grey would probably not be happy to find him standing. He dropped to his seat, just in time.

Mr. Grey cleared his throat. "Okay, now we may continue with our studies," he said derisively, with a stern look at the Trestle boys.

163

All had been quiet for some time when Trey suddenly felt a prick in his back. His heart squeezed tight. He knew more trouble was brewing. The pain from the pricking grew increasingly intense. He clamped his lips together, trying not to leap out of his seat.

The black-haired boy had decided it had been such great fun when Sorryl had leapt out of his seat and yelped that he wanted to see if he would get the same response from the little boy's brother. He had come to the conclusion that it was no use to try not to involve the older brother since he obviously already had him upset, though he couldn't understand why Trey would want to stand up for his little brother.

Finally, Trey could stand the pain no longer. He, too, leapt out of his seat. His eyes filled with frustrated tears and he hurriedly blinked them back.

The teacher glared at him, "You, too, have learned to leap out of your seat?"

The black-haired boy sat serenely on his bench as if he knew nothing about the boys' strange behavior.

Trey began to explain, but he, too, was quickly cut off.

"You may come up here and share your brother's spot. As I do not have another dunce cap, you shall have to take turns. Now, stay there. And no more leaps," Mr. Grey demanded severely as he switched the cap from Sorryl's head to Trey's.

The brothers stood desolately facing the class. The students kept glancing at the Trestle brothers with haughty airs.

Trey and Sorryl's feet grew weary. Their hearts longed for their father to take them in his loving, strong arms, give them a hug, and tell them it was alright.

Sorryl reached back and felt his back. It still stung. Mr. Grey shot him a displeased look and he hastily dropped his hand to his side.

Finally, it was time for recess and Mr. Grey allowed Trey and Sorryl to vacate their positions at the front of the room. "Perhaps you boys have learned to behave," he told them sternly, dearly hoping they had.

Trey and Sorryl only nodded and ran outside to join the other students. Mr. Grey didn't bother to stop them and reprove them for running. He was too worn out already. He wasn't accustomed to such behavior.

The brothers' black-haired tormentor, Gary, watched them nervously as they emerged from the schoolhouse, prepared for their imminent attack.

Trey and Sorryl came to a sudden, confused halt when they noticed all the students walking slowly about. A few were talking with each other, but the rest were walking purposelessly around the yard, hands behind their backs.

"They must not be able to think of something to play," Trey said, looking at Sorryl with a puzzled crease in his forehead. He quickly forgot about his sore back.

"Yeah. I guess we better give them a suggestion," Sorryl said thoughtfully. "Let's see... we can play leap frog."

"Oh! Good idea! Hey! Everybody!" Trey shouted, working up some courage.

The students turned and stared at him, eyes wide.

"Hey! We can play leap frog!" he continued, not to be shaken.

The students continued to stare at them for a moment, then one of the older boys stepped forward. "Number one, we don't shout," he began firmly. "And number two, none of us know what leap frog is."

"You don't know what leap frog is?" Trey repeated incredulously, forgetting in his surprise that 'they didn't shout'.

" No. What is it?" a curious girl of about eleven asked.

By this time, Gary had decided that, by some miracle unknown to him, the brothers had forgotten his little trick, so he cautiously meandered over to join the group.

"Oh! We'll show you!" Trey answered excitedly. "You all line up like this. Then you get down like this," he demonstrated. "And leap over everybody in front of you."

Sorryl leapt over Trey to show them how. "And then the rest of the people behind jump as soon as the person that jumped over them is out of the way, see? And you go all over. Here, let's line up," Trey suggested, putting the children in place. He wondered at their awkwardness, but soon forgot about it in his excitement. "Then squat down. Go ahead," he prompted when they hesitated. "Like this."

Finally, one by one, the students awkwardly squatted down and ducked their heads. They had never played a game like this before. They usually just walked around or read a history book. This idea was foreign to them. They didn't remember ever being told not to play. Of course, they had tried to run and been reprimanded, but this was not running. The pupils grew increasingly interested as Trey kept explaining, and then leaping over everybody.

Then Sorryl started leaping over them too. He turned back and waved the girl behind him on. She was staring at him and hadn't begun jumping yet. "It's your turn, you can start now," he said, excitement glowing in his friendly blue eyes.

She hesitated a moment, then awkwardly leapt over the girl in front of her. She laughed, "Oh! That was fun!"

Sorryl approached a larger boy and attempted to leap over him. He didn't make it and ended up straddling the boy's back. He began to giggle, "I guess I need help."

The boy Sorryl had landed on didn't know what to do, but the girl Sorryl had just leapt over stood up and lifted him over the boy's head. "There you are," she said.

Sorryl giggled again and beamed a thank you.

The students forgot, at least for a time, to be suspicious of these boys, or to give them the 'test' which any new students usually underwent, especially 'outsiders' like the Trestles.

Inside the schoolhouse, Mr. Grey kept hearing sounds he was quite unaccustomed to. He finally rose and went to the window. There he stood stock still for a moment, watching the children. "What on earth could they be doing?" he wondered, so amazed he forgot that they might get their clothes dirty. He scratched his head in wonderment, forgetting himself. "That looks like great fun!" he exclaimed to himself as he caught on to what the children were doing. The stern teacher watched, enthralled, from the window for a few moments longer. One of the boys leapt over another and landed on his face. Mr. Grey cringed and urged quietly, "Gotta jump further." The boy made it over the next child and Mr. Grey cheered quietly, "That's right!" Suddenly, he indignantly drew himself up to his full height. "What are they doing? They should not even have started such a... a.... an operation." He marched angrily to the door and furiously rang the bell.

The children had no sense that they were doing anything wrong, but obediently lined up in front of the teacher when they heard his bell. "Yes, sir?" they all wondered, a bit worried.

"Who, I would like to know, started that outlandish operation I just witnessed you children carrying out?"

The children were quick to look at Trey and Sorryl, who hurriedly glanced down, blushing. They somehow knew Mr. Grey was displeased, though they had no idea why.

"As I thought. It was you impertinent boys. Come immediately into the schoolhouse," he said to the brothers. "The rest of you are free to continue your exercise. I will not hold this against you. However, do not let me ever catch you at such... amazing activities again." With that, he whisked into the schoolhouse behind Trey and Sorryl.

The students stared a moment, wondering what had so displeased Mr. Grey, then resumed walking slowly about the yard.

Mr. Grey indignantly stood Trey and Sorryl in front of him, "I have never seen such as your likes for making trouble," he began sternly.

The boys looked at him questioningly.

"Oh, don't tell me you didn't know you shouldn't have started that game. Recess is for walking about and stretching your legs, not behaving like... rabid kangaroos. Now, hold out your hands. I shall give you each a licking with my ruler. Perhaps that will make you behave," he finished almost in exasperated tones. "Trey first."

The boys obediently held out their hands. They bit their lips to keep from crying out as Mr. Grey applied the ruler to their hands.

"Now. You may sit in your seats until recess is over," he instructed sternly.

The discouraged brothers obediently trudged to their seats, heads hanging and brains whirling, trying to figure out what they had done wrong.

"No. Wait. I will split you up," Mr. Grey decided.

Trey and Sorryl glanced fearfully at each other. Could it get any worse?

"Trey, you move back two rows and sit there with Bill. Sorrel, I will move you to sit with Gary, the seat behind you. They have had their own seats 'till now, but they may as well share and hopefully keep you in line."

When the students filed into the schoolhouse at the ringing of the bell, Mr. Grey explained the new arrangement to them.

Gary rolled his eyes and muttered low enough that the teacher would not hear him, but loud enough for Sorryl's ears, "I gotta baby-sit now."

Sorryl left Gary, his black-haired tormenter from earlier that day, as much room on the bench as possible. He was very grateful Gary didn't try anything more that day, for his small back was still quite sore. Unfortunately, in his efforts to leave Gary enough room, he fell off his bench. Exasperated, Mr. Grey only gave him a severe look and continued with his lesson.

Trey found his sullen seatmate left him alone, except for jogging his pencil occasionally.

As soon as school let out, the weary brothers came together like magnets and headed eagerly to the shop and the haven of their Daddy's presence.

Chapter 15

Spencer glanced up as the boys entered the shop. He had long ago given up hope that perhaps *this* time it might be the boys, for he had eagerly looked to the door nearly every time it had opened, hoping it was time for Trey and Sorryl to arrive. His heart gave a bound of joy when he realized who it was and he rushed happily from behind the counter to give his dear boys a hug and swing them about in his arms. They laughed and, for the moment, forgot the turmoil which the school day had wrought within their young hearts.

Charlie appeared from the back room then, wiping his hands on a rag. "Ah! My wonderful helpers are back!" he exclaimed.

"Mr. Brendt says hello back to you," their father reported, smiling at them.

Charlie nearly dropped his rag, but managed to cover his surprise well. *Imagine Mr. Brendt saying hello... and to them! He rarely even talks to the most 'righteous' people here,* he thought. After a moment he smiled and clapped Spencer on the back, "Your Daddy has been doing some good stuff today. Guess what?" he asked, kneeling down in order to speak more easily to the boys.

"What?" both boys asked.

"Your Daddy told me how to have Jesus living inside me. And I took the gift God was holding out to me and I feel the wonderfullest that I've ever felt!" he exclaimed, opening his arms wide in his excitement.

Just at that moment, a customer entered the shop. He quickly dropped his arms and went behind the counter with much more energy than he had ever dared display in that town before.

His customer glanced at him curiously, then, with a shake of his head, began searching for what he needed.

Trey and Sorryl rushed up to him, delighted to be back to their old job. "Do you need a basket, sir?" Trey asked.

"No, I don't need one. But thanks," he replied, even offering a little smile.

Trey and Sorryl went back to their father and took his hands, glad to be back with him. Whoever invented school anyway? They'd rather stay with Daddy and learn from him. They'd heard their parents talking about teaching them at home before their mother had gotten sick, but it had never happened.

Spencer laughed warmly, gently freeing his hands, "I've got to get back to work." Catching the disappointed look in their eyes, he added, "But you can come back and help me."

Trey and Sorryl eagerly followed him into the back room. But they didn't forget their own jobs. Whenever the bell rang announcing a new customer, they would dash back out to the front of the shop to greet them and see if they needed help. But they always hurried back to join their father.

When they arrived home that night, Spencer took them fondly on his knees. Kissing each of them on the top of the head he asked, "So how was the first day of school here for my boys?"

As he voiced this question, a somber cloud passed over the boys' faces and they looked down, toying with their daddy's buttons.

After a difficult pause, Trey answered penitently, "We were both naughty and had to have a pointed hat on while we stood up with the teacher. And we got our hands smacked, too."

"Ah. What did you do to bring that upon yourselves?" Spencer inquired gently, finding it hard to believe they would get themselves into so much trouble. Back in New York he and Annaleah had always been complimented on how well their boys behaved in school.

Sorryl began explaining quietly, "Well, the first time we were punished, Gary, the boy sitting behind me, poked me with a pin and I jumped out of my seat and yelped. The teacher didn't like that one bit. Then the boy did it again, harder and harder 'till I couldn't stand it and had to jump up again. So the teacher made me stand up front with him. But I don't think he knew I had been poked, and he wouldn't let me explain why I was jumping out of my seat," he added. Tears gathered in his eyes and he blinked them away.

Spencer swallowed hard, attempting not to grow indignant. It made it even harder when he saw Sorryl's efforts to make his teacher appear in a better light.

Then Trey spoke up, "And then the boy did it to me and made me jump out of my chair. So I had to stand up there with Sorryl. But at least Sorryl didn't have to stay there by himself."

Spencer sighed and hugged his boys, trying to comfort them. Why couldn't the world just be perfect? Finally, he said, "Well, I guess there was a mistake there. I hope the children don't give you any more problems. Why did you get your hands smacked?" he asked.

With a confused sigh, Trey answered, "Well, I'm not exactly sure what was wrong the next time. It was during recess when we taught the other students to play leapfrog. Mr. Grey came out of the schoolhouse all mad and asked who started the 'outlandish',... something. I don't remember the word he used." Trey sighed, "I think he meant our game of leapfrog, but I'm not sure. Everyone said Sorryl and I started it, so the teacher took us inside and told us not to act like rabbit kangaroos or something and gave us each a whacking with his ruler. Then he separated us and made us sit with other boys instead of together," Trey finished sadly.

"Oh dear," was all Spencer could say for a moment as he groaned inwardly. He gave a long sigh. He wished for Annaleah to come back. He wished he could fix all their problems. He wished he knew what to do. To make matters worse, he thought he had seen someone watching from the mountain as he and the boys were playing tag when they had gotten home from the store that evening. It could have been one of the townspeople, it probably was, but now Spencer was a bit paranoid.

He hugged his boys close, "I don't know what it was that displeased Mr. Grey, but we'll hope – and pray – that it goes better tomorrow, hey?"

The weary boys snuggled up close to him and nodded, glad to be back with their daddy.

The next morning, Spencer glanced up the mountain. Nothing seemed out of the ordinary. He shook his head at himself and headed off to town with the boys. He was still wondering what to do about the boys' situation at school. He wasn't used to dealing with problems like these, but he knew he was not going to put up with his boys being misused. If it had been a case of one of them getting beaten up by a student, well, he was used to that. But the teacher misunderstanding them and thinking they were doing wrong when they played a game? Well, that had him stumped.

The boys reluctantly parted with him at the shop door and trudged to the schoolyard. On the way, Sorryl found a grasshopper. He chased it and finally caught it. The brothers giggled as they gently passed their treasure back and forth while they walked the rest of the way to school. When they reached the yard, the grasshopper suddenly leapt free and the boys dove after it. They weren't worried about being late for school because they knew they were early. As students arrived at the school, they stopped to watch the Trestle boys. They stared in puzzled silence.

One girl finally worked up the courage to ask, "What are you doing?"

Trey threw his answer over his shoulder as he made another wild dive for the elusive grasshopper, "Catching a grasshopper! Oooof!" He landed with a thud, then leapt to his feet in victory, "Got him! You wanna see?" he offered, addressing his appalled classmates.

Their curiosity aroused, all the students quickly crowded around the Trestle boys and began gently examining the grasshopper. The schoolchildren couldn't help exclaiming over it:

"You can see the hairs on his legs!"

"And what big eyes he's got!"

"Amazing! I never knew they looked like that!"

They noticed how gently Trey and Sorryl handled the grasshopper and copied them.

Mr. Grey appeared at the schoolhouse doorway, wondering where the students had gotten to. They weren't late, but he was accustomed to them quietly filing in to find their seats with disinterested faces and sad eyes. But not a one had entered the schoolhouse yet.

When he saw them all gathered around Trey and Sorryl, he was curious at first, then angry. He could only imagine what the outlandish boys had started this time. All the townspeople had long ago given up trying to convert the Trestles to their way of thinking. There just seemed to be no way to get through to them. No, that wasn't quite right. You could get through to them, they just refused to be tempered by all the town's rules and seemed not to even understand them or that they actually existed. It surprised everyone very much that not a one of the Trestles had broken the law or done anything to get into serious trouble. Most of the townspeople fully expected that to happen, and soon. Mr. Grey stalked resolutely back into the schoolhouse to retrieve his bell, returned to the doorway, and began ringing it furiously. Trey and Sorryl came running into the schoolhouse ahead of all the others, their young faces flushed from dashing around. The rest of the children were close on their heels, alternately walking and jogging, for they dared not run.

Mr. Grey was exasperated once again. He hardly knew what to do any more. "What were you all doing out there?" he asked, a touch of irritation etching his tones. He had decided to ignore the fact that Trey and Sorryl had been running.

A girl answered calmly, her eyes shining, "Looking at a grasshopper, Mr. Grey."

Mr. Grey looked around at all the children. Their faces were flushed, and they looked eager and healthy, an appearance he was completely unaccustomed to. He could find nothing wrong with looking at a grasshopper, so, seeing that all his students were present, he bade them take their seats and began lessons for the day.

The stern teacher was surprised that the children seemed more attentive and interested in what he was telling them that day. He couldn't find a logical reason for it. Although he didn't realize it, he was beginning to speak with more fluctuation and emphasis in his voice, and the children had been enlivened by the short exercise they had gotten by jogging to the schoolhouse, their minds had been awakened as they were studying the grasshopper, and they had begun to take an interest in learning because of that small wonder of God's vast creation.

Sorryl was determined not to get into trouble today. When Gary reached over and began thumping his leg with a pencil, Sorryl resolutely clamped his lips together and ignored it. Then he felt a tug on his shirt from the boy in the seat behind him. Whenever the unsuspecting teacher turned his back, Sorryl received some sort of bop on the head or shoulder by someone's hand or pencil.

Trey was experiencing much the same thing. The pupils were giving the Trestle brothers 'the test' to find out what they were really like. The point was to try to annoy the unfortunate pupil and see how he would react. Trey and Sorryl strove to ignore the constant provocations, irritated at first. Suddenly, Sorryl was struck with how funny it was that all the pupils within his reach were trying to get their hands on him in some way or other. He smiled, barely managing not to let his giggle out.

Trey saw Sorryl's shoulders shaking in silent laughter. He wondered what Sorryl found so funny. He tried to guess and then he, too, realized how comical their situation was, and that it was no use to get mad at their classmates. A smile played at the corners of his mouth.

All afternoon, they were continually pestered. Just before the hour for recess approached, Trey, in an effort to pull his pencil out of his seatmate's taunting grasp in order to continue writing, accidentally bumped his eraser with his elbow and sent it bouncing across the floor.

The teacher testily looked up to see what the cause for the noise had been. He was growing desperate now.

All the children suddenly sat up straight and ceased pestering Trey and Sorryl. They turned their challenging eyes on Trey to see if he would confess, for they had seen what had happened. They half expected him to blame his seatmate.

"Who threw their eraser?" Mr. Grey asked sternly. "Was it you, Thomas?" he asked of the least liked pupil in the school. The children avoided him because his mother and father weren't as 'good' as theirs.

Trey quickly stood up, "No, sir, I accidentally bumped it with my elbow." He watched Mr. Grey fearfully, wondering how his new, seemingly unreasonable, teacher would react.

Mr. Grey studied him irresolutely for a moment, sensing the boy was telling the truth, though he had never before had a student willingly admit they were the one who had done something that displeased him. "Well, you may go pick it up then."

Heaving a relieved sigh, Trey rose to obey and the pupils turned back to their work. Little did Trey know that he had gained much respect from the students, especially the unfortunate Thomas, that day. Not many of the students would have done what Trey had, for they knew Mr. Grey was quick to jump to conclusions and that they very well could be punished. They put on a show of being good and righteous, as they had learned to do by the example of their parents, but they would have been very hesitant to confess when they just as well could have kept quiet and saved themselves, even if it was at the expense of others. Their goal was to *look* good, not necessarily *be* good. The children had never been taught to love others. They had just been taught to do good for others so that they themselves could get to Heaven. Or else to follow rule after rule that seemed to have no meaning. Yet, there was some inward sense that seemed to swell their young, callusing hearts, telling them that what Trey had done was very honorable, even if it wasn't at all expected. Somehow, it made them trust him more than they had ever dared to trust one of their other classmates before. It was puzzling. Weren't their parents always telling them that Trey and Sorryl were bad and to stay away from them? Sure, the brothers didn't seem to follow many of the rules the rest of the town did. But they seemed to always be caring and thinking about other people and enjoying it. And something seemed to be whispering to them that this was the most important thing. They knew Trey and Sorryl had rules to follow, but they somehow seemed to treat the rules differently than the townspeople. It was as if there was some reason for the rules; some underlying thing that helped them decide what to do in each situation rather than just mundanely doing something just because it was a rule. The students didn't realize it, but the law that God had written in their hearts, that shows people what is right and wrong, was what had caused them to recognize this.

When recess was once more called, the children filed slowly out the door. Trey and Sorryl gratefully dashed into the sunshine ahead of them all, and the rest of the students soon gathered around them as Trey began telling Sorryl a story with great animation. The students were enthralled and soon were seated at the boy's feet as he continued his exciting story.

"Of course, I just made it up, it didn't really happen. Except for the part about Daddy jumping off the back of the truck when it started to move," Trey finished.

"Do you have another one?" they pleaded eagerly.

"Well, I do. But we can save those for another time. Don't you want to move around some? We've been sitting all day!" Trey had been running to and fro as he acted out his story, but he didn't count that as 'moving around'.

At this odd speech, the students all looked at one another. They couldn't understand how this boy could be tired of sitting, for they were used to never moving about much or using their imaginations.

Sorryl gave an exaggerated moan as he stretched, "Yeah, my legs are as stiff as trees with mile-wide trunks from sitting so long."

There was silence for a moment as the students wondered where on earth Sorryl had ever seen a tree with a mile-wide trunk and how his legs could feel like one.

Finally, one of them asked, "So what are you going to do?"

The children watched the brothers, eager to find out what the strange boys would do next.

"I'm going to turn a summersault," Trey replied, a sparkle glowing in his lively blue eyes.

"A *what?*" the students returned with wide eyes. They had never heard of such a thing.

"A summersault," Trey repeated, wondering why these children acted as if he had said something like, "A zoombobber." He finally ducked his head and demonstrated for the astonished children.

Soon, the younger students were turning summersaults while the older ones looked on jealously. They were afraid to destroy their dignity by turning about in such a fashion. But one by one they finally gave in and were soon laughing along with the rest of the children.

Only Jake remained standing disconsolately by himself, too proud to join the fun. He finally could stand it no longer and tauntingly picked Sorryl up, dangling him in the air in order to plague him and make himself feel better. It only made him feel worse, though, and, to complicate matters, Trey defensively stomped up to him.

"Hey! He doesn't like that, you put him down!" This was more the sort of behavior Trey and Sorryl were used to, for they had been the smallest boys in their classes back in New York City and had been teased incessantly as a result. They were easy prey.

"Don't have to," Jake sulked.

"Then I'll get the teacher."

The schoolchildren were gradually gathering around the three unhappy children.

"No you won't," and Jake triumphantly swooped Trey up as well.

Trey kicked and squirmed, trying to free himself as the rest of the children looked on. He finally gave up. "Why are you picking on my brother?" he asked hotly.

"I'm not picking on him. I'd never do any such thing," Jake replied indignantly.

"Then what *are* you doing?" Trey demanded.

Jake was silent for a moment, then stuttered, "You guys are having all the fun, and I can't join you."

"Oh, if that's all," Trey said, cheering up, "We'll let you join us. I didn't know you felt like we didn't want you to do it. It's great fun. Here, put me down and I'll show you guys something even more fun!"

Jake slowly set the boys down, feeling rather ashamed of himself. Somehow, Trey's attitude made his actions seem so... so cowardly and mean.

"See the hill? If you roll down it, you'll go faster and faster until you get to the bottom. It's more fun than sledding sometimes! Watch!" He launched himself down the hill while the astonished students looked on and wondered what on earth sledding was.

When a slightly dizzy and wobbly Trey staggered back up the slope, Sorryl took his turn. Laughing from the bottom of the hill, he called to the children, who were staring in awe from the top of the hill, "Come on! It's fun! It's like rolling in a barrel... only better!"

Having never rolled in a barrel before, the students just continued staring. Finally, they decided they may as well try it seeing as Trey and Sorryl hadn't gotten hurt and seemed to enjoy it so much. Soon, every student, including an at first reluctant Jake, followed suit and were laughing and shouting as they rolled down the hill.

Mr. Grey once more approached the window to see what was going on, not really sure he wanted to find out. He was immensely surprised at what met his gaze. "Those Trestle boys are just... impossible," he muttered, shaking his head despairingly. "And none of those children thinks they are doing anything wrong." He paused a moment in deep thought, then said as if he had struck a new revelation, "Perhaps they aren't. I mean, what can possibly be wrong with playing when you've finished all your work? And it makes them learn so much better." The teacher shook his head once more and went back to his desk, at a loss for what to do.

When school let out, the boys skipped down the road. Today had been much better, though they had no idea the turmoil they had left their poor teacher in. Or the surprise parents were in for when their children arrived home, rosy cheeked and happy for perhaps the first time in their young lives.

When the schoolhouse was cleared of students, Mr. Grey lingered a little longer than usual, trying to collect his wits and figure out what to do the next day. He finally left, still perplexed. He had come up with no answers.

When Trey and Sorryl entered the shop, they ran to their father and hugged him tightly. The customer who was standing near looked on in wonder. Finally, she shook her head and returned to her shopping. She was used to being surprised by this strange trio by now anyway. The whole town was surprised at how much those three seemed to love each other. Even more confusing was how they seemed to care about everyone in the town, most of which had turned a cold shoulder to them. And their love was such an unselfish love, too. You could feel that they weren't looking for anything in return, they just loved.

"How was your day today?" Spencer asked. He waited a little anxiously for the answer; he wasn't sure he wanted to hear it.

"Fun! And we didn't get in trouble one bit! Except that Trey knocked his eraser off his desk by accident and Mr. Grey blamed someone else. But Trey told him it was his fault and then it was all okay," Sorryl said.

Spencer was pleasantly surprised. He let out a deep sigh of relief, but silently warned himself, *This doesn't mean all the trouble is over, Spencer, my man.* He looked into his sons' happy faces and ruffled their hair, then he turned to help the shopper who had just approached the counter.

As their daddy turned away, Trey eagerly whispered to Sorryl, "Oh! Do you remember what tomorrow is?"

"What?" Sorryl paused a moment, perched on one foot with his eyes fixed on the ceiling as he tried to recall what was so special about tomorrow. "Oh!" he exclaimed aloud, then quickly clapped both hands over his mouth and giggled as shoppers turned a curious and perhaps displeased look on him.

Spencer looked up at him and smiled, then turned back to the customer.

"Oh, now I remember!" Sorryl whispered this time.

"What?" Trey quizzed.

"Tomorrow is Daddy's birthday!" he said this even quieter as Trey put a warning finger to his lips and glanced at their daddy.

"Yeah! We can give him a surprise for his birthday after school!" Trey said excitedly, glancing at Daddy to be sure he hadn't overheard.

Sorryl's eyes lit up, "Great idea, Trey!" he whispered as Starlight entered the store with her mother. He contained his excitement and went over to them, "Hello, would you like a basket?"

Emma Bolton shook her head primly, "No thank you."

Trey said, "We didn't miss you today. You usually come when we would have been in school and so we thought we wouldn't see you today. But I'm so glad!"

"Me too!" Sorryl agreed. "We were so sad to miss everybody, but you most of all and now... well, now we get to see you anyway!"

Emma shook her head, trying not to let the boys penetrate her aching heart. But she finally gave in a little and smiled gently at them. At this encouragement, they flung their arms about both ladies at the same time. Emma stood stock still, stunned. But Starlight was overjoyed and warmly returned their embrace.

The moment Starlight and Emma turned to their shopping, the boys began eagerly discussing what to do the next day for their father. Spencer cast curious glances their direction from time to time, but he wasn't worried that they were up to mischief.

When they were tucked snugly into their beds that night, the boys continued to finalize their plans. They giggled excitedly, thinking of what Daddy would do when he found out what they had planned for him. They simply loved surprises. When Spencer finally poked his head into their room and gave them a warning look, they settled down and dropped into a deep, refreshing sleep.

As Spencer lay in bed that night, his mind wouldn't stop racing. He was glad the boys were doing better at school... at least, it had gone better today. But he thought he had seen someone up the mountain again that night when they had come home. He had realized, as it skipped away, that it was just a mountain goat, but he had locked the doors before going to bed anyway, something he hadn't done since they had moved here. Maybe they should find a better town to live in. This place was too gloomy anyway. With that thought, he finally rolled over and fell into a restless slumber.

Chapter 16

The following afternoon, the boys hurried home from school, chattering excitedly about their plans. They dashed ahead of the other students until they reached an almost hidden path into the woods. There they left the road and disappeared into the trees. They reemerged a little while later with their arms filled to overflowing with leaves and colorful flowers of many different varieties. Some of the schoolchildren caught up to them and gazed curiously at them.

By now, Trey and Sorryl were used to the strange looks the children were casting their way. Deep down, they wished it wouldn't happen anymore. But they cast that feeling aside and greeted the others before they began planning again.

"Now," Trey said excitedly, "Mr. Charlie should be able to distract Daddy in the back room. When I asked if he could keep him out of the store part, he told me he had lots of work for Daddy back there and winked at me. I think that means he's got a good plan. So we can hide all this," with a nod at the articles they were carrying, "and then go in the store and say hello to Daddy. Then, when he's busy in the back, we can hurry and get started. Mr. Charlie promised he wouldn't let Daddy come out 'till we were ready."

Sorryl nodded and began skipping, but he stopped as quickly as he had begun, for he found this activity dislodged his flowers and leaves, throwing them to the wind.

Trey looked over at him and giggled.

The schoolchildren finally gave up trying to figure out what the boys had been talking about and began listening to Trey as he told them a story while they walked along. Usually the townspeople, including the children, meandered along, seemingly with no purpose. Their discouraged hearts had lost interest in truly living. But it wasn't so with the schoolchildren today as they unconsciously swept along at a lively pace with the Trestle brothers.

As they entered the more populated area of town, Trey and Sorryl glimpsed Mr. Brendt walking dismally down the dusty street. They dashed up to him and asked the astonished man, "Hey, Mr. Brendt, would you come to the store for Daddy's birthday celebration? We're giving him a surprise!"

The students who had managed to keep up with the excited brothers stood at a safe distance and gaped. First of all, they couldn't believe Trey and Sorryl would dare get that close to the cranky old man who had given every one of the children severe speeches or cold, callused glares all too often. Second of all, an invitation to a birthday celebration or something like that? How interesting.

Trey and Sorryl earnestly included the schoolchildren in their invitation. Trey added, "Of course, you had better ask your parents first."

Mr. Brendt nodded his agreement, swelling with pride as if he himself had taught Trey and Sorryl to obey their parents. Lifting himself to his full height in a pleased fashion, he muttered to himself, "See, I knew those boys would do the right thing, even if they don't follow all our rules."

If anyone had chanced to overhear this little remark, no one would have understood what it was supposed to mean saving the pious old man himself. What could he mean, "They do the right thing, even if they don't follow all our rules"? Wasn't following all of the town's rules doing the right thing? And how could you be doing the right thing if you weren't following all the rules?

Though he didn't realize it, Mr. Brendt was beginning to see that having to follow rules wasn't what was important. Life was about loving others! "Love your neighbor as yourself"... and, he conceded rather reluctantly, perhaps God too. Couldn't that be the underlying reason for following rules? He had seen the way the Trestles seemed to love God. It was all very confusing to him. Hadn't he grown up thinking he had to painstakingly keep a million rules, however ridiculous, and, "Do good in order to please God and escape His terrible wrath and get to Heaven"? Then these Trestles had made their eccentric appearance and begun changing his perspective. Could he himself be filled with the joy the Trestles were overflowing with, even though he had lost his only son? This thought carried him to the time Sorryl had mentioned how much God loves everyone. It had been when Mr. Brendt had sternly informed him he better be real good or God wouldn't love him.

The little boy had exclaimed with tears in his eyes, "God loves us all no matter what! It's the bad things we do He doesn't like, the stuff we do against His Word. He loved us so much the Father gave us His only Son, Jesus, who loved us too. And Jesus, who is God – you know, they're like a family with the last name 'God'. There's the Father and Son, that's Jesus, and the Holy Spirit… and they're all God. Just like we're all Trestle – Well, Jesus loved everybody so much that He died on the horrible cross so our sins could be cleaned… you know, He paid for them so we wouldn't have to. But don't worry," Sorryl continued, noticing Mr. Brendt's unconsciously worried expression, "He came back alive, so now the Father has Him back in Heaven with Him. And we get to see Jesus someday and be with Him in Heaven. That is, if we believe He really did that for us and we let Him pay for our sin. 'Cause otherwise we'll have to pay for it, and the payment is death. Like, really death, not just dying. It's going to Hell and not being able to be with Jesus, who loves so, so much. You'd have to be with Satan, who hates and is mean. But God loves everyone! You can tell, 'cause the Father let His Son come and pay our punishment, and the Son, Jesus, came!"

Awestruck not only at the length and earnestness of the little boy's speech, but also at the words, Mr. Brendt had stood there, wondering at the boy's words and the love that flowed with them. He was sure it was that love which had made Sorryl want to talk about God so much… he could tell the boy was grateful to Him and that he had learned to love Him an awful lot. Mr. Brendt wished he had the love and joy this boy, and all three of the Trestles, seemed to possess. He also wondered if *his* son could 'come back alive' to him. Even though he pretended to be angry at his lost son and say he never wanted to see him or even hear his name again, deep inside he just wanted his Danni to come home and wished he'd never lost his temper that fateful night... But, never mind, that didn't matter. What was he thinking?

Leaving the bewildered Mr. Brendt and schoolchildren to ponder their unexpected invitation, Trey and Sorryl hurried on their way. They excitedly poked their heads into Jerry's shop as they passed.

"Hi, Jerry!" Sorryl called from the doorway.

Jerry looked up. When he saw who it was, he immediately brightened and hurried over to the door. "Come in! Come in!" he invited.

With the air of a grownup, Trey answered rather regretfully, "Oh. We can't stay. We just wanted to tell you we're having a party for Daddy and to come over to the store in about half an hour if you like," he finished with dancing eyes.

"A party, huh?" Jerry answered with a trace of a twinkle in his eye. With a quizzical look, he glanced at the things the boys were carrying.

Sorryl nodded. "Yup. We better go now. Daddy'll wonder if we don't hurry!" With that, the boys dashed away. A leaf fluttered from their piles and landed in front of Jerry's doorstep. He stooped to pick it up and then watched the little whirlwinds race across the street and disappear behind the general store. He chuckled as he recalled their earnest faces, then he returned to his counter as a customer entered his pizza shop.

When they reached the general store, Trey and Sorryl quickly deposited their loads behind the building and rushed into the shop. They hoped Daddy wouldn't notice how late they were.

As he took a rake down for a lady to inspect, Spencer caught a glimpse of them entering the store. After handing the customer the tool, he went over to them. "How are my boys today, 'ey?" he asked. He swooped them up in his arms and kissed them on top of their heads.

The boys tried not to giggle. If they did, Daddy might guess the surprise.

Trey answered, "School went really good! Today was great! Mr. Grey never yelled at us." The boy ended with a giggle in spite of himself.

"But he rubbed his nose a lot. I'm not sure, maybe he didn't yell because he was sick," Sorryl added with a puzzled frown.

Mr. Grey had the unconscious habit of scratching his nose when he wasn't sure what to do. All day today he had wondered what to do about the new boys and the effect they had on the other pupils, thus he had scratched his nose all day. It was certainly a different atmosphere at school the past few days, but he wasn't altogether sure whether to think of it as good or bad. Nevertheless, he was beginning to think he liked teaching better since those Trestle boys had made their eccentric appearance. Mr. Grey was beginning to join the growing number of people who had ceased expecting to find the Trestles in trouble with the law.

Spencer laughed and ruffled Trey and Sorryl's hair as he set them down to put the rake back up for the astonished lady who had overheard their conversation.

As soon as the unsuspecting Spencer turned his back, Charlie winked at the boys to let them know he hadn't forgotten his promise to keep Spencer busy in the back room. He soon had Spencer moving things around back there, the door shut, "To keep the dust from flying into the front of the store," Charlie explained to the boys with a grin, proud of the brilliant excuse he had concocted.

As soon as their father was shut up in the back room, Trey and Sorryl dashed back outside to retrieve their treasures. They nearly ran Martha Geller over on their way back in. She had entered in their absence and they couldn't see where they were going very well with the piles of 'decorations' blocking their view.

"Oh, I'm sorry!" they both exclaimed, trying to keep quiet lest Daddy hear them and wonder what was up.

"That's all right," she answered absentmindedly as she gazed curiously at their burdens.

Trey set his down and asked, "Do you need a basket, Mrs. Geller?"

She shook her head, still not really paying attention to her answer. She was still wondering about the leaves and flowers the boys had just carried in. She turned and began her shopping, but, along with the rest of the customers, she couldn't help glancing at the busy boys every once in a while.

Trey and Sorryl dragged chairs here and there as they used them for stools in order to reach as high as possible with their decorations. They dashed about, their disarming young eyes sparkling in anticipation. Each time a new customer entered the store, one of them would hop down from their chair to greet the newcomer and see if they could help with anything.

Once, the boys heard Daddy shout from the back room as his voice grew closer to the closed door, "Hey, Charlie! What do you want me to do with these boxes?" Trey and Sorryl anxiously watched as the back room's door handle jiggled a bit.

Charlie dashed over to it. He winked at Trey and Sorryl as he slipped inside. He had suddenly discovered how much he missed winking at the little boys in Lottie. He'd tried it on this town's boys, but wasn't met with the same feeling of camaraderie as he had been in Lottie, so he had quickly stopped using this affectionate gesture. But these Trestle boys now, they knew what he meant by a wink.

Trey and Sorryl gave a sigh of relief and giggled at their narrow escape as they returned to their work with renewed vigor.

Presently, Charlie reemerged from the back room and winked at the boys again, "He should be busy for a while yet."

Rising to his tiptoes on his chair, Trey beckoned to Charlie and asked him in a loud whisper, "What about that other thing?"

Charlie knew exactly what the boy meant and tipped his head toward the refrigerator, "Way in the back of that thing," he answered with a merry chuckle. "I had lots of fun with it."

Trey gave an excited bounce and clapped his hands, then threw his arms about Charlie's neck and whispered, "Thanks!"

"Hey, Mr. Charlie," Sorryl said, coming towards them, "We're all done except for this." From beneath one of the shelves he pulled a home-made sign carefully lettered with, "Happy Birthday Daddy (Spencer)!" It had little hearts drawn painstakingly across the entire length. They had hidden it under the shelf the day before so it would be in the store, but somewhere Spencer wouldn't find it.

"We want it hung way up there, but we can't reach. Would you put it up for us, please?" Sorryl asked.

Charlie scratched his head. He hadn't been up on a chair, or anything else, since he had moved to this place, unless it was to stock shelves. But he would have to climb up there in front of all his shoppers, Martha Geller of all people! And hang some sign that the town was sure to think was preposterous. Martha would undoubtedly deem his actions as too 'different' and 'unpredictable'.

But how could he turn these hopeful boys down just because of his pride? That decided it. He cleared his throat and smiled, "Of course I can." He stood on the chair and took the sign from Sorryl, then carefully pinned it above the doorway. "There," he said, stepping back to admire the boys' work. "That's a lovely sign," he added softly. It touched his heart to see the obvious love the Trestles had for each other. He hadn't seen that kind of love since he had moved to this town.

The shoppers stopped and stared at the sign and then the beautiful flowers and leaves adorning nearly the entire store. As understanding dawned, they forgot their duties entirely. The idea of a celebration of any kind was completely foreign to them. They shouldn't be wasting time on frivolous celebrations. The time would be better spent in helping the poor and thus doing more good works to get to Heaven, wouldn't it? In their efforts to be good, the glum townspeople seemed to have forgotten about serving the Lord with gladness and putting joy into hearts. If they were going to please God, they couldn't have fun, could they? A little leap of joy seemed to flood some of them with more energy than they had experienced in a long while as their hearts caught at the rising hope that perhaps they *could* have fun even *while* they served God.

At that moment, Jerry entered the shop and Trey and Sorryl gladly rushed up to him, "Oh good! You came!" they exclaimed in hushed tones. They had been eagerly watching for him, as well as for Mr. Brendt and the Boltons. Before Starlight and her mother had left the store yesterday, Trey and Sorryl had invited them to the party.

Trey and Sorryl peered hopefully out the door and were delighted to see Starlight and her mother making their way down the dusty street.

Starlight was eager to see what Trey and Sorryl were going to do for their daddy. Often, she had wished to do something for her own father when she was growing up, but, alas, the most she could manage without incurring a fierce scolding from her mother, and various appalled townspeople, was to give him flowers. He always loved that, and sometimes would take her on his knee and tell her of the times when he was young and his mother and father had celebrated his birthday, or any number of things. Once, he told of how he used to run in the fields or ride his horse, Dancer, just for fun. When she was young, Starlight wondered why he never told those stories when Mother was near, but now she understood. He couldn't. Her mother would have just sniffed and called him 'preposterous', advising him to leave those memories behind.

When Emma entered the store and saw the decorations, especially the sign, she stopped and stared. She had often overheard the stories her husband told Starlight with such animation and joy. Joy she had seen him slowly lose the longer he lived in Los Ciegos. The joy and energy she now realized was what had drawn her to him in the first place.

Trey and Sorryl hadn't been able to get away to invite anyone else to their 'party' without the risk of drawing unwanted attention from their father, but they knew Martha would most likely be there anyway. She usually was on that day.

Just as they were giving up hope of anyone else coming, Mr. Brendt entered the shop. He stopped and gazed at all the decorations. Driven by an odd curiosity to discover what Trey and Sorryl had been talking about, he had found his rusty feet directing him toward the general store. Besides, his heavy heart somehow seemed to grow lighter whenever he was with the Trestles, surrounded by their... Well, he guessed you would call it love; love that didn't care who you were or what you did; love that seemed to be like the love Sorryl had told him God had for everyone, even the worst sinners.

Completely unaware of the sensation they were creating, Trey and Sorryl whispered delightedly to Charlie, "Now we can get Daddy and sing to him!"

Charlie took his cue and called out, "Hey, Spence!"

A muffled, "Yeah?" came from the back room, followed by a grunt as Spencer evidently set a large box down.

"I need you out here a minute!" Charlie replied.

The entire store was even more silent than usual as shoppers paused, breathlessly waiting to find out what would happen next.

Spencer appeared, brushing his hands on his pants. He looked up, "Yeah, Charlie? What is it you wan..." his query broke off abruptly as his eyes scanned the decorations and the people gathered around, staring at him. His eyes came to rest on the sign, beautiful in its own way. Speechless in surprise, Spencer attempted to regain his composure. Finally he laughed. "I thought you forgot my birthday," he told the boys with a smile. "You didn't say anything about it this morning."

Trey and Sorryl giggled.

"We didn't want to spoil the surprise," Sorryl said.

The boys began singing "Happy Birthday", motioning Charlie to join them. They had taught Charlie the song, for nobody here ever sang it and Charlie was having trouble remembering it from where he had previously lived. Huddling in a corner of the store whenever Spencer was in the back room in search of some item, they had practiced the song while curious shoppers tried to pretend they weren't straining their pharisaical ears to catch a phrase here and there.

Spencer laughed as they began singing. The rest of the shoppers just stood and stared.

When the song was through, Jerry walked up to Spencer and shook his hand heartily, throwing aside the ever-ready qualms over what people would think, "Happy birthday! So how old are you now?"

Spencer laughed, "I'm an old man, Twenty-five to be exact."

Jerry laughed at Spencer's idea of old and patted his shoulder, "Just wait 'till you're my age."

"Lookie here!" Charlie said as he returned from digging in the back of his refrigerator. The townspeople turned toward him. He was bearing a gaily decorated cake, which Trey and Sorryl had convinced him to decorate since they had no way of doing it themselves without their father finding out.

When Trey and Sorryl caught sight of it, they exclaimed over the brightly frosted cake, however unorganized the adornments may have been.

"Oh, it's perfect!" Sorryl exclaimed.

Trey nodded in agreement.

Charlie beamed, "I'm glad you like it." He set it on the counter and raised his voice, "Everyone's welcome to some!"

For a moment, complete silence reigned as the people stared. They were unaccustomed to celebrations and wondered if they would be 'wrong' if they took a piece of cake.

After a confused moment, Martha Geller decidedly stepped forward and took a piece. The rest of the shoppers stared. Martha Geller? Taking a piece of that cake? They still weren't sure what to do, but, seeing as Martha was taking one, they figured they may as well, too. One by one the shoppers hesitantly stepped forward, wishing Spencer a happy birthday as they passed him.

Everyone had soon finished their cake with more relish than they cared to admit. They resumed their shopping, a deep imprint of the day and the Trestle boys' affection for their father etched forever on their minds.

Jerry had to hurry back to his shop, though their boisterous birthday song had attracted nearly everyone who had been on the street to the general store, including some of the schoolchildren with their previously reluctant parents.

Jerry clapped Spencer on the back, "You be sure to visit me soon, okay? I'll even give you a free pizza," he added, a bit of light shining in his once dull eyes. They always grew brighter when he was with the Trestles.

"Of course!" Spencer answered with a fond pat on Jerry's shoulder. "We love seeing you!" He laughed, "Besides, your pizza's delicious, too."

Presently, a lady slowly approached the Trestles with one of Trey and Sorryl's schoolmates, Thomas, close beside her. The woman's eyes glanced furtively in first one direction, then another. She seemed to feel awkward and afraid of what people would think of what she was about to do. She spoke to Trey in a burst of bravery, "I just wanted to thank you for not letting Thomas take your punishment. You know, when the eraser dropped on the floor and Mr. Grey blamed Thomas."

Trey blushed. He answered with light shining in his blue eyes, "I'm glad I could do it. It wasn't his fault, so I just did what I ought to."

Thomas' mother seemed close to tears. After a thoughtful pause, she replied softly, "Well, no one else would have done that – especially not for my Thomas. Thank you."

Trey looked down, unsure what to do, and answered, "Jesus would have done it. Actually, He took *our* punishment… except, if we don't realize that He did, we'll have to take the punishment too."

With a quiet, "Mmmm," Thomas' mother nodded and turned to do her shopping.

Trey smiled at Thomas as the boy turned to follow his mother. There was a sad note to Trey's smile though. When he saw Thomas with his mother, he was reminded of how he used to shop with his own mother sometimes.

Trey and Sorryl hadn't had enough money for a gift, but Spencer valued their decorations and thoughtfulness more than anything money could have bought. He took them in his arms and hugged them tight, "Thanks boys. I think that's about as good a party as your mama would have got up if she had been here."

Trey and Sorryl's hearts bubbled to the brim with joy. It made them feel special to know they had done something as good as their mama would have.

When they arrived home that evening, it was still light out and the boys begged for a birthday swim. Spencer agreed with a laugh, so the adventurous threesome changed as fast as they could.

"Volcano!" Trey shouted as he threw himself into the water.

"Whale!" Sorryl yelled gleefully as he followed Trey.

"Butterfly!" Spencer cried, gracefully sailing into the water.

In the middle of an animated chase, Sorryl stopped short, treading water as he listened, "What's that?"

Trey and Spencer paused too, "What?" they wondered in unison. Then they, too, heard the noise and glanced toward the road as a dusty truck pulled into their driveway. Curiously, the drenched onlookers climbed out of the water to greet their visitor.

A tall man stepped from the truck and started toward the dripping trio, "Hey! Imagine that! I should have known I would find you doing something like that! They told me I'd find you out here when I stopped and asked in town. Seems every last person knows you guys here," their visitor finished with a laugh.

With a simultaneous shout, Trey and Sorryl raced toward the man with their dripping arms wide open, "Officer Joe! Officer Joe!" They leapt into his arms, laughing.

"Well, I'm just Joe now," the suddenly damp traveler corrected. He chose to leave the culprits happily unconscious of their crime of transferring their water to his clothes. "I'm not an officer anymore. I quit my job and decided to come down here with you guys so I could have some more fresh air and warmth," he laughed at his last remark. "I couldn't let you have all of it, now, could I?"

"Of course not, Just Joe!" Trey laughed.

Joe laughed with him, "Nice joke, Trey." He looked down at the wet dog that had warily greeted him. Its bushy tail now waved back and forth in a wide arch, "And who is this loyal guardian?"

"Oh, that's Trooper," Sorryl answered. "We came home one night and found him there almost dead, but he's okay now," he added.

Joe smothered a grin and put Trey and Sorryl down. "Oh! It's so good to be with you guys again, I missed you! You know, when you left New York, all the sparkle seemed to leave the city with you."

"We missed you too, but I guess you could tell," Spencer responded with an apologetic look at his friend's damp clothes. He reached out to shake Joe's hand. Suddenly, he laughed and exclaimed, "Now, that'll never do!" He threw his arms around Joe.

Trey looked up at Joe, "Would you come swim with us? We were having lots of fun!"

Almost comically, he looked down at his soaked clothes, "Okay, let me dig something out to wear. I need to wash all this traveling dust, ahem, or mud, off anyway." In a teasing voice he added under his breath, "Though these are already so wet I don't see why I need to change."

Catching Joe's reference to mud and his muttered teasing, Spencer smiled another apology. He knew he had added to it with his hug.

Trey and Sorryl stared at Joe's wet clothes, then at their own. Their eyes widened.

"Oh, I'm sorry, Joe! We got you all wet!" Trey exclaimed.

Sorryl nodded, "Yeah, I forgot I was wet when I saw you. I was just too excited I guess."

Joe laughed, "That's all right. I really don't mind."

"So you're really going to swim with us?" Sorryl asked again.

"Yup. I sure will," Joe said.

Trey and Sorryl hurrahed and danced around as Joe went back to his truck. They had their Joe back! Joy filled their hearts.

"Would you like to stay here at our house?" Spencer asked, following Joe to his truck.

"Sure! If you'll have me," Joe answered, delighted to be back with his wonderful friends. Really, he couldn't comprehend how he had ever lived before he had known the Trestles. He gave a quiet grunt. He *hadn't* lived before he met them. Not really. They had taught him how again.

"Of course we'll have you! We'll help you bring everything in after we finish swimming," Spencer offered.

"Okay, thanks!" Joe said.

He soon joined them in the pond, laughing joyfully. He had missed this family.

"Let's play blind man's bluff!" Sorryl said.

"Okay, you're it!" Spencer agreed, brushing water from his eyes.

Sorryl shut his eyes tight and began counting. When he reached ten, he paused, quietly treading water as he listened. For a moment, there was complete silence. Suddenly a light splash sounded to his left. He leapt in that direction and missed Trey by an inch. Joe laughed at the boy's narrow escape. He couldn't help himself. Sorryl immediately dashed in his direction and Joe laughed again as he leapt out of the way. Then began a jolly chase with Joe laughing his way around the pond while he was hotly pursued by the relentless Sorryl. Finally, with one, last, mighty leap, Sorryl pounced on his still laughing victim. The boy's dancing eyes flew open, "You're not supposed to laugh! If you're quiet, I won't know where you are!"

Joe, still laughing, just shook his head, sending streams of water spraying in every direction. It was then that they noticed it was raining. Trey shrugged his shoulders and they continued their game, paying the rain no mind. They were already wet anyway, it didn't matter.

It was Trey's turn to be "it". After hopelessly chasing everyone around the pond he paused to listen, unwittingly right next to his daddy. Suddenly, a huge thunder clap sounded across the rapidly darkening sky. He jumped and his startled eyes flew open. Seeing his daddy right next to him, he laughed at how close he had been and said with a sheepish grin, "I guess I cheated."

Laughing, they splashed out of the water and pulled Joe's truck close to the house. Adventures like these were so fun!

"We better wait to bring your stuff in!" Spencer shouted to Joe above the rising wind.

Joe nodded and they all dashed into the house against the now driving wind and rain.

"This is the worst storm I've seen since we moved here." Spencer panted, catching his breath by the stove.

"Where's Trooper?" Sorryl suddenly asked.

Spencer looked up and scanned the room. Where *was* Trooper? Growing worried in spite of himself, he answered, "I'm not sure."

Fear clutching their hearts, Trey and Sorryl dashed about the house, calling out anxiously, "Trooper! Trooper! Where are you, buddy!"

Spencer and Joe leapt up and went to the porch, calling Trooper's name too.

In a moment, Sorryl came rushing out with Trey close on his heels, "He's not in the house and I didn't see him for a long time! We've got to find him! He might be sick like the last time! He always comes when we call... Oh, Daddy!" Sorryl finished in a sob. Then, before anyone could stop him, he dashed off the porch and was lost to sight in the driving rain.

Spencer took off after his son, yelling over his shoulder, "Stay on the porch, Trey! Sorryl! Sorryl! Come back!"

But Sorryl couldn't hear him above the pounding rain and rushing wind.

A tree cracked loudly. A dull thud sounded as it hit the ground. Spencer's voice rasped in his anxiety, "Sorryl!" He stopped and strove to penetrate the thick wall of rain with his eyes. His heart flooded with fear. "Sorryl!" he cried desperately once more. But there was no answer. He looked back to where the house stood, but it was lost to view. The rain was driving hard and the sky had grown ominously dark. Helplessly, Spencer surveyed the yard once more, but he couldn't see or hear anything above the pounding rain and wind and the claps of thunder. For a split second, a flash of lightning illuminated the yard, but his searching eyes could still see nothing because of the rain. "Oh, God! Take care of my son! Please..." he begged brokenly as streams of rain poured down his face. His heart ached furiously. He dashed back to the porch in near panic. "Joe! I can't find him! You've got to help me! He could get under a falling tree!"

As if in reply to his anxious words, another tree snapped and fell with a sickening crash. In a heart-wrenching panic, Spencer leapt for the stairs again.

Joe darted to Spencer's side, and put a restraining, yet comforting, hand on his friend's dripping shoulder. "I don't know if it would do any good to go out there. He can't hear you. None of us can see anything," he paused a moment before continuing in calming tones, "Let's pray. I think that's the best thing to do."

By this time, Trey was thoroughly frightened for his brother and had completely forgotten about Trooper. He grasped his daddy's hand and sobbed, "Is he okay, Daddy? Is Sorryl all right?"

This was the exact cry of Spencer's heart. Only his plea was directed toward his Heavenly Father. All he could think of was how Annaleah had so suddenly disappeared without even a chance for a goodbye. He would always remember and treasure that last hug before she had left for the store and be eternally grateful she had gotten him into the habit of doing that. His aching heart throbbed, *Not Sorryl, too! Please. Please. Please.* At every crack of a tree, his fears grew. Spencer's voice was husky when he answered, "I don't know, Trey. I don't know. But," he added as he stooped down, taking Trey's shoulders gently as he struggled to catch hold of the courage he felt had fled him, "We can trust God. Joe has the best idea, let's pray." He picked Trey up and held him with one arm and laid his other hand on Joe's shoulder. He began to pray in a shaky voice, "God? I don't know where Sorryl is, but you do. Please watch over him. I know you have total control over the rain and wind and over everything. You have proven that in many ways, one of them was when Jesus calmed the sea when He was on earth. Please, would You keep our Sorryl, *your* Sorryl, safe? I give him to you, Lord. He's yours to take care of." His voice trembled and he trailed off as he struggled to hold back the sobs that rose in his chest.

"Amen!" Joe breathed, clasping Spencer's shoulder tightly in an effort to encourage his friend.

Sorryl frantically dashed through the icy rain, crying anxiously, "Trooper! Trooper!" But the wind caught his young voice in its unyielding grasp and hurled it uselessly into the air. Sorryl halted, his hair dripping water into his worried eyes, mingling with his tears. He turned to go back to the house in defeat... But where *was* the house. His heart suddenly filled with a new panic. He couldn't see anything! Oh! Just to catch a glimpse of that wonderful, warm, friendly house! Or his Daddy. That would be even better.

Suddenly, just above him, he heard a threatening crack. He turned and fled. Sorryl raced on, his worry for Trooper now turned to terror of being crushed. Without warning, he ran head-long into a tree and was thrown to the ground. He rubbed his stinging face as frightened tears coursed down his cheeks with renewed vigor. Suddenly, he realized there was something sticky on his hand. He couldn't see what it was in the darkness, and it soon washed away in the driving rain, but he guessed it was blood. Gingerly, he picked himself up and looked around. All that met his longing gaze were the dark, looming shapes of the trees surrounding him, and even those were barely visible in the darkness and heavy rain.

"I've got to get out of here!" he panicked aloud, instinctively realizing the danger of being surrounded by trees in this wind. Fear gripped his heart, sending his brain into a discombobulated whirl.

Just then, a flash of lightening illuminated his surroundings. Hope filled his fast-beating heart as he strained to catch a glimpse of his cozy home, but, alas, he still couldn't see far, for the uncaring rain was driving fast. When he heard another frightening crack nearby, Sorryl decided all he could do was try to get away from it. As he ran, he called out frantically, "Daddy! Daddy! Oh! Daddy!" But the relentless wind whisked his cries into the sky, rendering them useless. He cried out again with quivering lips as he stumbled on, "Oh, dear Jesus! Please help me! Please, please help me!"

Another sickening crack sounded above him, sending him racing as fast as his tired legs would go. Where? He knew not. Just away. Away from the cracks of weakening trees. Away from the frightful thuds as the graceful pictures of strength gave way to the formidable winds. He was glad he had Someone more powerful, and full of love too, Whom he could trust. Something brushed his back as one of the magnificent trees thudded to the ground and he knew it had just missed him. With a shiver, he realized he had just barely escaped death. He stopped, attempting to get his bearings and clear his foggy mind, rendered more so by the terror now clutching at him. But another crack sounded and he dashed away from that as well.

He continued dodging cracks, not knowing where he was going and wishing with all his heart that the rain would stop and the beautiful sun would come back. But he knew it had probably gone down by now, even if the terrible, dark clouds did part to let it shine through. His heart kept up a constant plea, "Jesus, please help me! Please! Please. Please..." At that moment, he ran face first into something hard and rough, then, with a terrified cry, he heard a loud crack directly above him just before he sank into darkness.

Chapter 17

Spencer, Joe, and Trey stood on the porch, staring into the black expanse that had descended so quickly, straining their ears for any sign of Sorryl. But all that met their longing ears were terrifying cracks and thuds as tree after tree gave way in the bitter wind.

Joe finally encircled Spencer's shoulders and led him inside. He could see that Spencer and Trey were shaking from the cold and perhaps from emotional exhaustion.

Spencer reluctantly allowed himself to be directed into the house, carrying Trey with him. Absentmindedly, he helped the trembling boy change into dry clothes, and then tucked him into his bed to warm up. The weary Trey soon dropped into a troubled sleep.

Joe and Spencer changed as well, but Spencer couldn't sleep. He sat worriedly in the living room and each time the wind seemed to let up a bit, he would leap up and venture onto the dark porch, hoping it would have let up enough to go out and find Sorryl. But the relentless storm gave no indication of departing.

The fourth time he leapt up, Spencer almost stormed back inside and angrily kicked the door shut. Throwing himself into a chair, he sputtered furiously, "I wish we'd never found that dog! He's just been trouble!" In his heart, Spencer knew this was far from true. He didn't feel so anxious about letting the boys explore the outdoors when they had Trooper with them. And the dog was a loyal friend to them all. But in his anger, he cast aside these realities and chose to blame his son's danger on the unfortunate Trooper. Somehow it made him feel better, at least for the moment, to have something to blame.

Joe didn't respond, but waited for Spencer to finish. He longed with all his heart to comfort him.

"I need my son! What more is God going to take from me? He's already got my Annaleah. And…" Dropping his weary head into his hands, he almost sobbed, "I'm sorry, God. You have been very good to me. Oh! Please just help me!" When his aching heart could utter no more, he paused, striving to hold back his tears.

Joe placed a comforting hand on Spencer's shoulder, "I don't know where Sorryl is, but God knows, and He loves him far more than you or I ever could."

"I know, I know. I just… Ohhhh!" Spencer finished with a moan. His strong shoulders began to shake as tears burst past the barricade that had stood firm for so long. Sobs racked his body. He sobbed because he and Annaleah hadn't been able to have children. He sobbed because God had been so good to give them Trey and Sorryl. He sobbed for Sorryl and the danger he was in. Finally, he sobbed for Annaleah, something his aching heart had desperately needed for a long time.

Joe just sat there and let his grieving friend weep. Finally, when the sobs quieted a little, he laid a comforting hand on Spencer's shoulder again. He was glad God had brought his lonely self there that night.

Spencer sat up and rubbed his eyes, wondering why he was on the couch. He looked out the window. Pitch black. Then his weary gaze traveled to the fire cheerily burning in the fireplace.

With a small smile, Joe rose from adding a log to the fire and brushed his hands off. It was then that Spencer remembered with an aching heart why he was in the living room. He could hear the rain still pounding on the roof. He sighed and cried out to Jesus for Sorryl.

"That was a short nap. I was hoping you'd sleep until morning," Joe said, coming towards him.

Spencer sighed, "*I* was hoping the rain would be gone."

He didn't know how, but he soon dropped into a disturbed slumber once more.

A while later, Spencer awoke again, rubbing his eyes. He looked out the window. The early morning sun was streaming through the windows as if the storm had never come and Sorryl had always been safe. With hope beating in his chest, he rose and looked out into the yard. Fallen trees littered the ground, but there was no sign of Sorryl or Trooper. He sighed and opened the door, venturing out onto the porch. He didn't notice the birds cheerfully singing as they searched for new abodes among the remaining standing trees, but he called out eagerly, "Sorryl! Sorryl!" No answer. He stood looking about him for a moment, hoping to catch sight of his dear son. But his little boy seemed to be nowhere to be found. It didn't seem right for the sun to be shining, or the birds, which he finally noticed, to be singing. Turning dejectedly, he trudged back inside.

Joe was just waking. He blinked in the brightness and stretched, noticing the sun with delight. In New York City, he rarely got to see such a sight. His gaze traveled to Spencer when the worried father grabbed his shoes, saying, "I'm going to look for him." Joe's light spirits fell with a thud as he remembered the missing boy.

At that moment, Trey entered the room. He asked worriedly, "Sorryl's not back yet?"

Joe shook his head.

Trey noticed his father putting his shoes on. "Can I come too, Daddy?" he asked hopefully.

Spencer looked up at him, undecided. Finally, he nodded, "Sure. Joe may as well come too, if he wants."

Joe jumped up, "Of course I want," he said. So they all three hurried their shoes on.

"Let's head in the direction of town first, maybe we'll find him on the way and, if we don't, we can ask the townspeople to help us search for him," Spencer said as he hurried out the door and led the way through the woods.

They had been laboriously picking their way through the fallen trees for quite some time when Spencer suddenly stopped, staring at a branch not far off the ground. There dangled a piece of Sorryl's blue shirt. With great feeling, Spencer knelt down, gently releasing it from the branch. Bowing his head, he held the scrap of cloth to his face for a moment, sending a prayer of thanks to God for this sign of his son. Then he begged for Sorryl's safety and that they would find him soon. He wasn't sure whether it was good or bad that they had found this scrap of Sorryl's shirt here. It led into the deepest part of the woods. He looked up, striving to keep the fear that clutched at his heart from reaching his voice, and nearly whispered, "I guess we're on the right track, anyway."

Trey took his hand and they started off once more, but they reached Mr. Brendt's property, the first on the edge of town, without finding another trace of Sorryl.

Spencer sighed and started across the yard to ask Mr. Brendt if he would help in the search for Sorryl. He didn't know if it would do any good to ask, but he figured he may as well try. He picked Trey up as they made their way up the stairs. Joe rang the bell. They could hear someone moving around inside, but it took everlastingly long for them to come to the door.

Early on the morning after the storm, Mr. Brendt meandered across the yard to his shed. He had left his sweater out there when he had grumpily returned a hoe to its place just before the rains had come last night. No, of course he hadn't been using the hoe himself. One of his servants had left it out and had been nowhere to be found, so he had returned it to its rightful place himself, not willing that it should succumb to rust. He mumbled grumpily to himself all the way, growing angry when he noticed that the back window of the shed was open.

After he retrieved his sweater, Mr. Brendt stormed around the back to shut the window. He stopped when he saw a tree had fallen there, just missing the shed. Growing even more irritated, he surveyed the tree, wondering how he was to get to the back window with this enormous barricade blocking his way. His traveling gaze came to a startled halt as it settled on something blue hidden just beneath the tree's branches under the window.

In his shock, he forgot his irritation. He strained his eyes in an effort to find out whether his first impression had been right or not. With a doubtful shake of his head, he muttered, "My! That looks like a boy!" The graying man was a funny sight climbing over branches as he tried to reach the little spot of gently fluttering color. As he drew nearer, his certainty that it was a boy grew, and he suddenly recognized it as Sorryl Trestle.

Unheeding of the scratches he was receiving, the usually immaculate Mr. Brendt didn't stop a moment to wonder how Sorryl had gotten there, but worked even more diligently to reach him. He found that the boy was badly scraped up on his face, but it appeared the larger branches had missed him and that he had curled up under their protection.

Indeed, the crack Sorryl had heard just before he blacked out after ramming his head into Mr. Brendt's shed had been this very tree. He had come to a few moments after it fell, and, finding he was too exhausted to move and that the leaves provided some protection from the driving rain, he had curled up and fallen to sleep amid the cracks of thunder and flashes of lightening.

Realizing he had unconsciously carried his sweater over the tree with him, Mr. Brendt carefully lifted the small, soaked boy, trying not to wake him, and gently wrapped him in the comparatively large sweater. Once Sorryl was safely in his arms, he made his way back through the branches and hurried to the house with his precious burden, forgetting completely about the window, which had so angered him just a few moments before.

As he bore the dirty boy through the door, Sorryl stretched and yawned, then wearily opened his eyes. At his surprise of seeing Mr. Brendt looking anxiously down into his face, he came fully awake, but he had strength only to smile slightly before his sleepy eyes closed once more.

"Meg!" Mr. Brendt called curtly for his housekeeper as soon as he entered the house, "Get me some warm blankets."

She came hurrying in with them, wondering at her employer's strange request. His servants were used to his gruffness and self-righteous air, so she was not at all surprised at his stern tones. What puzzled her was the touch of anxiety that had entered his voice, and that he had called for blankets on a perfectly warm morning. When she arrived, she nearly dropped the blankets in surprise, for lying on his clean sofa was a small, extremely dirty boy whose face was covered in blood. She gasped, wondering which of the servants had dared to bring him inside. She never dreamed Mr. Brendt himself would do such a thing. "Oh, I'll remove him right away," she exclaimed apologetically, suddenly flustered.

Mr. Brendt glared at her, stopping her with his icy eyes, "You will do no such thing."

Meg halted abruptly in her hasty steps toward the couch, confused, "Well, then, I'll clean him up and..."

Mr. Brendt glared harder, "You will do no such thi—"

Meg didn't let him finish, "But you can't just leave him like that."

"What do you take me for? A dimwit?" he growled.

She finally resorted to silence.

"That's better. Now, get me some warm water and clean rags," he instructed. "And call Nancy to watch him while I look for some clothes upstairs!" he called after her. Meg nearly let out a surprised exclamation at these words, but managed to hold it back and continued on her mission.

When Mr. Brendt emerged from the attic, she did let out a surprised exclamation, "Why, Mr. Brendt! No one's supposed to touch those clothes!"

He glowered at her, "They are *my* clothes. That was *my* rule, and I can do what I want with them." The objects of this heated dispute were boy's clothes, just a tad big for Sorryl. Mr. Brendt softly stroked the little shirt. They had belonged to his son, Danni… Memories flooded back to wash over his hardened heart as he remembered that terrible night five years ago when he had gotten into a fight with his seventeen-year old son, his only son who had been his life. With these memories, his long-dead heart began to throb with a dull ache.

On that fateful night, Danni had stated feelingly, yet respectfully, in his impulsive way, "Father, life shouldn't be about all the rules. I wish we could just love people and God."

Thinking his son was referring to his refusal to allow Danni to get up some sort of play for Christmas, Mr. Brendt had countered in a rage, "I make the rules around here. Now you listen to me. Don't you dare get strange ideas into your head! And don't ever sass me again. Now, go stack firewood until I tell you you may stop."

His heart breaking over his father's reaction, Danni tried to reason with his father whom he knew could not be reasoned with, feeling he had been misunderstood and determining it would not remain that way this time. Finally, from the depths of his wounded heart, he had shouted, "I'll find somewhere more cheerful to live! You can't keep me here in this gloomy town where nobody loves anybody but themselves!" He had dashed for the door to escape before the hot tears he felt pricking his eyes could break past his barrier.

Mr. Brendt had grabbed him roughly, halting him in his desperate flight. Holding Danni's shaking shoulders so that the heartbroken boy had to look him in the face even as he continued to fight the relentless tears, the irritated father growled in low, angry tones, "I can, too, keep you here. You're my son, and I've given you everything you need…"

Here Danni mumbled bitterly, "Except love." Sadly, Danni didn't realize his father did love him, but here in this town, with so many rules without meaning, there was no room to display it.

Choosing not to heed his son's hurt words, Mr. Brendt rushed on, feeling his pride had been hurt by this threat to leave,

"…and you have a duty now to stay with me. But," he added in a low threatening voice, "If you do leave, be assured you can never set foot in this home again." *And you'll break your father's heart,* his very core added silently. Alas, if only he had voiced this longed-for indication of love.

At these words, Danni had desperately broken free of his father's grasp before his tears could spill over and made good his escape with his bleeding heart torn in two.

As the night waned, Mr. Brendt stomped to bed, determining to give his 'wayward' son a punishment when he returned. Danni had never done anything like this before, he was always so kind and understanding, and Mr. Brendt fully expected to hear him enter the house sometime during the night.

The next morning, Mr. Brendt realized his son had been in earnest, but he stalwartly refused to let anyone search for him. Then started the 'dark days' of the town, for Danni had always managed to find some way to cheer people up, but without him, everyone kind of got lost in their methodology.

It was then that Mr. Brendt had changed. Though he had always had great pride and wouldn't stoop to any dirty task, the servants remembered a time when he used to care and love to talk with whomever he met. True, he hadn't ever found a good way to show Danni he loved him, especially not after the boy's mother had died when he was only three, but he hadn't always been a cranky, clammed up man.

No one in that town had seen or heard of their bright, cheerful Danni for five years and Mr. Brendt would not allow anyone to so much as mention Danni's name or touch his possessions.

Meg and Nancy stared in surprise. They couldn't believe what they saw with their own eyes. Mr. Brendt was carefully dabbing the despised Trestle boy's bloody face with the warm water and rag Meg had brought. He had never even done anything like that before he had turned cranky and silent when Danni ran away.

This alone astounded them. But, even more, it appeared that he had gone to the attic and searched his long-lost son's belongings himself and fully intended to put this boy into little Danni's rich clothes. They had quickly recognized Sorryl, who was still despised by many in the town. That fact only served to intensify their shock.

Mr. Brendt turned on them, "Well. Haven't you got something to do?"

Meg and Nancy quickly collected themselves and hurried off to their tasks, wondering greatly at the miracle they had just witnessed.

A while later, Sorryl coughed and woke. He looked up at Mr. Brendt, "Hello, Mr. Brendt," he greeted weakly. The boy winced as Mr. Brendt gently dabbed his face.

"There," Mr. Brendt said, rising. "You had quite a cut up face," he told Sorryl, giving him a rusty smile.

Sorryl just smiled back. He didn't have the strength to say anything more.

"You need a hot bath, and then we'll change your clothes," Mr. Brendt said. He lifted his voice, "Meg! Nancy!"

When the flustered housekeepers appeared, he instructed gruffly, "Get a hot bath ready for this boy."

They rushed off to do his bidding, returning shortly to tell him it was ready. They watched, amazed, as Mr. Brendt carefully lifted the boy and took him upstairs.

Meg reached for the clothes in order to bring them up for him, but Mr. Brendt stopped her with a severe look, "Those, you do not touch," he demanded protectively. When he returned for the clothes a moment later, he cast a stern gaze the maids' way. This sent the amazed ladies racing for their duties once more.

Mr. Brendt soon returned a clean, but tired, Sorryl to the couch and covered him with the clean blankets Meg had brought. Then he sat by him and watched the boy as he slipped into a peaceful sleep.

At first, Mr. Brendt was relieved, but this soon turned into an anxious watchfulness as the peaceful slumber changed into a feverish tossing. The cold and wet had not been kind to the small boy. He tossed and turned, crying out, first in terror, then pain.

Mr. Brendt anxiously called for Meg and Nancy, sending them racing for lukewarm water and a clean rag. He paid them no heed this time when they remained hovering over the small boy and his peculiar nurse. The man's full attention was on the tossing Sorryl. He bathed the boy's hot face, dodging whenever he flailed his arms and legs. Once, Sorryl nearly slipped off the sofa, but Mr. Brendt caught him just in time and placed him gently back on the soft cushions.

Sorryl finally calmed down for a moment, and that was when Mr. Brendt heard the doorbell. Giving the maids withering glances when they turned to get the door, the nurse of sorts went himself. He poked his rarely disheveled head out the door. Seeing who it was, he opened the door wider. "Oh. Come in, come in," he offered with a quizzical glance at Joe. He turned perceptive eyes on the worried Spence and added, "Just the person I needed to see." He showed signs of leaving poor Joe outside since he didn't know him, but he seemed to think better of it and let the stranger in as well.

They immediately noticed the flushed Sorryl lying on the sofa.

Mr. Brendt held a finger to his lips, "He's got a fever. That cold and wet last night wasn't good for him."

Spencer, Joe, and Trey were extremely anxious to know how and when Sorryl came to be at Mr. Brendt's house, but they were relieved just to have found him. In spite of himself, Spencer lifted his arms toward Heaven, whispering, "Thank you Lord! Thank you!" This was all he could say, for gratefulness choked his heart along with fear— his son did not look well. He sent up another prayer for him, glad that God didn't mind him asking for so many things so close together. Tenderly, he and Trey knelt by the sofa and took over bathing Sorryl's brow. Nevertheless, an anxious Mr. Brendt remained hovering about them.

When Sorryl was having one of his restful moments, Spencer finally asked, "How did he find your house?"

"I think he must have run his head against my shed, I found him there with a tree nearly on top of him. It appeared he had been there when it fell and decided to stay there. I'm kind of curious myself," Mr. Brendt added. "I found him when I went to close my window in back of the shed, otherwise I would never have even gone back there, nor would anyone else, for that matter. So I carried him in here and got him cleaned up and then he started up with the fever. Poor little guy."

Meg and Nancy, who remained in the room with them, looked at each other with wide, astonished eyes. They had still believed that one of the servants had found Sorryl and carried him in, so were completely astounded to find that Mr. Brendt himself had found the boy and carried him into the house, however dirty he was, and laid Sorryl on his expensive sofa which he normally protected with a stalwart determination.

Spencer was amazed too, but for a different reason. When he found his voice, he nearly whispered, "God is so amazing! It's like he directed Sorryl here and you behind the shed."

Mr. Brendt added, "I wouldn't even have gone to the shed if I hadn't had to put a hoe away just before the rain last night and left my sweater out there. I would never have noticed the window, and then I wouldn't have seen Sorryl."

Joe shook his head in wonder.

"You think it was God, huh?" Mr. Brendt asked.

"I know it was God. I asked him to watch out for Sorryl and He did. He's always faithful. I should never have doubted," Spencer finished ashamedly.

Mr. Brendt, Meg, and Nancy were puzzled by Spencer's words of faith. Whoever heard of God doing something like that? Wasn't He there to make sure you were doing what was right, and if you did enough good, He might let you into His Heaven? Spencer apparently didn't think so. And they were beginning to feel he was right and that he had something they wanted, and desperately needed, but couldn't quite lay their finger on. Deep down, they were beginning to feel like all their righteousness was like filthy rags next to God's righteousness and that they never *could* be good enough to get to Heaven or have a relationship with Him and stand before His holiness. This placed within their hearts a growing desire to know how to *really* get to Heaven and be reconciled to this God they suddenly wanted to know better.

While the adults conversed, Trey had begun making his way about the room, gazing in awe at the spectacular carvings and rich draperies.

Mr. Brendt watched him with a fond smile and realized that the Trestles weren't accustomed to such wealth. "Why don't you stay here for lunch?" he asked.

Meg and Nancy were by now growing accustomed to being surprised and managed not to show their extreme astonishment this time. Mr. Brendt hadn't asked anyone to dine with him, let alone allowed anyone into his house, since his son had stormed out the door five years earlier.

Spencer looked to Joe, then Trey, and finally the ailing Sorryl. "I would be delighted to, thank you! You've been so kind and hospitable to us!" he replied gratefully.

Mr. Brendt nodded, "Good, I'm glad you'll stay."

Suddenly, Spencer said, "Oh. I'm sorry! I never introduced you! This is Joe Reaper. He was our friend back in New York City. He just arrived in Los Ciegos last night. Good thing, too. I'm not really sure if he's planning on staying or if he's just visiting," he looked toward Joe inquisitively.

"I'm hoping to stay," Joe said, smiling.

"And this is Mr. Brendt and, I assume, his housekeepers," Spencer continued.

Mr. Brendt nodded in affirmation, "Meg, Nancy," he indicated them as he spoke their names.

Sorryl suddenly cried out and began tossing and turning again. They flew to his side. Spencer had been bathing his face the whole time they had been talking, but he had jumped in surprise at the boy's terrified cry.

When Sorryl quieted down, everyone, including an anxious Meg and Nancy hovering in the background, sat studying him with concern.

Mr. Brendt finally observed bluntly, "We should send for the doctor. Perhaps he could do something for him."

Spencer sadly shook his head, "I don't know if I would be able to pay for one."

Mr. Brendt glared at him, "But I can. Nancy, go call the doctor."

Spencer had to give in, and, really, he was grateful of it.

Chapter 18

When Doctor Chense had somberly examined Sorryl, he showed Spencer how to cover the boy with his feet showing and put minced garlic with a little oil on the bottom of his feet.

"Also make sure he gets plenty of water if he can drink it." Doctor Chense handed Spencer some medicine that might help the boy's condition, but he shook his head in concern.

He took Mr. Brendt aside and quietly confided, "That boy has a very high fever, if it climbs much higher, he could die." He had wanted someone to know the boy's danger, but felt Spencer would overreact. He had hoped Mr. Brendt would understand and take the news coolly. But when he received the crotchety man's reaction, the poor doctor wondered if he should have told Spencer instead.

Mr. Brendt glowered at him and countered hotly, "That boy will be just fine. He has to be." After a slight pause he continued, "Besides, he's got a father who knows how to really talk to God. Spencer seems to think God takes care of us, especially when we ask Him to. And I'm beginning to think he's right."

The doctor shook his head, not believing anyone could really have a better handle on God than Mr. Brendt, the most pious person in the town. "Well, give him that medicine. Hopefully it should keep his fever down," Doctor Chense ordered gravely.

He approached Spencer again, feeling he must tell the boy's father *something* about his condition, the doctor tried to make the situation sound more hopeful than he thought it really was, "Your boy had quite the experience. He has a high fever, I'll do all I can to help him. Keep bathing his face and be sure to give him that medicine. A tablespoon every hour. Hopefully it will bring his fever down."

He added quietly to himself, "I think that's about all we can do."

The doctor hadn't thought his words were loud enough to be heard, so he was surprised when Spencer spoke quietly, "No. There is one more thing we can do, which is more effective than anything else, and that is to pray."

The doctor just shook his head. Of course they always prayed for healing, but not one of them connected the actual healing with God.

"Thank you, Doctor Chense," Spencer said when the doctor didn't respond aloud, "I appreciate your help very much."

"You're welcome. I should be back in a couple hours to see how the boy is," Doctor Chense replied, placing his hat on his head as he headed for the door.

When he was gone, Mr. Brendt sighed, "Well, Sorryl is quiet and lunch is ready, shall we eat? We can eat out here so we'll be on hand if Sorryl needs us."

Nancy and Meg brought out the food and, after a very stiff prayer, they began their silent meal. Alas, in spite of the tempting food, no one seemed to have a very good appetite.

Spencer picked at his food, glancing at Sorryl between bites.

Even Mr. Brendt was having troubles getting his food down. He was not so distracted that he didn't notice Trey's good manners at the table, though. He shouldn't have been surprised, because he had seen the Trestle boys' manners before, but he was. Along with the rest of the town, the pious man had harbored a notion that they would lack manners since they had no mother.

Finally giving up on attempting to eat, Mr. Brendt pushed his plate aside, "Say, Spencer. Have you done any more of that talking to God lately?"

Spencer nodded, "Yes, I don't know if I've stopped talking to Him since this morning."

With a satisfied nod, Mr. Brendt answered confidently, "Good. Then the boy will be okay."

Giving the usually pessimistic man an inquiring glance, Spencer asked, "How do you know?"

"Well, He answered you this morning. He even set everything up last night so it would happen right this morning. And you say He loves us, so why wouldn't Sorryl be okay?" Mr. Brendt asked.

Spencer shook his head. Mr. Brendt seemed to trust God even more than he did. "Unless it's better for us for Sorryl to...," he nearly said die, but quickly substituted as he choked on a sob, "not to... get better."

"Well, I don't see how that can be if He already saved him from being pounded to death by that tree. Or any of the other ones for that matter," Mr. Brendt said, not losing an ounce of courage.

Spencer had to agree that this made sense, and a small amount of his fear began to subside as he began to trust God a little more. Mr. Brendt's confidence and reasoning were good for Spencer, for, though he wasn't aware of it, much of his trust in God had been shaken by Annaleah's death. And it helped his trust that, in light of what Mr. Brendt had pointed out, God had just shown Spencer that He still cared. He had miraculously saved Sorryl so far. Wouldn't He make him well, too? Spencer tried not to hope too much. But Mr. Brendt was openly confident.

Nevertheless, when the doctor returned, he shook his head even more hopelessly, "That's the best medicine I've got, and his fever has only climbed higher."

With a worried leap in their hearts, everyone sensed the doctor's intense concern and were forced to admit that what their hearts had known all along was true, the anguished boy was not doing well at all.

As if confirming their hearts' agonized qualms, Sorryl suddenly cried out and began flailing, "It's dark! I can't! Oh! I shall die!"

Doctor Chense gave Spencer a knowing, yet compassionate look.

Suddenly, Sorryl lay still. In a panic, Spencer hurriedly felt for his pulse. He sighed with relief, it was still there. Silently reproving himself, he muttered, "Where is your trust in God, man?"

Four more hours passed of watching the boy thrash about in pain. Four more hours of prayer. Joe stood by Spencer and laid a reassuring hand on his shoulder.

Seeing Trey's quivering lips, Spencer took his worried son in his lap. Trey buried his face in his father's shoulder and cried for his brother.

The doctor came and went, always looking grave. They moved Sorryl to a bedroom, where he had less danger of falling off the wide bed.

As the men transported Sorryl, Meg whispered in shock, "He's putting him in there? There are dozens of other rooms! Why'd he pick that one?"

With raised, inquisitive eyebrows, Nancy answered, "Well, it *is* the most comfortable."

"Yes, but in *Danni's* room? I just don't believe it!" Suddenly, Meg clapped a hand over her mouth. They weren't supposed to speak Danni's name and it had been the first time she had uttered it since he left. She sighed. He had been so bright and courageous. The dear boy had brought glimmers of joy to the large home and even managed to make the whole town seem not so gloomy. He never had been one to keep all the ridiculous rules or to care what people thought because he didn't keep them to a 't'. Some of the townsfolk had found it amusing how different, yet how alike, father and son had been. Now there were barely any traces of Danni's manner in the grumpy man.

Sorryl continued to cry out and thrash about. By now, the whole town was aware of the Trestle's situation, and they were all talking about Mr. Brendt allowing someone besides his servants into his house. They couldn't imagine it and, though they would have been horrified to admit it, they were jealous of the 'intruders' who had been lucky enough to gain the privilege of crossing the esteemed man's threshold. Even more shocking was the rumor that the proud, cold man had found and carried the dirty little boy into his house of his own accord.

Many tried to visit the boy, though most were ashamed to admit that, rather than an honest concern and a desire to see the boy, it was more curiosity and a devious way to get into the coveted house that motivated them to approach his door.

Nevertheless, the perceptive doctor insisted it was best that no one disturb the boy, and many doubted whether Mr. Brendt would have allowed any of them to enter his home anyway.

Many of the townspeople actually thought it would be a good riddance if the boy should die. There would be one less indescribable, unpredictable person traipsing about the town, free from the oppression of their constant meddling. Perhaps if he died, the other two would come to realize their errors and set things right, or leave the town altogether.

The sun's rays began to slide across the horizon and the sky grew dark once more. It had been a long day. Mr. Brendt insisted that the Trestles, and Joe, stay at his house, "We can't move the boy, and of course you want him with you," he reasoned. "And we can't throw out the police officer," the usually stern Mr. Brendt added with a playful twinkle in his eye.

With a much-needed, though unconvincing, laugh, they all went to bed in their benefactor's spacious mansion. Even through their anxiety they couldn't help but notice the softness of the sheets and delightful springiness of the mattresses.

Spencer slept by Sorryl's side so he would be there if Sorryl needed him in the night. He slept restlessly and awoke at every sound.

Mr. Brendt was having trouble sleeping as well. He crept into Sorryl's room to check on him every few minutes. On one of these occasions, Spencer got up and said, "Why don't you just stay in here with us. I can't sleep either."

Mr. Brendt grunted for answer and pulled two chairs up to the bedside. The two men sat there, so oddly different, yet, deep in the core of their hearts, anguished for the same boy. They lapsed into a thoughtful silence as they anxiously watched Sorryl's troubled slumber.

The sun was just beginning to etch the sky with a silver light when Sorryl suddenly cried out louder than he ever had before. Everyone in the house raced to his bedside. He cried out again and again, tossing and turning for nearly a quarter of an hour. Mr. Brendt was about to call the doctor when Sorryl suddenly stopped and lay still. Once more, Spencer hurriedly checked his pulse. Everyone anxiously watched his face. They gave a sigh of relief along with him as he gently laid the pale arm back on the bed with a quivering smile. The boy was alive.

Suddenly, Sorryl gave a deep sigh. He rolled over and fell into a restful slumber for the first time since the fever had come upon him.

"Thank you God!" Spencer breathed, close to tears. He was almost afraid to believe what he saw.

Trey turned anxiously to Spencer, "Is Sorryl all right now, Daddy?"

Caressing Trey's chestnut curls, Spencer answered with a small smile, "Better than he has been in a long while. But we need to keep praying, he's not all the way better yet."

A few hours later, the concerned doctor arrived. He looked as though he wasn't sure he wanted to hear what had taken place in his absence. But when he beheld Mr. Brendt's rarely smiling face, he took heart and asked, "How is he?"

Mr. Brendt's eyebrow twitched, perhaps in humor, perhaps in victory and to say 'I told you so'. He answered proudly, "Been sleeping peacefully since about five o'clock this morning. And we took his temperature, too. His fever's nearly gone."

At this news, Doctor Chense hurried up the stairs. He greeted Spencer and Joe as he entered the sick room. Quickly taking out his thermometer, he took Sorryl's temperature. Everyone watched as the doctor removed the thermometer from Sorryl's mouth. Doctor Chense gazed at it with a look of disbelief. Finally, he methodically shook it down and announced in tones of confidence he did not in actuality possess, "As I thought, he's back to normal. Our patient should mend quickly now." He finally decided not to try to hide his amazement and shook his head in wonder, "The little fella' sure had me worried though."

Spencer smiled, "But God is always faithful." He had needed this encouragement from God. A growing flame of hope filled his heart.

Sorryl woke shortly after they had all eaten breakfast. He looked around at everyone's faces as they smiled at him. Finally, he asked in a scratchy voice, "Where am I?"

"You're at Mr. Brendt's house. He took you here after the storm, remember?" Trey answered.

Sorryl gazed at Mr. Brendt. Recollection slowly began to dawn in his pale face. "Oh yeah," he said, too worn out to say much of anything else, though he worked up enough strength to observe quietly, yet earnestly, "I'm hungry."

They all laughed.

"I've got some grapes downstairs, do you want some of those?" Mr. Brendt asked.

When Sorryl nodded eagerly, he dashed down the stairs before Meg or Nancy had time to respond. They stared after him. They couldn't believe he was actually running to do something himself. And how had he even known they had grapes or where they were?

Mr. Brendt soon returned, huffing to catch his breath. Sorryl gratefully accepted the grapes, then he weakly settled back on the soft pillows and fell into a peaceful slumber.

By suppertime, he was sitting up and talking to his numerous nurses. But they wouldn't let him out of bed.

"Tomorrow," Daddy promised.

Sorryl sighed, "Okay."

To make up for him having to stay in bed, they ate supper in the bedroom with him so he didn't have to be alone. Truth was, not one of them wanted to leave him in order to eat supper anyway.

In order to keep proper form, Meg and Nancy, who Mr. Brendt allowed to dine in the room with them for serving purposes, sat on the opposite side of the room.

Sorryl kept glancing over at them. Finally, he asked, "Why don't they want to be over here?"

Mr. Brendt looked between Sorryl and his maids. He opened his mouth to explain, then shut it again. Finally, he laughed and said, "You may as well eat over here, Meg and Nancy."

Then he added for Sorryl's benefit, "In rich folks homes, servants don't eat with the other people, that's why they were over there."

Sorryl's eyes grew large, "Boy! I'm glad I'm not rich then, if it means you can't be friendly!"

Everyone, except Trey, who wholeheartedly agreed with Sorryl and demonstrated it with an exuberant, "Yeah!" tried not to laugh.

Behind Mr. Brendt's smile was a sad look. He remembered Danni expressing Sorryl's sympathy many times.

The following day after lunch, the trio headed home. Spencer carried Sorryl, who was still a bit weak.

Raising his head from his daddy's shoulder, Sorryl asked, "Where's Trooper?"

Spencer sighed, "I don't know, honey. I forgot all about him when you got lost." He suddenly understood a little more how much God must love him to send His only Son, Jesus, to die for him. True, God knew His Son would rise from the dead again, but He also knew Jesus would suffer much because of His great love for the human race and His desire to make a way for them to be reunited with God after the fall of man. Without Jesus' payment for their sin, they couldn't come to the holy God.

"Maybe he'll be at home waiting for us," Sorryl said hopefully.

But when they arrived home, their loyal Trooper was nowhere to be found.

Chapter 19

Trey went around the back of the house calling, "Trooper! Trooper! Where are you!" But the only answer was the cheerful singing of the birds.

When Spencer had carefully settled Sorryl in the house, he left him in the care of Joe and went in search of Trey. He was not long in finding the worried boy who was still wandering the yard, eagerly calling for Trooper. Sighing, Spencer went to his son. He laid a comforting hand on his shoulder, "We'll ask people in town to keep an eye out for him, okay?"

Spencer turned back to the house, loathe to leave Sorryl for long.

Trey reluctantly turned to follow his daddy toward the house and asked, "When? When will we go and ask people to watch for him?"

With an understanding sigh, Spencer answered, "Well, Sorryl shouldn't be going anywhere for a few days. We better at least wait until tomorrow."

Trey looked up at his daddy, "I'm real glad God helped us find Sorryl and is making him better." He paused a moment and bit his lip, "But I'm still worried about Trooper. We have to find him sometime soon, or else he might die." Tears welled in his eyes, "Besides, Maybe Trooper will help make Sorryl better. Maybe he'll cuddle him and keep him warm."

Spencer smiled and ruffled Trey's hair. The dear boy had such a big heart! "Well, maybe Joe can bring you to town while I stay with Sorryl, and in the meantime we can pray."

Trey's clouded face lit up, "Oh! That's a good idea! God can help the best. And if Joe goes with me to town, I can introduce him to everybody!"

When they walked in the door, Trey immediately bombarded Joe with their idea, "You can come to town with me and ask people to look out for Trooper!" Suddenly, Trey paused, blushing, and added, "That is, if you want to. Would you come with me, please?" Putting his hands behind his back, Trey chewed his bottom lip as he anxiously waited for the answer. It wasn't long in coming.

With an amused laugh, Joe said, "Of course I'll come with you! It'll give me a chance to meet some of the townspeople, too."

So Trey and Joe headed back to town.

Trey skipped along, pulling Joe with him, "Come on," he laughed. "Daddy always skips with us."

Finally, Joe gave in and began skipping along with Trey, clumsily at first, until he grew re-accustomed to the action.

Suddenly, Trey stopped skipping, "Suppose the people don't know where Trooper is? What if he's still lost?"

Joe looked down at Trey and smiled encouragingly, "Well, even if they don't know where he is, God does. And with so many people looking, we're bound to find him somewhere."

At these words, Trey smiled, taking heart once more, "Oh yeah! I guess I forgot God knew where he was."

Smiling at Trey's simple outlook, Joe followed Trey as the boy began skipping and whistling down the road again. Every time he hit the ground, there was a little break in his boyish whistling, making the tune sound very interesting.

When they reached the town, Trey stopped skipping and eagerly approached a lady he vaguely recognized, "Excuse me, ma'am. Have you seen a big dog? He's black with brown patches and a little white. You know, our Trooper." Trey looked down sadly, "He's missing since the storm. But we did find Sorryl, and he's okay 'cause God helped us. But we want to find our dog too."

"No, I haven't seen a dog like that. But I'll keep my eye out for him," the lady said with an understanding smile. As an afterthought she added, "And I'm glad you found Sorryl."

"Me too!" Trey answered.

Other times, Trey was coldly ignored. This pierced his tender heart to the quick. Seeing the boy's hurt face, Joe would squeeze Trey's shoulder in a gesture of comfort and lead him to someone who looked more promising.

The two searchers had not been in town long when they met a very thoughtful Mr. Brendt walking aimlessly down the road. In spite of his strict orders not to speak Danni's name, the recent happenings had made the man's crusty heart disobey this order, and the tabooed name was indeed the subject occupying his thoughts at that very moment.

"Hello, Mr. Brendt," Trey greeted. "Have you seen our dog, Trooper? He's gone since the bad storm. That's why Sorryl was behind your shed. He ran to find Trooper before Daddy could stop him and then he got lost and nobody could find him and we were all really worried."

Mr. Brendt paused in the road, "I haven't seen him, but I'll watch for him."

"Oh, thank you! We really need to find him, because he needs us and we need him. That's why God brought him to our house, you know," he added confidently. A small smile brightened his face.

"Ah. Good to see you smiling again," Mr. Brendt commented in his gruff way.

With a little quirk of his head, Trey asked, "Do you smile Mr. Brendt? I think you would look even handsomer if you smiled."

Surprised, Mr. Brendt gave a little sniff and straightened. "Humph!" was all he said. Then, as if thinking better of it, he patted Trey's shoulder encouragingly and then set off on his way again, this time with more purpose in his step.

Trey looked quizzically at Joe, wondering why Mr. Brendt was acting so absentminded and distant.

With a confused shrug, Joe started off down the street again.

Trey tugged on Joe's shirt, halting him in his steps. Looking up at Joe with eager eyes, he suggested, "Let's pray for us to find him. I've been asking God myself, but it'd be nice to pray together."

"Good idea," Joe replied, turning back to Trey and taking his hands.

Just as the two finished praying, Trey looked up and caught sight of Starlight as she exited the bakery. With a happy bounce, he exclaimed, "Oh! Starlight!"

Turning toward the direction of the call, Starlight searched for the owner of the voice. When she spotted Trey and Joe, she started eagerly toward them, "Hey! How's Sorry!?"

Trey's eyes lit up, "He's good. God helped him get better!"

Starlight's face broke into a radiant smile, "Good!"

Trey looked up at her, "But Trooper's gone. Have you seen him? He's missing since the storm."

"Oh dear. That's not good. I haven't seen him, but I'll keep my eye out for him," she answered, stooping down to lay a comforting hand on his shoulder.

Trey looked down, disappointed, "That's what everybody says. Or else they ignore me," he added sadly. "Maybe Trooper's not here anymore. Maybe he went to New York."

A shadow fell across the ground and Starlight looked up to find that her mother had joined the little group standing in the middle of the road. With a sigh, her gaze traveled back to Trey, who was gazing dejectedly at the dusty ground at his feet. Trying to divert his troubled mind, she asked, "And who is this friend you have with you?"

Trey's face brightened, "Oh! He's Joe. He's the first one that found us, you know."

Quizzically, Starlight glanced at Joe, wondering what the boy could mean.

Poor Joe was blushing to his roots. He knew Trey was referring to the time he had roughly captured them when they were newly orphaned. He wondered at Trey's forgiving heart, for there was no malice in the youngster's tones.

Clearing his throat as he tried not to choke on the tears that rushed to his eyes, Joe spoke, feeling an explanation must be made, "When they were orphans, I found them on the street. I must say I wasn't very nice to them, though," he added, blushing again.

"Oh, but you didn't know us then," Trey comforted. He leapt into his friend's arms and added fondly, "You're the best now!"

Joe just laughed, shaking his head, "You boys are so forgiving."

After a thoughtful silence, Emma asked, "What are you doing here in town and not in school? I heard you say something about a dog."

Trey sobered and began toying with Joe's shirt collar, "Yeah, Daddy said not to worry about going to school until Sorryl is better. He said even tomorrow we pro'ly won't go and we can look for Trooper. He's missing since the storm and we can't find him. That's how Sorryl got lost. He ran to find Trooper before Daddy could stop him." He slid from Joe's arms.

"Oh. That dog," Emma said contemptuously. "I haven't seen him for a while." But when she glanced up and looked into the boy's pained eyes, something awoke within her crusty heart. After pausing in thought for a moment, she suddenly said, "Actually, I remember seeing a dog that looked like him out in the back yard just after the storm began."

Suddenly, a new light sprang into Trey's eyes and he clapped his hands, "Finally! Someone has seen him!"

"He's bound to be somewhere," Emma added encouragingly.

Gazing rapturously at her mother, Starlight smiled. It had been a long time since she had seen this tender side of her mother. Usually she was too busy putting on a good show and making sure she got to church and did everything right to stop and think about the actual people. Even when she made quilts for the poor she wasn't at all concerned for them. She did it for herself, to hopefully earn her way to Heaven and to look good amongst all the likeminded townsfolk.

But Emma took no notice of her daughter's surprise and joy. For once, she had forgotten herself and was thinking only of the boy before her. He had looked ready to cry. "I'll keep watching for him, okay?" she promised, laying a gentle hand on Trey's shoulder.

Trey nodded, "Thanks. I hope we find him soon. We asked God to help us, so I guess we will." He smiled again at this thought.

A little taken aback at his remark, Emma suddenly straightened. It wasn't at all unusual to hear someone say they would pray about something. In fact, they did that almost constantly. But to expect it to do any good, why, that was a foreign idea to her. She smiled gently down at the boy, not knowing how to respond but somehow feeling he might be right.

Starlight gazed happily at her mother's face, transformed even by the shadow of a smile. She had not seen her mother smile or even give many kind words since she had been a very little girl before her father had died.

"Well, we better get on and see if anyone else has seen Trooper," Joe finally said, taking Trey's hand.

Emma and Starlight watched as Trey and Joe made their way down the street.

Half in a daze, Starlight said, "You look lovely when you smile, Mother."

Suddenly taking her eyes off the departing figures, Emma started walking briskly so that Starlight had to run to catch up. "Humph," Emma grumped as she huffed away. These newcomers were just too much.

Chapter 20

A little while later, the two searchers approached Martha Geller's house. So far, they had been unsuccessful in finding anyone else who had seen Trooper. As they drew near her house, Joe and Trey noticed Martha sitting on her porch, industriously working on a quilt.

"Mrs. Geller! Hello!" Trey called as they approached her.

She looked up and her stern countenance softened.

"Have you seen Trooper?" Trey asked as he came onto her porch. Seeing Martha Geller's quizzical expression as she evaluated Joe, Trey smiled, "Oh, this is Joe. He's our really good friend from New York." Then he added proudly in a confidential whisper, "He was a policeman."

Joe overheard the whispered boast and laughed.

Rising from her seat, Martha held out her hand. She had decided Joe was alright, at least for now, "Nice to meet you, I'm Martha Geller." Then she turned to Trey and sadly added, "As to the dog, I haven't seen a speck of him."

Trey sighed, "He's been gone since the storm. That's how Sorryl got lost in it. He ran to find Trooper before Daddy could stop him, and then he couldn't find our house and got sick. And now we need Trooper to make Sorryl feel better," Trey confided.

"Hmm. Well, we'll have to watch for him," she said comfortingly. "And how is our Sorryl," she continued. A bit of anxiety crept into her tones in spite of herself.

"He's doing lots better. God rescued him by Mr. Brendt and now He's making him get all better," Trey answered. His eyes beamed.

"Ah. I've heard the story." Martha shook her head wonderingly, "I don't see how Mr. Brendt ever came to do it. That proud man never... Well, that's a different subject," Martha interrupted herself. "I'm glad Sorryl's doing so well."

"We all are," Joe responded warmly, unwittingly furthering Mrs. Geller's conviction that he was okay. Except that he was so disconcertingly joyful, just like those Trestles.

Joe continued, "It was nice to meet you. I think we had better get on asking others if they will look out for Trooper now, though. The only one that's seen him is Emma Bolton."

Martha nodded her head in acknowledgement and they turned to be on their way.

It was a discouraged twosome who traveled home that evening after scouring the town. They had found no trace of Trooper.

"He's got to be somewhere," Joe said in an attempt to encourage the boy at his side. Then he suggested, "Let's skip." He tugged Trey's hand and began to hop forward.

He was rewarded by Trey's sudden laugh. "You're not skipping, you're trotting," he giggled. He knew Joe was purposely messing up to tease him.

Joe laughed, too and teased, "Oh, so I'm a horse am I? Well then, my dear expert, will you please unveil the correct operations of skipping for me?"

Trey giggled once more and instructed, "Like this." He started to skip.

Joe grinned and swung into the motion with Trey, "There, now I have it."

Trey giggled and grinned knowingly at him.

Joe returned the grin.

When they arrived home, a healthy looking Sorryl came to the door to greet them, "Did you find him?"

"No," Trey answered honestly. "But Mrs. Bolton, Starlight's mother, saw him before the storm," he added, trying to look on the bright side.

Sorryl's eyes clouded. He shut the door behind Trey and Joe as they entered the house.

"Hey! How did it go?" Spencer asked. As soon as he took in their faces, he knew the answer. After a moment, he suggested, "Sorryl's feeling lots better. Trooper loved to be in town, so maybe we can all spread out and look around for him there again tomorrow. Maybe you just missed him."

Trey looked down, that wasn't likely, Trooper would have come as soon as he heard or saw them. But he agreed it was a good plan to look again tomorrow.

The next day after breakfast, they eagerly started for town. At first, Trey went with Joe while Sorryl followed Spencer. But after a while, Sorryl and Trey asked if they could go toward Martha Geller's house together while Joe and Spencer each went a different direction in case Trooper was running around town and they chanced to miss him.

"With three sets of people looking, we might find him better," Trey reasoned.

Seeing that Sorryl seemed fine, Spencer cautiously agreed.

As Trey and Sorryl approached Martha Geller's house, they saw that she was engaged in a very disagreeable conversation with her neighbor, Mr. Right. The earnest disputers didn't notice their visitors as Trey and Sorryl made their way up the walk. Trey and Sorryl tried to make the quarrelers aware of their presence as best they could while still being polite, but they remained unnoticed.

"I'll tell you what, Mr. Right. You always think you're right, but you're absolutely wrong!" Martha huffed in an angry, yet controlled, voice typical of the town. The whole quarrel had gone on in the same self-righteous way nearly everything in that town was done in.

"Oh. Is that so now? Well—"

Martha cut him off sharply, "I will not have you feeding your greedy cows on my lawn merely because your fence blew down in the wind and you are too lazy to fix it."

"What! You know I'm not lazy. I always have my boys out there on the spot to fix things. I tell you, it's because the store has no posts left and mine were carried off somehow," he said this accusingly, as if to imply she had taken them.

The quarrel seemed to have no signs of coming to an end soon, so Trey and Sorryl finally turned around. They sensed Mrs. Geller wouldn't want to talk right then anyway.

Choosing not to notice Mr. Right's implied accusation, Martha continued smugly sewing her quilt, "And you should know, Sir Right," she added, emphasizing 'right', "That I am in higher standing than you. You know very well that you missed church last week…"

"I was sick!" he defended angrily.

She took no notice of his interruption, "And that I have done many more good things and substantially less bad things than you. I say, I shall get to Heaven far easier than you, you self-righteous Mr. Right!"

At these words, Trey and Sorryl quickly turned around again. They cared very much about these people and felt they must tell these two the truth. They walked back to the quarrelers and Trey politely cleared his throat. But the adults still took no notice of the youngsters.

Mr. Right sputtered and worked his angry lips for a moment before he managed, "Oh, so you think you're better than I am. Well. I'm beginning to think that this whole town is self-righteous and boring and that those Trestles are the only ones that have whatever it is people need to be happy. And to get to Heaven," he added significantly.

Trey finally resorted to tapping Mr. Right's arm.

Instantly, the argument halted and the startled adults looked at the two small boys.

They were too young and innocent to become puffed up at Mr. Right's last sentence, but they did catch at his words. Trey spoke in respectful tones, looking down at his foot as he traced the boards with his bare toe, "Excuse me. Umm… Well, if you want to go to Heaven, being good's not the way."

"Oh, yes. I remember you told me that before," Martha was still in a sour mood from the argument.

"Oh!" Sorryl exclaimed, spontaneously he threw his arms around Martha Geller's stubborn neck, "I want to see you in Heaven too!" he finished almost despairingly. "Won't you take Jesus' gift?" he pleaded with tears trembling in his gentle eyes.

"What's this about a gift?" Mr. Right asked curiously.

"Oh! You don't know either?" Trey asked concernedly. "Boy, it seems like nobody told anybody here," he added as if he felt someone had done the entire town an extreme injustice.

Mr. Right nearly smiled at the boy's tones, but asked eagerly, "Well, what is it?"

Trey answered in wondering tones, realizing Mr. Right truly didn't know, "It's the gift. Jesus died for our sins and rose again and now He's alive. And the only way to Heaven is to take the gift, Jesus dying in your place for your sins. Because the payment for sins is death, being separated from God forever. But Jesus died so we could go and live with God and not have to live with Satan when we died. And now He is giving his gift to everybody who will take it. Then, when you take it, the reason you are good is because you love Him, not in order to get to Heaven."

"That sounds… amazing!" Mr. Right responded wonderingly.

Martha spoke up in her curt way, "So is this what you Trestles have that we don't that makes you so… full of bubbly… joy?" she faltered, searching for the best word.

A bit confused, Trey stammered, "I-I guess so. We have Jesus living inside of us, because that's what He does once you accept His gift and tell Him you want to belong to Him. It's really great to belong to somebody who can take care of you so well and loves you so much. And it's so really neat because He can live inside of everybody at once. Because He is God and God can do anything that's good."

"Well, how do I take the gift and belong to Him and have Him live in me?" Mr. Right asked as if the boy should have told him already.

Still wondering why no one had told these people about Jesus, Trey answered, "Just tell Him you believe what He did for you and let Jesus wash you. And ask Him to come live in you and help you live like He did."

"Well then," Mr. Right said nervously. Clearing his throat, he began with a will, "Uh. God? I don't really know how to talk to You. I thought I did, but now I feel like I don't. In fact, I don't really even know You. But I want to tell you that I believe in You and about Your Son, Jesus, who I've read and heard about so many times. I just didn't get it that that was how I was to get to Heaven, to live with You for eternity. Well, I believe now that Jesus paid for my sins and that it's not my own goodness, but Jesus' goodness that will connect me with You." He took a deep breath, "Thank You for dying in my place. I accept Your gift. I need it so much. I see now that I can never be good enough to stand before Your holiness. I want to know You. I want to be Your possession. It seems like You'll take so much better care of me than even I would. Please, come live in me." The words caught in his throat and he took a deep breath before uttering almost inaudibly, "Amen."

A shining light sprang into his eyes, "Well, I guess He cleaned me and took me as His, because I feel different somehow, like... wonderful!" He threw his arms into the air and turned toward the shining sun. "Oh! Thank You, Jesus! Thank You! Thank You!" he cried. He suddenly felt very light, as if a heavy burden of being perfect because everyone was watching had fallen away. Now he didn't care. He felt God had done the cleaning up and now he just wanted to obey Jesus who cared so much about him!

Trey and Sorryl looked eagerly at Martha Geller, but she showed no signs of wanting to talk to God just then. She wasn't ready to take all this new information in. She looked mildly interested, but rather puzzled at the same time.

"What was your errand?" she asked curtly in order to change the subject.

"Oh!" Trey and Sorryl exclaimed together, suddenly remembering their mission, "We were still looking for Trooper."

"Ah! That dog of yours that always follows you around," Mr. Right said. He somehow felt free, like he wanted to leap and skip and jump... or something... and it revealed itself in his voice.

"Yes. We miss him. He got lost in the storm," Trey explained, though he didn't sound as sad as he had when they first began the search. It somehow seemed impossible to be sad when someone had just become a part of your 'family' and been reunited with God.

"Well, I did see him just before the storm," Mr. Right responded thoughtfully. "He was out back. I was wondering what he could be up to down here since he rarely goes that far without you guys."

"Oh! I wish somebody would find him!" Sorryl exclaimed.

Moved, Martha smiled at the usually quiet boy's feeling exclamation. "I'm glad you're feeling better, we were all worried about you," Martha said, laying a hand on the boy's head.

Sorryl smiled shyly, "Me too. God took care of me like He always does." He added earnestly, "I hope Trooper's not sick like me. We've got to find him soon!"

At that moment, Spencer and Joe appeared, "There you guys are!" Spencer said, hurrying up to his boys. He picked Sorryl up tenderly, "How's my little, lost boy doing?"

"Oh, I feel fine!" Sorryl answered with a little smile, as if to tell his daddy not to worry.

"And so do I," Mr. Right added.

Spencer looked at him curiously, surprised at the light tones in the man's voice. "How so?" he asked.

"Well, these two boys of yours just told me about that wonderful gift of Jesus'. And I talked to God about it… in quite a different manner than I'm used to talking to Him. I usually use a written prayer," he added regretfully. "Well, I feel wonderful! I really do believe Jesus is inside me like they said He would be!"

"Oh, He always keeps His promises," Sorryl assured him.

Mr. Right laughed, truly laughed, for the first time in a long while. He felt free and wonderful. He tried it again and found he liked laughing. It made his heart actually physically feel good!

Spencer was beaming, "That's awesome, Mr. Right!"

Mr. Right smiled, "Yeah, it sure feels awesome anyway!"

After a moment of silence, Trey asked, "Did you find Trooper, Daddy?" He already knew the unwanted answer.

Spencer shook his head, "Not a trace. I think we ought to try the woods again. I know we didn't see him when we were looking for Sorryl, but… that's probably where he is."

"Mr. Right saw him in the back of his property," Trey spoke up, hope etching his tones. "And so did Mrs. Bolton, so he might be back there somewhere."

"I wonder why he was over there. He never goes that far without one of us," Spencer puzzled, scratching his head. Then, with a sigh, Spencer patted Sorryl's leg, "Well, I suppose we better get going. Oh. This is Joe Reaper from New York. He's thinking on moving out here with us. And this is Martha Geller and Ray Right," Spencer said.

"Yes, I met Mrs. Geller yesterday. Pleased to meet you, Mr. Right," Joe greeted as they shook hands.

"Well, now I guess we really had better get a move on. Time is crucial I think. Do you mind if we go through your back yard?" Spencer asked Mr. Right.

"Not at all, you go right ahead," Mr. Right permitted warmly.

So Spencer led the way through Mr. Right's back yard and into the thick wood behind his house.

It was rather dark under the dense roof of leaves, and it took a moment for their eyes to adjust, but they were soon hurrying through the trees.

The four had been tramping around, fruitlessly calling for Trooper for nearly two hours. They were about to give up when Trey suddenly stopped, "Listen! Did you hear that?"

Everyone paused a moment as they strained their ears. Then they heard it, too, a quiet whimper off to their left.

"Trooper!" Trey called out, hope beating within his chest right alongside fear that it was some wild animal that would attack him.

As the searchers listened again, it sounded as if the whimpering grew more anxious.

Slowly, cautiously, the foursome crept toward the sound, hoping it was their Trooper and not some other animal.

Suddenly, they caught sight of the dog slowly limping towards them. With painful lumps in their throats, they held back tears –

they nearly didn't recognize him. His fur was matted, his left front leg was wounded and appeared to have been bleeding, and the poor animal looked quite weak.

With a joyous whoop, half smothered in tears, Trey and Sorryl ran to meet their loyal friend. They threw their arms about his neck. "Trooper!" they exclaimed, relieved to have at least found him.

Trooper licked the boys' faces eagerly, but he seemed antsy and soon turned around, limping back the way he had come.

Trey and Sorryl looked at him, confused. "Trooper! That's not the way home. Come this way," they pleaded.

"The poor guy, he's so worn out he doesn't know what he's doing," Spencer said sympathetically. He knelt down to coax Trooper back to them.

But Trooper only looked over his shoulder at the little group. He refused to budge a step in their direction.

"Come on, Trooper! Let's go home!" the boys called anxiously.

Finally, Joe suggested quietly, "Maybe he wants to show us something. Suppose we follow him for a bit and humor the fellow."

Spencer raised his eyebrows, "I hadn't thought of that." It seemed impossible, but he shrugged and started cautiously toward Trooper with the rest close behind him. As soon as they took a step toward the dog, Trooper began limping away again. Slowly, they followed him, wondering where he was going and whether he was trying to get away from them or actually was leading them somewhere.

Finally, Trooper paused, sniffing something on the ground.

The little group strained their eyes, trying to see what it was.

He put his head down and sniffed it as if making sure it hadn't been harmed, then he lay down next to it and dropped his head wearily.

They looked at each other, then cautiously approached Trooper and the object he seemed to be trying to protect. When they reached him, they hesitantly peered around Trooper to see what sort of disgusting 'treasure' the dog could have discovered.

With an exclamation of surprise, they turned to stare at each other with wide eyes.

Spencer was the first to find his voice, "Why! It's a baby!"

The boys knelt down next to it, gently wiping dirt off the child's tear-streaked face.

Sorryl looked up at his daddy, "She must be a girl, see her dress? And she has pretty curls the color of mine," he added.

The girl looked up at them with terrified, though curious, eyes. A tear traced its way down her cheek.

With his heart pulsing in compassion, Spencer gently scooped her up while Trooper anxiously watched. As soon as Spencer had the girl safely in his arms, Trooper laid his head down again, seeming to feel he had completed his mission. The loyal dog had had a very weary night watching over the little one.

The child had no blanket or coat on, just a ragged short sleeve dress with pink rosebuds on it. As Spencer hugged her close to help warm her up, her shivers of fear gradually ceased. The weary little girl warily stared around at the four strangers.

Spencer suddenly realized his shirt was growing damp from the soaked girl. He gazed into her searching eyes. She looked so hungry. His heart gave a sob.

"We better get her into someplace warmer and change her clothes. We can bring her home with us," Spencer said decidedly, turning to walk home.

"What about Trooper?" Sorryl worried, looking back at the dog. Trooper hadn't moved.

"Trooper! We're going home now!" Trey called coaxingly.

But the loyal dog only lifted his head for a moment, then let it flop wearily back on the ground as if to say, "Go on, I'll come home later."

"Poor Trooper, he's too tired," Sorryl said.

Unwilling to leave the girl's protector behind, he went back to the dog's side to stroke his soaked head.

Joe turned back to the dog, "Maybe I can carry him. He's big, but I think I can manage. Come along Trooper," he soothed as he scooped the injured dog into his arms.

About an hour later, the tired but triumphant group emerged from the woods. They made their way to the road and continued on to their home.

As the search party passed Martha's house, she was pleased to see that they had Trooper with them, though he didn't look very well. She gave a start as she noticed the little bundle Spencer was carrying so tenderly. In the typical nosey curiosity of the town, she called out, "What have you got there?"

"Trooper. And a little girl," Trey answered solemnly, as if people found lost babies and took them home every day.

"I think Trooper saved her," Sorryl added proudly, stopping in the road. "He wouldn't let us leave without her."

Shocked almost into silence, Martha wondered incredulously, "Where on earth did you find her?"

"About an hour's walk into the woods," Spencer answered.

"What are you going to do with it? It could have a disease you know," Martha queried in a disgruntled manner as if afraid she would contract a disease from the child by merely looking at her. "We wouldn't want the town to get it."

"I think she's okay. And even if she isn't, she deserves a chance," Spencer answered quietly but firmly.

The boys looked from their daddy to Martha, wondering why Martha seemed so worried and didn't appear to be excited about the little treasure they had discovered.

"She might be an orphan like us, only now we're not orphans, 'cause Daddy made us his. And Mommy did too," Sorryl spoke up compassionately.

Martha hardly seemed to notice Sorryl's remark, "So what do you plan to do with it?"

"We're gonna ask if she belongs to anyone, and if she doesn't, we're gonna keep her. Then we will have a little sister!" Trey answered excitedly.

Martha's eyes grew wide in astonishment. She nearly fell off her bench. "*Keep* it?" she exclaimed as if the little girl were an animal. Horrified, she looked at Spencer to see if Trey was telling the truth.

"Of course," Spencer answered.

Martha just stared at him, not knowing what to say and thinking to herself, *What a strange set of people these are!*

After a moment of silence, Spencer said, "Well, we better be getting her home, we'll see you later!"

Martha absently waved, and the foursome continued their journey home, leaving the bewildered quilter staring after them. "They can't keep that here," she huffed to herself. "Who knows where it came from, or what disease it's carrying. It will just destroy our town," she grumbled. "I imagine they'll change their mind after they've had it for a couple days. They'll see how much work a baby is. After all, none of them have had one before. Not even Spencer, he got his boys after they were older." She gave a satisfied nod and returned to her quilting.

Chapter 21

When they arrived at the house, they carefully gave the small girl a bath. After she was cleaned up, they gave Trooper a warm bath too, and then they gently bandaged his injured leg. Afterwards, they created a soft bed for the little girl out of a box and some sheets and laid her near the stove. Then they put some blankets on the floor next to the stove for Trooper and laid the dog there.

When the two were quietly sleeping, Spencer asked Joe, "How old do you suppose she is?"

"Oh, I was thinking somewhere around a year old," he answered, thoughtfully rubbing his chin. "Maybe a little younger."

"That's what I was thinking," Spencer agreed. After a pensive silence he spoke again, "I wonder if we'll find anyone she belongs to. It seems kind of strange to find her there in the middle of the forest. Who can we ask anyway?"

"Well, people abandoned their babies in the streets back in New York City, they must do it here too, and I rather suspect that's what happened," Joe answered sadly.

"But, why?" Spencer asked incredulously.

Shaking his head mournfully, Joe responded, "I don't know. I really don't know. Perhaps their hearts had gotten hurt and hard like mine. Or they were desperate."

After a short pause, Spencer spoke again, "How can we spread word that she's found though?"

"Well, we can file a found person report at the police station. And we can travel to the next town and ask. That's probably where she came from," Joe answered.

"That sounds like a good idea. Do you think you could go place a found person report while I watch the children?" Spencer queried. He wanted to act as quickly as possible. Someone must be deathly worried about their little girl.

"Sure, I'll head out right now. The sooner we get word out the better. I could call, but I wanted to talk to them about a job anyway, and I'd rather do it in person," Joe said, reaching for his hat. "I have a feeling this whole town knows about her already. News travels fast around here," he added with a half-chuckle.

Spencer laughed. "You're probably right. Well, see you when you get back," he said as Joe started on his way out the door.

"Yup. Have fun," Joe chuckled, indicating the two sleepers.

After Joe left, Trey mused, "I wonder what her name is. I don't think she can tell it to us."

Spencer laughed, "Well, hopefully we find her folks. They'll know her name."

"Daddy," Sorryl spoke up, his eyebrows knit together worriedly, "Before you wrapped her in the blanket, I saw her foot. Why was it all crooked?"

"Crooked?" Spencer asked, suddenly a bit alarmed. "I didn't see that it was crooked. It was probably just turned funny or something."

But Sorryl was sure. "No, it was crooked, and she couldn't move it very well," he persisted.

Giving his concerned son a curious glance, Spencer rose and went to the baby's box. He gently lifted the blanket so he could see her foot. Scratching his head, he muttered to himself, "I'll be. I wonder why I didn't notice that."

"Is it crooked, Daddy?" Trey asked, coming over to him and peeking in the box.

Spencer was quiet a moment, he had more on his hands than he had thought. Finally, he answered slowly, "Yes. It seems so."

Trey's tender heart went out to the tiny girl, "Oh! Poor little girl! Is it broken?"

"I don't know, Trey. I guess we'll have to check it out when she wakes up. I don't want to disturb her now," Spencer answered worriedly.

By now, all three Trestles were crowded around the small girl's little box, peering anxiously down at her.

Sorryl broke the silence, "Dear Jesus, please help the little girl's foot. And help her not to hurt too badly. And if she doesn't know You, help her to soon! Amen."

Spencer reached down and tenderly ruffled Sorryl's hair. "Amen," he echoed softly.

Trey added, "And please help Trooper, too, Lord."

A little while later, Joe returned, "I placed the report." Suddenly, he noticed Spencer's sober face, "What's the matter?" he asked worriedly. "Is she okay?"

"Yeah, she's fine... mostly anyway. She's been sleeping this whole time. But we just discovered something. Come here a minute and tell me what you think," Spencer said, leading Joe to the baby's box and pulling the cover back. "See her foot?"

Joe peered at the tiny foot for a moment. "It's crooked! When did you notice that?" he asked in surprise.

"Sorryl asked me why it was crooked just after you left. When I pulled back the blanket to see what he was talking about, I realized he was right. I couldn't believe I hadn't noticed it before," Spencer answered.

"What are we going to do? Do you think it's broken?" Joe asked.

"I don't know. We should have Dr. Chense take a look at it when she wakes up, don't you think so?" Spencer said, sounding like a worried father.

"Yeah, I think we better," Joe answered.

Worried at the mention that the doctor would have to see her Sorryl asked anxiously, "Is she hurt? Will she die?"

"No, I think she's okay. We just need to check her foot out and see what the matter is," Spencer said. At least, he hoped it would be that simple.

The girl stretched her arms and yawned, then opened her eyes and stared at the people in the room. She studied them as they talked.

Spencer returned her gaze and slowly reached out to touch her small fingers, "Well, I suppose we may as well go now since she's awake."

"Can we come too?" the boys asked eagerly.

"Of course you can," Spencer answered, fondly ruffling their hair.

Trey and Sorryl raced to the car and Spencer followed with the small girl. He carefully settled her between Trey and Sorryl in the back seat and Joe got in the front seat beside Spencer.

When they arrived at the doctor's they anxiously approached his front door and knocked, then waited breathlessly.

This is silly, Spencer reproved himself. *It's not like she's dying or something. Why am I so worried? She isn't even mine.*

Finally, the doctor opened the door.

"Well, who do we have here?" he exclaimed as he peered out his door. Then he caught sight of the little girl Spencer held tenderly, "Ah. I'd heard you had found a baby girl, but I didn't believe a word of it."

Joe gave Spencer a knowing look, "I told you everyone would know," he laughed quietly.

Spencer chuckled and nodded, trying to shake off his nervousness.

"Well, come in. What can I do for you?" Doctor Chense asked curiously, ushering them inside.

"We discovered something wrong with her foot and wondered if you would check it out," Spencer explained.

"Well, let me see here," Doctor Chense said. He gently took the tiny foot in his large hand and carefully examined it. His fingers probed the bones in her ankle, then he gently bent her foot from side to side and up and down. After a moment, he looked up, "It looks like it was broken a while ago and wasn't taken care of properly so it mended crooked." He shook his head, "It's a shame. If it doesn't get fixed it will probably cause her some pain the rest of her life, and she'll probably never walk properly. Or at least not run. A shame. Pretty little girl too."

Spencer turned to Joe and said almost indignantly, "Maybe that's why she was in the woods out there. Maybe her family didn't want to deal with a crippled girl so they abandoned her."

"It could be fixed, but it would cost quite a bit of money," Dr. Chense spoke up.

"How much?" Spencer asked.

"I don't know exactly, probably a few thousand. She would have to be sent to a special doctor. They would have to break it and then set it properly."

Spencer looked down and swallowed. He didn't have near that much money. He'd be lucky if he could come up with even a hundred dollars.

But Trey and Sorryl weren't bogged down with discouraging facts.

"Then let's fix her!" Sorryl exclaimed excitedly, bouncing on his chair in his enthusiasm.

"We don't have enough money to do it, honey," Spencer answered sadly.

"Well then," Sorryl said after thinking a moment, "I bet the town has enough, we could ask them to help!"

"Oh, yeah! And then she can walk and run with us!" Trey agreed delightedly.

A light came slowly into Spencer's eyes. "That just might work," he answered.

Joe nodded.

"But first we have to figure out if she has someone who wants her back," Spencer reminded.

"Oh, yeah," the boys remembered, disappointed.

Doctor Chense just shook his head. He didn't think anyone would want to help a crippled girl who was right in their own town. They would consider her dirty and ungrateful, no matter how young she was. They'd rather give to some far-off child in a foreign country. Such an act would receive more credit from their neighbors than helping some wretch that happened upon their own town, who would most likely plague them with her unwanted presence for the rest of her invalid life if they did help her.

The next day, Spencer went back to work and reluctantly left the little girl home with Joe. Soon he'd have to find something else to do with her though, because Joe had gotten a job at the police station, if it could be called that. The almost insignificant establishment boasted one officer and a little building in the middle of town. Joe's job would be to take care of paperwork and phone calls. He wasn't trusted enough to be made an officer yet. He began that job the day after next and Spencer would have to find something else to do with the little girl by then.

Trey and Sorryl made a fuss as Daddy took firm hold of their hands and led them from the house and the presence of the little girl. "You have to go to school, boys."

"But, Daddy, don't you need someone to watch the little girl while you work?" Sorryl coaxed with a frown hovering behind his pleading eyes.

Spencer sighed, "Joe's doing that."

Trey added his reasoning, "How are we supposed to think about school when you're having all the fun at the shop and with the little girl?"

Spencer shook his head, "I'm sorry, boys, but I really think you need to get back to school before you get too far behind."

Scowling, Trey and Sorryl followed him to the shop and veered off for the schoolhouse. It was tempting to turn back for the house and tell Joe school wasn't in session that day. But, in spite of their bad mood, the boys didn't want to disappoint their daddy. One thought of how his discouraged and hurt eyes would gaze sadly into their own made the reluctant scholars resolutely set their faces toward the school. By the time they reached it, the beautiful day had brightened their spirits some. Besides, it wasn't any fun to sit there and pout when no one was there to see it and feel bad for you. And it made them feel so much more terrible when they pouted anyway.

That day at work, Spencer was questioned numerous times about the little girl they had. People wanted to know if it was true that they were going to keep her and were awed to find that the answer was 'yes' as long as they didn't find her family, especially since many now knew the little girl was crippled.

Near the end of the day, Spencer approached Charlie almost fearfully. He cleared his throat nervously.

"Yes, Spencer? Ask away," Charlie said cheerfully, glancing up from organizing his candy shelf.

"Well, today I left the girl we found home with Joe. But, as you know, he starts his job the day after tomorrow, so he can't watch her after that. I was wondering, would you mind if I brought her here with me? It would probably be a nuisance for you. I could find something else to do with her..."

Charlie laughed, "Don't look so worried, Spence! I'd love to have her here!" He turned a beaming face toward Spencer, "You don't know how much I miss the kids all tumbling into my store begging for candy." He paused with another laugh, "It might sound crazy, but I even miss the babies crying while their mothers shop. It seems like this dreary town has a severe shortage of babies."

"Are you sure?" Spencer said, surprised at Charlie's response.

"We can try it, but I'm fairly certain it will be just fine," Charlie chuckled. He knew Spencer would have a hard time finding anyone who would take care of her anyway. All the ladies were appalled to hear that she had a lame foot and they were worried about diseases too, despite the fact that Dr. Chense had declared her perfectly healthy other than her poor foot and being rather deprived of food and water.

When the boys and Spencer arrived home, they eagerly dashed through the door and over to the girl, who was sitting on the floor playing with some blocks.

Trey and Sorryl immediately joined her, making funny faces and knocking the piles over just to hear the giggles their antics drew from her. She didn't seem afraid of them at all. In fact, she appeared to be a mite fond of them. But when Spencer or Joe would approach her, she would sometimes shrink back and a terrified look would come into her eyes. But as soon as they spoke or gently stroked her hair she would smile and hold out her arms. They guessed from this reaction that she must have had a bad experience with a man, wherever she came from.

"What should your name be?" Trey asked her, fondly pulling one of her curls.

She just giggled and tugged on one of her chestnut curls too.

"She's the best and prettiest one, isn't she Daddy?" Sorryl asked with a fond sparkle in his eyes.

Spencer laughed, "Well, I sure think so."

"We need a name quick! We've got to call her something," Trey said.

"I think we better wait and see if we find who she belongs to before we go about naming her," Spencer advised. He didn't want Trey and Sorryl to get too attached to her.

Trey and Sorryl reluctantly relented, but not one of them could help subconsciously trying to find a name for the adorable treasure they believed God had led them to through Trooper.

In the evenings after work, they would all pile into the car and travel to one of the nearby towns to find out whether the lost little girl belonged to them or if they knew who she was. Each time the townspeople declared they didn't even recognize her, the Trestles sighed in relief even as sadness crept into their hearts. The little girl must be missing her real family, and they couldn't seem to find them, whoever they were.

Two mornings later, Spencer had to take the girl to work with him. As soon as he walked through the door, Charlie began hovering over her and making cooing sounds and funny faces, laughing every time she giggled, which was nearly all the time.

A few minutes after Spencer arrived at the store, Jerry popped his head through the door, "Hey, I've been so busy with the pizza shop lately – you know, painting it and all – that I haven't had time to say hello! And I just had to see this little girl of yours!" He entered the store and surveyed the girl Spencer still held in his arms. "Oh! She's adorable! I wish I had found her. But then, I wouldn't want to have to take care of her, so it's just as well you're the one that found her. That way I can just visit her."

Spencer laughed, "I'm glad you like her. Seems Charlie and yourself are the only ones who even want to be within a yard of her."

"Aww. No one likes you?" Jerry said to the girl, tickling her toes. She giggled, drawing a laugh from Jerry.

At that moment, Starlight and her mother entered the store and Jerry immediately resumed his nonchalance, saying, "I guess I better be off to my shop now." He gave the little girl a last gentle pat before he departed.

"Oh! Is this the girl you found?" Starlight asked excitedly, approaching the trio.

"Yup," Spencer answered, gently bouncing her in his arms.

"Starlight!" her mother's reproving voice rang sharply, "Do you want to get us sick?"

Starlight laughed softly, "She won't get us sick. Even Doctor Chense said she was fine." She reached out and traced one of the little girl's delicate fingers, "She's lovely. Look at her dimples!"

Spencer nodded. He had noticed her dimples, too. They had made him think of Annaleah, who had had one in her left cheek just like Sorryl did.

"Starlight!" her mother said more severely.

Starlight turned from the little girl. "I'm sorry Mother. But she won't get us sick, I promise," she said.

"Well, even if she won't, why would you want to be associated with a lame child?" her mother huffed.

"I don't mind, there's nothing wrong with a lame person," Starlight said.

"Humph," Emma countered with a toss of her head as she began her shopping.

With a sigh, Starlight followed her mother.

Coming over to Spencer, Charlie offered, "Here, I'll take her so you can stack those bags that came in yesterday."

Spencer laughed. "You're pretty fond of her, aren't you?" he teased.

"Well..." Charlie hesitated. Then he admitted, "Yeah. But I'm glad I'm not the one that has to figure out how to take care of her."

Spencer laughed, "Oh, it's not hard. Besides, I've got two boys who have plenty of suggestions..." His voice took on a regretful tone, "Although none of the ladies here seem to want to give me any tips."

With a slight bob of his head as if in sympathy, Charlie held out his arms and Spencer reluctantly handed his bundle over.

When school was over, Trey and Sorryl raced to the shop, "Hi, Daddy!"

"Hi, little-girl-that-we-can't-name!" Sorryl added, giving her a kiss on the cheek.

She giggled and Trey gave her a kiss too, bringing another giggle from her.

"Can we watch her now?" Trey asked eagerly. "We can teach her to play checkers."

"I guess this means the end of my babysitting job," Charlie mourned as he reluctantly handed her over. He had managed to get Spencer to let him hold her quite frequently throughout the day.

The boys laughed and swept their treasure away to the checkerboard.

"Be careful she doesn't fall off the bench," Spencer called after them.

"We're putting her in the chair," Sorryl assured him as if that would ensure her safety.

For one long month the girl's caretakers waited anxiously for an answer to their found person report. They visited nearby towns in an effort to find her family while they waited. To their relief, no one would claim her.

Each time the now unwelcome telephone rang at the Trestle abode, they all waited anxiously as Spencer answered it, worrying that someone had called to claim the little girl they had all come to love.

One Saturday morning, the small group started off for the last town they were going to check. Joe had told the Trestles the evening before when he returned from work that the law had determined the Trestles could pretty much assume the girl was theirs since no one had replied to their lost person report and no office had received a report of a missing child fitting her description. But Spencer insisted they try this one last town, just in case her family was there, longing for her.

As they drove through the "Town of Glooms", as Sorryl had dubbed Los Ciegos, it seemed everyone had found some excuse to be outside to witness their departure.

Emma turned to Starlight as the Trestle vehicle drove by, "I sure hope they find that girl's family. We don't want her living here."

"But mother, she's such a dear! I was rather hoping she would be ours to keep. Or rather, theirs to keep," she corrected herself with a smile as she realized she was thinking of the enchanting girl as belonging to the entire town.

Emma just shook her head and returned to her weeding.

A little while later, the search party left the last town they were going to search.

"Then she's ours!" Trey and Sorryl exclaimed excitedly as they drew away from the town. With a simultaneous, "Woohoo!" the boys skipped down the road to the car they had left a little way outside the town they had visited. Soon, they came racing back to rejoin Spencer, Joe, and the little girl. They chattered to the girl as they walked along, "You're really in our family now! We get to keep you for ever and ever!" She cooed at them and clapped her hands.

As they drove through Los Ciegos on the way home, many prying eyes tried to peer through the car windows to see if the baby's home had been found. But they couldn't tell whether the car still held the lost girl or not and they gazed curiously after the vehicle as it made its way to the Trestle home.

Meanwhile, inside the car, the boys were singing and playing with the little girl, happily oblivious of the peering eyes.

Sorryl suddenly said, "We have to name her now. We can't just keep calling her 'little girl'."

"Yes, what should we name her?" Spencer asked thoughtfully, excited to finally be able to christen the little girl.

A deep silence settled over the car. In spite of their constant subconscious search for a good name, not one of them had yet found one they deemed 'perfect'.

"Hey!" Sorryl suddenly exclaimed, "How 'bout we name her Treasure. We found her kind of like a treasure and she's so sparkly and it sounds perfect!"

The little girl clapped her hands and her dimples flashed as she laughed.

The rest of the occupants of the car were silent as they repeated the name to themselves, looking at the little girl.

After a moment, Spencer said, "That sounds like a good name! She's our little Treasure!"

Trey nodded enthusiastically and gently tugged one of her curls as he tried the name out, "Hey, Treasure, do you like your new name?"

She bounced and laughed, answering in her baby voice, "Yeah, yeah, yeah!" although she really had no idea what Trey had asked her.

That settled it.

When they arrived home, they piled out of the car.

Trey carried Treasure into the house, "Now that we know you're ours, we can try to get some money to help your foot!" he told her excitedly.

Treasure cooed at him and giggled. She was happy enough now, but sometimes her foot started aching really bad and she would cry or whimper for hours. Then they would try everything they could think of to help her feel better, but to little avail.

"We can put our notice up in Mr. Charlie's store now!" Sorryl said eagerly. In their excitement, they had created a sign asking for help for Treasure's foot even before they knew they were able to keep her.

Trey ran to retrieve the sign. "Okay! Let's go!" he urged in his impulsive way, sliding his shoes back on.

The shrill ringing of the telephone stopped him in his tracks.

Spencer answered it and Joe watched as the man's face grew paler and paler, until it seemed to have no color left to it. By the time he dropped the phone onto its hook, every eye, even Treasure's, were trained on him.

Chapter 22

With a shaky breath, Spencer sank into a nearby chair and looked around the room. How could he tell them? Was there any way to break this crushing news without suffocating the hearts represented here? Breathing a prayer for comfort and strength, Spencer quietly murmured, "That was the Dallas police station."

Joe's face suddenly went pale and Trey and Sorryl's eyes grew round and worried.

With another deep breath Spencer continued, "He said a couple contacted them saying they were missing a little girl of much the same description as—" his voice broke, "Treasure. They're on their way to our house now to see if she belongs to them."

The room was filled with an agonized silence for a moment, then Sorryl rose and went to Treasure, who had crawled into Spencer's lap and nestled in his arms, somehow feeling something was amiss and that she was in danger. Sorryl leaned his head on his daddy's shoulder as a silent tear shimmered down his sun-tanned cheek. Then he sighed and suggested bravely, "Maybe we should put on her best dress and comb her curls. Then if she *is* theirs they'll be so happy to see how beautiful she is."

Spencer smiled shakily and ruffled Treasure's curls, "That's a good idea, Sorryl."

When a hesitant knock sounded at the Trestle door a while later, they were all seated in the living room, trying not to be nervous. All eyes turned to the door when they heard the knock.

Spencer rose and set Treasure with Trey and Sorryl, who were seated on the floor. Then he went to answer the door.

What met Spencer's gaze on the other side of the door were a very tearful young woman and a worn-faced young man. The man had his arm wrapped comfortingly about the lady's shoulders, for she was just that, a lady, in spite of her poor clothes and tear-streaked face.

Spencer lost his voice for a moment at the touching scene before him. But he soon recovered it and heard his own, deep voice greet warmly, "Come in. Come in."

Trey and Sorryl were now standing. Trey held Treasure in his arms while Sorryl rested a protective hand on her shoulder.

The young lady turned longing eyes toward the beautiful little girl. The color drained completely from her features, and then slowly returned to her lovely face. The man's features went through much the same process while Trey and Sorryl gazed up at them with fearful, but sympathetic eyes. These people looked so sad.

When the couple said nothing, Sorryl ventured timidly, tears trembling on his dark lashes, "I-is she your Treasure?"

Unable to speak, the lady turned pleading eyes to her husband.

He said nothing for a moment. Finally, he swallowed hard and answered with a trembling smile, "I feel you will all be relieved when I say, 'No, she isn't.' But she appears to be very much *your* Treasure."

A glad light leapt into the Trestle's eyes at the same time a sad look brought tears to them.

The lady blinked rapidly and the man tenderly patted her shoulders.

Spencer broke the silence, holding his hand out congenially, "My name's Spencer Trestle. This is Joe Reaper, a friend of ours, Trey, and Sorryl, and of course, Treasure."

With a brave tilt of his head, the young man accepted the hand warmly, "I'm Cameron Westgate, and this is my wife, Lily."

The young lady nodded and dried her eyes, lifting her trembling chin a trifle.

251

Spencer motioned to Joe who disappeared to the kitchen for some teacups and to put on the kettle, "Why don't you sit down a moment. I'm sure you've had a long journey."

Seeming relieved to be able to sit down and recover, Cameron and Lily tried to smile their gratefulness.

Trey and Sorryl ventured over to the couple and leaned confidingly on their knees in their trusting way as they told the story of finding Treasure. They proceeded to tell of the time Spencer had fallen into the Bolton's pond, and then about their 'split' pizza. Before long, Cameron and Lily had heard about nearly all of the children's favorite townspeople, though, if they chanced to meet them when the Trestles weren't around, the couple would have had a hard time knowing how they came to be described in such a manner.

Realizing they were grateful for the children's enlivening talk, Spencer let the boys be, smiling warmly into Cameron and Lily's eyes as he poured their tea.

"We had a Mommy once. Actually, we had two Mommies," Sorryl was saying. A longing look welled in his frank eyes. "Our Mommy that adopted us was a lot like you. Only she was a little different."

Lily returned his tremulous smile and he continued.

"When she…" his voice faltered, "When she died and didn't come back anymore, we moved here. But I like you, 'cause you're sweet like my mommy, even when you're so sad."

Impulsively, Lily reached down and hugged the little boys.

A grateful light crept into Cameron's eyes when he saw her long lost smile.

By this time, Spencer and Joe had taken a seat at the table, too. Now Cameron turned his gaze toward them as Treasure climbed into Spencer's welcoming embrace, "We're very grateful you let us come and see this girl you so obviously love."

Spencer smiled softly, "We were pretty scared. But that love made us want her to have her family if she could." Then he added warmly, "We'd love to hear your story if you want to share it."

With a questioning look to his wife, who gave him a gentle nod, Cameron answered, "You know, we haven't really told our story to many people, other than those it was necessary to share it with to find our daughter." Tears came to his eyes then, "But none of them really cared. I think you do, though, and we'd like to tell you our story."

Lily nodded in agreement as tears sprang to her eyes again.

"One night, about a month ago, Lily was walking with our—" Cameron's voice quivered, but he continued with a swallow, "Our little Wynne in her arms when a rough looking man bumped into her. The next thing she knew, he had snatched Wynne from her arms. We've been searching for her ever since, finding only that the ruthless man had tried to sell her numerous times before disappearing completely. When we heard your report, we were almost afraid to hope," Cameron looked down sadly, "I'm glad we didn't have to take your Treasure away, though."

Spencer didn't know what to say, so he just sat silently praying for these hurting people.

Cameron sighed and stretched, "We better get going. We've got three hours of travel ahead of us and it's getting late."

Spencer tried to convince them to stay, but the couple sorrowfully refused. If Cameron didn't get back in time, he could lose his job. So, with sad farewells and promises to see each other again sometime, they parted ways, somehow feeling their hearts had received something beautiful in that short hour.

When the door was shut, Trey lost no time in saying, "Well, she really *is* ours still! Let's go put up the sign!" He was already back to pulling on his shoes.

"Hold your horses!" Spencer laughed. "We should eat supper first. I'm starved. And I'm sure Treasure must be, too," he added, brushing her cheek with his finger.

Trey reluctantly removed his shoes again, "Okay. But let's hurry!"

Joe was quiet a moment, stroking his chin. Finally, he said, "I have an idea!"

The boys eagerly looked up at him, "What? What's your idea?" They were clinging to his arms now.

Joe laughed, and started warningly, "Only if it's okay with your father." He paused dramatically. Everyone's eyes were riveted to him.

"We could go to Jerry's and get some pizza, my treat," he finished persuasively, with an impish grin Spencer's way.

"Oh! Yes!" Trey and Sorryl agreed excitedly, jumping up and down. "That'll be perfect!"

Little Treasure squealed and clapped her hands energetically, not really knowing what the excitement was about, but sure that if Trey and Sorryl thought it was good, it must be.

Spencer laughed softly and ran his hand through his hair, "Okay, Okay. You've got me convinced. Let's go."

At these longed for words, the boys skidded across the room and threw on their shoes again. As soon as that was accomplished, they each grabbed one of Treasure's shoes and gently put them on her tiny feet. By the time they succeeded, Spencer and Joe were ready as well.

"Let's go!" Spencer said, leading the way out the door. "We should probably drive."

With a whoop, Trey and Sorryl dashed to the car, more than ready to be on their way.

After making sure everyone was safely in, Spencer started down the driveway.

They had gotten nearly to the end when Trey suddenly shouted, "Stop, Daddy!"

Spencer slammed on the brake with a fast-beating heart. "What?" he asked, scanning the driveway in front of him for something he would have run over.

"We forgot our sign!"

With a relieved laugh, Spencer relaxed in his seat, "Oh, was that all?"

But Trey was already half-way back down the driveway. A few moments later, the little tornado came whirling back, nearly out of breath, "There we go. Now, let's hurry!"

And they were on their way once more.

As the celebrating group drove up to the pizza shop, curious townspeople peered at their vehicle wondering why the unpredictable Trestles were back so soon and what had come of the strange visitors everyone knew had visited their home. The citizens eagerly watched as the occupants of the Trestle vehicle excitedly piled out. When Spencer came around to the side and lovingly drew the little girl from the back seat, kissing her before he settled her safely in his arms, the townspeople gasped. So, she was here to stay. They watched, stunned, as the five happy travelers traipsed into the pizza shop.

Jerry welcomed them heartily, "Well! So does this mean the little girl is ours to keep?" he asked happily, oblivious of his possessive statement of 'ours'.

"Yup! She's all ours!" Trey answered proudly.

"I guess this calls for a celebration. Pizza's on me!" Jerry said.

Joe stepped forward with a smile, "I'm afraid I already claimed that privilege."

With a dismissing laugh, Jerry rebutted, "Well, you can't very well pay if I don't charge you!"

Spencer looked at Joe, then back at Jerry, "Well, I suppose not if you're in earnest."

Jerry chuckled again, "Of course I'm in earnest!"

Spencer grinned at Joe, "Sorry, Joe, looks like you're beat this time."

Joe smiled back, his eyes sparkling, "*This* time."

Jerry winked at Joe, then said, "Now, choose any spot you want, no one else is here." With a sparkle in his eye he chuckled, "I know just what you want to order. Comin' right up!" Then he added in a confidential whisper, "I'll even throw in the cheesy bread sticks you always want but never buy!"

Trey and Sorryl gave an excited whoop.

When Treasure saw Trey and Sorryl's excitement, she squealed and clapped her hands.

Spencer smiled and turned to find a place to sit.

But Trey and Sorryl were ahead of him, "Can we sit right here?" they asked eagerly, racing to their favorite table in the center of the room.

"Well, no one's taken it, so we may as well," Spencer laughed as he gazed about the completely empty pizza shop. "Let's go hang this poster while we're waiting for our food," he suggested.

With a nod in agreement, they all followed him to the door.

It seemed half the town had gathered outside the pizza shop, trying to discover what was going on inside without being conspicuous. Their gaze followed the merry group as they skipped down the road a little ways to Charlie's store where Spencer hung the poster in the window.

After it was securely fastened, the group stepped back to survey their work.

Sorryl's eyes were shining. "Perfect!" he exclaimed.

The others nodded in agreement as they looked at their colorful poster with a touching sketch of Treasure and an exaggerated view of her crooked foot. Then in bold, colorful letters it read, "Help Treasure walk and run like other children. Give today to help pay the doctor for surgery. Special box located inside store for donations."

As soon as they vacated the storefront and disappeared into the pizza shop, townspeople crowded around the sign, wondering what it could mean. They knew of the little girl's foot problem and also the costly remedy, for the doctor had told someone and it had spread like wild fire from there. They couldn't figure out what was meant by 'Treasure', though. The only thing they could think of was that it might be the girl's name. But that couldn't be! Or could it? This was the Trestles they were speaking of. With a shake of their heads, the townspeople tore themselves from the captivating sign. Who would want to help a child who was lame? Maybe if the child were far off in a distant land, but one wouldn't be elevated in peoples' opinions for just giving to help someone in their own town who had a lame foot.

The Trestles and Joe had returned to the pizza shop and been comfortably seated for only a few minutes when Jerry approached them with their pizza.

As they began their meal, the bell above the door tinkled and one of the townspeople walked in. She solemnly ordered a pizza. No sooner had she left the counter and sat down than the bell tinkled again, and then again, and yet another time as the townsfolk filed methodically through the door until the pizza shop was filled to capacity.

The Trestles looked around wonderingly for a moment. They had never seen such a crowd of people in the pizza shop before! But they soon forgot about the stoic occupants as they enjoyed their pizza.

A little while later, Charlie entered the shop. He stopped abruptly when he saw the crowded tables. With a quizzical look at Jerry, he shrugged and confided, "I decided I'd get some pizza today... apparently the rest of the town had the same idea, 'ey?"

Jerry laughed and jabbed a thumb in the Trestle's direction, "That little girl has drawn the crowd, I'm afraid," he chuckled.

Charlie nodded knowingly, "I see. I wonder if the popular Trestles would mind if I joined them."

"I think they'd love to have your company. I wish I could sit down with them and chat, but..." he chuckled once more, indicating his full shop.

"Can you get me a couple slices of pizza?"

Jerry laughed and shook his head, "I'm a little behind on orders. I'm not used to so many at once. But I don't think the Trestles would mind sharing a couple of their weird slices for now."

Charlie laughed as he saw they were eating it in true 'Trestle' style, cheese on one side and sauce on the other.

"Here, maybe you can take them a couple extra napkins," Jerry chuckled, handing Charlie a sizable stack.

Charlie laughed good-humoredly and approached the table that held the famous attraction, "Hey! Mind if I join you?"

"Not a bit! Help yourself," Spencer invited, then added with a laugh, "Jerry's treating us, but I don't think he'd mind if you swiped a few pieces."

"Nope, he told me to steal a few of yours. He's a little behind on orders."

Spencer and Joe looked around the packed pizza shop and smiled.

"So, did you find her a name yet?" Charlie asked.

"Yup. She's called Treasure!" Trey answered, his eyes sparkling.

At this announcement, there was a nearly audible gasp from the townspeople, who were carefully observing the Trestle's table.

Mr. Brendt had arrived just as Trey told Charlie Treasure's name. He looked at the townspeople and guessed the reason everyone had gathered there. With a sniff of disapproval, he turned his back to them and faced Jerry instead.

"I suppose you haven't got any pizza left," he grumped.

Jerry smiled apologetically, "Nope. I'm cleaned out. I've got more baking, though."

"It's a shame to come in here and just watch them. If they want to know what's up, why don't they just ask?" Mr. Brendt muttered, looking at the full tables. "Guess I'll just go home and see if Nancy can cook up anything for me," he finished gloomily. After a hesitant pause, he approached the Trestle's table, "How are you doing?" he asked, looking at Sorryl first.

"Fine, sir!" Sorryl replied happily, gazing up at the man with fond eyes.

"So you're keeping her?" Mr. Brendt addressed Spencer gruffly.

"Yes, we are!" Spencer said, his eyes lighting up.

With a grunt, Mr. Brendt muttered to himself, "I don't know how you ever thought up a name like Treasure." Then, with a shrug, he said, "I better be getting along home now."

Spencer chuckled at the man's blunt manner.

"Bye, Mr. Brendt!" the boys said.

The pious man, who never spoke to anyone lifted his hand in a brief farewell and was gone.

Spencer chuckled again and turned to Joe, "I don't think he knows it, but beneath all that prickle he has a heart softer and sweeter than honey."

Joe laughed softly and nodded in agreement. He could relate. Hadn't he once been gruff and apparently uncaring, yet just dying inside to be able to care?

As soon as they finished their meal, Spencer rose, "Okay boys, we better get home and to bed. You've got school tomorrow."

Trey and Sorryl groaned, "Can't we stay home with Treasure?"

"Nope. You'll see her when you get back. I'll have her with me at Charlie's, same as always."

With a deep sigh Trey and Sorryl relented, "Okay." Then, on impulse, they simultaneously hugged Treasure and exclaimed, "We're gonna miss you!" as if they had to part with her that very moment and might never see her again.

Spencer laughed, "Okay, let's go. Goodnight, Jerry. And thank you!"

"Goodnight!" Jerry called after them as they went out the door.

As they parted ways, Spencer clapped Charlie on the shoulder, "Goodnight, Charlie, see you tomorrow."

"Yup. A good night to you too. Be sure and bring that Treasure tomorrow!" Charlie reminded.

Spencer smiled almost sadly as his charges piled into the car, "I can't forget. I'm the only one to watch her."

One by one the townspeople followed the Trestles out of the pizza shop. On their way home, they unconsciously filed past the colorful sign again. Now they understood about the 'Treasure'. After a short pause in front of the sign, they shook their heads and continued on.

Spencer hadn't seen the 'man' on the mountain for some weeks, but tonight as he tussled with the boys and Treasure on the lawn, he happened to glance up and saw what looked like a man walking along the ridge with a bundle in his arms. Quickly, he wrapped up their game and herded the children inside, making sure he locked the door. At Joe's quizzical look, Spencer just shrugged his shoulders with a weak smile. "Paranoid I guess," he explained sheepishly, heading to his room to get Treasure ready for bed.

When all were tucked in and cozy, Spencer checked the door once more to be sure it was still locked, then he headed for bed.

Joe was going to be staying in town after tomorrow. The Trestles were going to help him move his few possessions tomorrow evening into a house he had found there. Spencer sighed. With Joe and his guns around, he felt a lot safer.

With a soft laugh, Spencer murmured, "I guess I'll just have to trust You to keep my children safe, 'ey, Lord?"

He rolled over and shut his eyes to dream of opening his door only to meet a menacing man who was carrying a huge gun cleverly hidden beneath a blanket.

Chapter 23

The next morning the boys reluctantly started for school. They kept turning back to throw Treasure kisses until they rounded the bend and could no longer see her.

They arrived in the schoolyard just before the bell rang and dashed to their seats. Mr. Grey had ceased trying to stop them from dashing about with energy. Unconsciously, the other students had begun to move about with more purpose and enthusiasm too.

Mr. Grey actually liked the change. The students paid better attention to his teaching now. He didn't realize it, but a touch of interest had crept into his usually bored voice, making it easier for the students to pay attention.

But today, none of the students would even look at Trey or Sorryl. They turned the other way whenever the boys passed them and their seatmates moved as far away from them as possible. Trey and Sorryl wondered at this attitude, but tried to forget about it as lessons began.

At recess, they hurriedly dashed outside, where the animated boys were normally surrounded by eager students waiting for the Trestle boys' next exciting idea. But this time they were immediately deserted. They could see the students walking aimlessly about in pairs in much the same manner as that first morning of school the Trestle's had experienced in Los Ciegos.

Sorryl turned to Trey with a furrowed brow, "What's the matter with everyone?"

Shrugging his shoulders, Trey replied, "I'm not really sure." After a slight pause he finally suggested, "Let's ask."

"Okay."

But both boys stood still, gazing about for a moment.

"Well," Sorryl said pointedly.

Trey shifted nervously. "Okay," he resolved, lifting his chin bravely, "Let's ask Jake." Jake had become a good friend of the boys lately, despite the skepticism of their games he had displayed at first. He had begun to consider the little boys his special charges.

"Okay," Sorryl lamely agreed again.

Taking a deep breath, Trey and Sorryl slowly approached Jake, who was walking about almost dejectedly. When they reached him, Trey took a deep breath and ventured almost pleadingly, "Hey, Jake, what's going on?"

But Jake just pretended he hadn't heard and continued walking.

With a baffled look, the boys finally approached Bill, Trey's seatmate. With another gulp for courage, Trey queried timorously, "Bill, what's up?"

Bill started to ignore the young boy, but seemed to change his mind and turned to sneer, "We shouldn't talk to people who have diseased, crippled little girls for sisters, *especially* when they don't even know where she came from." With that, the ruthless boy turned on his heel and haughtily strolled away with his walking partner, leaving two very stunned boys behind him.

Trey stared at Sorryl with huge eyes and Sorryl returned his shocked gaze. Then, as if having come to a mutual agreement, they both took off after Bill. Hot, unwelcome tears forced their way to their blue eyes as they went. Stubbornly shoving them back, both boys placed themselves in front of Bill and confronted the bully. "She's not diseased, and it's not her fault she's hurt and doesn't know where she came from. She's perfectly lovely!"

"Ha! She's no good! It would have been better if you had never found her. Why don't you give her away so she doesn't plague our town?" Bill returned cruelly.

Trey and Sorryl's faces flushed red with anger.

"She's not a plague!" Trey shouted indignantly.

"She's the best one of us all!" Sorryl added, ending with a choking sound as he held back a sob.

Trey nearly punched Bill, but he remembered just in time that he was behaving rather meanly. Instead, he sharply sucked in his breath. Taking Sorryl's hand, he turned and they ran towards town as tears streamed from their eyes.

Mr. Grey heard a commotion outside and rose from his desk. He reached the window just in time to see Trey and Sorryl disappear out of the schoolyard. He shook his head. It was too late to stop them. Wondering where they were headed, he made a mental note to punish the prodigals when recess was over and they returned. He couldn't account for the strange feeling of reluctance to do so that rose within him. The students knew they weren't allowed to leave the yard during recess. Really, he wondered greatly that the Trestle boys had. He hadn't thought they would ever do such a thing. Little did the man dream of the unfortunate events that had taken place.

Trey and Sorryl dashed brokenly up the road and finally burst into Charlie's store, breathless. Fresh tears traced trails down their now dusty faces as they looked anxiously for their daddy. He would know what to do. But they didn't see him anywhere.

An astonished Charlie approached them, "School let out already?" he asked gently for lack of a better way to begin a conversation. He was almost certain it hadn't.

The boys just shook their heads.

Emma, Starlight's mother, was in the store shopping and looked on curiously with the rest of the customers, who all shook their heads reprovingly as if to say, "I knew that's what would happen to them without a mother." They continued with their shopping, but kept glancing over at Trey and Sorryl.

"Where's Daddy?" Trey asked shakily.

"I'm here," Spencer called, coming out of the back room as he wiped his hands on a rag. He caught the look on his children's faces and hurried over to them. He knelt in front of them. "What's wrong?" he asked, choosing not to mention the fact that they should be in school, at least not until he found out what was troubling them.

"They said Treasure was a plague and that they wanted us to give her away!" Sorryl wailed, burying his head in his daddy's shoulder. Trey followed suit and both boys clung to their daddy's comforting shoulder for a moment.

Spencer was shocked to hear this news. He assumed 'they' meant the schoolchildren, and perhaps Mr. Grey. He had known no one liked little Treasure, but he hadn't realized that was the way they felt. He couldn't understand it. Spencer hugged his boys speechlessly as agony filled his heart.

Brought to an unconscious pause in their shopping by this scene, Emma and the rest of the shoppers gazed at the grieving family. They hadn't thought anyone could possibly love that little girl so much. They simply regarded her just as the boys had said they had been told by the schoolchildren, as a plague. Every one of them sat waiting to find what damage she would bring, never thinking of her as a live being with feelings just as real as theirs. With a shake of the head, they shoved these pricking thoughts aside and resumed their neglected shopping.

At that moment, Starlight pushed through the door, "Mother, I couldn't find..." her voice trailed off as she saw the sad group in the middle of the store. "Why, what's the matter?" she asked, with a curious glance at her mother, who had unsympathetically continued with her shopping.

Trey and Sorryl turned at her voice, "The children at school said Treasure was a plague and that we should get her out of our town. But she's not! She's the best one of us all!" Sorryl finished with a heartbroken sob.

"Oh, honey! It's okay! Don't worry about what they think. You never have before. We know Treasure is a perfectly lovely girl. And a gift from God," she added, embracing the boys and stroking their hair.

"But they don't like her!" Trey mourned.

"That's because they don't know her, honey. You just wait. If they give themselves a chance to look at her for what she really is rather than thinking of her as they do now, they'll see that she's wonderful."

Trey and Sorryl looked up and smiled dimly through their tears, "Really?"

"Of course. And besides, even if they don't, we know she's special to God. He led you to her and kept her alive for a very special reason, don't you think?" she asked.

"Yeah! That's right," the boys agreed, forgetting some of their sorrow.

All the while, Emma was throwing Starlight reproachful glances, but the intended receiver never saw them.

Spencer and Charlie looked at Starlight wonderingly. They hadn't known she thought of God in that light. They assumed she viewed Him as the rest of the town did – keeping a record of her good and bad deeds and ready to pronounce destruction on her if she trespassed.

She noticed their incredulous looks, "What's wrong?" she asked.

Spencer said, "Well, I guess I didn't think you thought of God that way."

She smiled, "I've always thought God was something more than what the people said He was. My father seemed to think so, though he was too shy to say so. And when you guys came, I realized He was, and that you knew so." She paused reflectively for a moment, "But you all still seem to have something I can't quite grasp."

A slow smile spread over Charlie's face, "That's exactly what I felt, and Spencer here told me what it was the other day."

"What?" Starlight asked eagerly.

"Jesus." Spencer answered simply.

By this time, the shoppers were lining up at the counter to check out, so Charlie went to tend to them, but they still heard all Spencer said. Not one of them could make themselves leave without hearing him to the finish.

"Jesus? You can *have* Jesus?" Starlight answered incredulously.

Spencer smiled at her earnestness, "Yes. You can. You know all about Him, don't you?"

"I think so," Starlight answered doubtfully, "I thought I did, but I guess I didn't think you could have Him."

Trey and Sorryl gazed up at her, wondering how so many people could be ignorant of the fact that you could have Jesus.

Spencer smiled, "Well you can. The Bible says that as many as receive Him, to them He gave power to become the sons, or daughters, of God. Isn't that beautiful?" He went on to tell her what he had told Charlie about God's gift.

Starlight was awestruck. She sat in silence with her eyes large in wonder. After a moment she eagerly spoke in prayer, disregarding all the onlookers. She knew her Bible, and confusing passages suddenly began to make sense, "I realize now that I desperately need that gift You have given me that I didn't even realize You were trying to give me. Well, I accept that gift of Your own, precious life," she was nearly whispering now, close to tears. With a hard swallow she continued, "And I really am sorry for assuming I could somehow be good enough without You. Now I'll try to be like You, with your help. Please come live in me. I choose to serve you rather than sin. Please let me *have* You. Oh, Thank you!" she finished rapturously.

Emma looked over at her daughter with a bit of a confused expression, but a trace of longing crept into her countenance too.

Treasure was seated on the floor between them. She began to whimper.

"It must be her foot," Spencer said with a pained expression. He swooped her into his arms and told her gently, "I wish we could make it all better. I really do."

Suddenly remembering their sign requesting help for the little girl, Trey and Sorryl eagerly glanced over at the bucket placed by the counter for donations. Their faces fell. No one had given any money for Treasure's doctor bill.

Starlight spoke in an effort to distract them. Her mother had forbidden her to help, even with the little money she herself had, "Well, I was just on my way to get some pizza, I guess I better go over there before it's too late for lunch." She paused and smiled gratefully, "Thanks, I feel... wonderful!"

Charlie and Spencer smiled, and Spencer answered, "Congratulations! But be thanking Him, not us."

With a beaming smile thrown over her shoulder, she flew off to the pizza shop where a bored Jerry was sitting on the counter. He had had very few customers all day, and couldn't bring himself to think of anything else to do while he waited for someone to decide they wanted some pizza.

"Hey, Jerry, did you know you could *have* Jesus?" was the first thing Starlight blurted when she entered the shop.

Jerry started and slipped off the counter as quickly as he could, hoping he had done it in a manner that would prevent her from realizing he had ever been on it, "*Have* Jesus? What are you talking about? Have you lost your mind?"

Starlight laughed, "The Trestles have Jesus, and they just told me how to have Him. I'm so glad!"

"Well, then, how *do* you have Jesus?" he asked eagerly, betrayed into curiosity. "I knew the Trestles had something I didn't."

So Starlight readily explained, "He gave us a gift and a chance to restore our relationship with God. The gift is that He died for us so we could be washed of our sins..."

Jerry listened intently as she continued.

Once he found out it was possible, he took Jesus too. Afterwards, they both hurried back to the store.

"Guess what? I have Jesus too!" Jerry exclaimed happily as they entered.

Astonished customers stopped to watch as Charlie, Starlight, Jerry and the Trestles gathered in a circle and celebrated.

Jerry's words bubbled over again, "It seems like I'm in a new family or something!" He paused in thought a moment, "Hey, it's sort of like your little girl! It's like I was living my life trying to do what I had learned was right, but no matter how I tried I couldn't keep myself perfect, and I couldn't fix myself. She's got that foot that was broken and it's just stuck that way. She can't fix herself. She was lost and out in the cold rain. She would have died... and just like you came along and saved her life and took her into your family, Jesus came to me and saved me and wanted me to be in His family. Now he's mine and I am His! It's so cool!"

Starlight had been nodding and making little sounds of agreement all through this speech. "It *is* really neat! I never imagined..."

Sorryl laughed, "So now we have more people in our family! And even when things go bad, like when your mommy dies, you still have each other and can help each other... and Jesus will help you too."

Spencer tousled Sorryl's hair, "Yup. It *is* nice, isn't it?"

As Spencer turned back to stocking shelves, he suddenly remembered his boys were supposed to be at school. "Trey, Sorryl," he called gently.

The boys came running up to him. "What, Daddy?" they wondered.

"Do you remember where you're supposed to be?" he asked.

Both heads bowed dejectedly. They remembered all right.

"Daddy, we don't want to go back. Nobody will talk to us and they all hate us now," Sorryl said.

"Oh." was all Spencer could say. He hadn't heard that part of the story before. After a moment he said, "Well, I'll walk you to school and talk with Mr. Grey if Charlie can spare me. Wait a minute, okay?" he dashed to the counter where Charlie was.

A moment later, Spencer came back to them, carrying Treasure, "Okay, Charlie says it's fine, so I'll come with you."

"Oh, goody. Then you can make everybody see that Treasure is a really nice baby," Sorryl said eagerly.

Hearing her name, which she was already beginning to recognize, Treasure laughed and clapped her hands.

Spencer smiled at her, "Well, I don't know if I can do that, but we'll see what happens."

After a short silence he added in slightly reproving tones, "Boys. You shouldn't have run off from school without permission. You realize that, don't you?"

The little culprits squirmed by his side and nodded solemnly.

Seeming glad to have that over, Spencer added, "I'm glad you came right to me with your problem though. I'll always be there to help you when you need it, okay?"

Trey and Sorryl nodded again, the smiles returning to their faces. It was so sad whenever Daddy had to reprimand them.

"Of course we know that, Daddy. You always have been there for us before," Sorryl said feelingly.

His sincere words sent a warm rush to Spencer's heart and he smiled at his sons. It was good to be a dad.

Chapter 24

The foursome had reached the schoolyard now. The students had long ago filed back into the schoolhouse and resumed their studies. Much to Mr. Grey's dismay, they showed much less interest than they had the last few days.

Mr. Grey was worried about the Trestle boys by now. They were over an hour late. He was distraught because the children were not really paying attention to him anymore either. He hadn't realized what a miserable teaching job this had been before the Trestle boys had arrived.

Sighing heavily, the weary teacher glanced out the window. Suddenly, he caught sight of the Trestles' figures making their way up the road and his heart bounded in relief. Turning his gaze momentarily to the students, who were strangely quiet despite the fact that they were not really applying themselves to their lessons, Mr. Grey sighed again. With an admonishment to the students to behave, he left the schoolhouse to meet the Trestles in the yard. At least he didn't have to worry about Trey and Sorryl anymore.

Approaching the travelers in the schoolyard, the teacher was surprised to see Treasure carefully cradled in Spencer's arms. He hadn't seen her up close before. Neither had most of the students.

After a moment of almost amazed silence, Mr. Grey ventured rather stiffly, "Is this the... Treasure?"

"Yup," Spencer answered proudly, "This is our Treasure."

Trey and Sorryl were too disheartened to answer.

Spencer smiled fondly at his sons, "I brought Trey and Sorryl back to school. They were sad because some of the students were teasing about Treasure, so they came and told me about it. I'm sorry they ran off on you. That wasn't good of them. I explained that to them on the way here. They have something to say to you."

The boys looked down for a moment, gathering courage.

Presently, Trey turned misty, sincere eyes to Mr. Grey, "I'm sorry I ran off. I know I'm not supposed to leave school without permission."

"Me, too. I knew that too, but I got upset and forgot. I'm sorry," Sorryl said.

Mr. Gray smiled, surprised, "That's all right. Just remember not to do it again, okay?" He wasn't used to such sincere apologies. Normally, the students would have gotten a good whacking of his ruler and perhaps extra studies, but the repentance in the boys' faces somehow made him decide against this.

Trey and Sorryl nodded, "We'll remember."

After a hesitant pause, Mr. Gray tentatively traced a finger across one of Treasure's tiny fingers. "She's a cutie. Really sweet too," he said, smiling fondly. "What did the children have to say about her?" he asked curiously.

When Trey answered, a bit of his returning indignation crept into his tone as he remembered the injustice done to Treasure, "They said she was diseased and crippled and a plague to the town."

Spencer gently laid a warning hand on his son's shoulder.

Trey looked up at him and took a deep breath, trying to calm himself.

"Ah. Is that so? Well, I suppose I'll need to have a talk with them." Mr. Grey turned to look back at the schoolhouse and caught sight of all the students clamoring to see out the open window. He almost smiled at their shoving and jostling and turned back to the Trestles.

At that moment, one of the students pushed a little too hard in an effort to get a better view and poor Thomas, one of the less liked pupils, fell out with a thud.

In bewilderment, he stared straight ahead for a moment, then he rose and dusted himself off. Suddenly realizing his rather forced freedom from the stuffy schoolhouse, Thomas happily started toward the Trestles. When he reached them, he gazed at Treasure in silence. After a moment, he reached out and touched one of her wispy curls.

"She's a nice girl," the shy boy observed quietly.

By this time, the rest of the students were watching him enviously. In spite of their cruel words and attitudes against her, they wanted to see Treasure too.

Finally, Jake crawled awkwardly out the window, seeming to forget that the schoolhouse possessed a perfectly good door. Once he was out, he went to join the group in the schoolyard. When he reached them, he just stared at Treasure. The little girl returned his gaze with her sweet eyes.

At last the boy breathed, "She's wonderful!"

If the little party gathered on the school lawn had chanced to glance over at the schoolhouse just then, they would have seen a desolate door calling fruitlessly for the attention it was accustomed to, while the poor window tried not to burst as students clamored through its opening to freedom. They had decided it was safe to venture over since Thomas and Jake didn't seem to be in any trouble for vacating the schoolhouse. Shortly, one, then another and another of the students traipsed over to the little group and began exclaiming over Treasure.

Finally, Mr. Grey said, "Okay, it's time we got back to our studies, children. Now you see that we should never judge people by what we hear, or by how they look, or just because they're crippled," he added reprovingly.

He bade Spencer and Treasure goodbye, but as he turned to head back to the schoolhouse, his heart sang, *I can't wait for that Treasure to be in my school.* Impulsively, he turned back and gave her tiny toes one last tickle. Treasure giggled and bounced in her new daddy's arms.

As their teacher turned for the schoolhouse, the pupils reluctantly followed.

Spencer smiled and winked at his boys before he turned back towards the shop.

Treasure hung over his shoulder and watched the boys walk away. "Bye!" she called in her tinkling baby voice.

Trey and Sorryl turned and smiled at her, then dashed through the neglected schoolhouse door.

That evening after supper, the Trestles helped Joe move his belongings into his little house in town.

Trey and Sorryl didn't want him to go, but they knew he must. Even so, their feet dragged a little as they carried things into his new house.

Finally, unable to stand Trey and Sorryl's despondent faces any longer, Joe said, "Don't look so dreary. You can still visit me any time. And it'll be better than when we lived in New York City 'cause I'm not so far away."

Making their best effort to smile, Trey and Sorryl lifted their chins bravely. They wouldn't make Joe sad. Besides, he was right, they could still visit him.

The rest of the week Trey and Sorryl occupied themselves during recess by telling stories of Treasure's antics to their now eager listeners. Even Mr. Grey came out to inconspicuously listen at the door once in a while.

That Saturday, business at the shop was slow and Trey and Sorryl grew tired of waiting for someone to come to the store. Finally, Trey wandered to the back room where Spencer was stacking boxes.

"Daddy?" he asked.

Spencer stood up and wiped the sweat from his face, "Yeah?"

"Can me and Sorryl take Treasure for a walk? We need something to do."

"Sorryl and I," Spencer corrected with a teasing smile.

Trey sighed exaggeratedly. "Sorryl and I," he corrected himself almost teasingly.

"Well, if you're bored you can help me back here..." Spencer began with a twinkle in his eyes.

"Oh, Daddy," Trey laughed. "We would if we could, but everything's too heavy. We're not *that* strong. But we can carry Treasure," he hastened to add.

Spencer laughed outright this time and ruffled Trey's hair.

Just then, Sorryl poked his head around the corner, holding a giggling Treasure. "Did he say we can go?" he asked Trey eagerly.

Spencer ruffled his hair too, "Go ahead boys. Just stay on or near the road and don't get lost." He knew the townspeople were trustworthy, so he wasn't very worried. "And don't go too far – Treasure can't walk, so you'll have to carry her the whole way. Think you can do it?" He knew they probably could if they didn't go too far. The brothers usually insisted on carrying her at least partway to the store every morning since they had to pass the store on the way to school anyway.

"Sure!" both boys answered with confident grins.

"We'll take turns with her," Sorryl added.

With that, the excited boys dashed out of the shop with a giggling Treasure in tow.

"Onward Christian Soldiers, marching as to war!" Sorryl began singing as he tried to march and carry Treasure at the same time.

Trey enthusiastically took up the song, but Sorryl soon stopped in the road. "Here," he panted, "You can have a turn carrying her now."

Trey happily took Treasure and they continued with their song and marching. Trey had a little easier time carrying Treasure than Sorryl had, until she started bouncing in time to their song.

"Treasure, I can't carry you easy when you jump all over the place," he protested, struggling to keep a hold on her.

Treasure stopped bouncing because the boys had quit singing, but she just smiled at him and tickled his nose with her dainty finger.

"Treasure, you're gonna make me to sneeze," the hot boy protested, squirming to escape her tiny fingers.

She clapped her hands joyfully and laughed at Trey's antics, fully confident they were being carried out solely for her pleasure.

As the children walked along, grownup heads turned away from them, haughtily ignoring the youngsters, but children came skipping over to them to toy with Treasure's auburn curls or just to look at her until they were sharply called away by irate parents.

"Okay, let's go," Trey said, beginning to walk again. "But let's not sing," he added as Sorryl took up their song again and Treasure accordingly resumed her bounces.

Sorryl giggled, "She wants to march, too. That's all."

Trey's voice took on a sad tone, "But she can't even walk. I wish someone would help her be able to walk."

"Yeah," Sorryl sighed. "But I don't want to send her away without us either. I want to go with her."

Trey started. "Of course we would go with her! She couldn't go by herself," he demanded, suddenly alarmed.

"Really?" Sorryl asked, a touch of hope creeping into his voice.

"Well... I think so. Let's ask Daddy when we get back," Trey suggested with worry in his voice.

"Okay."

The boys looked up in surprise when they heard Starlight call, "Hello there!" Quickly altering their course, the weary travelers turned and crossed the lawn to where she knelt by the garden in front of her house.

Heaving a relieved sigh, Trey placed Treasure on the grass, and then shook his arms, trying to wake them up after having carried her all that distance.

"Do you want help?" Sorryl asked Starlight.

Starlight laughed, "Sure! If you want to."

"Of course we do," the boys answered at once, making her laugh again.

"I'm almost done, and then it's time to water it."

At this news, the boys gave a delighted shout.

"Oh! Watering is the funnest part!" Trey enthused.

Treasure bounced and squealed, getting caught up in the boys' excitement.

Keeping a careful eye on Treasure, Trey and Sorryl began weeding with energy. Before long, the curious little girl had crawled to where they were pulling weeds. She stuck her tiny hands in the dirt, trying to copy her brothers.

"Oh, not that one!" Trey exclaimed as she nearly pulled out a flower.

That's when Sorryl noticed it, "Hey! Now you have flowers, not just vegetables!"

"Oh, yeah!" Trey exclaimed in delight.

Their little mocking bird was heard to echo just as emphatically as her brothers, "Yeah!"

"Well, I liked how nice your house looked with the wonderful flowers out front, so I finally convinced mother, I really don't know how, to let me put some here. Don't they look beautiful? I noticed that Martha and Mr. Brendt had some out front too. Mr. Brendt I wasn't too surprised about, because he already had flowers in the backyard because of his wife, even though she's gone now..." her voice trailed off. Then she finished, "But Martha? I guess I always knew she was hiding a soft heart in there somewhere."

The boys laughed, "Oh, yeah. Now I remember seeing them!"

After a moment, Starlight stood, brushing her hands off, "Okay, now it's watering time. Whew! What a hot day!" she added. She brushed a hand across her forehead, leaving a streak of dirt behind.

"I'll get the hose!" Sorryl offered, running to the spigot and turning it on.

The surprised people on the other end of the garden were immediately sprayed with water.

"Oh! Turn it off, quick! I forgot to take the sprinkler off last time!" Starlight called.

Trey and Starlight dashed out of the spray, and Starlight pleaded again, "Turn it off for a second!"

But Sorryl was laughing too hard to work the handle properly and just turned the water on higher.

"Oh! Treasure!" Trey suddenly exclaimed, running back into the spray to rescue the wet little girl. She was giggling and trying to catch the little water droplets.

"Oh, what's the use," Starlight laughed at last, looking down at her damp clothes, "I'm already wet anyway. Besides, it's hot." With that, she dashed for the hose so she could unscrew the sprinkler from it. Now she was dripping with water.

"Hey! No fair! I'm hot too!" Sorryl said, running over to the dripping trio. "Here, spray me!" he suggested, spreading his arms wide.

With a laugh, Starlight twisted the sprinkler off and turned the hose his direction, sending a spray right into his face as she brought it down.

"Hey!" Sorryl spluttered, laughing as he blinked water from his eyes, "Not like that!"

"I'm sorry! I didn't try to," Starlight apologized, giggling in spite of herself.

Curious, Treasure crawled over to Starlight and grabbed the hose, pulling it from Starlight's startled hands.

"Whah!" she exclaimed as water sprayed her in the face.

The hose swung around, pushed by the water pressure, and began slithering about like a snake in Treasure's hands, drenching first one, then another of them as they almost playfully dodged the streams of water. All the while, Treasure helped it along by waving it back and forth, giggling and squealing happily at the funny dances it caused her companions to perform.

Dashing over to the spigot, Starlight quickly shut the water off.

When the hose ran out of water on the other end, a disappointed Treasure demanded, "'Ey! No bye, bye!" and waved the hose around, trying to get more water to come out.

"No, I don't think so, squirt," Starlight laughed, we're all done. And all wet," she added with another laugh.

At that moment, Emma came up the walk toward the house. She stopped stock still when she saw them, "What happened to you?"

Starlight spun around, "Oh, I didn't know you were back, Mother. Treasure was just having fun spraying us all."

"Yes, I'm back," Emma answered shortly. Then she went over to Treasure and knelt on the wet grass beside the little girl, who was still clutching the hose. "Did you do all that?" Emma demanded almost playfully, much to Starlight's surprise and pleasure.

"No, no! Es!" Treasure replied happily.

"Not quite all of it. It's hard to explain what happened," Starlight laughed.

"I see," Emma answered, peering at the garden. "At least the garden got watered in the process," she added with a hint of tease in her voice again.

Starlight laughed. "I guess it did!" she answered in surprise.

"You better get that Treasure home and changed before she catches something. No, wait here. I'll get her a blanket," Emma said brusquely.

Starlight stared after her in surprise. Her mother was actually showing concern for the little girl she had so despised not long ago?

Emma quickly returned with a blanket. She felt she must explain herself in order to preserve her image, so she stated in rather irritated tones as if someone had challenged her actions, "One can't be expected to let a little girl get sick, now, can she?"

Realizing Emma felt someone must disapprove of her actions, Sorryl quickly answered, "Of course not! God even said not to send someone in need away if you have something to give them."

With a quiet little sniff, which meant she didn't remember that, but was glad someone knew it was there so her actions could be explained, Emma gave the little girl one last pat and sent the children hurrying home before they could catch cold.

As they trooped across the lawn, she called, "Tell your father he can keep the blanket at the store, I'll pick it up when I go shopping next time. And make sure you all change into dry clothes soon!"

When the Trestle boys passed Martha in the road, she stopped them, looking rather worried, "What's the matter with her?"

"Oh, nothing. She's just wet from watering Starlight's garden and we didn't want her to get sick so we wrapped her up. It was Mrs. Bolton's idea," Sorryl answered since Trey was out of breath because it was his turn to carry Treasure.

Martha stared in surprise. Imagine! Emma Bolton!

When she didn't say anything more, the boys moved on, flashing her a smile for a goodbye.

"I like your flowers!" Sorryl called back as she watched them continue down the road.

After that, they were stopped again and again by worried ladies, and even a few men. They all wanted to know what had happened to Treasure and if she was alright.

Leaning over her delightedly, Trey informed the giggling little girl, "They're worried about you, Treasure. That means they're beginning to like you," he added in hopeful tones.

When they entered the shop, Spencer and Charlie both darted forward.

"What's wrong?" they asked at the same time.

"Nothing. She's just all wet from watering Starlight's garden. She has flowers in it now, and so do Mrs. Geller and Mr. Brendt and lots of others too," Trey added excitedly.

"Is that so?" Charlie said, rubbing his chin. As he tried to picture the houses in town, he suddenly vaguely recalled seeing flowers in front of some of them. He smiled.

But Spencer was too concerned about Treasure to give the flowers much thought at the moment. "I'm glad I brought an extra change of clothes for you," he told her as he disappeared with her into the back room.

"It's almost time for you to head home anyway, Spence!" Charlie called after him, laughing.

"That's okay! I'm changing her now anyway," he called back.

A couple moments later, he reemerged. Then the boys told all about how she had drenched everybody and how people kept worrying about her on the way home.

Spencer laughed in delight, "Is that so?"

"She's quite the teaser isn't she?" Charlie chuckled.

With a proud lift to their heads Trey and Sorryl answered simultaneously, "Yup!"

Suddenly, Trey remembered the question he wanted to ask his father. He turned a serious face to him, "Daddy."

"What, honey?" Spencer asked gently, noticing Trey's crinkled brow.

"Will Treasure have to go to that far-away doctor without us? Or can we go with her?"

Spencer stared at his son for a moment, surprised that he had even thought of this aspect. He wasn't sure what to say. "Well," he finally answered, "We don't even have enough money for her to go. And it would take quite a bit of extra money for us to go too since we'd have to rent a house or pay for a motel. I already checked and the doctor said it would cost about five-hundred extra dollars for me to stay at the hospital with Treasure. But they don't allow younger children to stay there unless they are receiving treatment, so if you boys were to come, it would cost at least an extra two-thousand dollars for us to stay at a nearby motel, plus food. So, if she goes, I don't really see how we can all go too," he finished gently.

"We'd have to find a way for at least you to go, we can't send little Treasure off on her own," Charlie protested.

"Yes, of course I'll go with her, but it would cost so much more to take you boys... I guess you would have to stay with Joe." He finished remorsefully.

Trey and Sorryl looked ready to cry. This was worse than they had thought. Now they would lose both Treasure *and* their Daddy all at once.

Finally, Trey asked, "Is there any money for her yet?"

Charlie took the can and shook it, then peeked inside. He shook his head sadly, "Doesn't look like it," he answered reluctantly. "We just have twenty dollars so far."

"That's what you gave, isn't it," Sorryl said, looking up at Charlie with eyes determined not to think about his daddy and sister leaving.

Charlie chuckled and answered after a little pause, "Some was from Jerry."

"But some was from you," Sorryl insisted.

Charlie chuckled once more and finally admitted, "Yup. How'd you know that?"

"Because I did," Sorryl answered matter-of-factly.

Treasure wiggled in Spencer's arms, "Ungy" she said.

Spencer laughed, "She's hungry. I guess we better get going home. Come on boys, we need to get you changed too, you're all wet. Bye, Charlie, and thanks for everything!"

"Not a problem, thank *you*!" Charlie called back.

At first it was a somber walk home without Joe, but Spencer began a game of chase as he carried Treasure carefully, hoping to erase the creases forming on Trey and Sorryl's foreheads.

~ ☼ ~

When Trey and Sorryl bounced into the store Monday after school, they were met by Spencer and Charlie's beaming faces.

"Look what we have," Charlie said, coming forward and drawing his closed hands from behind his back. "Here, close your eyes and hold out your hands," he instructed.

The boys obeyed curiously.

"Ah. Ah. No peeking," Charlie warned as Trey inched one eye open. The boy quickly snapped it shut again and Charlie swiftly placed something in each of their hands.

"Okay. Now open them," he instructed mysteriously.

The boys' eyes popped open, then flew even wider in surprise.

"What's this for?" Trey asked, awestruck.

"Is it Treasure's?" Sorryl asked incredulously.

Spencer and Charlie nodded.

"You bet your boots it is!" Charlie answered happily.

Leaping into the air, Trey shouted, "Whoopee!"

"Whoohoo!" Sorryl echoed, dancing across the room.

"All day people just kept coming in and putting something in that can. I couldn't believe my eyes. They just kept coming and coming. I couldn't wait for them to stop for a minute so I could see how much there was. Guess how much there is now," Charlie said.

"Uh… A hundred dollars?" Sorryl guessed.

"Three-hundred and forty-three," Trey said.

Charlie laughed at Trey's exactness, "One *thousand* three-hundred and nineteen dollars and fifty-two cents."

Trey and Sorryl gasped, amazed.

"Is that enough?" Sorryl breathed.

"Not quite. We need two-thousand-five-hundred for her and then another five-hundred in order for your daddy to go. And I hope we get an extra two-thousand so you can go too," Charlie answered.

"I don't know, Charlie, everyone's already given so much. It doesn't seem possible," Spencer protested.

"Ah, ah, ah," Charlie warned, wagging a finger at him. "You're the one that told me God can do anything, and I think He'll do this."

Spencer laughed, "Okay, I guess you've got me. But don't get your hopes up too high," he added warningly to the boys.

Charlie began playfully wagging his finger at him again and Spencer laughed.

"Two more hours here and then we go home for supper," Sorryl said, rubbing his belly. He was determined not to let the idea that he wasn't going to be able to go with them dampen the joy at the thought that Treasure's foot might get mended after all. "I'm starved."

All the rest of the week, Trey and Sorryl eagerly raced home from school to see what was in the can. Each time, they found a little more money, though not nearly as much as that first day.

"Two-thousand-eight-hundred and forty dollars and seventy-six cents," Charlie counted on Saturday night. "Including Mr.

Brendt's seven-hundred. I still can't believe he gave that much," the shopkeeper finished in awe.

"Remember," Spencer said, playfully wagging a finger Charlie's direction, "God can do anything." He felt rather bad that everyone had given so much, but glad at the same time that they seemed to care about Treasure more now.

Charlie laughed and pushed Spencer's finger away, "Okay, okay! Lesson taken."

The boys giggled.

"And if I throw in the two-hundred extra dollars I earned, that makes just enough for Treasure and me to go," Spencer said, his joy dampened a bit by the thought of leaving his boys behind.

"I think everyone's given as much as they're going to," Charlie added. "We only got two dollars today."

The boys dropped their heads. They had been desperately hoping that by some miracle they would be able to go too.

Spencer sighed and looked at Trey and Sorryl, "I have enough saved for their care while I'm gone, but not enough to bring them with me."

For a moment, the room was filled with a gloomy silence as everyone, except the happily oblivious Treasure, fought back tears.

Suddenly, Charlie reminded with forced enthusiasm, "Hey! We should be rejoicing! What do you say we finish it off with pizza at Jerry's? I think I can pay for that."

Trey lifted his chin bravely. "Okay. That sounds fun! And we can thank everybody at church tomorrow," the boy suggested, shaking off the lonesome sadness that threatened to overwhelm him.

"Right!" Spencer answered, "Thank You, Lord!" he exulted throwing his arms in the air. He tried not to think of the impending separation from his sons.

The following day, the Trestles walked to church since it was such a beautiful day. When they entered the church building, first one, then another and another of the townsfolk nonchalantly approached them and muttered a hello, pretending not to notice Treasure. But they always managed to, they thought, inconspicuously touch her dainty fingers or gently brush her cheek.

Joe smiled knowingly at Spencer, whispering, "I think they're beginning to come around. I guess we should have known that from all they've given."

Spencer smiled and winked at his friend, "They did this whenever they came in the store, too."

When the sermon had been delivered, Spencer and the boys eagerly rose, carrying Treasure to the front of the room.

Spencer's beaming face was enough thanks even for the calloused occupants of that religious town. He spoke with tears in his voice, "We would like to thank all of you who have helped Treasure. I am delighted to tell you that we now have two thousand three-hundred and forty dollars and seventy-six cents toward our trip. That's just enough, with the money I was able to save, for Treasure and me to make the trip and stay at the doctor's. We will be making arrangements for our trip this next week." He paused and swallowed hard around a lump in his throat before continuing earnestly, "Thank you all so much."

He couldn't understand how all these people could give so much, especially to newcomers who weren't at all like them. He was unaware that this was the first time any of the natives of the town had opened their eyes *and* hearts to one of the other resident's needs. He only knew that God had moved in the people's hearts and provided for them through the townspeople.

There were tears standing in many of the townsfolk's eyes by the time he finished. In truth, the usually grudging givers had anticipated a very different reaction, such as expecting the 'generous philanthropists' to give them more money whenever someone should have a 'need'. Somehow the sincere gratefulness of this little family with no mother touched their hearts in a strange, yet pleasing way.

On the way home, Joe accompanied the Trestles as far as his house. As they walked along, he struck up a conversation with his quiet companions, "Spencer, have you noticed the sermons lately? They seem to have taken on a brighter outlook and to talk more about how God is good and merciful rather than that He will pronounce judgment on you if you're not good. Come to think of it, they don't seem to be implying that 'you better do this and that and the other thing or you're in big trouble' all the time either. I even heard the pastor mention how Jesus paid for us to go to Heaven and how we can't earn that. How 'the just shall live by *faith*' not works."

Spencer pondered this for a moment, then added thoughtfully, "And people are beginning to look more cheerful and like they actually want to be there."

"And some even laugh," Trey put in as if this were the most important thing.

Indeed the people were changing. More and more of them were beginning to understand God for who He truly is. News was spreading fast of how the Trestles had Jesus living in them and were serving *Him*, not rules or sin. That was what the town was missing. This was the reason the Trestles could have joy even though they had suffered so much.

Spencer looked about him as they walked along.

Children were happily skipping home instead of dully walking along. Houses were painted in delightful colors rather than dark, somber ones. There were even flowers in most of the people's yards. But these were only a few of the outward signs of the changes taking place deep within the people's hearts.

"It's really getting to be a beautiful town," Spencer commented. "Just like Annaleah insisted it would be," he added, smiling sadly.

"Booful," Treasure echoed, making everybody laugh and unconsciously succeeding in erasing most of the sadness from Spencer's smile.

The next few days held much anxious waiting as the Trestles planned Spencer and Treasure's big trip. On Thursday it was finally decided that the travelers would leave the following Wednesday. They were going to drive the car over to the city near Houston, Texas, where the doctor lived, planning to arrive by Saturday. Dr. Chense had told them it would probably take three or four months before they could return. When the boys heard this, they clung to Treasure and their father. Three months seemed like *eternity*.

The days flew by at the same time they seemed to drag mercilessly. Only six days were left with their daddy and Treasure. How could they let them leave without them? They were delighted that God had provided for Treasure's foot to be able to be fixed, and they told Him so quite often. They tried hard not to be sad and only to focus on how God had blessed them, like their daddy had said to do, but it was hard and scary to let their daddy and Treasure go without them. They would miss them a lot. And then… what if they never came back? Just like their first parents had disappeared, and then their second mother too.

The schoolyard was a dull place during recess that Thursday. The students walked around in somber pairs, wondering what to do for the Trestle boys.

Trey and Sorryl sat with their backs against a tree, trying not to cry. They were each silently talking to the Lord, telling Him how they felt. The tears came as much as through gratefulness of how He had provided as through sorrow that they couldn't go with their father and sister. They were so absorbed in their conversation with the Lord that they didn't notice as Jake traversed the schoolyard, speaking to each of the students. Their gazes never looked up as the students gradually gathered in a corner of the yard. They didn't even see when Jake led the students toward the tree where they sat absently picking blades of grass and tossing them into the gentle breeze as their hearts conversed with the

One who was their comforter, savior, and provider... and so much more.

Finally, as the group neared them, Trey and Sorryl glanced up wonderingly.

"Hey, we've got a story for you," Jake announced with more enthusiasm than he felt.

The boys looked at him curiously. *They* were always the story tellers. Not one of the students had ever told *them* a story before.

Finally Trey answered rather listlessly, "Okay."

Jake looked at the students and winked. Immediately, they began their story, a bit awkwardly at first. But they soon comfortably slipped into their roles and each of the students told a part and vigorously acted it out, accomplishing a fairly good effect even in their inexperience at such activities. The students turned cartwheels and ran to and fro across the grass, throwing their entire hearts into this attempt to cheer their classmates. Before long, they were delighted to find Trey and Sorryl smiling; then giggling; and finally they were rewarded by a full-out laugh from Trey.

When it was over, Jake hastily groped for something else they could do to occupy the boys' minds and cheer them some more, "Hey! Want to play leap frog?" Mr. Grey had finally permitted them to play this game, unable to find any logical reason why they shouldn't.

"Well," Trey began hesitantly. "I don't know."

"Aww. Come on," Jake coaxed. Gently taking the boys by the hand, he led them over to the open area in the middle of the schoolyard. The boy forced his voice to sound excited, "Okay, guys! This time it's the figure eight!"

Immediate protests sounded from every corner of the yard.

Only one voice was raised in happy assent. It was Sorryl, finally showing some interest. "Oh! That's the fun one! Come on guys!" he encouraged, crouching on the lawn. It was no good to stay sad, and he was determined to enjoy this time with his friends. It touched his heart that their classmates wanted to help them.

Trey joined him, the anxious wrinkles smoothing from his forehead.

Wanting to keep the pensive look from the brother's faces, the rest of the students lined up, creating a figure eight. Before long, a vigorous hopping, laughing, and screeching began as the students tried to leap around the human chain just as fast as they could without colliding in the middle of the eight.

Mr. Grey smiled from the window. Somehow the tables were turned. At first it had been the Trestle boys who had cheered the rest of the children. Now it was the other children's turn to cheer the Trestle boys. He wished there was some way Trey and Sorryl could go with their sister and father, but he just didn't see how he could help. Suddenly, the teacher tipped his head in thought.

That day, when school let out, he started for town with much more purpose in his step than had ever before been observed in the methodical, stern teacher.

Chapter 25

That Saturday evening as Trey and Sorryl played on their lawn with Treasure, they looked up to see someone walking along the road toward their home.

Sorryl squinted and examined the portly outline of the person approaching. Suddenly he shouted, "It's Mr. Brendt!"

At his enthusiastic cry, Spencer came out on the porch. Seeing Mr. Brendt approaching the yard, he descended the porch steps to meet him. "Hello, Mr. Brendt! How are you?"

"Fine," the man answered in his short way.

"Hi, Mr. Brendt!" Trey greeted, racing to him and giving him his hand.

"Hello, young man. And you too, Sorryl. You look sadder than usual today. I'm used to jolly faces," Mr. Brendt told them almost admonishingly. Their faces had lit up on sight of him, but he could still see hints of sorrow behind the luminous eyes.

With a bittersweet smile, Sorryl explained, "Well, we can't go with Daddy and Treasure. But we're not *completely* sad, because at least Treasure can go and get better. God was good to give us enough to get her foot fixed."

"Ah. Well, it's good to look on the bright side I suppose. You're that sad about being left behind though, 'ey?"

The boys just looked at him, blinking back tears. It was hard to let their daddy leave them. Though they didn't want to admit it, they were actually afraid to let him leave without them lest he should never return. They knew he would if he could, but what if he *couldn't*... like their mother.

"It's for three whole months," Sorryl finally said.

"Is that so? Well, that's too bad. I'm sure you'll be fine though. The time will go quickly," Mr. Brendt comforted as he turned to Spencer. "You look as if there is sorrow behind your joy too."

Spencer smiled, trying to erase what sorrow the gentleman had observed, "Well, I guess I'm gonna miss the boys, too," he answered quietly. "But they'll be okay with Joe to take care of them, won't you?" he asked, gently ruffling their hair.

Trey and Sorryl looked up at him and Trey answered, "Yeah. We'll be okay." They smiled bravely.

Mr. Brendt shifted. He couldn't believe this family actually cared so much about each other. No one in this town seemed to care so much, even for their parents. And yet, even though he knew they were sad to be leaving each other for a time, he could still see the prevailing joy in their countenances.

Sorryl looked up at him. "You were really nice to give so much so Treasure could go. I didn't even know anybody *had* that much money. You *do* have enough left for you, don't you?" he asked with concern.

Mr. Brendt felt his eyes crinkle as he smiled at the boy, "I have *more* than enough left for me."

Sorryl's eyes widened, "Truly?"

"Truly."

"You must have a lot of money!" Sorryl couldn't help exclaiming.

Spencer laid a hand on Sorryl's shoulder, "We do thank you for your generosity. I never thought... I mean, I didn't know..." his voice trailed off and the corners of his mouth lifted slightly in a smile, "Well. I guess I just never expected to raise enough money... and certainly not for someone to be as generous as you were. I guess I didn't have enough faith that God could actually raise that much money, especially in this little town." He laughed lightly, "But then, He fed thousands with only a few loaves of bread and a couple fish, so I shouldn't be surprised. But I am. And I'm grateful too... and a little chagrinned that I forgot how

God always provides what we need… and often, as in this case, way more than that." He paused and looked at Mr. Brendt, then spoke again, his voice sincere, "Thank you."

Mr. Brendt didn't know what to say. He wasn't used to this attitude. And it sounded as though they were giving the credit to God more than to the people for providing, though they were grateful to both. Somehow it made his heart feel lighter and as though his gift held greater value because of their praise to God for it. He couldn't explain his reaction.

His voice was a bit rough when he answered, "You're welcome. I don't see how you're so happy about it when it wasn't enough to get everyone there though."

Spencer laughed, "Well, we couldn't expect that much could we? God provided for the most important thing, to make Treasure so she can walk and run without pain. What more could we ask?"

Mr. Brendt just looked at them for a moment. Trey and Sorryl seemed to be in agreement with their father, though he knew from their teacher that they had been quite distracted at school and hadn't initiated games at recess as they usually did. He smiled at the remembrance of how the incredulous teacher had told him it had been the other students who had pulled Trey and Sorryl into playing games that week. He knew they sorely wanted to go with their father… and yet they were happy that he and Treasure could go at all. The other children he knew would have been sulking around, actually angry that someone wasn't 'nice enough' to give enough money for them to go too. But their reasons for wanting to go would have been the adventure and fun they could have, not to stay with their father and sister as he knew these two boys wanted.

He finally spoke again, "What would you say if I told you Trey and Sorryl could go?"

Three heads snapped up, hope filling their eyes, only to simmer away.

"Don't tease us, Mr. Brendt," Sorryl pled. "You know we can't. That would be a whole two-thousand more dollars."

"Oh, is that all?" Mr. Brendt asked unconcernedly.

"*All!* That's like a million dollars, Mr. Brendt!" Trey exclaimed in awe.

"Wait a minute. I thought you said it was only two-thousand," Mr. Brendt rejoined.

"I did," Trey answered. "But it may as well be a million."

"Two-thousand is hardly a million."

Trey bobbed his head in acknowledgement, "I know, but they both seem so huge that they're almost the same to me."

Mr. Brendt felt a smile tug the corners of his mouth.

After a pause he pressed, "So, what if I said you could go and it were true?"

Sorryl looked up and a new shine entered his eyes, "Well, if it *were* true, I'd jump and leap and go with them."

Mr. Brendt smiled in amusement and looked to Trey and Spencer.

"Well, I'd take them with me, if it were true," Spencer finally answered. "But I don't want to think about it, because it's not true and it's better not to think about it than to daydream that it was true, and then be even more disappointed."

Much to Spencer's confusion, Mr. Brendt chuckled softly this time, a sound that was growing increasingly usual to hear from the once gruff man. "Well then, what do *you* say Trey."

Trey sighed wistfully, "I would go. And be happy, and hug you and Daddy and everybody." His eyes sparkled.

Mr. Brendt paused a moment, surveying the faces before him. He hadn't been sure when he had come. But now he knew what he wanted to do. "Then I'll say it. The boys can go with you."

Nobody stirred and Mr. Brendt looked from one to the other. "You don't believe me?" he asked, appalled.

They shook their heads.

"Listen. Remember that faith you were talking about, Spencer? Well, you must need to grab hold of some more of it. Now, I'll say it once more, and you better believe me this time: *the boys can go with you!*"

Sorryl looked up, finally daring to hope, "Really?" he questioned eagerly.

"Really! Here's the money to prove it, with an extra two-hundred dollars just in case," Mr. Brendt held it out to the astonished trio.

There was a moment of complete silence, and then all three erupted at once. Treasure added her delighted squeals to their shouts of joy, if they were happy, so was she!

"Oh! For really and truly we're going!" Sorryl shouted, doing a summersault, then a cartwheel, and then racing to embrace first his Daddy then Treasure and finally Mr. Brendt.

Trey yelped joyfully. Then, true to his word, he flew from one person to another, giving them each an affectionate hug.

Spencer hesitated, "But, we can't take that..."

"You must take it, for I'm giving it and I know you will use it," Mr. Brendt rejoined half sternly, but with a fond sparkle in his eye.

Spencer just stood with tears in his eyes, and when the boys were through giving Mr. Brendt another hug, he embraced the astonished man as well. Stepping back, he surveyed the older man's joyful face. "I don't know how to thank you enough—"

Mr. Brendt stopped him, "You don't need to. You've done more for me than I could ever do for you. You've helped me to find the way to have Jesus and come to accept what He did as payment for my sins. And He has come and set me free! You just keep thanking *Him*, not me."

This time Spencer did let out a whoop, "Then you know Him! You're one of God's sons! And that means my brother!" and he embraced him again.

Unused to anyone even wanting to talk to him, Mr. Brendt's warming heart thrilled and he laughed, "Yup, I guess I am!"

Now the celebrating was begun anew. The boys hovered around Mr. Brendt, insisting he stay for supper.

Mr. Brendt threw up his hands, "Okay, okay, I will. But only if you let me have Meg and Nancy bring over the supper."

Spencer chuckled and finally agreed, laughing that it would seem strange to have a lady preparing the meal again.

Mr. Brendt stayed late into the night helping the Trestles pack after dinner. The boys kept spontaneously running to him and giving him hugs. At first he felt awkward. It had been so long since he had let someone love him. But he soon grew used to it. The formerly stern man even exclaimed once, "This is wonderful to keep getting hugs!"

Spencer only laughed. "Now you know what a fortunate guy I am," he teased.

That evening when the Trestles had their time talking with the Lord, Mr. Brendt eagerly joined them. He had to smile at Sorryl's prayer. It echoed each of theirs in a simplistically deep way.

"Dear Father, thank you for people who listen to You, and for talking to them. Like how You made us able to go with Daddy through having Mr. Brendt help us. You already did so much for us, dying for us and taking our sin, and then You do more for us just because You really do love us. Thanks, God."

That Sunday, the Trestles told the people in church that someone had given a gift so Trey and Sorryl could go along as well.

"They want to remain anonymous," Spencer added with grateful tears standing in his eyes.

Looking at the beaming Trestles' faces, the churchgoers found themselves having a difficult time keeping a serene composure instead of jumping up and celebrating. In place of this previously forbidden display, tears gathered in many of their opening eyes.

As Spencer and his little brood resumed their seats, Mr. Grey looked across the church. He caught Mr. Brendt's eye and dropped his eyelid in a wink.

Monday morning dawned sunny and peaceful. The boys were helping their father pack. After a while, they grew weary of it and of being trapped in the stuffy house.

"Trey, don't poke my clothes," Sorryl demanded, irritated.

"I'm not, I'm just packing them down so there's room for mine," Trey returned hotly.

"You're not folding yours, that's why they don't fit," Sorryl pouted.

With a sigh, Spencer warned, "Boys."

Sorryl turned to his father with a flushed face, "Oh, Daddy, I'm hot and I can't breathe in here."

"Well, we only have a couple more hours until lunchtime," Spencer tried to console him.

"But, Daddy, my head is hot and I can't think," Trey said.

"Well... me too. Why don't we take a break now and go up in the cool hills for a while." Spencer suggested.

"Oh, yeah! Let's go!" Sorryl eagerly agreed, suddenly regaining his energy.

They all hurried to get ready. They soon left the stuffy house behind, Spencer carrying a delighted Treasure. Trooper ran off to explore on his own. He did that often if Spencer was with the boys.

"Daddy, what will it be like near Houston?" Trey asked as they worked their way up the mountain.

"I'm not sure, I've never been there," Spencer answered. "I know it's different over in East Texas than it is here."

"Well, I hope there are mountains. Mountains are the best. And I hope it's warm," Sorryl added.

"Me too," Trey agreed.

"Well, I'm pretty sure it'll be about as warm as it is here, maybe warmer. I know it's near the ocean, but I'm not sure if it has mountains," Spencer said.

"The ocean? Oh, that would be even more fun than mountains! I think I'll like the ocean!" Trey exclaimed, his enthusiasm growing.

"Me too," Sorryl agreed.

"Yeah!" Treasure put in, nodding her head vigorously.

"Can I carry her for a little bit?" Trey asked.

"Okay, but be careful," Spencer allowed, cautiously handing her over.

"I will— Daddy!" Trey suddenly shouted as his father disappeared into a hole that had been hidden by a loose rock he had just stepped on. Trey held Treasure tighter and stepped back from the new gaping hole. He didn't want her to fall in too.

Sorryl knelt by the opening and peered down anxiously. He could just make out his father's form lying what seemed like an eternity below him. "Daddy! Daddy!" he called. But there was no answer.

"We have to help him!" Trey cried franticly. "Here, you take Treasure, I'll try to go down and see if he's okay."

"Trey! You can't do that! You'll fall and get hurt." Sorryl was nearly in tears by now. He looked longingly off to the town. It seemed so far away! "I'll run to town and get help. You wait here with Treasure. And wave this if he talks to you," he added, untying one of Treasure's red hair ribbons and handing it to him.

"You won't see that," Trey said.

Sorryl was in too much of a panic to wait and find a better solution. "Oh, well. I'll just go." With that, he turned and ran down the mountain as fast as his legs could carry him. "Oh, Daddy! Daddy!" he cried softly to himself as he ran. Finally, he had to stop to catch his breath. Then he pressed on again as fast as he could. All of a sudden, he slammed into something and fell backwards to the ground. Looking up through the tears that blinded him, he saw a man with a shaggy beard and a little bundle held carefully in his arms.

Speechless in amazement and grief, Sorryl only stared. But when the stranger began reaching a hand toward him, the frightened boy panicked and leapt to his feet, turning to race back to Trey and his unconscious father for safety.

But the man caught him by the arm and held Sorryl back. Sorryl screamed and kicked against the man's legs with all his strength. He suddenly stopped squirming when the man spoke in a voice that was rather gentle, very much in opposition of his appearance, "Hey, little guy. I won't hurt you. Are you lost?"

Almost daring to hope, Sorryl turned back to the man. His young heart throbbed. If he looked past the dirt on the man's face and that awful, untrimmed beard, the stranger really didn't seem that awful. Suddenly relieved to have someone who might really know what to do, Sorryl nearly sobbed, "Oh! Sir! Come quick!"

"What's the matter?" the man wondered. He followed the frantic boy, carefully carrying his bundle.

"It's Daddy. And he's fallen in the hole and he won't say anything!" Sorryl explained hastily. "Oh! Hurry! He might be dead!" he finished with another sob, tilting his chin bravely as he warded off tears so he could see where he was going.

When the boy stopped at last, the stranger knelt beside the boys. "What's your daddy's name?" he asked softly.

Trey only stared suspiciously at this stranger his brother had brought back, but Sorryl answered confidently, "Spencer. He's Spencer."

The man leaned over the hole, calling, "Spencer! Hey! Are you all right?" But the man's echo, followed by an ominous silence, was their only answer.

The man gazed at Trey and Sorryl. In his calloused eyes, there was a conflicting gentleness springing from their depths. "We'll have to go to town and get some rope and strong men so we can have someone go down there and see him, and someone else to stay up here and pull them out."

The man seemed to have a raging battle within his heart for a moment. Finally, he sighed and said with a touch of mingled despair and bravery, "You boys wait here. I'll be right back." He hurried off toward the little town, leaving the boys with Treasure.

Treasure touched one of the tears that were sliding down Trey's face and shook her head as if to tell him not to cry.

Grasping her close, the boy could only sob, "Oh, Treasure! You don't even know what's wrong. Maybe we don't have a Daddy anymore."

"Trey, let's pray," Sorryl's quiet voice pled as he knelt close to his brother.

"Yeah. That's a good idea." Trey licked his lips. They tasted of salt from his tears. He raised his face to the sky and tears quietly slid off his chin, "Jesus? Daddy's down there and maybe he's dead. Oh! Please don't let him be, and if he is... well... then make him not be anymore, 'cause You're our Shepherd. And please, *please* bring somebody soon to help. Oh, *please* make Daddy be okay! I know You care about us. Thank You that You do, and that we can talk to You…"

Trey and Sorryl sat in silence for a moment, then Trey leaned rather precariously over the hole. "Daddy! Oh, Daddy! I can't lose both my Daddies!" When the echoes died away, he sat back and dropped his head into his hands.

"Oh, Daddy!" Sorryl groaned. He scooped Treasure up as she started to crawl away.

"Dada?" she asked Sorryl, looking around eagerly.

"Oh, Treasure!" the boy hugged her close.

But she squirmed impatiently, insisting, "Dada."

"You can't have Daddy, he's not here. He's… down there," Sorryl reasoned quite incoherently as more tears traced down his cheeks.

Treasure looked from one boy to the other, confused by their tears and refusal to find Daddy.

The stranger hurried down the mountain with mixed feelings, nearly trembling. There was no saying what would happen to him when the people saw him, but those boys needed help for their father. And he would do almost anything for this family. Yes. He knew them. Not really, but he had longingly watched them from the mountain as they played their little games or splashed in the pond. Yes, he had even dodged their tinkling voices as they played games on the mountain. Well, it would have come to this sooner or later anyway, on account of his little bundle.

He had almost sent the boys to town and stayed with their little girl. But they hardly looked ready to leave their precious 'Treasure', as he had heard her called many times, with some scruffy bearded stranger. And, after a moment's thought, he had realized neither boy was in any condition to run down the mountain and coherently ask for help. Well, his poor personage would have to carry out this difficult mission. Hopefully they would listen to him.

When he reached the first house on the outskirts of town, the man paused. After a moment, he shook himself and raced on to the pizza shop not far into town. Through the window he saw Joe conversing with the owner. They were the only occupants of the store, but they looked strong and healthy enough for the task he was about to request them to carry out. The stranger summoned courage and pulled the door open, stepping inside.

Both men looked up, startled.

When they said nothing, the stranger began, "You know Spencer, don't you?"

Suddenly giving this stranger their full attention, the men nodded warily. They sent a suspicious glance toward the vagabond's bundle.

"Well, I ran into one of his boys up on that mountain over there. I believe the boy's name was Sorryl. He was apparently running for help when I found him. He led me to where his father had fallen into a deep hole up there."

Joe and Jerry still said nothing, but their eyes grew anxious at the mention of Spencer falling into a hole. Jerry looked to Joe, feeling he, as a former police officer, would know better than a pizza maker whether the stranger could be trusted.

Something in this man's eyes made Joe want to believe him. Finally, knowing Spencer's life might be at stake, he chose in favor of the stranger, though he felt he would need to confront him about that bundle as soon as matters were taken care of. "Jerry, can you leave your shop for a bit?"

"For Spencer? Of course I can. I could leave it forever for that man." The expressive Jerry dashed from behind his counter, ready to begin at once.

The stranger spoke again, "We'll need some strong rope. He's really far down and someone needs to go in after him. He hasn't spoken."

Fear throbbed in Joe's chest now. He made himself think rationally, "Okay, you two get Dr. Chense if he's available. We'll need him if Spencer's hurt. I'll go get a rope."

The stranger started and blushed, then he stammered, "I-I'll just go on up the mountain and stay with those kids."

With a stern look the bearded man's way, Joe answered almost warningly, "As you wish."

Relieved, the stranger turned and exited almost too eagerly.

Casting a quizzical look Joe's way, Jerry started for the doctor.

A while later, Trey and Sorryl heard someone climbing the mountain below them. The stranger reappeared alone and knelt by them once more, "The doctor and two other men are on their way. Don't worry, boys, they'll be here before long, but I need to go…" how could he explain to these innocent boys who were looking up at him so trustfully and gratefully? With a sigh, he turned and sped away. After backtracking, he parted the bushes and watched as the men he had recruited approached the boys, who were bravely drying their tears and talking to the little girl.

"Here we are," Joe called out, puffing up to them with Jerry and Doctor Chense close on his heels.

Seeing the boy's tight faces, Joe stooped next to them, taking Treasure from the weary Sorryl as he soothed, "Hey, it'll be okay. He's down there?" He indicated the hole.

The boys nodded.

Joe looked around and sighed. The man who had come and alerted them was nowhere to be seen. But at least he had told the truth. "Okay, don't worry, we'll get him out. Jerry, you're the smallest, will you go down and see if we can get him out?" Joe asked, taking charge in his trained policeman manner.

"Maybe I should go down. That way I can see if we can safely move him," Dr. Chense suggested.

"Okay, that's a better idea. But we better not waste any time," Joe agreed.

The boys stood by as they waited for Dr. Chense to get down in that nasty hole with their daddy.

After what seemed like a torturing eternity, Dr. Chense called up, "He's breathing!"

A few more minutes passed and he called once again, "I think it's okay to bring him up! Just be very gentle. Can I have another rope down here?"

A scrambling followed as they set about sending another rope down. When Dr. Chense shouted that they were ready, the people above slowly pulled the ropes hand-over-hand until Doctor Chense and Spencer were out of the hole.

Doctor Chense smiled compassionately at the boys, "I think he'll be all right. He doesn't seem to have broken anything, just knocked himself out is all."

They all gathered around Spencer then, watching as Doctor Chense examined him more closely in the sunlight and dressed the wounds he had received in his fall.

Doctor Chense was nearly finished when Spencer stirred.

"Daddy!" the boys eagerly rushed toward him.

Joe quickly laid his hands on their shoulders, "Don't jostle him boys, he needs us to be calm and gentle."

Checking their speed, they slowly approached their daddy.

Spencer opened his eyes. "Where am I?" he wondered foggily.

"You were climbing with us and then you fell down a hole," Trey tried to explain.

"Huh?" Spencer asked groggily.

"You were..." Trey's voice trailed off as Joe laid a restraining hand on his shoulder.

"You're fine," Doctor Chense said. "You just had a little fall. Now we should get you home and to bed." He motioned for the makeshift stretcher they had brought along.

Spencer was placed on the stretcher and they carefully carried him down to his home.

Many of the townspeople were at the base of the mountain looking up and wondering if they should venture to climb its slopes. Even Mr. Grey and the schoolchildren had come when they heard of Spencer's fall. The stretcher was immediately surrounded and they followed them to the house.

"Give us some room, don't crowd him," Doctor Chense ordered quietly. "He'll be fine. He has a concussion and just needs some rest."

The doctor shook his head wonderingly. When these people had first arrived, no one had even wanted to talk to them, now practically the entire town showed up when they heard Spencer had been injured.

They carried Spencer inside. He was almost asleep as they situated him on his bed.

The boys were shooed from the room and they ventured back outside while the doctor made sure Spencer would be comfortable and had all he needed.

As soon as they reemerged from the house, their schoolmates crowded around them, "Your father is going to be okay, isn't he?"

Trey blinked back tears, "The doctor says he thinks so."

Sorryl looked at them, "And we're asking God to help him. I think He'll make Daddy better."

The students just stared at Sorryl for a minute. Finally, one ventured to ask, "So, you think God cares whether your father gets better?"

Sorryl looked at him, shocked, "Of course He does. He made each one of us and loves us all!"

"He does?" the student asked.

"Yes!" Sorryl went on to explain God's love and how people can know Him.

The students were silent after this fervent answer, contemplating the deep yet simple things Sorryl had told them. The talk traveled to other things then, but none of the people that heard could forget what had been said. Phrases of what Sorryl had told them flitted across their minds and laced their way into their hearts. *"God loves us all!" "But God is Holy… people who sin can't be near Him." "Jesus died… for you." "Then we can know God… He'll be an extra daddy, a perfect one, better than any other one that ever was. Even better than mine! He'll take care of us."*

Finally one of their schoolmates broke the deep silence, "We miss you at school. Too bad you have to skip it to pack. And then you're gonna be gone for a whole three months!"

"Yeah, we miss you guys too. But I'm still glad I'm going. I still can't believe it happened. We can actually, truly go with Daddy and Treasure!" Trey answered.

Doctor Chense went back outside after he had settled Spencer. He would sleep a lot the next few days... and probably have a bad headache. But he hoped he would be better in a week or so. He looked up and an amused smile touched his lips when he noticed that many of the people were still there, waiting to hear news of Spencer. "Folks, he's sleeping peacefully now." Everyone looked at him, but they didn't move to leave. He added, "He'll probably sleep until sometime tomorrow."

Hearing this news, townspeople began to filter from the yard toward town. As they passed Trey and Sorryl, many of them spoke encouraging words to them. The two boys looked remarkably peaceful now, though there were still traces of the tears from earlier.

When they had all departed, Dr. Chense warned the boys, "Just let your daddy sleep, he should be okay. Don't worry about him, alright? Joe's going to stay here. You can get him if you need anything."

The boys nodded and the doctor placed a hand on each of their heads, then he started walking down the long driveway. They followed him.

"I told Joe to let me know when your daddy wakes up," he said.

"Okay. Thanks for coming, Doctor Chense," Trey said, looking up at him.

Doctor Chense chuckled, "It's my job. And I was glad to." He turned from the driveway onto the road to town.

The boys waved, then went into the house where they found Joe giving Treasure something to eat.

"You hungry?" he asked them.

They nodded.

"Okay, I'll get you some lunch."

Meanwhile, the stranger watched from the mountain until Trey and Sorryl disappeared into the house. Then he carefully bore his bundle to the little cave he had been using for shelter and left it there while he went in search of food.

Chapter 26

The boys didn't want to go to bed without saying goodnight to their father, but he hadn't woken yet, and they recalled Doctor Chense's admonishment not to wake him, so they reluctantly trailed to bed after helping Joe get Treasure ready.

"Goodnight, boys," Joe called as they tumbled off to their room. "See you in the morning."

"Goodnight, Joe," they answered.

"Ni', ni'," Treasure echoed from her crib.

"Night, night, Treasure," her brothers replied, smiling.

A few moments later, Joe retired, only to join the rest of the household in their restless slumber. Sometime later, Joe slowly became aware of a crying sound and Sorryl's voice calling anxiously, "Daddy, Daddy!" Coming fully awake now, Joe threw the covers back and hurried to the boys' room.

Hastening to Sorryl's bedside, he sat on the edge of the bed and laid a comforting hand on his shoulder, "It's okay, Sorryl. Your daddy's sleeping in his room."

A whimper escaped Sorryl's lips. Suddenly, he darted up in bed. When he saw Joe, he stared for a moment, trying to get his bearings. Finally, he held out his arms and clung to Joe, still murmuring, "Daddy, Daddy."

"It's okay. Your daddy's sleeping," Joe soothed once more, hugging him.

Sorryl swiped a tear away, whispering tremulously, "I thought he was in the hole again."

"He's okay. He's right here and sleeping peacefully. Should we talk to God about it?"

Sorryl nodded. He paused to sniffle, then said, "God, I'm kinda scared for my daddy, but I know You don't want us to be afraid, and I also know You can take care of my daddy better than I can. Please, please help him. You're so powerful and caring; I know You can do it. I'm glad you watched out for us and nobody got hurt worse. Thanks, Lord."

Joe smiled and patted Sorryl's knee. His voice was almost a whisper, "Yes, Lord. Thank You. May Sorryl have peace from you that passes all understanding, and may his sleep be sweet and unafraid." After a moment, he laid Sorryl back down, "Do you think you can get back to sleep now?"

Sorryl nodded again and closed his eyes.

Joe stayed by his side until he was sure Sorryl was asleep. As he gazed at the boy's young features, he smiled tenderly. The boy was so sensitive... yet strong. He used to think the two could never coincide. Now he knew differently.

Trey was the first one up in the morning, but Treasure wasn't long after him. By the time Joe had awakened, the ambitious brother had already checked on his sleeping father at least five times and had Treasure dressed. Joe was amazed and relieved to find that the girl's clothes actually matched and were on correctly.

When Joe poked his head around the corner, it seemed Trey and Treasure had been waiting for him, for Trey promptly announced, "We're hungry."

Joe rolled his eyes and stretched. He wasn't even awake yet, how was he supposed to fix breakfast? *How does Spence do it? I tell you, I'd almost pity him if I didn't know he enjoyed it,* he mumbled to himself.

He had stayed with the Trestles before, but then Spencer had taken care of the meals and had gotten the children ready in the morning. He hadn't realized until now how much Spencer had done. Joe never had been a morning person. He yawned. He hated this groggy feeling. He was used to having collected thoughts and acting quickly at his job. But mornings were always like this until he had been awake for a bit. Turning to Trey, he answered, "Hold on a minute. If I get you any breakfast now I'd goof and fry up the egg carton and toast the bag."

Trey laughed at him, "You're silly, Joe."

Joe made a face and ran his fingers through his hair. "Yeah," he half agreed before he got up and stumbled to the bathroom to brush his teeth.

Trey quizzically watched his retreat.

Joe was just about to put his toothbrush in his mouth when Sorryl peeked in the doorway. Joe looked down at him, "Don't tell me you're hungry, too."

With wide eyes, Sorryl watched him brush his teeth for a moment. Finally, he answered a bit hesitantly, "But I am, so if I told you I wasn't it wouldn't be true."

Joe spit his toothpaste in the sink. "I only meant I hoped you weren't," he explained.

"Oh," Sorryl's eyebrows drew together as he evaluated this odd remark.

"I'll make something in a couple minutes. Let me wake up first, though," Joe said with a yawn as he went and sat on the sofa.

Sorryl stared at him. "You're already awake," he said.

"Well, only half-way," Joe answered. "I'll be fine soon. Don't you remember how I never woke up quickly when I was here before?"

Trey laughed, "You did always just sit on the couch in the morning for a little bit. Daddy always made breakfast while you did that. I thought you were just trying not to be in the way." Then he told Sorryl, "He said if he made breakfast now he would fry the egg carton and toast the bag."

Sorryl giggled, "You're silly, Joe."

Joe made a face again. "So I've been told," he mumbled with his eyes half open.

"Boy, you really are only half awake, huh?" Trey observed, going over to Joe and propping one of his eyes open the rest of the way.

Joe jumped in surprise, "Hey!" Then, sleepily, he wondered, "What was that you said?"

"Yup, he's only half awake," Trey confidently told Sorryl, deciding it was unnecessary to answer Joe's question since he seemed unable to hear them anyway.

Sorryl giggled, "Daddy doesn't half-way sleep. At least, not most times."

"Yeah, yeah, yeah," Joe mumbled good-naturedly. "That's why he's your dad, and I'm just Joe."

Trey and Sorryl giggled.

"Ungy!" Treasure informed the little group from across the room, wondering why Daddy hadn't come and given her breakfast yet.

"Okay, okay," Joe relented, stumbling to his feet and out to the kitchen.

Sorryl got the eggs out and offered eagerly, "We'll help you."

"Sure," Joe answered. "Uh. We need the syrup to put in the eggs," he said as he broke eggs into a bowl.

Trey and Sorryl looked at each other and tried not to giggle. "You make eggs funny," Sorryl informed him while Trey went obediently for the syrup.

"Uh huh," Joe agreed amiably as he stretched and yawned.

Trey handed him the syrup a bit hesitantly, "Here you go."

"Thanks." Joe poured some syrup into the bowl, then looked at the jar and back to the egg mixture, "Hey! This is syrup!"

Sorryl stared at him, confused, "That's what you asked for."

Trey giggled at Joe's expression. "He must have still been half asleep when he asked for it," he whispered to Sorryl.

"Well, these are gonna taste… interesting," Joe said finally.

When breakfast was ready, the boys washed Treasure's hands and set the table. Then they all sat down to eat.

"Sorryl's turn to pray today," Trey said.

"Okay." Sorryl said, then he began, "Dear God, thank you for this interesting food and that Daddy's okay and that Treasure is here. Amen."

"Amen," Joe and Trey echoed.

Trey gingerly lifted the eggs to his mouth. After a moment, he exclaimed with an agreeable smack of his lips, "Mmmm. Eggs are good with syrup!"

Sorryl nodded vigorously as he took another bite, "Yeah, they are."

Joe, finally waking up, tasted his. "Yeah, they do taste pretty good." With a self-pitying groan, he added silently, *And Spencer's gonna have my neck for teaching these little guys to like syrup in their eggs.*

"Um! Um! Um!" Treasure announced as she smacked her lips together just like Trey had. The boys giggled.

After breakfast, Joe sat down with the children to read to them. He had gotten the day off work so he could stay with them.

Whenever Trey and Sorryl thought they heard a noise from Spencer's room, they would dash over to see if he had woken yet. Joe good-naturedly paused in his reading each time they left.

After many such dashes, the anxious boys finally decided their daddy wouldn't be up for quite some time and put their minds to the words Joe was reading.

After lunch, Joe retired to a cozy corner with a book. Lunch preparation had gone much better than breakfast, though he had only made sandwiches. He was thankful there weren't many dishes to clean up after sandwiches. He couldn't believe how much work it had been to clean up after breakfast, even though Trey and Sorryl had helped him.

The children were playing together on the floor not far from Joe's corner. Suddenly, Sorryl looked up and asked, "Hey, did you hear that?"

"What?" Trey wondered, cocking his head.

"I think Daddy woke up," Sorryl answered.

Sighing, Trey gently rolled the little ball they were playing with to Treasure, "We thought that a million times."

"Well, I'll go see," Sorryl insisted.

"Okay, maybe I'll come with you," Trey decided.

"You boys are crazy," Joe said, looking up from his book.

But they were already gone from the room and all he saw was little Treasure disappearing around the corner as she shadowed her brothers. A moment later, he heard them shouting excitedly, "Oh! He is! He is! He did!"

Throwing down his book, Joe rushed to the room. "Good morning, Spence," he greeted quietly. Then to the boys he warned, "Don't be too loud." He turned back to Spencer, who looked rather pale, "How do you feel?"

"Tired. What happened, Joe?"

"You fell down a hole when you were out walking with the children yesterday morning. You slept a long time."

"Really?"

"Yeah, Daddy. Don't you remember?" Trey wondered.

"Nope, guess I got knocked out."

Immediately growing worried, Sorryl asked anxiously, "You got what?"

Joe laughed at the boy's worried face in spite of himself. He explained, "That's what happened to him when he was kind of sleeping and couldn't hear us. You call that getting knocked out."

Sorryl studied his father, evaluating whether he was sufficiently un-knocked out. "Oh," was all he said.

"You hungry?" Joe asked Spencer.

Spencer began to stretch, then winced as he discovered a large bruise on his leg. Deciding to forfeit the stretch for now, he answered rather distractedly as he found another bruise on his arm, "Um. Yeah."

"Okay. I'm supposed to call Dr. Chense when you wake up. I'll ask him if you're allowed to eat."

With a little twinkle in his eye which immediately betrayed him, Spencer retorted indignantly, "You mean you offered me food when you didn't even know if I was allowed to have it?"

With an impish grin Joe hastily retreated in order to make the call to the doctor.

Upon his return, Joe immediately took up where they had left off, having had sufficient time to produce an answer... and forget in the process of doing so to ask the doctor whether Spencer could eat. He had only told him Spencer was awake. In spite of his cool head in emergency situations, he never had been very quick when teasing back and forth. It was unusual for him to forget something, but then, this wasn't an emergency anymore. "For your information, Mr. Spencer, I only asked whether you were hungry, I didn't offer food."

The effect of Spencer's pout was spoiled by the twinkle in his eyes as he protested, "I should think the two statements were one and the same, if you ask my stomach."

Shortly, Dr. Chense arrived. After knocking and receiving no answer, he opened the door and ventured to Spencer's room. He halted in the doorway and stared. Trey and Sorryl were delightedly aiding Spencer in teasing Joe about offering food when it wasn't his place to do so. Joe waited almost laughingly for the times when Sorryl would deem Joe battered a bit too much and take that man's side, only to promptly return to his father's as soon as he dubbed Joe back on sure footing.

After greeting the doctor cheerily, Spencer turned back to Joe, "Trying to make my stomach growl, then, Joe?"

Turning his back to prevent his upturned lips from being seen, Joe returned in a pouting voice, "I only wanted to find out if you really would *like* to eat before I went to the trouble of asking him whether you could."

"Admit it, old fella, you just didn't think I was actually awake until you found out I wanted food."

Nearly bursting with the laugh he endeavored to muffle, Joe missed his line and Trey took his place.

"A*ha*. He assumed Daddy was just as much a half-sleeper as he is."

Joe cleared his throat, preparatory to replying to this accusation, but he was once again delinquent.

Sorryl's merry voice piped, "And he knew if Daddy's stomach growled, he was awake. That was to be his clue."

"Well, I... That is, I had no intention of hearing his stomach growl," Joe stumbled at last.

Spencer howled at this reply, "You had no intention of hearing it?"

Trey's indignant voice joined his father, "Why, Joe! You mean you meant to *ignore* it?"

At this moment, Joe had a very hard time refraining from open laughter, for Sorryl's innocent voice was heard to exclaim, "Oh! But he was only thinking that it wouldn't growl, weren't you?"

Joe managed with only a smile, "Rightly so, my lad."

With a satisfied nod at having gotten Joe out of this muddy spot, he promptly threw one of his friend's feet back in, "And he was half-asleep when he asked. That's why he stalled by saying he had to call the doctor. Because he knew he'd fry the egg carton and toast the bag if he didn't gain some time to wake up before he had to make some food."

Spencer and Joe very nearly turned red in their efforts to maintain a serious, injured expression.

Laughing silently to himself, Doctor Chense began checking Spencer over.

Finally recovering enough to trust his voice, Spencer turned a solemn face to Joe, "Oh, ho! Is this the story, then, my good fellow? Then you ought not to have asked me until you were good and ready to carry out your offer."

With a wagging finger, Joe reminded, "I already told you I didn't offer any food. I just wondered whether you were hungry."

Wagging his finger in like manner, Spencer returned, "And I already told *you* that that was altogether one and the same."

Doctor Chense chuckled and interrupted, "You look perfectly fine, Spencer. You were really fortunate. Or should I say, God was really watching out for you."

"Yeah, I would say it was the latter," Spencer agreed.

"You'll probably need to help out with the children the rest of today and maybe tomorrow, Joe." Dr. Chense turned to Spencer and the boys, "My suggestion would be for you to plan on leaving for Doctor Jamison's on Friday or Saturday. You shouldn't really be driving all that way these next few days, and definitely not tomorrow."

"Isn't this Monday?" Spencer asked incredulously.

"Nope. It's Tuesday, ol' fella," Joe answered.

"Wow, I guess I slept a long time."

"Yup. A reeeeaaally long time," Joe answered teasingly.

"Well, I suppose we had better call Doctor Jamison and tell him we'll be there late then. I think we'll leave next Monday. That'd probably work best."

"Good idea," Dr. Chense approved, relieved Spencer hadn't put up a fuss and insisted on leaving earlier.

"Boy. Spence thinks better after a concussion than I do after waking up in the morning," Joe commented dryly.

"Yeah, I noticed you were always kind of groggy when you woke up. I used to be once in a while, but not often now," Spencer agreed, laughing. "Is that why you asked me if I wanted to eat when you didn't know whether I could?"

With an exaggerated groan, Joe returned, "Must have been." Then, with a sudden rising of color in his neck, he turned hastily to the amused doctor, "Say, *can* he eat now?"

With an effort at composure, Dr. Chense stroked his chin and turned his eyes to the ceiling as if in deep thought, "I would say he had better not, but after all this torment of wondering if he can, I suppose he'd better before he begins to envision mirages of wonderful food never before eaten." So saying, Doctor Chense donned his hat, nodded good day, and walked out. He paused a moment on the porch, listening to the merry laughter spilling from the window by the porch. With a smile tugging at his mouth, he gave his cap a satisfied thump with his index and middle finger and continued on. He hadn't felt this good in a long, long time.

The next few days were a flurry of activity as last plans were made to leave. On Friday, Dr. Chense pronounced Spencer well enough to get up and even go outside.

Joe was more than ready to let Spencer handle the making of breakfast now. Truth was, he had let Trey and Sorryl make it that morning. After the meal, he headed off to work, almost reluctant to leave the children he had taken charge of the past few days. It had been fun, though hard, taking care of them.

That day, when they were taking a break from their packing, Spencer took Trey and Sorryl on his knee. After a moment of silence, he asked, "How did you find help when I was down in that hole?"

Sorryl bit his lip, not wanting to remember that awful morning. But at a prompting poke from Trey's elbow, which he supposed meant, "You're the one that ran for help. You tell," Sorryl told his father the story of running into some strange man who looked bad but turned out to be nice. When he was through, he said regretfully, "He disappeared and we couldn't say thank you at all after we had you safe. He looked sad, Daddy. It made me want to hug him."

All through this story, chills crept up Spencer's spine. He figured this must be the man he had seen on the mountain. The man with the dreadful gun concealed beneath a blanket. With a start, he realized that had only been a dream, but it seemed so real. At Sorryl's last words, he hugged his children close, murmuring thanks to God for protecting his boys from that man.

Suddenly, he realized Trey was pulling back and saying something to him.

"Daddy, maybe we should find him. He looked really hungry."

Spencer's laugh sounded hollow to his ears. That's what his heart was saying too. That he ought to find the man who had helped save his life. But he held back from doing this. Somehow he just wanted to live and let life be normal, or as normal as it could be. He didn't want to have to decide whether he had to turn someone over to the police or not, especially someone who had helped him. He realized it must have been difficult for some criminal to go into a town and request help. And Sorryl had noticed and told him about the fear in the man's eyes as he told the boy he would go to town and seek help. Sorryl had explained that he knew the fear wasn't about his daddy, though the strange man had seemed concerned about that too, but a fear of going to the town.

Now Sorryl was beseeching him with his eyes, "Daddy, we could go up on the mountain and find him. Maybe he wants a family, too. Like me and Trey and Treasure. Do you think you're better enough to go and look for him?"

Spencer smiled down at him gently, trying to explain, "I feel pretty well. But, honey, you can't simply go find just any person. This man might be a bad man who will steal from us or even kill us. We have to be careful."

Sorryl regarded his daddy with almost reproachful eyes, "Daddy, we didn't think that about *Treasure*. Only just the town did and made her sad. Besides, he can't be bad. He helped us and smiled at me and helped me up." To Sorryl, this had been enough to assure him that the man was a good one. He had seen plenty of bad ones in New York City, though his heart went out to them too. His heart had always held a special place for those that other people thought were worthless. But he hadn't seen enough evil to destroy his trust in mankind – not even scruffy bearded, blood-shot-eyed men who lived on mountains and were afraid of people. The man had helped his Daddy, and thus gained his full confidence and, as a result, his heart. Besides, hadn't Joe turned out to be just perfectly wonderful?

Spencer sighed. How was he to explain this matter to his sons? He would seem to them to be changing his mind, for he hadn't cared where the little girl came from. But little girls weren't the same as potential murderers. He sighed again. If only he could talk it over with Annaleah. Then they could have figured it out together. It helped him make a decision if he could talk something out. With a smile tugging at the corners of his mouth, he ruffled Sorryl's hair. He could see her now. Yes, she would have appealed to him, if not with her voice, then with her eyes, to go find the man who had helped him, just as Sorryl and Trey were doing now.

He sighed, *Lord, what do I do?*

Go.

Go? To the mountain to find that man?

There was silence. All he could think of was the words from the Bible, *"Strive not with a man without cause, if he have done thee no harm."*

I'm not striving with him. I just don't know if it's safe to go looking for him, Lord.

Have I not said I will be your confidence and keep your foot from being taken?

Spencer was silent for a long time, battling within his soul to trust his Lord.

Finally, he sighed. *Okay, Lord. I'll trust You"*

When he looked up, Sorryl asked, "Are you done talking with God yet?"

Spencer smiled softly and nodded. After a moment he asked, "Well, boys, what do you say we take a little walk to the mountain."

Trey and Sorryl threw their arms around him with joyful shouts.

"You mean we will go find him?" Sorryl questioned just to be sure.

"We'll try to find him. But we have to be very careful," Spencer warned. He didn't want to tell anyone about the man. It might just make his life miserable. Besides, Joe would have told the police station by now and they would have looked for him if they wanted to. But this was his matter. He didn't want Joe to feel like it was his duty to report the man. So Spencer made the decision to go alone, wishing he had followed the example of the rest of Texas and purchased a gun for himself. He'd never felt the need for one in this little town… until now.

Unknown to him, the town's police *had* conducted a search for the man with well-armed men from the town. But they had found no trace of him and assumed he had moved on. They were now discussing whether to inform other stations of the man. On account of his goodness in helping Spencer, the little town would have let him go, but there was that bundle…

Spencer thought about leaving Trey and Sorryl behind with Treasure, but he finally decided to let them come. Joe had gone home, and what if the mountain man snuck down here and took all his kids while he was out looking for him? So he helped all three get ready for the trek with much trepidation, wondering if he was doing the right thing.

I did hear you right, didn't I, Lord?

The only answer was a wave of peace washing over his soul.

Finally, they were ready to go. He advised the boys to be quiet, just in case the man didn't want to be found, knowing himself that the man wouldn't. So they walked on in silence, Spencer carrying Treasure and making sure Trey and Sorryl were close to him. They scoured the mountain without seeing a trace of the man.

"I don't think we'll find him," Spencer said at last, the slight anxiety seeping from his heart as he gave a relieved sigh. "He probably left since everyone would know he was here now."

Disappointed, Trey and Sorryl looked at the ground and scuffed their shoes. Their hearts suddenly felt as though someone had thrown too much water over them and they had wilted like the sunny buttercups who were giving up their quest for sunshine. They had so longed to find that man. Especially Sorryl. His little heart loved him in spite of what Daddy said about him maybe being dangerous.

When their Daddy started walking again, this time toward home, Trey and Sorryl followed

As they passed by their cave, Trey suddenly lifted his head with a surge of hope and suggested, "How 'bout we look in there."

Spencer sighed. He hadn't checked there because the man must know they used it and would avoid it, but he redirected his steps to appease the boys.

Trey and Sorryl started to dash ahead, but Spencer held them back. "Me first, just in case," he commanded a little more gruffly than he intended, handing Treasure to Trey.

When Spencer had nearly reached the cave, a man suddenly leapt from within its black mouth and grabbed him, wrestling him away from it.

Trey and Sorryl screamed as panic rose in their throats. Trey hastily backed away to protect Treasure while Sorryl stepped forward, ready to help his father.

"God, please help my daddy. Please!" Sorryl breathed.

Spencer fought bravely, but he was still weakened from his fall into the hole and this man was very strong. Thinking of his children and what would happen to them if he lost this battle, Spencer threw himself into the fray with renewed vigor, ignoring the pounding headache that pushed at his eyes at his exertion. The doctor had told him to be careful not to do anything strenuous. Now he knew why.

Suddenly, Sorryl strangled a frightened cry. His daddy's attacker had produced a knife, obviously intending to use it. He couldn't stand being a useless spectator any longer. With a cry of desperation, the small boy leapt forward with something very much like the Indian war whoops he used in their frolics on the mountain.

Suddenly, he was thrust back by a strong hand on his shoulder.

Trey screamed.

Sorryl glanced up just in time to see a figure dash past him and leap onto the man who had come from the cave. He had just positioned the knife above Spencer, ready to strike, but he was halted mid-swing by the new man.

Suddenly, a light sparked in Sorryl's frightened eyes. *This* was the man! It never occurred to the boy that this stranger might help the other man who was already fighting his daddy.

With a cry of rage, the first man glanced up at his new attacker, snarling angrily, "You!" as if he was already acquainted with him.

Now freed from his foe, Spencer leapt from the ground and grabbed the man's hand that held the knife, pinning it behind him. The new man grabbed the attacker's left hand and did the same while Spencer tore the knife from his right hand.

The captive was now shouting angrily, "Leave me be! You're going to pay for this, you scoundrels!"

Sorryl had retreated to stand with Trey, tears tracing their way down his cheeks as he tried to calm Treasure, who was frightened too.

Spencer gasped for air as he tried to ignore the pounding in his head. Now that he was still, it seemed to be receding somewhat.

Suddenly, a baby's cry echoed from within the boys' cave and the captured man renewed his struggles with a vengeance, but the other man had tied him up with the ropes left behind from Spencer's rescue earlier that week. He forced the man to the ground and, before Spencer knew what had happened, had dashed into the cave. In a moment, he rushed back out with the little personage who had uttered the cry. He ran around the other side of the cave, as if terrified of something precious being taken away from him, and tried to disappear. The crying had ceased.

Ignoring his returning headache, Spencer raced after the man, who was hampered by his burden, and grabbed him, halting him in his steps. With a defeated cry, the man turned around, his face hardened and nearly white. Hanging his head, he muttered in despair, "Okay, now you've got me."

In a panic, Spencer looked at the little girl the man held, then quickly glanced to where Trey and Sorryl were watching him from across the bound man lying on the ground. With a sigh of relief, he turned back to the man. For a moment, he had thought the child this man held was his Treasure, but she was still with Trey and Sorryl. Taking a firm grip on the man, he led him back toward Trey and Sorryl and halted in front of them. The boys gazed at them, still too stunned to speak or move.

Finally, Spencer cleared his throat, trying to catch his breath, "Are either of these your man?"

Suddenly able to move again, Trey and Sorryl simultaneously rushed to the man Spencer firmly held. When they reached him, they threw their arms around him crying breathlessly, "Thank you, sir!"

The man's smile was almost cynical, but fully sad, as he murmured after a slight hesitation, "You're welcome." For a moment, his hardened features softened, but only for a moment.

Afraid to let the man go in order to pull his sons from this stranger, Spencer looked on anxiously. Wetting his dry lips, he asked, "Is this one him?"

To his relief, Trey and Sorryl backed away from the man to speak to their daddy. Their eyes shown as Sorryl answered, "Yes. He's the one I ran into." The little boy added almost indignantly, "I don't know who the other one is."

The man Spencer held looked down quickly, swallowing hard as his face grew red. Spencer wondered whether it was caused by anger or embarrassment, but was almost certain it was because of the mention of the other man.

Trey and Sorryl watched their daddy wonderingly. Why did he seem afraid of this man? Why didn't he trust him? And why was this man holding a little girl? Suddenly, Sorryl remembered that the man had been holding something the other day too, but he hadn't been able to see what it was. Now he recognized the blanket as the same one the man had been holding before and realized it must have been the girl the man had carried the day his father had fallen into the hole.

Spencer turned to the man he still firmly held, startled to find that the stranger's eyes were watching him. A tear had escaped the man's eyes and trickled down his cheek. It nearly brought the tears to Spencer's own eyes.

The man looked away quickly, unable to wipe the tear away. One of his arms was still held by Spencer and the other tenderly encircled the little girl he carried.

Swallowing around a sudden lump in his throat, Spencer asked quietly, "Is she yours?"

The man held the girl closer and turned his eyes once more to Spencer's, his gaze pleading with him to understand. He finally answered huskily, "She is sort of mine."

Spencer shifted his weight uneasily as worry attempted to grip his heart. This situation just grew increasingly complicated. The girl was 'sort of' this man's. What could that mean? Unconsciously, he pressed a hand to his hot temple, trying to stay the throbbing in his head.

God I don't know what to do! Please send your Holy Spirit to help me!

When the pounding had calmed a bit, he decided on a different approach, "Do you know that man?" indicating the unfortunate man still lying on the ground. The captive had ceased his outraged cries, grunts, and demands to be set free and now just lay with a seething face, glaring at the man who held the child.

It was some time before the man could speak, but he finally answered, nearly in a whisper, "Yes, I know him." There was anger and indignation in the man's tones as he met the bound man's eyes, which seemed to be challenging him with a deadly threat.

Panic grew within him. He was going to have to get to the bottom of this, and somehow he knew it wasn't going to be a simple story. He must know what this was about or he couldn't decide what to do. He wasn't going to turn this man in if he hadn't done anything wrong, though he strongly believed he had. But he hadn't hurt either of the men in his fighting, and he had no grounds on which to take him to the police even if he wanted to, and he was beginning to believe he didn't want to. Turning his eyes back to the man he held, Spencer queried, "And how is that?"

With a desperate look to the man on the ground, the questioned man pled, "Please, sir…"

Spencer sighed. He just wasn't cut out for this 'interrogation' thing. His heart wanted to let the man be… but that girl.

All this time, Trey, Sorryl and Treasure looked on with wide eyes, knowing they shouldn't interrupt.

Spencer sighed, half in confusion and half in relief that his headache was receding, "Well, then. Were you his partner?"

At this, the man blanched white and Spencer's heart scolded him severely. He should never have asked that question. Now that he knew he was a partner to this man, at least by his reaction to the question, it made it more possible he should have to turn him in. But he needed to know. He wasn't going to let a criminal run around freely and hurt others. And what if this girl were stolen?

Chapter 27

But the man's vehement voice jolted Spencer from his anguished thoughts. "No!" the answer was emphatic, almost filled with contempt. Spencer was inclined to believe he was lying. But the man wasn't through. The stranger realized he must tell more now, though he hated to do it.

In a strangled voice, almost too quiet to be heard, the man continued, "This man was walking the streets in some towns further east, trying to sell this little girl."

At these words, the man on the ground gave another outraged screech and struggled to sit up and work his ropes loose. After a moment, he fell back to the earth with an angry grunt and lapsed into a moody silence.

Spencer's eyes grew wide as he glanced to the bound man.

The man Spencer held continued in an almost indignant tone, "I knew he wasn't feeding her properly or keeping her warm. I couldn't do much better for her, but I finally decided I *had* to do *something*. I had been following him around, I don't know why, and I knew where they were. One day, I approached him when he was on his way out of the town we were in and offered my money for her. He must have been desperate, because, after realizing I had no more than the small amount I offered, he promptly took it and sold her to me." Tears were now trembling in the man's eyes. The bound criminal, for so Spencer now regarded him for trying to sell a little girl, lay silent after a few sniveling attempts to break into the story and insist it hadn't been him.

Trey and Sorryl just stared in disbelief as tears sprang to their eyes.

Spencer suddenly realized the man he held was bleeding from a cut he had received from the bound man's knife. He also noticed that the man looked very weary. His heart pulsing in compassion, Spencer gently led him to a place to sit down. "If you promise not to run away, I'll let you go while we talk. I need to figure out what's going on here so I know what to do."

The man gave a nod of his head. "I'll stay," he murmured almost broken-heartedly. "I've got to do something for this girl anyway." I haven't been able to find food to give her very well up here."

With a nod, Spencer released his arm. "First, what is your name, so I can address you properly?"

The man hesitated, regarding Spencer with searching eyes. Finally he answered, "Some people call me Jack."

Spencer smiled almost sadly. He knew that wasn't the man's true name. And if he needed to hide his identity, he must be some sort of outlaw... or something. Still, his honesty in admitting it wasn't really his name somehow made Spencer regard him with a sort of wary respect. "Okay... Jack, how did he come to have the girl again?"

Jack's brow furrowed almost in anger, but his eyes darted to the man on the ground with a touch of compassion. "I'm not sure why, but the man followed me here. I have no idea how. He must have spent the money I gave him and needed more. Yesterday, he jumped me with that knife and held it to the girl's throat. He threatened to kill her if I put up a fuss. I couldn't stand for that, so I let him have her, praying he wouldn't hurt her." Seeming to have forgotten his companions for a moment, the alleged Jack shook his head regretfully and muttered, "I should have left right after I went to town to fetch somebody to help you, but I just couldn't. Something kept me here. Somehow I just wanted to see—" he abruptly cut himself off and glanced fearfully at Spencer.

Spencer carefully turned his eyes away. He didn't know what this 'Jack' was talking about, but he sensed the man at his side had nearly betrayed himself. Spencer's conviction was growing stronger. This man had something to hide that would get him in trouble should he reveal it. His heart clenched in grief. What could Jack have done? This man who obviously had a heart of compassion beneath the rough front he attempted to put up. Spencer sighed. He knew he must ask the question he wished with all his heart to avoid. But time was running short, and he had to figure out what to do. When he finally spoke, his voice was gentle, "Why are you living up here? Couldn't you have gone to town and gotten some work to feed the girl? And yourself?" he added, noticing that the man was rather thin and weary.

Jack's laugh scared Spencer. He couldn't tell what it meant, but it seemed to be a laugh to cover up for a deep pain inside. Perhaps bitterness. It was this that scared him. A bitter man was not a man to be messed with.

Jack turned his head away, "I'm afraid I can't answer that question." Suddenly, he turned to Spencer and pled earnestly, "But, please, sir, don't think I did anything that bad. I just – couldn't go down there. And don't turn me in for this little girl. Please, I haven't done her any harm. I just wanted to help her. She was so little and helpless…" the man's shaking voice trailed off. "Please, sir."

Spencer studied this man. In a flash, he realized that, though this 'Jack's' suddenly frank eyes looked old, the man was younger than he himself – perhaps not by much… perhaps the same age. He didn't know what to make of the young man's speech. Ought he to believe him that he had done nothing wrong? Wait. He hadn't said *'nothing'* wrong. He had said he hadn't done anything *'that bad'*.

Gazing into Spencer's eyes, Jack saw him wavering in indecision. He had all he could do to keep from breaking his promise not to run away. What if this man should turn him over to the police? At this thought, his neck burned with shame. He would never live this down. Never.

His thoughts flitted far away to that fateful night… He wished he had never done it. He wished… Oh, what was the use? He *had* done it, and he couldn't undo what was already done.

When Spencer touched his arm, Jack started. Looking up, he found the man's honest eyes on him. Jack glanced at Trey, Sorryl, and Treasure, who had long ago seated themselves next to the men, unnoticed. Seeming to come to a resolution he wasn't sure he liked, Jack tenderly held out his little bundle toward Spencer. "Here." His voice was gruff with emotion, "I know you'll take good care of her. If you can't keep her, you can find a good home for her." He paused, and then continued barely above a whisper, "I trust you."

Spencer gently pushed the man's arms back to his rapidly beating heart, "No," he answered quietly, "You hold her for a bit." He resumed almost painfully, "But I need to know what it is you have done. Why you are hiding away." He sighed, realizing it was dangerous to admit this, "I really don't want to turn you in, but I feel I have to if you have done something wrong. And if I don't know what it is you have done, I'll have to turn you over to the police so they can figure it out."

Jack turned his face away. He could tell this young man beside him cared. He could hear it in his voice and see it in his eyes. Gulping down the lump in his throat, he turned back to this man called Spencer, having made his decision. They would probably know soon anyway, even if he didn't tell them. He could only hope they would understand. As he turned his eyes back to Spencer, he noticed the youngsters' eyes riveted to him. They were not hostile, nor were they suspicious... just trustingly curious.

Turning his gaze to his nervous hands that were gently clutching his precious bundle, he took a deep breath and began, "You see. I can't go down there. If it were any other town, I could, except for the way I look and the fact that they would have promptly taken the girl away and put her who knows where. I haven't called the police because I don't have a phone and I was afraid if I went to them, they would take her away and put her in an orphanage or that foster care thing and I was afraid they wouldn't love her wherever she went. I know I should have done that, and I had decided to give her to the police as soon as I got to a different town far away from here." He paused as if struggling to hold back a sob, then he continued with difficulty, "But I just couldn't make myself leave. Not yet. Not until I knew for sure."

He glanced sideways at Spencer, "You see, my father and I had a quarrel. I'm not really sure how it happened, but he was mad at me for some reason. All I said was that I wished we could just love people and not worry about all the rules, and he blew up. Well, it cut my heart to the quick, whatever he said. I don't remember it, really. The whole thing was a big blur after that. All I know is that he told me if I left I could never come back again. But my heart felt torn in pieces and I was going to break down crying and I felt I just had to get out of there, so I tore away from him and ran and ran. When I finally stopped, I made myself sit down to think. Then it hit me. Father would probably think I had run away. And now I could never go back again." The young man sat for a while, biting his lower lip as he fought to hold back the tears.

Spencer wisely said nothing.

Finally, the little girl Jack held reached up and touched a tear that had escaped and trickled down his cheek. Jack smiled sadly, then began again, twisting an end of the blanket around his fingers, "I suppose you know my father, Daniel Brendt."

Spencer gave a start. With much difficulty, he answered quietly, "He's your father?"

Jack smiled softly, but there were tears behind that smile, "Yeah. He's my Dad." Looking down ashamedly, he said, "I suppose I may as well tell you my name now. You see, I'm really Danni Brendt."

Trey and Sorryl were staring at this man with wide eyes. They couldn't believe what they had just heard.

The young man continued, "I suppose you know how this town is, you can't do anything strange. Well, I'm afraid I was much like I noticed you guys are, different. And unable to do what they expected. I don't know what they think of me in town, or whether Dad even remembers me. But, you see, I can't go down there, because Dad said I could never come back and he never changes his mind. Not for anything. He's probably turned the whole town against me. That's most of the reason I was afraid to admit to you who I was, I was afraid he had made me seem like a criminal to you and you would..." he swallowed hard, "Well, I'm not sure what I was afraid you would do. Maybe scoff at me and turn me in to the police station where everyone knew me and some dreadful story about me my father had made up to cover his shame at his son leaving. I know I'm foolish and mean to think so, but..." he broke off despondently. Another tear had escaped by now, but Danni let it trace its way down his cheek unheeded. He had held them back too long to care. He took a shaky breath, "It might have been different if Mother was still alive."

Spencer didn't know what to say. He had noticed the little clothes Mr. Brendt had given Sorryl and wondered how he had come to have them, and why he had held them so tenderly to his cheek after Sorryl changed out of them. Now he understood. They were Danni's clothes. Danni must still mean something to the man, but he wasn't sure how Mr. Brendt would take it if he were to find out Danni was right here. Would he be angry and send him away? The man had never even mentioned a son or wife. Nobody in the town had. He couldn't tell this to Danni, so he just reached over and laid a comforting hand on his knee. "I'm sorry I ever doubted you..."

Danni held up a hand, "No apologies, I know I look suspicious and one has to be careful."

Now Sorryl spoke up, "Oh, but I knew you were good. As soon as you helped my daddy, I knew. 'Cause you had that look in your eye that you cared."

Danni smiled gently, "Thanks, lad."

Spencer smiled sheepishly, "You should have heard him asking me to come look for you. Both boys were worried about you, you know."

Suddenly, the bound man gave an angry grunt. These preposterous people! If only they hadn't taken his knife away, he could have cut himself loose and been far away by now. They probably would never have even noticed he was gone.

Spencer turned to the bound man with a start. What should he do? "We've got to get him to the station. Poor man, we must have left him there for an hour." He turned to the young man sitting quietly beside him, "Danni, I think we need your testimony for any of this to make sense. I can't turn him in for trying to sell that girl if I don't have her. And I can't testify to some stranger giving her to me claiming he bought her from him…"

Danni sighed. After a severe inward struggle, he set his face and replied, "I guess you're right. I'll come down with you to turn him over to the police. But I've got to leave as soon as we're done." He paused fearfully, "Hopefully they'll let me go." Suddenly, he decided he *could* leave without finding out if his father even remembered him anymore.

Spencer rose with a commending nod, saying decidedly, "I'll make sure they let you go." Some of the worry receded from Danni's eyes and a slow smile of gratefulness lifted the corners of his mouth. Spencer knew it was hard for this young man to come with him, knowing his father might see him and perhaps renounce him again. He sensed that would hurt Danni's heart more than anything else, because he could see the love Danni had for his father in spite of what had happened, and the deep longing in his heart for his father to love him back.

Danni stopped him with a hand on his knee, "One thing. Will you promise to keep the girl with you until they find a good home for her?"

Suddenly, Spencer stopped and stared at the girl. After a pause, he nodded, "We'll keep her. But I just had this crazy thought. A couple visited us just a little while ago. They have lost their daughter who they said looked a lot like Treasure. All they could find out was that the man who snatched her from her mother's arms had tried to sell her, and then disappeared. I just was thinking, what if she's theirs? Danni, maybe she can go back to her *real* parents!"

Danni stared at Spencer, so stunned his voice came out rather quietly, "I sure hope you're right."

"They were planning on visiting us before we left for the specialist for Treasure's foot. Actually, they're coming tomorrow afternoon. I won't tell them about her, just in case she isn't theirs. I wouldn't want to disappoint them again."

Danni nodded in agreement as he rose. "Let's get this over with," he murmured. He knew the Trestles were leaving. In his bolder ventures nearer the town, he had heard much talk of their departure.

Spencer clapped him encouragingly on the back as they went to help the bound man to his feet. They had to untie his feet so he could walk, but they kept a good hold on him so he wouldn't run away. Spencer produced the confiscated knife just in case.

When they neared the town, Danni's face tensed and he stared straight ahead, refusing to acknowledge the looks sent their way.

Indeed, it was an odd sight. Two men with a rough appearance walked with Spencer while Trey and Sorryl hovered close behind, taking turns carrying Treasure. One of the rough men was tied up. The other was carrying a little girl tenderly wrapped in a blanket. If you looked closely, you noticed the stain on her blanket left by the blood that had trickled down the arm of the man who was carrying her.

Spencer ignored all the townsfolk for Danni's sake. He headed straight for the station. The man between them kept a moody silence.

When they entered the station, the sole policeman and Joe met them with startled expressions. After a shocked pause, they stepped forward.

Joe spoke first, "What's this all about, Spence?"

After making sure no one else was present, Spencer told the story, beginning at his fall and Sorryl's accidental meeting of the man next to him, whom he introduced as Jack. Danni sent him a grateful smile.

It was decided to lock the bound man up. Though he moodily refused the accusations of stealing the girl and Danni was the only witness, they decided to give him a short sentence for attacking Spencer. It was concluded that Jack could go free if Spencer would agree to watch him. And the girl would go with Spencer, especially since the police had no idea what else to do with her. They didn't think anyone else in town would take her, and they certainly didn't know what to do for a little girl themselves. The policeman now respected Joe very much and his opinion carried great weight, so, when he advised agreeing to Spencer taking her and Jack into custody, the policeman promptly gave his approval.

As soon as the bound man was handed over, Spencer gave the policeman the confiscated knife and turned to leave with his charges.

Danni wanted to go straight back to the mountain, but Spencer wouldn't agree to this without a fuss. "Come to our house at least for a bit. It isn't even in town, and I could lend you my razor and some clothes."

"I couldn't. I really shouldn't stay here at all. Besides, how can you know you can trust me?"

Spencer smiled, "I guess I can't. But I have a good idea that I can. Besides, you need some warmth and good food. And you could use a shave. No offence meant," he added hastily, realizing his words could be taken wrong.

"Yeah, we want you to visit us," Sorryl said. Trey nodded in agreement.

"Well… Just for a little while," Danni relented.

Spencer clapped him warmly on the back, "That's my man." He left Danni to the boys and took the little girl to wash her up.

Trey and Sorryl soon had Danni laughing, something his wounded heart dearly needed. They coaxed him into shaving and laughed as they made him look in the mirror with only half of his beard remaining. Then they convinced him to take a bath and put on some of Daddy's clothes. Danni finally had to give in with a chuckle.

A little while later, dragging a flushed Danni with them, Trey and Sorryl skipped into the kitchen where Spencer was preparing some food while he watched the two little girls who were now playing together on the floor.

Spencer turned at the commotion, "Well! If it isn't the handsomest man I ever laid eyes on. I knew there was a real gentleman behind all that dirt and beard." He said this almost teasingly, but he was seriously surprised at how the young man before him looked. If only he could get some more meat on Danni's bones and take away that weary, sad look that sprang to his eyes all too often.

Danni smiled his thanks. How long had it been since he had felt this sense of camaraderie with someone?

With a coaxing smile, Trey asked his father, "Can we have a picnic on the mountain? We pro'ly can't have one for a long time after we leave. At least, not on this mountain."

Spencer laughed, "That okay with you, Danni?" He already knew the answer by the pleading look that had entered the young man's eyes at the mention of a picnic.

"Sure. I'd like that," he answered calmly. No one would have guessed the effort it took him to refrain from shouting emphatically, "Yes, *please!*" He was uneasy staying here where his father might find him and say something that would hurt him more. He knew his father couldn't throw him out of a house that wasn't his, but he hated the thought of an encounter that would only refresh his longing for his father to love him. He almost wished he hadn't shaved or changed clothes, that way there would have been less chance of him being recognized. But there was no sense thinking about it now, the thing was done.

A little while later, the little group headed up the mountain with an abundance of good food in their baskets. When they had finished eating, Trey and Sorryl played with the little girls on a flat rock while Spencer and Danni looked out over the town in companionable silence.

Finally, Danni broke the stillness, causing Trey and Sorryl to leave the now sleeping girls and creep into their father's lap. "You know, I used to watch you guys every day from this mountain, wishing the whole world – and our town especially – could be as happy as you are. When I heard you had lost your wife – I don't remember how I did – I was so surprised!"

At the mention of Annaleah, the Trestle's eyes misted and they gazed off into the distance with a nostalgic expression.

Danni quickly continued, wanting to divert their attention. He feared the mention of her had caused them pain, something he wished never to inflict on them, "I was staying in that cave when Sorryl discovered it." He laughed, "Lucky for me there was a hidden hole carved into the back of it, though it was almost too small for me. I scrambled into it when they came in, flashing their light all around and Sorryl swinging some humongous stick as if he meant to use it."

Sorryl nodded seriously, "I did." At the quiet laugh from his elders, he added hastily, "But not on you, only if it was a bear and Trey needed help."

Danni and Spencer laughed again, and then Danni resumed his story. "Well, when they left, I hurried my way out of there, but they nearly caught me when they came back carrying that heavy log."

Sorryl's eyes popped wide in surprise, "Then maybe it was you I saw when we came back. I thought I saw something sneaking away, but then I decided it was nothing."

Danni laughed, "Yup. That was probably me." He added, "And then you three had to come up here and play whatever it was you played and you nearly ran me over several times. I was just trying to keep out of sight." Glancing down, he added, "I must confess, I stole one of your sandwiches. The poor girl was hungry and I couldn't seem to catch a rabbit or anything."

Spencer waved his hand dismissively, "Awe, Don't worry about that. I'm glad one of our measly sandwiches could help a poor, hungry little girl. I must say, though, you did have me quite scared. I even started locking the house up when we went to bed because I kept thinking I saw someone up here."

Danni looked down, sorrow etching his features. After a moment, he said, "I'm sorry. I never meant to scare anyone."

"Of course you didn't," Spencer said comfortingly. He chuckled softly. "Don't worry about it. It was foolish of me to get worried anyway."

Danni half-smiled and gratefully gazed into these people's caring eyes as a warm glow spread though his starved heart.

Spencer laid a hand on the young man's shoulder, "Danni?"

The young man turned and looked at him, "Yeah?"

"Do you mind if I challenge you?"

Danni smiled softly, "I don't mind, but I might not accept it."

Spencer nodded in understanding, "Your dad is a lot different now than when we first moved here." He hesitated a moment, "I don't know if you believe in Jesus, but your dad does now, and he's lots softer and lets his heart care in its own, gruff way."

Danni's eyes lit up, "I do know Jesus. There weren't many people who wanted to talk to a man who seemed like a vagabond and a rogue. How were they to know I was only an honest man who carried a deep hurt and a discouraged heart?

"But there was one man who seemed to care. He took me into his house one especially cold night. I had approached his home out of desperation, hoping whoever lived there would be kind enough to at least let me stay until the rain let up. That was before I had the little girl. Well, the old man took me inside and was so kind to me. I was embarrassed at the tears that pricked my eyes. I hadn't cried for a long time." He paused, and then added quietly, "It had been a long time since anyone cared. Well, he didn't waste any time getting to telling me about this wonderful Jesus Who cared more than he did. Then I really did cry, and I took Him as my Lord and accepted what He did for me," new tears pricked his eyes at the remembrance of that day. The strong, though thin, young man was ashamed at all the tears that seemed to come lately. Perhaps it was a good thing. Tears somehow made him feel better. He swallowed hard, "I was almost positive you guys knew Him, I could see His love in you. He's my hero, you know. The first one I really ever had. I'm real glad Dad has Him now. That was one of my biggest fears – that he would die without Jesus and go to Hell."

Spencer squeezed Danni's shoulder, "I'm glad."

Trey looked up at Danni, "Why don't you just go see your Dad? Maybe he wants you now."

Tears standing in his eyes, Danni looked to Spencer, "That's what you were getting at, wasn't it? That I should try to make up with my Father?"

Spencer nodded.

With a longing sigh, Danni nearly whispered, "I'll think about it… and pray. It just seems so frightening. What if he sends me away? That would be worse than wondering if he would take me back or not."

Spencer returned quietly, "What if he accepts you with open arms? That would be far better than wondering if he would take you back."

With a shaky smile, Danni admitted quietly, "You're right, of course. But it just seems so hard."

They sat in silence for a while longer. Then the little girls began stirring and Spencer stood and stretched, "We'd better get back to our house."

Rising with Spencer, Danni stood irresolute for a moment, "I think I'll stay up here for a while. I need some thinking time."

Spencer nodded understandingly.

Danni nodded in the little girl's direction, "You can take her with you. She'll be better off down there with you guys."

Spencer nodded again and scooped up the girl, who promptly held her arms out to Danni. He smiled. "I think she wants a hug," Spencer laughed as he handed her over to Danni.

Smiling softly, the young man took her and snuggled her close. The fresh smell of little girl filled his senses and somehow comforted him. Slowly, he handed her back to Spencer, "You be a good girl now, okay? I'm staying here, and you're going with this nice man and your little friend, Treasure, 'kay?"

She turned big eyes on him, and kept watching him as Spencer carried her in one arm and Treasure in the other down the mountain.

Chapter 28

That night, Spencer watched for Danni to come back to the house, knowing he probably wouldn't. Finally, he gave up his vigil and went to bed. But when he awoke in the night to a thunderstorm, he decided to go after the young man. Grabbing a flashlight, Spencer stumbled out the door. He was glad Trooper followed him. He didn't relish the idea of being out there in the wild darkness by himself. Now, where should he look for Danni first?

Just as he stepped off the porch, someone called challengingly from within the shadows of the porch roof, "Who's there?"

Spencer jumped and hastily shone the light in the direction of the voice. With a shaky laugh when he saw who it was, he replied, "It's just me. Spencer. What on earth are you doing out here?"

Danni sat up and stretched, "It was raining and I decided I preferred your porch to the caves."

"But why didn't you knock so we could let you in?"

Danni laughed incredulously, "I didn't want to wake you guys up."

"Awe, come on, Danni. I wouldn't have minded if you woke us up. In fact, I wouldn't have minded if you just came in. From now on our house is your house."

Danni regarded Spencer unbelievingly, "You're sure?"

"I'm sure," Spencer answered with conviction. "Now, come on, let's get you inside."

Reluctantly allowing himself to be ushered into the house, Danni tried to realize he wasn't dreaming. Someone actually trusted him and wasn't calling him a beggar, throwing him back out into the cold and rain. Instead, they were telling him this was his home.

"You're shivering! Here, I'll get you some dry clothes and heat up some tea for you," Spencer hurried off to his room, leaving a bewildered Danni staring after him.

Presently, Spencer returned and handed Danni some dry clothes. "There. Now you change while I get some hot water on the stove," he said gently

Unable to protest, Danni took the clothes handed to him and disappeared into the bathroom.

When he returned, Spencer handed him a warm blanket and set two steaming cups of tea on the table, pulling a chair out for Danni. He was still shivering.

With a grateful smile, Danni sat down as Spencer pulled a chair up next to him and sipped his tea.

After some time of silence, Spencer asked, "If you don't mind me asking, how old are you now?"

Danni smiled almost sadly, "Twenty-two. That terrible night when I ran from the house I was seventeen. It's been five years since I saw my Dad." After a thoughtful pause, he asked, "How 'bout you?"

"I'm twenty-five. We adopted Trey and Sorryl when I was twenty-three."

Danni looked at Spencer in surprise, "They're adopted?"

Spencer laughed softly, "Yup. But we found out that they belonged to Annaleah's sister after we adopted them. It was so neat! In fact, those pictures are of her and her sister." He indicated the photos hung lovingly above the mantle. "The one on the left is Annaleah. The other is her sister, who is the real mother of the boys."

Danni turned his gaze to the photos and shook his head in wonderment, smiling warmly. Yes. It was just like this man to adopt three children and continue taking care of them so well even after his wife was gone. He wondered how someone could love so truly and so much. Not the unpredictable, breathless kind of love that overwhelms you and then suddenly disappears without warning. It was a more fulfilling kind of love he saw in this man, one that made him bold enough to confront people, though kindly, and gentle and thoughtful enough to notice what someone needed in their heart as well as physically. It reminded him of his hero, Jesus.

After chatting companionably a while longer, Spencer stretched, showed Danni a bed where he could sleep, then stumbled sleepily off to bed.

The next morning, when Spencer entered the living room, Danni greeted him, "I made some eggs and toast." He paused fearfully a moment, "I hope you don't mind. I wanted to do something for y'all."

Spencer smiled, "Not at all. I've learned to like cooking, but I don't mind a break in the least."

Danni laughed at this last statement. He pointed towards the boy's room, "Sounds like they're up. We'd best get the girls."

After breakfast, Danni helped the Trestles clean up and then they all seated themselves in the living room. Danni fidgeted in his chair. Finally, he lifted his chin in determination. With a deep breath he said rather shakily, "I'm going to go see my Dad. If he'll see me." The last words were almost a painful whisper.

Spencer smiled encouragingly and laid a hand on Danni's shoulder, "May the Lord bless you, Danni. May you find peace with your father and have courage to do what you need to."

Danni smiled tremulously, "Thank you, Spencer."

Spencer smiled and nodded, "I'll keep praying for you."

With an almost imperceptible nod, Danni started slowly for the door. This was going to take all the resolve he could muster. *Oh, Lord. I can't do this. I'm... I'm... afraid. I need Your help. Please help me to do this right, to make up with my dad. And... and please help him to understand. To... to... love me.*

By the time he could see his home from the road, he was trembling. This wasn't going to be easy. At the end of his childhood driveway, he paused, sucking in a deep breath as he tried to calm his quaking heart. What was the matter with him? He tried to convince himself that, should his father send him away, it wouldn't be any different than it was now. But he knew that was a lie. It would be horribly different. At least he had a small hope to cling to this way – a hope that maybe someday he would be loved by his father at last.

He squared his shoulders. *Okay, Danni. Time to get on with it.* He dragged himself to his father's door. His childhood home that held almost all of his fond memories. He knew that the outcome of this encounter would either ban him forever from this beloved place and his beloved father, or, by some slim chance, open the door for him at this dear, dear home.

He lifted his hand to knock, and noticed that it was shaking. Blinking back tears, he let his hand fall on the door with a dull thud that sounded frighteningly like his heart felt. Empty and dim. Once, twice, three times. There. If there was no answer, he'd walk away and leave this painful place far behind forever. With a lump rising in his throat, he waited. And waited. Finally, Danni could stand the tension no longer. He turned with an almost desperate lunge off the porch. Blindly, he ran. He knew he shouldn't have given up so soon, but he couldn't stand the pain of waiting any longer. He was leaving forever, he knew. Tears blinded him as he raced down the driveway. Suddenly, he was brought to an abrupt halt as he ran up against a sturdy man. Looking up, Danni's face blanched white and he stumbled backward. His heart cried passionately, *Dad! My own, dear father!* He willed his eyes not to look too long. The more he looked, the more it hurt to realize he was seeing his last glimpse of this person he loved so well.

Mr. Brendt stared at the intruder he had unconsciously caught when the young man had run into him and nearly fallen down. The man seemed not to realize he was being supported. He seemed to be in a violent struggle with tears and unable to run, though he appeared to desperately long to. Suddenly, he gazed more intently at the trespasser. Could it be? Could it possibly be true? Yes! Yes! This was his Danni! Oh! How he had missed him! He caught himself and stiffened his shoulders. He had forbidden the boy ever to return. Rebellious boy. He was about to shove his son away, even though the thought of doing so tore his heart in two, when the story of another runaway son told of in the Bible pushed its way toward the front of his mind. That boy's father had welcomed his son home, just like God welcomes his children back when they choose to come to Him. Tears sprang to Mr. Brendt's eyes and he suddenly clasped the astonished young man close, crying softly, "Danni! My Danni! I'm so sorry... so sorry!"

Unable to speak, Danni's tears finally spilled over and he was sobbing on his father's shoulder. He finally managed to stammer, "N-no, D-d-dad. *I-I'm* sorry."

Neither of them said anything for a long while after that. They just leaned on each other while tears traced their way down their cheeks. When they finally released each other and looked up, they were grateful no one was around. What would the stoic townspeople think of two grown men sobbing in such a manner? Let alone the pious Mr. Brendt and his son.

Finally, Danni spoke, "Dad, I really am so sorry!"

Mr. Brendt smiled and placed an arm around his son's shoulder, "I forgive you." He looked down and swallowed, then looked back up at Danni, "I'm sorry too, Danni. Forgive me?"

Danni gazed at his father's sincere face. His voice came out almost in a whisper, "Yeah, Dad. I do."

Mr. Brendt hugged him again. After a moment, he pulled away and exclaimed, "Welcome home, my Danni!" With that, he ushered the speechless boy up the driveway and across the forbidden threshold.

When Meg heard the door open, she came hurrying up to ward off whatever invader had burst into the solitary Mr. Brendt's home uninvited. She assumed they had grown impatient when no answer was given to their knock and barged into the house. When she rounded the corner, she stopped stock still.

Nancy came rushing in behind her and nearly ran into Meg before she, too, halted in amazement.

Meg finally stuttered, "I-is this Danni? *Our* Danni?"

Mr. Brendt drew the suddenly shy young man forward, answering proudly, "This is our Danni."

Silent tears pushed their way to Meg and Nancy's eyes while they stood dumbly, wondering how this could have happened. Then they were hugging him and calling the embarrassed, but pleased, young man, "Our little Danni!"

In the middle of their fond exclamations, the front door banged open and the gardener came in. He stopped dead in his tracks. After a momentary pause, he threw his arms into the air, crying, "Hallelujah! The sunshine has returned!" He didn't know how else to express his surprise and delight at seeing Danni.

Nobody could help laughing at this remark and the ringing truth it held. A healing merriness spread to their hearts with the laughter.

Before long, Danni found himself alone with his father in the living room, sharing his side of the story of that fateful night. Tears traced their way down Mr. Brendt's cheeks as he listened to Danni's true heart. He was suddenly ashamed, for the first time in a long while, for not understanding. A resolve to listen to others more rather than always assuming he knew what someone's motives were grew within him. And when Mr. Brendt resolved, that resolve was almost sure to remain and be the cause of some drastic changes.

A while later, father and son strolled arm in arm down their driveway, having decided to walk to the Trestles' house to let them join in the celebration, since they were the ones who were largely responsible for bringing father and son together again.

Starlight was just leaving Charlie's store when she noticed them ambling down Mr. Brendt's drive. Her basket slid from her fingers unheeded and she stopped and stared. If she didn't know better, she would declare that was Danni Brendt walking with his father. In a sudden surge of boldness mingled with disbelief and a silent chiding to herself not to be outlandish, she ran impulsively forward a few steps and called tentatively, "Danni!"

When the young man turned around, she knew it was him and disregarded all thoughts of the shocked townspeople's sure disapproval at seeing her race the rest of the way to greet the pair. She was mystified. How had Danni come to be here? And how on earth had that proud light for his son entered Mr. Brendt's eyes?

"Danni!" she cried again in happy disbelief as she threw her arms about the tall figure of her childhood playmate – really the only one she had had, since the rest of the children were too 'good' to enjoy her whims and capers.

He laughed and returned her embrace while Mr. Brendt stood back, smiling to himself.

Suddenly crashing back to earth, Starlight released Danni and glanced fearfully at Mr. Brendt, knowing he had never really liked her. He had always scolded her, claiming that if it weren't for her and her wild ideas and unusual ways, his son would be perfectly normal. She knew that wasn't true. They were both just naturally so full of ideas and energy that they couldn't harness them as easily as the rest of the town seemed to be able to. Perhaps that was because their hearts really didn't want to.

But the sour old man was actually beaming at her. When he met her gaze, he looked down at the dusty road for a moment, and then met her eyes again, "I ought to ask your forgiveness, Starlight."

Her eyes widened.

"I always blamed you for Danni's ways. But I know it wasn't your fault, though you two egged each other on all the time," he smiled fondly. "Well. Anyway, I'll tell you, I think we would have done good to follow *some* of your enthusiasm, and I'm sorry for scolding you all the time. I'm actually beginning to like the energy you both – and those Trestles, too – put into life," he smiled again. "But Danni and I had best be on our way. We were headed to the Trestles' just now. You two can catch up tomorrow or later tonight."

Starlight was shocked when he winked at her. Sour Mr. Brendt winking? She'd never known him to do that, not even before Danni had left. But, after all, he had Jesus now, and wasn't worrying about the town's senseless 'do this, don't do that' rules and was instead thinking of loving his neighbor. She smiled and nodded, "See you later, then."

The astonished damsel watched the pair walk away, and then dashed home to tell her mother, wondering what she would say to Mr. Brendt winking and apologizing. Starlight laughed. No telling what her mother would say. She was so different lately, since she had told Starlight she finally decided the Trestles must be right about Jesus living in you and changing your outlook and that she had invited Jesus to live in her. Suddenly, Starlight stopped in her tracks. "Oh, dear! I believe I left my basket back there where I dropped it." She turned and raced back to the front of the store to retrieve it, unmindful of the stares as she whisked past people. Her heart felt so light… so free… so happy. When she had her basket, she turned for home again, whistling as she walked.

Meanwhile, back at the Trestle abode, excitement mounted as they prepared for the arrival of their new friends, Cameron and Lily Westgate. If this *was* the couple's little girl, they'd be so happy! What a fuss went into making sure she was spotless and had on the most beautiful dress she could borrow from Treasure.

They had hoped Danni would be there to tell the story of this little girl, but they realized that a more important mission was hopefully being accomplished – the reunion of Mr. Brendt and his son.

As the hour drew near for the Westgate's arrival, Trey and Sorryl couldn't keep themselves from the window. They would bounce back and forth between the little girl, who was playing with Treasure, and the irresistible casement.

Spencer just watched them with a fond smile as he fixed what he hoped would be a good lunch. He couldn't help but sigh. Annaleah had always gotten up the best meals, and enjoyed the process even more when company was expected.

Although the crushing pain that used to assault him so often when he thought of Annaleah had faded and rarely presented itself now, a new kind of hurt had taken its place, almost a soft sorrow mingled with sweetness at the memories it brought with it. Hearing steps approaching on the porch stairs, he hastily brushed a wayward tear from his cheek. Trey and Sorryl were racing to and fro, shouting, "It's Mr. Brendt and Danni! Daddy! I think it worked! I think it worked!"

Spencer smiled at his boys' enthusiasm and raced to the living room, throwing the door open for Danni and his beaming father. "Welcome! Come in!" he exclaimed warmly, his heart filling with joy as he saw their happy faces and knew things had gone well for the manly, though gentle, Danni.

Trey and Sorryl offered the pair a seat on the couch and promptly seated themselves, one on each lap, making room for the little girl who ran to Danni and claimed a spot on his lap too.

After Mr. Brendt and Danni shared the story of their meeting and what had come about, Danni absentmindedly twirled the little girl's curls, "You know, I suddenly realize how wonderful it is that God takes us back when we come to Him with repentant hearts." He swallowed hard and grateful tears sparkled in his eyes, "I didn't realize how precious God's love was to me until now."

Mr. Brendt's eyes were misty too. And to think he had almost turned the boy away! He was glad that hateful old pride of his had been stamped down at least this once. It was well worth it. He had felt so much better when it had disappeared. Was it possible God had changed him and it wouldn't return?

Suddenly, Trey and Sorryl leapt from their places as they heard car tires on the driveway. Danni quickly disappeared into a bedroom with the little girl. He would bring her out once greetings were through.

Soon, Trey and Sorryl returned to the house, pulling a laughing Lily and Cameron along.

"What's the rush, Sorryl?" Cameron laughed, attempting to keep up with the boy who held his hand.

The little boy flushed. How was he to keep the secret without lying? "Nothing... really. Well... I mean... Umm. You'll have to wait and see. We're happy to see you." He tried to distract them.

Cameron laughed.

Then Sorryl blurted, "And we might have a surprise for you." He couldn't refrain himself.

"A surprise, huh?" Cameron asked with a twinkle in his eye. "Is it a new puppy?"

Sorryl just laughed and Trey giggled, "We're not telling."

Cameron pretended to pout, "I see. That's how it is. No one will tell us what this surprise is."

Trey tried to keep a straight face, "But it's not a surprise if we tell you."

"Okay, okay. We'll wait," Cameron relented, putting his arm around Lily. With pleasure, he noticed the laughter in her eyes.

"Hi! How are you!" Spencer greeted them at the door.

"Good, thank you. It was a rather dusty trip, though," Cameron answered, pretending to brush dirt off his clothes.

Spencer laughed, "Yeah, it has been rather dry. Well, come in and have a seat. This is our good friend, Daniel Brendt. His son, Danni, is here too, he'll be out shortly. And this is Cameron and Lily Westgate," Spencer finished the introductions.

This was the cue for Danni to come out with who they hoped was little Wynne. They didn't plan on saying anything. They didn't want to dash any hopes and they knew that if it *was* their child the Westgates would recognize her as soon as they laid eyes on her.

Danni appeared just then, tenderly carrying the small girl. She was so lovely in the little white dress they had adorned her in that the boys' eyes sparkled with pride as they silently telegraphed to each other, "I helped do her hair…" "I picked out that dress…".

Danni spoke as he approached Cameron and Lily, his dark eyes searching their faces with a twinkle that wouldn't be repressed, "Hi, I'm Danni."

But there was no answer. Lily stood, gripping Cameron's arm as if her life depended on it. Their faces went white, and then their eyes filled with tears. Suddenly seeming to be set free, Lily dashed to Danni and color flooded back into her countenance. The little girl's protector joyously handed her over as he glanced to Spencer with a wink. They must have been right.

"Wynne! Oh, our precious little Wynne!" Lily cried as she hugged the girl close.

After a moment of studying Lily, the girl's face lit up like the sun breaking over the horizon. She flung her little arms around Lily, crying in her clear, lisping voice, "Mama!"

Then Cameron joined his wife and daughter and there were cries of, "Dada!" "Wynne. My Wynne!"

With a sudden start, Cameron fearfully faced Spencer, dread filling his heart, "Is this another girl you adopted?"

But Spencer was beaming, "No. She was a little girl Danni found and I thought she might be yours. I didn't tell you in case she wasn't... She's all yours!"

Then Danni told his story.

A glad light lit Cameron's eyes, "We've found her! Oh! Thank you, Jesus!"

This called for a celebration cake and Lily made herself at home in the kitchen, playfully shooing Spencer to the living room with the other men. "I've got it all handled. You've done plenty – and a wonderful job, too – making the lunch. This is *my* job."

Spencer gave in with a soft laugh, "Okay, okay. I won't say I mind the least bit."

Lily shoved him toward the doorway, "Now go enjoy your company. Little Wynne is all the help I need."

Sure enough, Wynne was there clinging to her mother. Cameron soon joined them and Spencer chuckled to himself. Lily didn't shoo *Cameron* out of the kitchen. When Spencer reappeared in the kitchen doorway, teasing about Cameron helping and not him, Lily promptly ordered him away again, "Now, now. *He* doesn't get to help every day. Besides, Wynne wants to see her daddy, too."

Spencer laughed again and retreated to the living room to stay.

Mr. Brendt was with the children, telling them a story while Danni looked on with shining eyes. Sorryl's fondness for Danni had only grown and he was sitting on his lap as he listened to Mr. Brendt.

Before long, Lily poked her head into the living room, "Okay, boys, men too, it's all ready. Come and get it!"

Sorryl giggled, "That's just what Daddy always says, 'Come and get it!' But it's funny to hear someone else say it."

Spencer ruffled his son's hair, "Let's go wash up."

When they were all gathered at the table, Spencer prayed, "Lord, thank You for all You have done today. Thank You that You care about us and work in our lives and that You have redeemed us. We can't begin to thank You enough! And, Lord, thank You for this food we have to eat too. In Jesus' name, amen."

"Amen," the others echoed with deep feeling.

All through the meal, laughter permeated the conversation. If it wasn't because of one of the little girls' antics, it was just from sheer joy. So much reuniting had taken place, who wouldn't be happy?

After devouring the food with as many manners as a small, hungry boy can remember, Trey pushed his plate aside, "I'm done. Now let's have some cake." With a sudden blush of embarrassment at his lack of manners, he added with an inquiring glance to his father, "May we, please?"

It was good he remembered his manners in time, for the boys' little shadow copied her brother. The others couldn't help smiling, for it was accompanied with the dainty ways of a girl, "Uh huh. All done. Ake now!" Then, with a sweetly imploring face meant to mirror Trey's, she questioned, "Pease?"

Spencer laughed and looked to Lily with a nod. She disappeared into the kitchen to fetch the cake. 'Oohs' and 'aahs' were breathed as she set the beautifully decorated cake on the table.

Sorryl's eyes were beaming, "Charlie did a good job with Daddy's, but Lily did even better!"

Cameron beamed, "She's the best cake baker in the world!"

Clapping his hands in anticipation, Trey enthused, "Then let's have some!"

So the cake was dispersed and devoured with much praise for the baker.

But the best praise of all was little Treasure's hearty, "Mmmmm!" as she clapped her hands in delight.

Chapter 29

After the celebrating group had gathered in the Trestles' cheery living room, Spencer looked to Lily with a compassionate face, "Lily?"

She looked up from bending over her little Wynne with a happily flushed face.

Spencer cleared his throat as if what he was about to say pained him. He glanced at Cameron, then back to Lily's wondering gaze, "Do you think you could identify the man who took Wynne if you saw him?"

Her eyes sprung wide and Lily stammered, "I I'm not sure. Why?"

Spencer gazed into her face, hoping she wouldn't be frightened by his next words, "Because we think we have him in the town's jail, but he won't admit to it. Danni here is a witness, but we need two..." his voice trailed off.

Lily's face had gone white. Suddenly, it flushed a deep red and her usually gentle eyes snapped almost angrily, "I'm not sure I could recognize him, but I'll go look and see if I do." Her chin was tilted bravely and Cameron's arm encircled her comfortingly.

Spencer nodded, "Thank you, Lily."

Lily looked to him with anxious eyes, "When can we go?"

Surprised at the eagerness in her voice, Spencer replied, "Why, I suppose we could go now if you wanted."

"Then let's go now and get this over with," she said, rising as if in preparation to depart.

Cameron rose, too, "Yeah, we may as well go now."

They were soon bumping down the road, tightly packed in Spencer's car.

When they arrived at the police station and had explained their story, the policeman led them to the man's cell. Joe followed. When the startled prisoner caught sight of Lily carrying Wynne, he blanched white, but tried to pretend nothing was wrong.

The officer addressed Lily, "Is this the man?"

She nodded confidently, surprised that she recognized him when she hadn't been able to describe him very well before, "Yes, that's him."

The man's face grew even paler. He actually jumped when the officer spoke to him.

"Do you recognize this lady?" he demanded sternly.

Defeat marked the man's haughty eyes. After a long, sullen silence, he finally answered defiantly, between clenched teeth, "Yes."

The officer continued, "You stole this little girl from her, isn't that right?"

Setting his jaw, the man stared stonily, muttering, "Didn't steal her, just borrowed her for a bit."

Ignoring the man's wheedling, the officer asked threateningly, "And are there any other stolen people we ought to know about?"

Now the man started wining. He figured they must know, or they wouldn't be asking. And the officer sounded so confident. "Hey, now, let's not be too hard on a man..." he began in a sniveling voice.

The officer interrupted him. He had his answer, but now he needed to know who it was that had been stolen. He stared the man coldly in the eyes, "I only asked who you stole. Please give me a straight answer."

Looking at the officer angrily, the man shut his mouth. How did these aggravating people know so much? His glowering voice mumbled, "Only one other little girl. I had just gotten started with this operation when you guys ruined the whole thing."

Spencer and Joe looked at each other and, in spite of the seriousness of the matter, half-smiled at the man's accusing tones.

"And where is this other little girl."

The man assumed a careless attitude, "Dunno. I left her in the woods when she got to crying too loud because of a storm. Figured I was through with the brat. She had a crooked leg anyway."

Spencer started and stared hard at the man.

The officer's voice broke through Spencer's racing thoughts, "Which woods? Near here?"

With something almost resembling a snarl, the man finally gave in, though sullenly, "Oh. Don't bother me. You know very well it was this very town's woods and that this plaguing man has the girl now."

Truly stunned now, they all turned to stare at Treasure.

The man suddenly regretted his confession, beginning to think perhaps these people hadn't known.

The officer turned back to him gruffly, "And where did you get her from?"

Trey and Sorryl were clinging to Treasure now, realizing they were about to find the girl's true family and would have to give their dear sister up.

The man's eyes grew even harder. He'd already confessed everything. It'd be better if they knew right off. "Stole her from an overstuffed orphanage," He grumped. "They didn't need or want her anyway," he added as if he had done the poor little girl a favor.

When the town's officer didn't say anything, Joe stepped forward, "And what is the name of this orphanage?"

"Grey's Orphan Home in Oklahoma," the man spit through clenched teeth.

Producing a piece of paper and a pen, Joe pressed, "And what would the address of this establishment be?"

The man smiled maliciously, "Don't know it. So there."

Joe finally weeded the city's name from the stubborn man. Believing the criminal was telling the truth that Treasure was the only other one he had stolen, Joe left him to his burning conscience. At least, he sincerely hoped it was burning.

In a shocked daze, the others followed the officer and Joe into the office.

"Now what?" Spencer wondered, plopping into a seat with Treasure on his knee. He hugged her close.

Joe knew what he meant, "We find out the phone number of this orphanage and enquire into the matter. But for now, you guys should get home and get some rest. We'll let you know when we find out about this orphanage. It might take a while to locate the information we need."

Resigned, Spencer nodded and reluctantly started for the door.

Unable to bear the weary droop of his dear friend's shoulders, Joe stopped him, "I wouldn't worry, though. If she really did come from an orphanage, you can probably keep her."

Spencer nodded his thanks. Trying to keep his heart from thudding to the ground at the thought of losing his dear Treasure, he led the children to the car.

On their way home, Spencer dropped Mr. Brendt and Danni off at their house and then proceeded home with the Westgates. They had decided to stay until Monday to see the Trestles off when they left for the specialist for Treasure's foot, if Treasure was still to be theirs. Cameron and Lily wished they could stay longer, but, once again, work called them home earlier than they would have liked. But it wouldn't do so for long. Cameron was to help in the general store with Spencer soon. Charlie could use the help, especially if Spencer was going to be gone for a while with Treasure. And the Westgates had found an enchanting house in town they were planning to move to in a month or so.

That evening, the telephone startled Spencer as he was reading to the children, trying not to think about what would happen if they had to part with Treasure. Softly laughing at his jumpy nerves, he went to answer it, not sure if he wanted to know who it was or what they were going to say. What if Joe had found out Treasure had to go back to the orphanage and they wouldn't let someone so far away adopt her? His hands shaking, he picked up the phone and forced himself to croak, "Hello?"

"Hey, Spence!" Joe's voice was full of energy. Then he blurted, as if he could no longer hold his words back, "Treasure was a true orphan and they say you can keep her! There's just a few forms you need to sign."

Spencer barely heard the last sentence. He threw the phone down and leapt into the air. "We can keep her! She's ours!" Everyone started hugging and dancing. Then they hoisted Treasure into the air and paraded around the room with her.

Suddenly, Spencer raced back to the phone. With flushed cheeks he sheepishly picked it up and questioned, "Joe?"

He was met with laughter on the other end of the line, "I'm still here. I wished I'd been able to see you guys just a minute ago, it sounded like a circus or something. But I guess hearing your shouts was enough to pacify me."

Spencer laughed at his friend's good humor, "Thanks for calling, Joe."

"You're welcome. Oh, and they're transporting this guy to the city he stole Wynne from for a trial. I thought you might want to know."

"Sure thing. Thanks!"

"Okay, see you tomorrow for church?"

"You betcha'."

"'Kay, bye."

"Bye."

After a restless night of sleep and a rush to prepare for church the next morning, the Trestles and Westgates happily swung down the dusty road to the church. They met Mr. Brendt and Danni as they passed their house and walked the rest of the way with them.

News had traveled in typical small town manner of the man in the jail, the two little girls, and Danni showing up. Thus, when the Trestles entered the church with the Westgates and Brendts, everyone turned and stared, mostly at Danni, who nearly all of the townspeople recognized with a sudden leap of their long-dormant hearts. Soon, a hushed whispering was heard among the parishioners.

"Is that him?" One lady inquired incredulously. "I didn't think he would be so fresh and young-looking after living like a vagabond for so long."

Her companion lifted a warning finger to her lips as she glanced Mr. Brendt's way, "Shush! Don't let that old grump hear you say that. I hear tell he's fond of Danni."

"I knew he was. You couldn't help but notice the sad look in his eyes when something reminded him of his son," the other lady replied.

The whispers didn't last long, however, and the Trestles, Westgates, and Brendts were soon surrounded by questioners inquiring whether this fact or that were true of the numerous stories they had heard about the happenings of the last few days. Danni was ignored at first. The shrewd townspeople were productively 'skipping two lakes with one stone', as Trey and Sorryl put the phrase since Sorryl insisted he didn't want to kill any birds, but skipping stones was wild fun. While they found out the particulars from the Trestles and Westgates, the wary townspeople studied Danni with sharp eyes.

Danni smiled quietly from his dad's side as he watched people stare at him, as if sizing him up. He nearly laughed when the townsfolk seemed to decide all at once to come and greet him.

When Pastor Ryan stepped to the pulpit, he surveyed his flock gathered joyously about the Trestles, Westgates, and, most particularly, the Brendts. Who would have thought his serious little town church could ever be so noisy? Or hear the laughs now bouncing off the stiff pews and bare walls as Danni answered a cynical statement in his old disarming, witty way. His gaze traveled to the bare walls and he realized that, here and there, they were bright with flowers Starlight had taped to them in honor of Treasure's trip and Danni's arrival.

The townspeople were fondly patting Danni on the arm now, happy to have 'that Danni boy' they had all secretly loved back.

Martha finally managed to edge her way over to Danni. He watched her warily, for she had been his most harassing and severe scolder. His eyes popped wide in astonishment when, instead of a stern scolding, her gentle voice was heard to say, "Dear, let me give you these." She handed Danni a bulging bag of food supplies as if his father weren't the richest man in town and couldn't buy whatever he pleased for the boy. "You be sure to get some meat on those bones," she admonished in a motherly way.

Then the lady leaned closer and confided, "That man who found you, he's a real gift. Well, maybe it's them children. Or both. But whatever it is, they finally have me convinced about Jesus. Knowing Him and having Him in me seems to have put a shine in everything."

Suddenly, she glanced down in shame, then looked tenderly into Danni's astonished eyes and rushed on, "I'm sorry for being so... so... scolding. I know my focus was in the wrong place and that you were right to want to care about people without meaningless stipulations." Tears misted both their eyes now. Tentatively, she reached out and gave him a motherly pat.

Impulsively, Danni threw his arms about this lady who had been one of the first to recognize his true heart. "Thanks," was all he could manage to whisper.

Stunned for only a moment, Martha nodded in acknowledgement.

Suddenly, everyone seemed to notice Pastor Ryan smiling down on them from the pulpit and there was a frenzied rush for the pews such as had never occurred before in the history of the town.

When all was quiet, Pastor Ryan spoke with a smile in his tones, "It seems God has been working mightily here. You all know the stories," he laughed lightly, "however mixed up they may have become through the 'grapevine'. Let's just praise the Lord Jesus right now for His goodness and love." With that, Pastor Ryan spontaneously lifted his hands into the air without a thought of the townspeople's reaction. The highest a hand had ever been raised there must have been to dry an imaginary tear meant to make the pastor think someone was touched by his message.

But no one seemed to notice, for they were all busy drying true tears of joy, or else bowing their heads to this suddenly real God.

When church let out, the Trestles were immediately surrounded by townspeople. With contagious enthusiasm flying
around so thickly, it seemed every lady in the town was eager to
invite the Trestles to their home, "As a good-bye token." Deep
down, they were grateful to this once ostracized family, for they
had brought back the equally despised Danni. Beneath their hard
shell, they had loved him. When he was gone, they realized how
much he had contributed to their lives… his joy, his constant eagerness to help people, his compassion. In truth, they wanted to
invite the Brendts, too, but didn't dare put such a proposition to
the cranky Mr. Brendt.

Meanwhile, the 'old crank' stood back and watched in silence
for a bit. Finally, he leaned over and confided to Danni, "I've
never seen anyone invite someone over after church before." He
clicked his tongue and shook his head, amused.

Danni was watching the whole scene with sparkling eyes.
Spencer had been right, his Dad *was* different. And so was the
rest of the town.

Now the people were starting to get into little arguments
while the Trestles stood by, watching with interest. One lady
claimed to have first rights to them since she asked first. But, of
course, another lady had *thought* of it first. This argument brought
on many more such claims, until Spencer was nearly laughing at
the commotion of the recently stoic town.

Danni looked on in amusement, but he gave a start as his father spoke to him.

"I'm gonna go over there and settle this thing once and for
all." With that, the man strode over to the argumentative group.

Danni hurried after him, afraid of what his father's plan
might be.

Mr. Brendt cleared his throat authoritatively, then called out
in an almost teasing manner, "Little children, I have somewhat to
say to you."

Everyone stopped and stared at Mr. Brendt's stern, yet jolly,
features.

"Let's *all* have them over for a meal…"

Suddenly, incredulous murmurs ran throughout the church. "*All* have them over?" "Why, what a weird idea." "Danni's return must have addled Mr. Brendt's head or something."

Sorryl and Trey looked at each other, raising their eyebrows suggestively. Boy, they sure were going to be stuffed if they went and ate at everyone's house today.

Mr. Brendt raised his voice, "Hey! I'm not done. I'll tell you how we can do this."

Now everyone hushed again and stared at him, wondering how anyone could find a way to accomplish this amazing feat.

"We can have a big picnic lunch with everyone bringing something to share!" Mr. Brendt finished.

The air was still except for Trey and Sorryl, who immediately began hopping up and down and clapping their hands.

The townspeople's minds whirled. A picnic? The word was almost foreign to them! How could they all bring something to a picnic and share it?

The townspeople swarmed about Mr. Brendt, skeptically inquiring how this could be carried out.

"We just need lots of tables for all the food. Then we can go by them in a line and get what we want. We can hold it in my back yard if you like."

At this longed-for proposal, Danni glanced at his father and spontaneously hugged him, oblivious of the surprised onlookers.

But Mr. Brendt didn't seem to mind one bit.

At the numerous nods and approving statements for his idea, everyone decided to meet in Mr. Brendt's spacious back yard in about two hours to carry out this astonishing, yet delightful-sounding, idea.

Danni just stood where he was, blinking back tears of joy. This was living. This was what he had longed to do for ever so long. Just to love with a true heart. He couldn't remember ever having anyone over before, though when he was younger he had begged for it. Now his father was doing it of his own initiative. Amazing!

Oh, God! I don't even know how to thank You! You have transformed me... and my father... and so many others. You have fulfilled us! You have changed our outlook and our responses to others. You have renewed our hearts. I don't know how we ever even lived without You. Really, I wouldn't say I was living before I had You. Not really." Danni's eyes sparkled with unshed tears of joy. What he had longed for was now becoming a reality… and it was all because of Jesus.

Chapter 30

Danni dashed across the wide deck in the back of their house, "I've got more plates here, Dad!"

Mr. Brendt took them from him, "Thank you. We should have told everyone to bring their own plates."

"Oh well. Maybe they will anyway. And it's not that far back to people's houses if they need…" Danni's voice trailed off and his mouth fell open when he caught sight of the man who was stumbling across the lawn under a heavy load. Realizing it was Jerry, Danni ran to help him. "Here, I'll take some of those for you."

Jerry just grunted and paused for Danni to transfer some of the plates he was carrying to his own arms.

Mr. Brendt was still over by the table he had just set up, gaping at the huge stack of plates Jerry was now trying to carefully set on one of the tables. "What on earth…" he finally managed to exclaim.

Jerry grinned, panting, "I was makin' some pizzas for y'all and I suddenly thought to myself, 'Now, how on earth are we all goin' to eat without plates?' So I brought these over and now I'll go back for those pizzas."

"W-why thank you," Mr. Brendt stammered in surprise.

Danni eyed Jerry suspiciously, "Just how many pizzas do you plan to carry over here?"

"Oh, ten. I figured maybe I could somehow balance them all and…"

Danni's rich laugh that had caused many a stoic townspersons' mouth to curve upwards, if only for a second, rang out. "I've got a better idea! I'll come over to help, and we can use that wheelbarrow to carry some of them."

Jerry glanced at the barrow. "Wa'll I guess that'd be lots easier. But it'll probably make the pizzas as scrambled as a hen's egg after an earthquake."

Danni hid a smile.

After a slight pause, Jerry stroked his chin, "And I had to leave a few plates behind since I couldn't carry them all, maybe we can stuff them in there too."

Danni shook his head, "Jerry, you sure do beat all."

Jerry laughed, "Only when you or Starlight or the Trestles are around. 'Course, now just about anybody can make me come up with zany ideas."

Mr. Brendt stared at him, aghast, "With *what?*"

Jerry laughed, "Zany ideas. You know, bizarre, wacky, strange…"

"All right, all right. I get the point now," Mr. Brendt chuckled.

Danni laughed too, then retrieved the wheelbarrow and threw a blanket over it to keep the pizzas they were going to bring back with them clean. This done, Jerry and Danni set off for the pizza shop.

When they returned, Starlight had arrived and was engaged in arranging the plates and silverware.

Laughing, Danni announced, "Jerry insisted on packing these plates in… and this silverware." He plopped a heap of the silver unceremoniously onto the table where the Brendt's silverware was already stacked.

Starlight set her hands on her hips, "I just finished setting those up all nice, and now look what you did."

Danni glanced at the mess of utensils and grinned apologetically, "As far as I can figure, we could leave 'em like that and fish for the ones we need."

Setting her lips, Starlight swatted him playfully, "Go get some chairs or something. I'll set these to rights so people don't go *fishing* through them." A chuckle escaped at the end of her little speech, giving her away, and Danni sauntered away. As he departed, he threw a wink toward Jerry over his shoulder.

When the Trestles arrived, they eagerly set to work, though Starlight and the Brendts insisted it was their 'party' and they shouldn't do any work to get it ready.

"But that's all the fun part," Trey insisted earnestly. "We like doin' stuff!"

So they were permitted to carry on.

Trey and Sorryl traipsed about the yard laying blankets on the ground and dragging chairs to various shady spots while their little shadow crawled close behind since she couldn't walk. She 'helped' by rearranging nearly every one of the chairs. When they were through with this task, the boys gazed at the numerous flowerbeds in admiration. They had never been in Mr. Brendt's back yard before, except for the time Sorryl had rammed his head into the shed. But he had hardly been in a state to notice beauty then.

Dusting his hands off, Sorryl turned to proudly survey the setup they had created. He grinned at the zigzag formation of most of the chairs and patted Treasure's head as she 'fixed' the last chair. He looked at Trey and shrugged. Who cared if they were zigzaggy? At least people could sit somewhere.

Next, Sorryl turned his gaze to the rather plain tables. His forehead puckered in consternation. Suddenly, he dashed to Mr. Brendt. Looking up with a shy but luminous smile, he said, "You have really beautiful flowers!"

Mr. Brendt's face flushed as he nodded.

Sorryl searched his face eagerly, "Can I pick some to put on the tables?"

Danni glanced at his father quickly. He had strictly forbidden Danni to do that when he was a boy. The town's scorn for having flowers to decorate anything had greatly weighed the scales toward this restriction, but Danni suspected the real reason was that his father didn't want to be reminded of his wife, who had planted them. It was amazing that Mr. Brendt even had flowers, since the rest of the town hadn't until recently. Flowers had always been despised as frivolous in Los Ciegos. But Mrs. Brendt had loved flowers and, seeing as they were in the back of the house, Mr. Brendt had allowed her to plant them as she wished. Once she was gone, he adamantly refused any suggestions to remove them. He had even hired people to take care of the beautiful garden that seemed to claim nearly half the huge backyard.

Much to Danni's amazement, Mr. Brendt smiled widely, though a bit sadly. His voice was tinged with a husky note as he answered, "Sure! It's been entirely too long since those flowers have graced one of our tables."

With a surprised, though happy, glance at his father, Danni watched the unsuspecting Sorryl send Mr. Brendt a beaming smile and scamper off to artfully gather some flowers with Treasure tagging along to smell them and tuck a few in his hair. She thought it only proper since he had tastefully arranged some in her own hair. So, to amuse his little sister, Sorryl happily traipsed about with a long-stemmed tulip gaily bobbing at either ear, until they kindly bounced themselves out, much to the relief of the boy's tickled ears.

When everyone had arrived, the pastor prayed for their food. Afterwards, everyone stood where they were with confused expressions, gazing helplessly at the food on the tables, and at the chairs and blankets scattered across the sprawling lawn.

Realizing they had probably never done anything like this before, Spencer stood, surveying the hesitant townspeople for a moment. Then, scooping Treasure into his arms and beckoning Trey and Sorryl to follow him, he approached the tables of food, "We can all just take a plate and serve ourselves what we want." He chuckled, "Obviously we'll never be able to eat some of everything. Parents better help the children," he added, demonstrating by beginning to dish bits of food onto Treasure's plate as well as his own.

Suddenly reassured, everyone rushed for the table, but then no one knew who should go first, so Spencer commented, almost as if to Treasure, "See? It's just like at the store, everyone in a line to check out, only this time we select our items while we're in the line and don't pay for it." His eyes took on a merry twinkle as Mr.

Brendt suddenly started handing people plates and telling them they were next.

Getting situated on the lawn was another confusing matter, but Spencer came to the rescue again, "Just find a seat, in a chair or on a blanket, and have a nice chat with the people near you while you eat. It's like the pizza shop, find your seat." With a soft laugh, he gently seated Treasure on a blanket and Trey and Sorryl plopped down next to her.

Gathering courage, the rest of the people followed suit.

When everyone seemed to be through eating and were exclaiming over what a wonderful idea this had been and how much more fun it was to eat outside than in, Pastor Ryan stood and cleared his throat to gain his parishioners' attention.

Soon, everyone had tears in their eyes as Pastor Ryan announced the coming departure of the Trestles.

"We've grown to love them dearly. They have added sparkle and life to our little town," Pastor Ryan said amid assenting nods from the listeners. He smiled jokingly, "It's a good thing we still have our Danni and Starlight. They'll keep us living until the Trestles return."

There was a quiet murmur of amused chuckles from the listening townsfolk while Starlight and Danni glanced at each other with suspicious twinkles in their otherwise innocent eyes.

"The Trestles will be leaving tomorrow afternoon. Any of you who would like to meet them to say one last goodbye are welcomed to their home tomorrow," Pastor Ryan concluded, resuming his place on the lawn.

As the party broke up, it seemed every townsperson had to shake Spencer's hand, pat the children on the head, and, after summoning their courage, fondly smile at Danni or pat his arm.

The next morning, the Trestles were astounded to find their lawn spilling over with townspeople.

When Trey emerged from the house with a large box to put in the car, he was immediately surrounded. He glanced back and forth in confusion as offers came from every side, "I'll take that for you, honey." "Here, dear. I can carry that." A smile crept across his face and he gave the box into their hands for them to argue over while he retreated to the house for another. When he reemerged, he passed Sorryl who was on his way back inside. They grinned at each other. Sorryl had been just as eagerly relieved of his burden. They found it rather amusing. They didn't mind carrying the boxes at all, but it seemed they were not to be allowed to carry them all the way to the car. So they began bringing the last few boxes out and handing them to whoever held their hands out first.

When the car was packed, Trey and Sorryl sadly stood beside it, reluctant to get in and leave.

"Bye, Trey. Bye, Sorryl. We'll miss you," one of the school children said. The rest emphatically agreed. They were sure they were going to have a dull time at school without Trey and Sorryl to invent games for them to play or projects to do for some invalid of the town.

"Yeah, us too," Trey and Sorryl said, blinking back wayward tears as they hugged their classmates.

Trey smiled at Jake, "Jake will be sure to give you suggestions if you don't know what to do at recess. Won't you, Jake?" he asked eagerly.

Jake combed his hair with his fingers in mild embarrassment before answering with bravado, "Sure I will." Then, suddenly losing courage, he added despairingly, "If I can think of anything."

Trey smiled encouragingly and presented a piece of paper. "Here's a list of things you know to do and play. Then you'll always have something to do," he offered.

Jake smiled and reached out to take the paper, his spirits lifting a bit as the dismal prospect of school without the Trestles grew a bit brighter.

Then Trey added, "And if that doesn't work, just think of somebody who's sad or lonely and make them something they'd like."

Jake smiled bravely and hugged these boys he had once tormented so ruthlessly. He much regretted that day and was glad for the times when he had been able to help them since.

"Take good care of Trooper and our house," Sorryl reminded Joe.

"I will, honey, don't you worry," Joe said, glad the tears that were pricking his eyes didn't spill over.

Spencer reluctantly turned from speaking with some of the people gathered there and opened his car door, "Okay, boys. Time to load up. We better be on our way." After making sure the children were situated comfortably, he climbed in his own seat and shut the door. Every window was rolled down and the children were hanging out of them, waving. Spencer smiled, "Bye! And thank you all so much! For everything!" his voice choked.

"Bye, drive safe now," someone answered.

Charlie called out, "Don't forget! Your job is waiting for you when you return!"

Spencer laughed and waved, "Thanks!"

The boys stuck their heads further out the windows and put their arms around the precariously dangling Treasure, "Bye! We'll miss you all!"

Spencer looked at the people they had come to love. It was hard to leave them. His gaze swept to his children, seated in the car behind him. He smiled. Yes, they had merry hearts now. Just what Annaleah had said they needed to help them get. His heart thrilled as he realized this mission had been carried on to the rest of the people gathered on his lawn as well, and to Treasure. They had all received merry hearts. All because of Jesus' love and sacrifice. Now that tiny spark of joy was being fanned into a blazing fire that spread to others as those who already possessed it passed it on. He was almost unaware that, as he endeavored to pass Jesus' love to others even through his pain, his broken heart had been made merrier as well.

Reluctantly, he put his foot on the gas and began their new journey. As they rolled from the driveway, Spencer, Trey, Sorryl and Treasure each waved in their own fashion. The people gathered on his lawn lifted their hands in farewell with tears of love in their eyes. Tears and love that were made possible by the journey their hurt and callused hearts had begun. The journey home to the God who had created them and knew how to bring healing to them.

As they left the drive, Treasure stuck her curly head out the window again and called out some of the few words she knew, "Bye, Bye! God bwess oo!" Her hair danced in the breeze, playing about her face like flames of gold. She threw the watching people a kiss and it washed over them like a balmy breeze. The townsfolk found they were already longing for the Trestles' return. Perhaps then the family would help their hearts continue the journey home they had begun rather reluctantly. They were reluctant no longer. And somehow they knew that, even with the Trestles gone, God Himself would complete the work He had begun in each of their hearts... the journey home.

About the Author

ASHLEY ELISABETH CROOK GREW UP WITH A LOVE for writing and for Jesus Christ, her Lord. Her heart reached out to those that other people had given up on and longed to tell them about Jesus, who could bring them life and joy. She endeavors to do that through her writing. She lives in the gorgeously painted hills of Western New York, where her imagination is sparked by God's vast creation. Much of her writing takes place in her spacious backyard surrounded by state forest, where she says she feels 'closer to God' and like she is 'set free and refreshed'.